Beloved Captive

**Center Point
Large Print**

Also by Kathleen Y'Barbo
and available from Center Point Large Print:

Fairweather Key Series
Beloved Castaway

**This Large Print Book carries the
Seal of Approval of N.A.V.H.**

KATHLEEN Y'BARBO

CENTER POINT PUBLISHING
THORNDIKE, MAINE

This Center Point Large Print edition
is published in the year 2010 by arrangement with
Barbour Publishing, Inc.

The text of this Large Print edition is unabridged.
In other aspects, this book may vary
from the original edition.
Printed in the United States of America
on permanent paper.
Set in 16-point Times New Roman type.

ISBN: 978-1-60285-780-3

Library of Congress Cataloging-in-Publication Data

Y'Barbo, Kathleen.
  Beloved captive / Kathleen Y'Barbo.
    p. cm.
  ISBN 978-1-60285-780-3 (library binding : alk. paper)
  1. Family secrets—Fiction. 2. Large type books. I. Title.
  PS3625.B37B44 2010
  813'.6—dc22

                                              2010000555

CHAPTER 1

May 2, 1836
New Orleans

It was a terrible thing to wish.

With every roll of the carriage wheels, Emilie Gayarre fought the urge to pray that her arrival would come too late. The request she'd traveled so far to make stood a greater chance of being granted were she begging the funds from her father's estate rather than making the request to him personally.

Yet if she were made to return to Fairweather Key without funds to build a school for the children, Judge Campbell would see to it that the children were sent off to neighboring keys where the price for their education had already been paid. "If only the old grouch would pry open the coffers and do what's right."

"My friend is not an unreasonable man, you know." The Reverend Hezekiah Carter, her elderly traveling companion, reached over to pat her sleeve. "Perhaps you will change your mind and visit upon the morrow rather than rush to his side."

She'd been thinking of Judge Campbell when she spoke her musings aloud, but the words certainly had a bearing on her situation with her father. Emilie stayed her fidgeting fingers and swung her gaze toward her father's oldest and dearest friend.

How easy it would be to agree, to avail herself of a warm bath and a good night's sleep before attempting the visit she dreaded. But the letter had been marked urgent, the words sure in their insistence that the daughters of Jean Gayarre see to their father's last wish: an audience with him at the family home should he survive, and a reading of the will should he perish before their arrival.

"No, Reverend Carter," she said, even as she hated it. "Time appears to be of the essence. I'll not disappoint my father by delaying in meeting his last request."

Though I've sorely disappointed him in other matters.

The old preacher merely nodded.

As the carriage rocked over uneven streets, the earthy smells of the city pushed away the stench of the docks. To their right, a fruit vendor juggled samples of his freshest produce, while across the way a woman sold pastries right from the folds of her apron.

"Are you fearing your father tonight, lass?"

Emilie swung her attention to Hezekiah Carter. "Fearing?" She gave the question but a moment's thought. "I don't suppose I ever feared my father, though I surely disliked him on occasion."

Leaning heavily on the silver-topped cane, the reverend shook his head. "A clever response, Emilie, but not a direct one." His piercing gaze challenged her. "Shall I rephrase the question, or will you rephrase your answer?"

She sighed. This man knew the Gayarres far too well. Any hope of deflecting the true meaning of his query disappeared under his persistent stare. "Indeed," she began, "I do wonder what awaits me, though I'd not call my feelings fear." Emilie paused. "I believe I am yet in awe of the man as much as I am reluctant to return to his home."

Reverend Carter reached across the space between them to grasp her hands. "Then it is well you chose not to face this alone."

"I chose?" A grin threatened. "Would that I'd known there was a choice."

He affected a surprised expression. "Dare I believe a woman of your quality would travel unaccompanied? One must be concerned with the dangers of ruffians who ply the shipping trade nowadays."

His grin joined hers at the reference. Some two years past, the reverend's own son was one of those ruffians. Now Josiah Carter's sole enterprise was to love his wife and his God, dote on his newly born son, and make his living saving others from the ravages of the Florida seas as a wrecker. Emilie smiled at the reminder of the man's transformation from infidel to husband. Her smile broadened when she thought of his wife, her half-sister Isabelle.

"A penny for your thoughts, my dear," the old preacher said.

"I was thinking about Isabelle and Josiah," she said, "and what an interesting life one lives when following God is one's priority."

"Indeed you speak the truth," he said.

Too soon the carriage rolled to a halt, and the coachman called out. A moment later the iron gates gave entrance to the courtyard, where the news of their arrival had brought a collection of servants running.

Her smile faded. In this home, she had first learned of Isabelle. An errant slip of the tongue by a gossiping housemaid had sent Emilie on a quest to find the young quadroon woman who shared her father. Here the plans were made for freeing this slave who was her half-sister.

Here, too, I will likely have to atone for the success of those plans.

Emilie tugged at her gloves to disguise the shaking of her hands. When the carriage door opened, she straightened her back and closed her eyes to offer an entreaty to the Lord that she might not be thrown in the Cabildo as befitting her crimes.

"Welcome home, mademoiselle."

Emilie opened her eyes to see Nate, the husband of Cook. "Thank you, Nate," she said with a genuine smile. "It's wonderful to see you again."

He tipped his hat, then lifted her down onto the cobblestones. "It's right nice to have you back here again."

One step into the courtyard, and Emilie's concern returned. The home seemed less of a home and more of a haven for the dying. Lamps that never went unlit were dark, and curtains in rooms that once invited guests to enter now stood closed.

"My father?" she asked of Nate.

"Up there waiting for you last I heard," he said as he gestured toward the second floor.

Reverend Carter glanced up at the darkened windows, then shook his head. "On the morrow, perhaps?"

"No." Emilie squared her shoulders, and head held high, she walked toward the front door. "I shall not wait until then," she whispered. Trembling fingers formed a fist, then with care rose to come near to knocking on a door that swung open on silent hinges.

Cook took two steps backward and clutched at the scarf at her neck. "Miss Emilie, Lawdy mercy and bless my soul. My prayers done been answered. You've come home!"

The housemaid's cry brought a half dozen familiar faces running. Each exclaimed as if a lost treasure had been suddenly found.

Emilie nudged past and walked into her father's home as if she were certain he would receive her. In truth, she had no idea whether Jean Gayarre would welcome her or whether he'd merely sent for his daughters to exact some measure of revenge. *Or did he seek only Isabelle's counsel and not wish to see me at all save to banish me?*

The question had lain dormant as Emilie boarded the vessel in Fairweather Key, and until she saw the gates swing open and heard her footsteps echo in the long hallway that led to her father's room, she felt no need to disturb it.

Too soon, however, the lamplight chased her to her father's door. Just once could she remember breaching the sanctum that was Jean Gayarre's chambers. As a small child, she'd had the great misfortune to lose a button off her favorite doll's dress beneath the heavy cypress door.

A moment's worth of demanding ended when a hapless servant girl, no more than a child herself, had agreed to go in and fetch it. Even now the sound of the girl's soft knock echoed in Emilie's mind, followed by the creak of the door. Emilie remembered peering inside at the heavily curtained bed positioned before windows that were swagged and festooned with matching tassels and loops.

The servant girl had crept toward the button on hands and knees, and Emilie shadowed her despite warnings to the contrary. What great fun it seemed to a child of no more than six or seven.

And then a sound from the bed. Her father, his voice thick and nearly unrecognizable, called an unfamiliar name and then repeated it. "Sylvie, *ma chere, c'est vous?*"

Much as in the present, fear had held Emilie's

lips shut tight and kept her feet glued to the floor.

"No, sir," the servant had said. "I'm D–d–daisy, sir. I k–k–keep the girl when my mama's busy."

A rustle of bed coverings sounded, and then a man rose. Bold as you please, he stumbled toward them without bothering to don a dressing gown or cover the stench of his breath.

"Sylvie," he repeated, ignoring Emilie completely, then swept the poor servant girl into his arms and deposited her behind the bed curtains. Only when the servant girl's bloodcurdling scream chased her from the room did Emilie flee.

After that, Emilie had never gone near the door again.

"Would you like me to go in with you?"

Emilie started at the sound of Reverend Carter's voice. "No," she said. "Thank you," was added as an afterthought.

His nod was hasty, as was his retreat, despite the impediment of the cane. "I shall have Cook prepare a light supper for you," he called. "Perhaps some of her biscuits and red eye gravy."

In truth, the thought of food did not hold any appeal. Neither did opening the door, yet she must.

One hand on the knob and the other pressing against her furiously beating heart, Emilie somehow managed to find herself inside. She blinked hard to get her bearings. The same heavy velvet curtains were now drawn against the afternoon sun, casting a pall across the mountain of quilts piled on the grand bed. In the midst of it all, the skeletal form of Jean Gayarre lay propped on more pillows than could surely be comfortable.

"Miss Emilie, that you?" This from the girl who'd fetched clean water for her bath more times than Emilie could count. Yet she knew not the girl's name.

"It is," she said, tossing aside the reminder of her formerly self-centered life. Before she left, she would know this girl's name, but now was not the time to ask. Not with Papa watching.

And watch he did, his eyes clear and bright even as his face wore no expression. A week's worth of travel had not been in vain, for Jean Gayarre had not yet gone to his reward. His mouth opened and closed, putting Emilie in mind of a fish in want of water.

Was he working to find the breath that would order her from the room or welcome her home? A sound escaped from the old man's mouth, something akin to a baby's soft whimper. She held her finger to her lips, halting. "Don't try to speak, Papa."

"Ma belle fille," emerged from cracked lips in a breathless gasp.

She grasped his hand and held it, painfully aware of the lack of strength in his icy grip even as her heart softened at his tender greeting. *"Oui,* Papa, *c'est moi. C'est* Emilie."

The old man looked past her. "But where is . . . ?"

14

"Isabelle?" she offered. "She was unable to make the journey."

To say more seemed unwise, so Emilie kept her silence and turned her attention to the bed-chamber's condition. The windows were shut tight against the danger of draft, and a great fire had been laid in the massive fireplace, wrapping the room in oppressive heat.

With her free hand, Emilie shrugged out of her wrap and passed it off to the nearest housemaid. "Thank you," she said to the young woman's retreating back before returning her attention to her father.

"Never . . . thank . . . a servant," he said. "Makes them . . ."

The rest of his admonition was lost in a fit of coughing that left Papa struggling for each breath. Finally, the old man's eyes closed, and he rested. For a moment, she thought he might have breathed his last. Then he stirred. A look came over his face that could only be described as disappointment.

"I summoned two, yet only one of my daughters has arrived." He paused and seemed to collect either his breath or his thoughts.

"Isabelle is abed with child, Father, and unable to travel," Emilie said.

"And you. You're Sylvie's girl," he whispered.

Sylvie. Emilie's gaze darted from the bed curtains as her heart lurched. Did her father remember that long ago day? What significance did this name hold over a man who would repeat it after all these years?

"No, Papa," she said as she forced her attention back on the old man's nearly lifeless form. "My mother was Elizabeth, your wife." She added what she hoped would be a smile in order to placate him. "I'm told I resemble her."

"Ha!" The force of his statement startled Emilie, as did the flash of anger on his face and his sudden move to rise up on one elbow. The motion sent pillows flying and caused a tray of what looked to be sweets to fall to the floor. As the servants surged forward to clean the mess, her father banished them all from the room.

The moment the door closed behind the last of the startled household help, Jean Gayarre fell back onto the remaining pillows. Emilie hastened to arrange them, then stopped when Papa motioned for her to move away.

Before she could step away from his grasp, Emilie felt her father's hand encircle her wrist to hold her captive. Despite his pallor and the exhaustion written in dark circles beneath his eyes, Jean Gayarre still held some measure of his former strength.

"Indeed you resemble your mother." Brown eyes slid shut, and his grip loosened. "*Trés jolie*, my Sylvie was," the old man muttered as he pointed to the bedside table, then allowed his hand to fall to the coverlet as if the effort caused him the last of his strength.

"But, Papa, my mother was . . ." The breath died in her throat as she spied the lone portrait at his bedside. The woman smiling back at her from the bonds of the silver frame could have passed as Emilie's twin.

CHAPTER 2

As Emilie stared at the tiny painting, the thought occurred to her that she'd reached the age of one and twenty without ever knowing the image of her mother, either in person or in portrait. The artwork suddenly became important, essential, to who she was.

An odd consideration given the fact that she had known from her earliest days exactly who she was. The privileged daughter of Jean Gayarre had only to look around her to know she'd been to the manor born. From the silks and satins adorning her cradle to the silks and satins she wore to the finest balls in New Orleans, Emilie Gayarre wanted for only two things: a father who stayed sober past dark and a mother to offer a kiss and a bedtime prayer.

Neither seemed terribly important until this moment. What she lacked, she'd made up for in the early and unwavering understanding that the Lord filled the empty spaces in her heart and held her in the blackest of nights. Cook saw to her saving knowledge of Christ even as she swore Emilie to secrecy over the matter.

But neither God nor Jean Gayarre had found a replacement for her mother.

"Might I . . . ?" She reached for the miniature, and the effort of keeping her fingers steady made speaking impossible. Only the knowledge that Papa seemed too absorbed in studying the pattern on the bed coverings kept her from making an excuse for it.

"It's yours," he said as his fingers traced the petal of a rose on the bed curtain, "for I'll be seeing her soon enough." A shuddering sigh silenced him for a moment. "Although like as not, St. Peter will bar the gates once my list of transgressions are read."

"The Lord forgives, Papa," she said. "As far as the east is from the west, that's what He does with our sins if we ask Him."

Her father's silence continued. This discussion would go no further tonight. It never did.

"Thank you, Papa," she finally managed to say as she felt the cold weight of the portrait balanced on her palm. "I shall treasure this image of my mother as no doubt she did."

"It was done from memory. She never saw it." A fierce look came over his pale, drawn features. "Leave me now. Go."

Emilie bit back a sharp retort and patted her father's shoulder. "Of course. Your rest is most important." She affected a smile that nearly cost her composure. "I've many stories of the children under my tutelage back on the key. Perhaps tomorrow I can tell you more."

"Tutelage?"

Was this the opening she sought for making her request on the children's behalf? Emilie swallowed hard, then proceeded carefully. "Yes, Father. In a curious twist of events, I've found myself an educator. The island children are quite eager to learn, although they often lack for the most basic of—"

Brittle laughter shook the silk-covered walls, then faded into a fit of gasps. "You, a cosseted pet, now a common tradeswoman? A teacher?" he finally managed.

The word seemed to taste ill in his mouth, such was the expression on his face. In his struggle to rise from the pillows, Papa slid dangerously close to the edge of the bed.

Emilie remained rooted in place. Heartless as it might seem, she had no further desire to comfort a man who took pleasure in laughing at her expense.

"Do be serious," he finally managed after settling himself nearer to the center of the bed.

Then she took a deep breath. "I am serious," she said carefully. "I have found a gift for educating. I rather enjoy it, actually, although I must say I perform my work under the most primitive of conditions."

Her father reached for the silk handkerchief on the bedside table. Likely an announcement that she'd decided to sell her wares in a bordello or sail off to a life of pirating would have displeased him no less.

Anger, her well-hidden companion, threatened mutiny. Best to leave now rather than risk any further breach in her relationship with the dying man.

Leave. She squared her shoulders. *Yes. That's what I'm to do.*

Emilie cleared her throat. "I shall leave on the morrow, Father, likely never to return. I do, however, extend the warmest invitation for you to visit my humble home in Fairweather Key once your recovery is complete."

She turned on her heels and made for the door, eyes focused on the ornately carved wood. A rustling behind her signaled her father had moved, but she continued walking. Only if he begged her to stay would she consider it.

Too soon her fingers touched the cold doorknob. Deliberately slowing her motions, Emilie gave her father one last chance to cry out, to stop her.

Silence.

The door swam before her as renegade tears pooled. Emilie straightened her backbone and blinked hard, refusing to swipe at her wet cheeks lest her father be watching. She yanked hard, and the door opened. Before she could change her mind, Emilie stepped into the dark hallway, disappearing, she hoped, into the shadows.

There she remained for an eternity, the only

sound the ticking of the monstrous clock at the opposite end of the hall. Finally, shaking knees threatened to give way, so she turned to glance one last time into the bedchamber of her father.

Jean Gayarre had turned his face to the wall, and in the pale firelight she saw—or perhaps she only imagined—a tear sliding down his cheek. His right hand held tight to the coverlet, his fingers clenching and unclenching as if making a fist, then thinking better of it.

As if even now in the throes of death he fought on.

Emilie clutched her hands across her middle as the realization struck. Death would soon take another Gayarre. Had it been only two years since she lost her brother Andre? Soon there would be none left save her and Isabelle.

She spied the miniature and felt the sharp pain of reminder. Indeed, she had a mother somewhere. Philadelphia, she'd once overheard, but that was so long ago. Papa might know.

Like as not, he'd refuse to answer even if she found a way to ask. Then again, the odds he knew were slim to none.

"Father, forgive me," she heard him whisper as his fingers stilled. "For I knew exactly what I did and cared not."

She waited for him to move again, prayed he had not stepped into the afterlife while she watched. Finally she could remain still no longer.

"Papa?" She burst from the shadows, compelled to move toward the curtained bed.

"Leave him be, child. He gets this way of an evenin', but he's generally recovered by breakfast time."

Emilie whirled around to see a familiar face standing in the doorway. The woman who'd once conspired to help her now seemed sorry to see her. "Mama Dell. I wondered if you were still in his employ."

A movement stirred beneath the blankets, and her father's voice crackled once more. "I daresay Delilah will be in my employ as long as my wretched life continues."

"He's right," she said, her dark eyes never straying from the old man's face. As soon as the words were out, her expression softened, and she moved toward them. "You look tired, Mademoiselle Emilie." Her petticoats swished as she walked. "Perhaps Sadie can draw you a bath."

In reality, such luxury was the farthest thing from her mind. "Thank you, but I think not," she managed to respond.

"Indeed, she shall," her father said. "But I would have you see to it yourself." He paused. "Immediately."

The old woman looked as if she might argue but apparently thought better of it. "Of course," she purred softly.

When the door closed, Emilie felt her father's

hand on her sleeve. "I would have you remain here with me." He paused to stare into her face. "I require it."

The shock of his demand rendered her momentarily speechless. "You require it?" she finally managed. "I don't understand. I came when summoned, and I am quite available to you while I am here, but . . ."

She searched for the proper way to tell her father that while she loved him, he had less need of her than the children who were going without instruction in her absence.

"But?" Dark eyes stared almost without blinking.

He is my father. The children are but my temporary charges.

The cost too high to count, Emilie allowed a long breath and a short prayer. "As long as you have need of me, I shall stay."

Later, while lying in a tub of water heated on the stove and infused with lavender, Emilie had to wonder why she had agreed so easily. The education of Fairweather Key's youth gave her life purpose and meaning. Staying with her father only added to the pain she'd been building on since childhood.

Yet a part of her would never stop being the little girl desperately seeking her father's approval. She blinked back a tear.

And looking for her absent mother's love.

She'd finished her bath and donned her night-gown when Mama Dell knocked. "Might I comb your hair for you?" she asked, obviously reluctant to enter the room uninvited.

"Yes, please," Emilie said. "And while you do, perhaps we can have a long-overdue talk."

Emilie seated herself at the vanity, then handed Mama Dell the silver brush. For a moment she felt transported to childhood when, as a child of the manor, she'd done very little for herself. Indeed the dressing, combing, and everything else but the feeding, it seemed, was done by the servant women of the Gayarre house.

And of them, Mama Dell and Cook vied to be the leader until a truce was had. Mama Dell was queen of everything upstairs, and Cook reigned supreme over the downstairs. So while Cook might curry Emilie's favor with her favorite sweet treat, Mama Dell would entertain her with stories and games.

In all, it came out a tie and gave Emilie a wonderful childhood, even though Mama Dell left to take on the raising of Isabelle.

"There," Mama Dell said.

Emilie looked in the mirror, stunned to see that her hair had been combed and braided so quickly. "I'd forgotten how fast you work."

Mama Dell replaced the brush on the vanity and stood a moment, giving Emilie the idea she wanted to talk. Emilie swiveled on the stool and turned to face her.

"There's a conversation to be had, isn't there?"

"Only if you want to, Miss Emilie," she said, her face unreadable.

"I do. I think I would like very much to discuss what happened with Isabelle." Emilie gestured to the chair nearest her. "Please do sit." She waited until Mama Dell complied before continuing. "Where to start?"

Indeed, she did search for a place to begin. What had started as a simple, well-intentioned decision to teach a slave girl to read and give her a Bible had quickly grown into so much more. When Emilie overheard that this girl would be sold as a concubine to one of her father's friends, she decided to take action. Involving Mama Dell in the plan had been much more difficult, though not impossible.

Eventually Josiah Carter, Hezekiah's wayward son, had been duped into taking not only Isabelle, but also Emilie and her friend Viola Dumont aboard his London-bound ship. When the vessel was wrecked on a Florida reef during a storm, the group had landed in Fairweather Key.

"You know, of course, that Isabelle found love with Reverend Carter's son."

Mama Dell nodded.

"And Viola, she's found a love of medicine. The doctor's employed her as his nurse. She delivered Isabelle's son a few days before I left."

Again the older woman merely nodded. Finally,

she cleared her throat. "And you? What is it that keeps you in that place? Some man, perhaps?"

Emilie smiled even as she shook her head. "The children." She paused. "I'm their teacher."

Mama Dell rose. "Then it's all worked out as it should."

"I suppose it has," Emilie said. "I only hope Papa wasn't upset at your part in all of this."

She shook her head. "I know too much about that old man. He doesn't dare get upset with me." The older woman paused. "Child, you're looking troubled."

"I'm worried about Papa," she said. "And," she continued slowly, "it has occurred to me that you may be able to tell me about my mother."

"Ah," Mama Dell said. "You were always a direct child. Never one to mind her words."

"It got me in trouble more than once." She studied the hem of her gown, then gazed at Mama Dell. "Am I like her?"

"Your mama?" An unreadable expression crossed her face. "In some ways, yes. In others, I'd say you're more like your papa."

"And Isabelle?" she asked, knowing Mama Dell had raised the woman Emilie now knew as her sister.

"She's like neither. I can't imagine how such a sweet child came from such a woman."

Her statement and the strength with which she said it stunned Emilie. She'd only heard good things spoken of the woman called Sylvie, but then, she'd also only heard them whispered, never spoken in the open.

"How so?" she dared ask, praying Mama Dell's good humor and propensity to speak on this subject would continue.

Mama Dell helped herself to the chair nearest the door. When she'd settled her skirts around her, she leveled a direct look at Emilie. "Your mama was the sweetest thing ever drew a breath. Before I took on Isabelle, I raised Sylvie until she went off to be with your daddy in that house on Burgundy Street."

The statement confounded logic, but Emilie let the old woman talk. There would be enough time to figure it all out later.

"When he married Miss Elizabeth, it near broke Sylvie's heart. I believe that's what killed her and not birthing you."

Words formed and fell away, refusing to shape themselves into anything that made sense. Oblivious to Emilie's state, Mama Dell kept talking.

"When he scooped you up from your mama's bed and brought you to me, I thought, Oh no, what has he done? It wasn't until Miss Elizabeth's time came the same day that I knew what he was thinking. Two baby girls with the same dark hair and the same daddy." She looked away as if reliving the moment. "I looked down in that cradle, and I asked myself who but the Lord and your papa would know what he done 'cept me."

Emilie began to shake. A response was well beyond her ability.

"So I thought, Well, if I help him do what he's gone do anyway, then at least I've got myself a nice life ahead of me." When she lifted her gaze to meet Emilie's incredulous stare, tears brimmed at the corners of caramel-colored eyes. "I know I'm gonna answer to this someday when I meet my Savior, but right now I wish Isabelle was here to ask her forgiveness."

"You're serious," Emilie managed.

"Serious?" She shook her head. "What do you mean?"

"My father switched the babies, and you helped him. I grew up in this house believing my mother to be Elizabeth when, in fact, she was . . ."

Emilie couldn't say it. Couldn't wrap her mind around the fact that she had lived a life she did not, indeed, deserve.

Her mouth opened of its own volition, then closed. Words begged to be spoken but went unsaid.

"I am . . ." Emilie's breath failed her.

"A slave just like me?" Mama Dell rose. "I'm afraid so, Miss Emilie," she said as she slowly crossed the distance between them.

"And I should have . . . that is, Isabelle was meant to . . ."

She gave up speaking and fell into the soft pillow of Mama Dell's chest.

"There, there, baby girl," Mama Dell whispered as she wrapped ample arms around Emilie. "The Lord, He sees it all. What happened is past, and neither you nor Isabelle can change it."

"Isabelle." Emilie leaned away and looked up at Mama Dell, her image swimming through the veil of Emilie's tears. "She knows."

"I reckon she does," Mama Dell said. "Though I thought you did, too. I told your papa he ought to write those letters to set things straight while he still could. Andre was to take them to both of you."

"He did," Emilie said, "but Isabelle read hers, then threw both letters into the fire." She paused as tears fell afresh. "She said they weren't fit for a lady to read." Her lips trembled, and the room swam. "She knew, and she chose not to tell me. She chose to remain a slave so I could stay free."

"No, child," Mama Dell said. "You're as free as she is. Your papa signed the papers, and it's all done. Why, the Reverend Carter, he made sure it was done."

"Reverend Carter knew?" She struggled to make sense of it all.

"Yes, he knew. Your papa, he knew he'd likely not live to an old age, what with the life he lived. So, he asked Reverend Carter to see to the freeing of his daughter with Sylvie on her twentieth birthday. I believe that's how it was to go."

"But Isabelle escaped."

"That's right," Mama Dell said. "And I let it

29

happen. I knew I couldn't leave with you ladies. Someone had to take care of your papa. So, I did my best to look like I'd changed sides. I hated it, but I had to do what was best for Jean Gayarre. He would've died sooner if both of us had left him at the same time."

Emilie looked at the woman and realized she'd never really known her. "You care for my papa, don't you?"

Mama Dell looked surprised. "I suppose I do, in my own way. He's been good to me, though I'll never know if it's to keep me happy or keep me quiet." She stepped back and lifted the corner of her apron to dab the tears streaming down Emilie's cheeks. "Now, I'm gonna leave you to get used to this idea of who you really are in private. You've got every right to be mad at all of us," she said, "but just you know that what we did, we did out of love for your mama. Sylvie, she was special, and so are you."

The older woman cupped Emilie's face in her callused hands, then gently tilted her chin until their gazes met. "The Lord, He don't see color, and He don't see slave nor free. That's the evil in this world speaking. His Word says He looks beyond those things to what's inside."

"But I lived the life I did not deserve."

"Baby girl, none of us get what we deserve," she said softly. "But I know for a fact, it all got paid at Calvary, and now I don't have to fret about it."

CHAPTER 3

May 4, 1836
A day's sail from the
Caribbean island of Santa Lucida

Fletcher, I find this ruse tiring." Caleb Spencer set aside his pistol, then reached for the ridiculous scabbard at his waist and gave it a tug. "Long as their bellies are full and their pockets are lined, I'm certain none of the reprobates and brigands aboard this vessel care that they are transporting someone on the opposite side of the law."

The man who served as mentor and substitute father nodded. "Aye, lad, 'tis enough for them to know they are escorting a Benning home."

"I am a Spencer." His fingers clenched, and the cold metal bit into his palm. "Never forget that. And my home is not in this godforsaken place. I am a legislator, not a farmer."

"Well, that's a good thing," Fletcher said, "for your grandfather was not in the business of farming, either."

"I know that all too well."

"You only know what you've been told, lad, and I'd wager that information is sadly incomplete." Fletcher's dark eyes narrowed beneath bushy gray brows. "For all his reputation as a man of the sea, Ian Benning was also a man of the land. What do you know of the many families he helped by allowing them to work for a living wage in his fields? Of the advances in the growing of indigo and cane he pioneered?"

In truth, Caleb remembered only brief snatches of time spent in the great white house beside the green sea. A vague image of his mother standing at the ocean's edge was the sole picture his mind could manage. Even that was blurry, worn at the edges by time and yellowed by forgetfulness.

"I was but a child," he said. A smile threatened, but Caleb resisted. Much as he hated the Benning legacy, the time spent with his grandfather had indeed been the stuff of youthful adventure. But then, what lad did not play the occasional game of pirate? In his case, however, the play was all too real.

"And now you've the chance to return a man grown into his responsibilities as head of the household." Fletcher shrugged. "I daresay the Lord has a purpose in all of this."

"Head of the household?" Caleb's laugh held no humor. "Hardly. I am merely a dutiful son heeding his widowed mother's call for assistance. As for the Lord's purpose, likely my mother will soon find a substitute better skilled in agriculture than me, and I shall be released to continue my practice of the law in whatever location Attorney General Butler decrees. I pray the Lord will speed the process."

Another yank of the sash, and the weight tore free and landed easily in his hand. Too easily.

For a moment, he allowed the cool metal to slice through the years and bring forth a memory of another scabbard, another sword. One he'd sworn to his father never to pick up again. Yet here he stood aboard the brigantine *Cormorant* heading across a light chop for the familiar green waters of the Caribbean. To make matters worse, the moment the vessel hit open seas, the rapscallions had seen fit to hoist the green and gold Benning flag.

Now he bore not only the Benning lineage, but also sailed under their dubious banner. Neither would set well with his staid and stodgy supervisor under the authority of the attorney general.

A glint of sunshine on seawater caught his attention, and he crossed the uneven floor to the lone porthole. From his reckoning, Caleb figured another good hour of daylight lay ahead before the sun began to set. When it rose again, the *Cormorant* would be within sight of Santa Lucida.

Almost without thinking, Caleb tightened his grip on the hilt and turned the great weapon toward the swaying light of the lantern. Its razor-sharp blade gleamed with a promise that would go unfilled.

It must if he were to salvage the life he'd paid so dear a price for.

Caleb lowered the sword and sheathed it in the

scabbard that had once belonged to the great Ian Benning, then thrust the weapon toward Fletcher. "Take this. I have no use for it."

Something akin to sadness fell across the older man's face, quickly chased away by what could not be anything but anger. Slowly, his chest rose as he took in a deep breath, then let it out with great leisure.

It was a gesture Caleb knew too well. From the time he'd been sent as a lad to study under Fletcher's tutelage, the pause between anger and speech had become a moment of reckoning. Whatever transpired next, the words would be carefully chosen.

"Were I to take that weapon from you, I'd be obliged to thrust it into my heart." He took a step back. "For though you choose to ignore the Benning blood coursing through your veins, I warrant the Lord has not."

It was Caleb's turn to pause before he spoke. Unlike his mentor, he'd never quite perfected the ability.

"What business has God with my mother's kin? I've heard enough talk of the Bennings on this voyage to last a lifetime." He fairly spat the words. "All but a few of the pirate clan have denied the Lord when called upon. Would you wish this on me as well? Rather, I think of my mother as a Spencer than relegate her to an association with murderers and thieves."

Fletcher gave a long-suffering sigh. "We'll not revisit the ghosts of the past," he said, "but neither shall we ignore them. Aye, you've a history bespeckled with heretics and the like, but your mother can never be counted among them, now can she?" He gestured to the sword. "Would you now deny her the proper homecoming of her only son and the aid which you shall render?"

"Deny her?" Caleb's words exploded above the mask of civility he'd worked hard to maintain. "Did I not request six months' leave from Attorney General Butler to attend to family business despite the fact that I could well be putting next year's promotion to assistant attorney general in jeopardy? Am I not standing in my father's stead to run a plantation neither of us wanted?"

Fletcher listened impassively, his expression giving no indication of an opinion both already knew. The older man's silence only served to fan the flames of outrage that had been licking at Caleb's heels since he locked the door to his suite of rooms near the Capitol.

"My father's only crime was falling in love with the daughter of a pirate. Despite the fact he lived in the shadow and doubtless under the constant pressure of Ian Benning, John Spencer remained a man of unbending principle and a defender of the law until the day he died."

Fletcher's nod was almost imperceptible. "Aye, he did, may he rest in peace."

"So then, how is it that I, the son, am now expected to take my place in the tug of war between law and lawlessness that has characterized our family ever since my parents' marriage? You know that is what I will be facing once this vessel ties up at the Benning dock. Have I not risen sufficiently above that?"

"Risen above?" Fletcher seemed to consider the statement a moment. "Is that the question, or are you asking whether you've earned the right to ignore your place in the family in order to serve your own ends?"

The flames of anger rose until Caleb could feel them in his face and in his fists. Indeed, his mother had long desired his triumphant return to Santa Lucida from what she termed his exile in Washington, D.C. What his mother deemed exile, however, Caleb counted as gain.

His letters to her were peppered with references to conversations with many influential persons including Attorney General Butler, in whose employ he now found himself; certain higher-ups in the naval department; and even President Jackson. Indeed, the senior statesman never failed to begin his conversations with Caleb by stating, "When I was military governor of Florida, your father was invaluable to me."

More than once, Caleb had bit back the question of whether his father's value lay in his service to the United States as judge and chief prosecutor in the Florida territory or as son-in-law to Ian Benning, a man who could feed the president's love of whiskey and horses with the ease of one who could obtain either quickly and without question. Of course, it was all conjecture and speculation. Like as not, his father had kept his association with the notorious pirate a secret from all.

Caleb sighed.

That the bulk of his forbearer's trade was not in politics but in piracy had no bearing on his mother's pride. Perhaps it was true what Fletcher asserted. Perhaps his mother truly had no clear idea of her late father's family business.

As soon as the thought occurred, Caleb pushed it away. As daughter to a fortune built on the treasure of others, Mary-Margaret Benning Spencer knew well the deeds of her relatives, though likely not in detail. Years spent in Florida as wife and mother quickly gave way to a return as a widow to her homeland of Santa Lucida and the Benning Plantation.

"And the old man," Fletcher continued, "only Jesus Himself knows whether Ian Benning's last words were yes or no to the offer of eternal life."

"Indeed."

Caleb let the scabbard fall onto the bunk he'd found abominable but necessary given the poor weather and heaving of his gut. Finally, he sank beside the weapon and rested his head in his hands. The scrape of wood against wood told him

Fletcher had helped himself to the lone chair in the room.

While the ship rolled beneath his feet, Caleb let his thoughts swim ahead as well. The ruse would continue, at least until he could make good his visit and subsequent escape from Benning Plantation.

If only he'd asked for a shorter leave.

"I must speak my mind, lad." The old man shifted positions to rest his elbows on his knees. "When I'm done likely you'll wish I'd kept my silence."

"Speak then," he said. "I'll not stop you."

For a moment, the only sound was the creak of the old wood and the sound of waves lapping against the *Cormorant*'s hull as she cut a brisk path south. Caleb loosened the ties on his shirt and waited. Fletcher never seemed to speak until he'd thought out each word carefully. Rarely did the wait bite against Caleb's nerves as it did now. He rose and walked to the desk, where an aged Bible sat atop the captain's log. He moved the Bible aside and opened the log. There in his grandfather's hand the name of the vessel and the date October 23, 1814, had been scrawled across a page that was otherwise blank.

Caleb turned the flyleaf and began to read. "On the twenty-third day of our Lord in the year of eighteen hundred and fourteen, I did find this vessel fair and seaworthy as she made the voyage from . . ." He stopped, unable to read the next word due to what appeared to be water spots on the page.

"Cartagena." Fletcher swiveled in the chair to face Caleb. "She left from Cartagena under a sky so blue it hurt your eyes to look at it. Such was the chop of the wind that we found our sails full enough to blow us all the way back to Santa Lucida with but one stop."

Caleb shook his head. "Yes, that's exactly what it says, but how . . ."

"How did I know?" Fletcher scrubbed at his face with his hands, then sighed. "I wrote it."

"But my grandfather . . ."

"Aye," he said. "He was a fine man, but the truth is he wasn't much given to the finer points of sailing when there were others aboard who preferred the job. Without a man who loved her at the helm, the *Cormorant* might have long ago been lost. Indeed, she's like a woman. Some are still fine and fair in spite of age."

Caleb closed the log. The man he'd known only as Fletcher and who for nearly all of Caleb's twenty-seven years had served as teacher, mentor, and surrogate grandfather was an academic, not a sailor. He searched the old man's face for a break of humor and found none.

"You jest," Caleb finally said.

"All right, then." Fletcher rose and made for the door. "I'll say no more, for I can see you're not of a mind to hear it."

He watched the man's broad back and noted his brisk gait. Caleb had sparred often enough with Fletcher to know when he bluffed and when he did not. This time, he did not.

"Halt," he called as he settled once again on the bunk. "Return and tell me your tale. I warrant this time you'll find an eager listener."

"Your grandfather, he was in much the same kettle of stew as you now find yourself."

"Which is?"

Above them, the watch bell rang: a reminder that time still marched forward. In this, Caleb found both good and bad.

Fletcher leaned against the doorframe and crossed his arms over his chest. For a moment, he seemed to be in another place and time. "His obligations didn't match up with his calling," he finally said.

Interesting. Perhaps there was yet another lesson to be gleaned from his former tutor. "What, dare I ask, did he do about this conflict?"

The old man smiled, his grin quick and genuine. "That, lad, is what I hope you'll discover once we arrive in Santa Lucida."

Once again the bell above decks sounded. Even with his limited knowledge of seafaring ways, Caleb knew this could mean only one thing: trouble.

CHAPTER 4

Trouble it was, the likes of which Caleb had not seen during his staid life as aide to the attorney general's assistant. Silhouetted against the orange sun off the windward side, a vessel under full sail seemingly charged toward the *Cormorant*.

Around him, confusion reigned. At least it appeared so, although upon closer inspection, the men were performing in unison.

From the past, a dusty memory beckoned—a game he and his grandfather had played during idle times aboard this very ship. While the great Ian Benning would stand lookout, Caleb's wooden sword would slash at imaginary enemies.

Depending on his mood, Caleb would raise a flag or two, sometimes more, on the length of twine Grandfather fashioned on the quarterdeck for Caleb's use. He'd learned the colors—white for pursuit, black for attack, red for no quarter—and plied the seas at his grandfather's side, striking and raising them at will.

Of course, the only missions accomplished during those voyages were the fetching of new agricultural samples for his grandfather's plantation and the occasional visit with some seaman whose age had forced him to hang up his oars.

"Cast loose your guns," the captain called, drawing Caleb back to the present.

"I would have a look," he said.

Upon the captain's nod, the second-in-command rushed for a spyglass.

Until Caleb lifted the glass to his eye, the banners snapping from the other ship's topmast were indistinguishable against the nearly blinding glare of the sun. "There are two," he said as he handed the glass to Fletcher. "One red and the other black."

Fletcher bit down on his pipe and uttered an oath. "Black for battle and red for no quarter."

Yes, I remember. All a part of the game.

But this was no game.

Above them, the lookout skittered to the highest reaches of the rigging while others moved about fore and aft. Due west, the sun still rode high enough above the horizon to be trouble.

"What'll ye have me do, sir?" the captain said.

"We'll not stand by and have them board us so take the necessary actions." He glanced over at Fletcher, who gave a slow and almost imperceptible nod. "You are in command here, Captain. I am but a passenger, albeit one willing to defend the vessel."

The captain of the *Cormorant* barked orders to load. He addressed Caleb, offering an amateur's version of a courtly bow. "Beggin' yer pardon, but ye might want to go below until this bit o' bluster's done. Your mother would have my hide if yours is damaged."

"I am no babe in arms, sir." Anger flashed white hot. "Would that I had the time to answer such an affront."

"She'll be upon us soon, lad." Fletcher returned the spyglass to Caleb. "What'll you be defending yourself with?"

The vessel now bore down on them, her name easily read through the glass in his hand. *Hawk's Remedy.* Caleb pushed away the fear in his gut and stared down into the wide eyes of the captain. "Have a man fetch my grandfather's—my sword and pistols."

Once the order was given, the captain looked to Caleb for further instruction. He looked up at the *Cormorant*'s mainsail and found it empty.

"Where is the Benning flag?"

"If you recall, you wished it removed some days ago," Fletcher said. "I felt it prudent to honor that wish, at least until we come within site of Santa Lucida."

"Raise it once more," Caleb called as the first volley of shots rang out. "And fly the red banner beneath her. The only response to an unprovoked attack is to let the infidels know we'll take no quarter."

"Would that we might discuss this," the captain said.

Caleb pointed to the advancing ship. "Do those ruffians look as if they'd like a discussion or a fight, good sir?"

A second later, the *Hawk's Remedy* sent a volley of shot hurtling near the forward bow, and the time for action was upon them. A second round of shot found its mark just shy of the quarterdeck. Splinters of wood peppered Caleb's face and arms, but a smoldering coil of hemp leaning against the mainmast stole his attention.

Should the hemp ignite, the mainmast would be next. Bounding toward the potential disaster, Caleb gathered the rope into his arms and tried not to think about the flames as he raced to the gunwale and threw the rope overboard. The rope sizzled and smoked as it hit the churning water and slowly disappeared beneath it.

That accomplished, he fell into action beside those around him, heedless of the wounds now rising. Another explosion hit near the vessel, and the *Cormorant* shuddered but remained true and seaworthy.

When the attacking vessel came about, Caleb reached for his pistol but found no clear shot. A second try proved just as fruitless when a rising blister on his palm caused him to jerk at the last minute and miss his target, a large and vocal fellow wearing a top hat and strutting about the foredeck shouting and pointing.

"Likely he's the captain of that tub." Caleb turned to see Fletcher standing beside him, the spyglass at his side. "You've got your grandfather's instincts, lad, and that fellow knows it."

With the spyglass, he pointed to the *Hawk's Remedy*. "He'll not make the same mistake. I saw his face when he knew you'd found him in your sights."

Caleb watched the wake from the smaller vessel lap against the sides of the *Cormorant*, attesting to the near miss. "Had I my grandfather's instincts," he said, "perhaps my—" Another shot from the attacker's cannon prevented further debate.

Someone peppered the deck with grapeshot, causing Caleb to dive. Fletcher followed, landing nearby. A moment later, Caleb glanced up at the mainmast, then with difficulty climbed to his knees and peered over the rail.

"They've tacked away." Fletcher rose and limped toward the aft deck, shouting something about the colors to a lad who had the misfortune to cross his path. Caleb watched the older man a moment, then returned to the cannon crew.

"You almost got 'em," one of the sailors remarked.

"Indeed that's fine shooting," another said as he prepared the wadding and stuffed it into place. "You're a real Benning, you are."

Rather than comment, Caleb fell into position and waited for the cannon's fire before joining with the men to repeat the process. The ropes he held tore at his palms and chafed against his bare arms, but he ignored the petty aches by doubling his efforts and urging the others to do the same.

Several volleys hit their mark, but none managed to sink the agile vessel.

"Look at that," the fellow next to Caleb said as he pointed to the center of the ship.

Caleb held tight to the rope as he glanced over his shoulder. There above the fray was a lone figure shinnying up the mainmast with the Benning flag in his teeth.

"What in the world? He's going to get himself killed." Caleb dropped the rope and ran toward the mainmast, reaching for his pistol. Thankfully, the enemy ship was too far away for anyone to fire directly at the youth. When he slid down, his grin broad, Caleb was waiting to upbraid him for the careless act.

"It was an order, Mr. Benning, I mean, Spencer, sir," he said, eyes wide. "When I joined up with this crew, the captain said I was to do what I'm told and that's what I did."

"Is that so?" Caleb looked around for the source of the child's irresponsible order but found all hands otherwise occupied. Turning his attention back to the lad, Caleb forced a smile. "Good work, sailor. Now get yourself off to someplace safe until this is over."

The boy tipped his hat and scurried aft. Out of the corner of his eye, he saw a flash on the deck of *Hawk's Remedy*. A second later, something exploded just above the head of the retreating youth.

Caleb watched the boy skitter away, thankfully unharmed; then he turned to see from whence the shots had come. On the deck of the vessel stood the scoundrel in the top hat. With a flourish, the villain bowed at the waist, then straightened to aim his weapon directly toward Caleb.

The fact that the man's gun could not reach the distance between the ships seemed to be of no concern to the madman who captained *Hawk's Remedy*. Caleb stood his ground, his fear fading as anger grew.

Whether it was because of the skilled aim of the *Cormorant*'s crew or the green and gold banner that flew above her, the marauding vessel struck her colors and made to limp away.

"After them," Caleb shouted over the din of the celebrating crew. "We've promised no quarter, and we shall give none."

"Lad." Caleb felt the weight of the captain's hand on his shoulder. "Why give chase to cowards? Likely they'll not trouble us further."

"But they wished no quarter. We must grant that wish." He began to pace, his mind reeling as he sought to justify the argument to pursue. "If allowed to escape, they may return to plague us again."

"If they do, then they've earned what we give them." The captain paused. "Of course, this is your vessel, and you'll do as you wish, although I suggest seeing to your wounds as a priority."

Caleb wanted to argue but found nothing to counter the older man's logic save his own anger. "Others are in worse need of doctoring, Captain," he said. "But I'll take my turn when they have been seen to."

"Aye, Mr. Benning." He shook his head. "Er, Spencer."

Caleb stepped past the captain to stride to the rail, being careful not to impede the progress of those still at their tasks. Heedless of the debris floating around them, gentle waves lapped against the hull as if pushing her toward home.

The ship's home, not his. The litany began to play in his head, a series of thoughts all leading to the same conclusion: The choice had been made long before Caleb was given the chance to make it himself.

From the corner of his eye, Caleb saw Fletcher approach.

"See that you record this encounter in the log, Fletcher." He flexed his fists, then paid for the effort with a pain he ignored. "I'll not be wanting to forget the name of the scourge who plagued us this day."

"Indeed."

Caleb gave him a sideways glance and noted red stains on Fletcher's sleeve and shirtfront. "You're bleeding."

"It's nothing. Now, if you've no further need of me, I'll see to the recording of the log."

Fletcher turned away, leaving Caleb to stand amid the chaos. Caleb looked down to see his palms showed both the blisters from the smoldering hemp and the marks of the rope he'd held to balance the vessel's short gun.

Splinters from a percussion shell had torn holes in his shirt and peppered the skin below, and his left arm likely had been grazed by the same weapon. Swiping at the blood with the back of his sleeve, Caleb took a strange satisfaction in watching the fleeing vessel grow smaller as the shadows grew longer.

As darkness fell in heavy shadows around him, satisfaction turned to confusion.

Less than two weeks ago, he had sat behind his desk and thought that was where God wanted him to be. Now, as he shook the splinters from his hair and inhaled deeply of the sulfur-tinged salt air, Caleb was no longer so sure.

For a man who had vowed to uphold justice and the word of the law, taking those things into his own wounded hands was a heady and fearful thing. Heady because of the great pleasure it gave him, and fearful because there seemed no end to it.

"Beggin' yer pardon."

Caleb whirled around to find one of the young riggers standing a short distance behind him. He shifted from side to side as if his bare feet were touching hot metal.

"The old man what boarded with you?"

49

"Aye," Caleb said, "that would be Mr. Fletcher. What of him?"

The boy removed his cap and held it against the tattered rag that served as a shirt. "I reckon he's near to done for, sir. Leastwise that's what I heard the—"

"Take me to him." As Caleb fell into step behind the boy, revenge—a new and curiously invigorating emotion—took hold and wrapped around his already conflicted heart. If Fletcher was dead, then every last hand aboard *Hawk's Remedy* would have to die as well.

In the time it took Caleb to reach his old friend's side, a promise had been made. An accounting would be made of each sorry soul aboard the *Hawk's Remedy*, and payment would be extracted in hide rather than in coin.

Much as his Spencer blood called for justice, his Benning blood boiled for revenge.

Caleb balled his fingers into fists as he ducked beneath the low beam to enter the galley that had been turned into a makeshift hospital. Bloody rags and the stench of sulfur permeated the room, while the sound of men suffering played in harmony with the creak of the ship and the lapping of the waves.

Once his eyes adjusted to the gloom, Caleb found Fletcher immediately. Propped against a barrel, he had been stripped to the waist. Bandages covered his torso and right arm, and a nasty bruise had spread across one cheek. His right eye had swollen shut. Still, he held the ever-present empty pipe between his teeth, even as his good eye followed Caleb.

"Can he speak?" he asked the surgeon, an affable fellow whose last call of duty had been in a dental office in Boston.

"Of course I can speak," Fletcher said. "I'm just having a bit of trouble standing." He swung his attention from Caleb to the young doctor. "Go work on someone who needs the help."

Nodding, Caleb sent the man off to the next wounded man, then lowered himself to his knees beside Fletcher. For a moment, neither spoke.

"I was told you were near death," Caleb said when he trusted his voice not to fail him. "I thought I'd have to manage without you."

"So did I." Fletcher removed the pipe to balance it in his hand. "Could be the confusion started when I woke up in this mummy suit." He looked down at his chest, then back up at Caleb. "I warrant the young surgeon's a bit overzealous with his bandages. I'm trussed up like an Egyptian being readied for the tomb."

Despite his true feelings, Caleb allowed Fletcher to believe he went along with the joke. "And a sorry excuse for a mummy you'd make." He sobered. "What happened?" he asked as he pointed to the bandages.

"Grapeshot," he said. "Even with the scoundrel's bad aim, the shot managed to catch me off guard. I attribute it to old age, lad, for I've no other reason to it."

"That ain't true at all."

Caleb looked over to where the heavily accented voice had come from. "Are you calling my man Fletcher a liar?"

"He ain't lying, but he sure ain't giving you the whole story." This from a man bundled beneath a greatcoat and bandaged about his head and shoulders.

"Is that so?" Caleb looked to Fletcher, who shrugged.

"I'll tell you what happened." The fellow leaned up on his elbows as his voice strengthened. The greatcoat fell away, revealing serious damage to his midsection.

"Enlighten me," Caleb said.

"The *Hawk*, it came about just as the Benning banner went up. I saw him, this redheaded fella on the other ship. He took aim right at you, Mr. Benning, whilst you were hauling that burning rope over the side, and well, your friend saved your life."

"Is this true?" Caleb looked to Fletcher, who said nothing.

"With the Lord as my witness, I ain't lying."

Caleb reached for the old man's hand and placed his atop it. "You risked your life for mine."

"It was nothing." Fletcher shifted positions. "One sailor to another on the field of battle."

One sailor to another. Caleb looked away. Fletcher's highest praise, no doubt.

Caleb turned his attention to Fletcher and found him staring. "I owe you my life," Caleb said. "You've gone far beyond the call of duty."

"No. Long ago I made a promise," he said slowly, his voice rough and his forehead now beading with sweat, "and even as I am guilty of much, I am a man of honor." He closed his eyes, then opened them again with difficulty. "Never forget you are a man of honor as well, Caleb Benning."

Benning? He started to correct the old man, then thought better of it.

Instead, Caleb called to the surgeon. "Have this man moved to my quarters, then inform the captain to raise all sails and make for Santa Lucida at full speed."

The youth nearly disappeared around the corner before Caleb called him back. "And give the order. All eyes will be watching for the vessel *Hawk's Remedy*. Should she be sighted, I will have her burned to the water line and her crew left to swim with the sharks."

A cheer went up all around. Fletcher alone kept his silence. Only later, when he'd been settled in Caleb's bunk, did Fletcher broach the subject.

"Where is the lad whose concern for the law and love of the Lord would not allow him to plot revenge?"

Caleb set down his quill and pushed away the log book. Several responses came to mind, but out of respect for his teacher, Caleb remained silent.

"Ignore me if you will, lad," Fletcher said, "but the truth is and always will be the truth."

" 'And ye shall know the truth, and the truth shall make you free.' " Caleb swiveled on his seat and rested his elbows on his knees. "See, old friend. I've not yet forgotten what you insisted I set to memory."

" 'Dearly beloved,' " Fletcher said, his voice strong and clear, " 'avenge not yourselves, but rather give place unto wrath: for it is written, Vengeance is mine; I will repay, saith the Lord.' "

Caleb heaved a sigh. "For that I have no rebuttal."

"That's a relief." Fletcher shifted positions. "It's of some comfort to know that even the grandson of Ian Benning knows he cannot trump the Word of God."

Even as the watch bell rang overhead, Caleb had to wonder if perhaps he couldn't have both religion and revenge.

CHAPTER 5

May 20, 1836
New Orleans

Emilie had long assumed that she and not her brother, now deceased, would be the one to see to their father in his declining years. What she did not expect was the difficulty of doing so, especially in light of her conversation with Mama Dell.

For the most part, Emilie had chosen to set that information aside, to proceed as if she'd never been told she was the daughter of a concubine rather than a wife. To acknowledge the facts would be to admit them, and she'd yet to decide how best to do that.

So she'd spent her time in the duty for which she'd been well trained: as the lady of the house. A woman raised to understand duty to home and family, she nonetheless struggled with her warring emotions. How could a man do what Mama Dell said her father had done? How could the reverend, a man of God, have a part in such duplicity?

If these things were true—the lies and the subsequent covering up of them—then her father's penchant to shut the world out by finding his focus at the bottom of an empty liquor bottle would make sense.

And how could she reconcile the past she had with the one that, if this story proved true, she deserved? Was it enough to believe, as Mama Dell stated, that only in heaven is life fair?

These questions and more kept her silent on the subject both in the presence of Mama Dell and in the time spent with Papa. Silence with him was the most difficult to maintain.

For eighteen days she had sat at his bedside, leaving him only to find respite in a few meager hours of sleep somewhere between midnight and dawn. On occasion, Jean Gayarre was delightful company, but by and large her father spent his hours grousing, groaning, or complaining.

Not that she blamed him completely. Like as not, she, too, would someday prove a difficult, impatient patient. Such was the Gayarre temperament.

Still, she took his jabs and jests in stride, giving each equal attention as she saw to the care and feeding of the man who, along with her mother, gave her life. Several times during the past week, she'd attempted to garner more information from him regarding her mother.

Was she yet living?

On the questions went, peppered carefully during conversations on such bland topics as the weather, the recent political climate, and the scent of the jasmine blooming each night in the courtyard outside the window. When Reverend Carter paced the room, his cane softly thudding against the thick carpets, she took her leave to allow the old friends their conversation.

She no longer concerned herself with whether aiding Isabelle's escape would be addressed. The topic of her transgressions, it seemed, was buried deep and intended to be left undisturbed. For this she felt a measure of relief, though the irony of the situation gave her pause.

The slave helped the free woman escape.

On days not dampened by the New Orleans spring rains, Emilie escaped her own gilded prison to take the long walks she'd become accustomed to in Fairweather Key. Some days, it was her only link to the place where she'd finally felt at home, thus she had become reluctant to share her time with anyone other than Nate, the coachman Cook insisted on sending to follow a close distance behind Emilie.

Today, however, she had no answer when Reverend Carter stated his intention to join her. To her great surprise, the older man proved an able companion, keeping up both the pace and the conversation without fail. Any temptation to grill him on the facts of her birth was tempered by the public forum in which the conversation was being held.

Thus, when they lapsed into companionable silence, Emilie felt no need to speak. Rather, she walked on and waited for the old pastor to speak again.

"So," he finally said, "I would have your opinion

on the state of my old friend. I will be blunt. Is he long for this world?"

Finally, the reason for tagging along. She hesitated but a moment. "I shall be honest."

His cane clicked on the hard surface of the sidewalk. "I would have nothing else."

Emilie nodded. "There are days when I fear he shall draw his last breath any moment. Other days, I fear he shall live so long that I shall surely arrive at the heavenly gates before him."

"I see."

"And his state of mind," she continued, "it never varies. He is but the same man I have always known, only there are moments when I fear he gives voice to thoughts he might have left in silence in years past."

The reverend nodded. "Indeed I have seen this." He stopped abruptly and reached for Emilie's arm, a look of alarm on his wrinkled face. "Has he perhaps said something that was harmful to you?"

"Harmful?" She thought a moment. "Nothing beyond his disdain for my calling to teach."

"And nothing further?" When she shook her head, his expression relaxed. " 'Tis a relief indeed. That you've been spared the brunt of his ill temper."

Odd his sudden concern for her feelings. Surely Hezekiah Carter, oldest and dearest friend to her father, knew that sparing feelings had never been something with which Jean Gayarre concerned himself. This he owed to his temperament, although often Papa was just too far into his cups to care.

"I fear I cannot remain indefinitely, Emilie," he said without breaking his stride. "I've word my congregation is suffering from my absence, as, I hope, is my wife. I fear I must make arrangements to leave within the week."

"I understand." Truly she did. Would that she, too, could pack her bags and step aboard a Florida-bound ship. "You are a good friend for accompanying me on this voyage. I shall not hold you here any longer."

"Then 'tis settled." He sighed. "I would beg you to join me, but my old friend tells me he requires your attendance at his bedside."

She walked on in silence for there was no need to respond.

Together they turned the corner at Royal Street. Up ahead, the Gayarre home loomed. "You do not have to remain here," Reverend Carter said. "You're a good daughter to him, Emilie, but he will not suffer in your absence. I warrant Delilah will see that he is well taken care of."

"He needs me."

"Does he now?" The pastor shrugged. "Or perhaps it is you who needs him. Perhaps," he said before pausing to allow a well-dressed couple to pass, "you are afraid if he dies you will not have answers to the questions you surely seek."

"Questions?" Anger flared white hot, and then on its heels came the guilt. He must have discerned her quest for funding for the school. "Do you assume I have come back to New Orleans only for my own purposes?"

"No," he said quickly, "although I do know there is some issue about funding our Fairweather Key school that might be resolved should your father contribute."

"Yes," she said slowly, guilt now dogging each step toward home, "this is true. I wish desperately not to separate children from parents in order for the students to receive an education, but the situation seems to be one that cannot be changed without a proper school for the children. If only the judge would . . ."

Emilie clamped her lips shut. Nothing good would come of further complaints. Judge Campbell was a man who would never waver once he made up his mind.

"Indeed, Judge Campbell seems to have a particular bent toward keeping the Fairweather Key coffers full to the brim," Reverend Carter agreed. "We've petitioned the Lord to deal with him, Emilie. What else can be done?"

She straightened her spine and bit back on the comment begging to be spoken. "Reverend, while I'm sure the families are doing their part in praying, I can't help but think that without action there may be nothing done."

"Dear girl, don't you understand prayer is action?" He shook his head. "Ah, the impetuousness of youth. There are situations where waiting is but the only solution."

"Waiting is not an option. If I cannot produce a school in three months' time, families will be praying over the decision of whether to send their children away or allow them to remain uneducated."

"And if you continue as you have teaching the children in the boardinghouse? What can he do, Emilie?"

"He can throw me in jail," she said, recalling the last conversation she had had with the unreasonable old judge.

"He wouldn't jail a woman, especially one of your quality and reputation."

Emilie gave him a sideways look.

"Indeed, he might, eh?"

She nodded.

Reverend Carter stopped once more, this time leaning heavily on the silver top of his cane. While his face bore no sign of distress, he seemed disconcerted.

"Are you ill, sir?"

Emilie reached for his sleeve, and the reverend stepped back. "I am fit and well, dear girl, but my heart is burdened. That much is true."

"You are concerned about me." She shook her head. "Do not be. I'm a grown woman and well aware of what I am doing."

"I fear we may no longer be talking about the education of children."

"No, but I will grant Papa his last wish even if it means I must choose him over my other responsibilities." She paused. "It has meant a great deal to me that your wife has undertaken the duty of teacher in my absence. I am beholden to her, though I know she cannot continue this indefinitely."

"My dear wife has loved every minute of this assignment," he said. "You're a young woman and perhaps would not understand, but when one reaches a certain age, it is comforting to know there is still value to be had and work to be done." He looked past her to the home where she'd lived all but the last two years of her life. "Come with me, Emilie," he said. "We've a talk to have that is long overdue."

To her surprise, Emilie found it difficult to keep up with the older man. In short order, she'd followed him up the stairs and into the front parlor, where he insisted she sit while he continue his pacing.

Finally, he halted. "I am an old man and a friend of this family," he said as he leveled a direct look at Emilie. "For this much, I have earned the right to ask of you a difficult question. Have you spoken to your father about the events that took you away from New Orleans?"

"The escape," she said softly. "No," came out in

a more bold tone. "He has not mentioned that I helped Isabelle escape her servitude, and I have not offered up the subject for conversation."

Reverend Carter gave a curt nod. "And shall you yet offer this up, or are you determined to ignore it?"

Emilie chose the words with care, her attention focused on the old pastor. "Truthfully?" When he nodded, Emilie managed a shaky grin. "I much prefer to let the subject lie dormant. I could face prison for having the daughter of my father's mistress freed." She shrugged. "Amend that. I did not have her freed. I planned it, then climbed aboard the boat with her. Oh, Reverend Carter, I only did as God instructed."

"Of course you did," he said. "And for that, He rewarded you both with the freedom He desired for you." He paused. "What of the letters from your father?"

Emilie thought back to the pair of letters brought to Fairweather Key by her brother and thrown into the fire. So he was ready to discuss the topic. Her heart quickened, as did her resolve to let Reverend Carter be the first to acknowledge the travesty Mama Dell insisted had occurred.

"Isabelle deemed the information they contained unfit for a lady and destroyed them in the chamber fireplace."

The reverend raised a gray brow. "And you did not question her?"

"I did not." She shrugged. "What could possibly be in a letter?"

He appeared deep in thought. "Then I suppose there is nothing further to say."

So he intended to let the subject go?

Unwilling to allow that, Emilie pressed on. "Indeed, there is one last question before we lay the topic to rest, Reverend Carter." She studied her hands for a moment, then lifted her gaze to meet his. "My mother."

"Your mother," the old man echoed.

Emboldened, she straightened her shoulders and rose, all the better to show the strength of purpose with which she intended to pursue the discussion. "You knew her."

It was a statement, not a question, for the reverend had been friend to her father longer even than he had been married to Elizabeth. At whatever point the mysterious Sylvie entered Jean Gayarre's life, Reverend Carter likely knew this as well.

She waited and tried to decipher the old man's expression, her heart pounding.

After what seemed an eternity, Reverend Carter looked away. "She was very beautiful."

"I was once scolded gently by a dear man for not giving a direct answer when asked." Emilie moved to the fireplace and rested her hand on the cold marble. "I will now return that gentle scolding, sir."

"Caught in my own net," the reverend said.

"Indeed, I met your mother on several occasions, though I regret I did not know her well."

"My mother Elizabeth?" She paused to pray for the strength to ask the question and then to withstand the answer. "Or my mother Sylvie?"

He looked as if he'd been slapped. "So you know."

"I would hear it from you, please."

Reverend Carter ducked his head. When he lifted his gaze, his features held compassion and, she hoped, regret. "I believe your father loved your mother—"

"My mother, Sylvie," she snapped.

"Yes, Sylvie," he said slowly, "but theirs was a love that could not be."

"Because he owned her."

"For a time," he said. "Though, as you know, he no longer owns anyone. Every member of his staff is free and paid well to remain here."

"I did not know this," she said. "I assumed . . ."

"They were slaves? No, though they all started out that way. I warrant the loss of Sylvie caused him to think differently on the practice. He freed them all while you were still in the cradle."

"All but Isabelle?"

He leaned on his cane and appeared to be contemplating the rug. "He often expressed the fear that he might lose her if she was set free. Thus the plan to allow her to believe she would be passed on to another when in fact he intended to free her."

The old man paused. "It was not a plan I approved of, though I regret I did allow him to use me as a part of it."

"Until I ruined it."

Smiling, Hezekiah Carter made his way to the settee and lowered himself onto the stiff cushions. "Indeed, I was quite angry about that, as was your father, as much for the disobedience as for the fact that my wayward son was involved. As it turns out," he said with a shrug, "it all worked out quite well, didn't it?"

"You mentioned that my father lost my mother." Despite the tears that threatened, Emilie took a deep breath and pressed on with the question she'd never dared to speak aloud. "Why did she leave?"

It was a shorter version of the real question that had plagued her since she'd been old enough to ask it: Why did she leave me?

"Was it my father who banished her?" she added.

"No, Emilie," he said softly. "For all your father's sins—and they are many—this one is not on his head." He rose to reach for his handkerchief and offered it to her.

Ignoring his gesture, Emilie swiped at her wet cheeks, caring not for the silk that would be ruined by her tears. "Then why was I given over to be raised by servants?"

The reverend placed the handkerchief in her open palm then wrapped her fingers around it. "Child, your mother is dead."

"Dead?" She slipped away from his reach, then put out her hands to stop his progress.

"Emilie, I'm terribly sorry."

Something inside her slipped ajar, and feelings she'd kept long guarded threatened to spill. One more question, and she would take her leave.

"So many times, I questioned Papa about my mother. At any time he could have relieved me of my hopes to see her again by telling me of her death." She paused to draw a deep breath, then let it out slowly. "Reverend Carter, did my father know of this and keep silent all these years?"

"Your father sought to keep this from you for the obvious reason, Emilie. To tell you of your mother's death would be to tell you who your mother was."

"So he allowed a girl to cry herself to sleep over a mother whom he knew would never return?"

The old man hesitated. "Yes," he finally said.

CHAPTER 6

May 21, 1836

The death of a stranger should never be so painful." Yet Emilie felt the loss of her mother all the more sharply because she was a stranger. For that matter, so was the woman in the mirror.

Where once she saw a person whose origins she thought she knew, now she just saw a woman. Did her curls, her lips, her skin color give her away as her father's or her mother's child? What did the combination of the two make her?

More important, did it matter, or was it as Mama Dell said? Save the fact that another had been held captive when in truth it should have been she, perhaps Mama Dell's philosophy might have worked.

"There are two things a person should never be angry at, what they can help, and what they cannot." A quote from the Greek philosopher Plato she'd committed to memory early in her formal education.

"Aren't I full of platitudes this morning?" she asked the woman in the mirror on her dressing table. "Well, that and a picayune will buy breakfast and coffee."

Emilie practiced a smile, then looked away. The fact that she sat at the table at this late hour was pure defiance.

Every morning since awakening in her old bed, Emilie had risen, seeing to her father's needs before attending to her own. This morning she'd pinned up her hair and donned her morning attire first, taking her time with each part of the process. Failing any further means of delay, she now found herself with a decision to make.

Emilie squared her shoulders and stepped out of her bedroom into the carpeted hallway. To the left was the back stairs leading to the servants' area, while to the right the front stairs led past her father's bedchamber. Always, her first steps of the day had led to her father.

That was before she knew about her mother. Maudlin as it sounded, everything in the time line of her life would reflect whether it happened before or after she knew she was orphaned by the mysterious slave woman. One last look to the right, and Emilie turned toward the back stairs and the delicious smells coming from the outdoor kitchen.

"We got a fine ham and red eye gravy this mornin', Miss Emilie," Cook called as she emerged into the sunshine. "Get on back inside and let me bring you a plate. You're about to waste away what with the little bit you eat."

"I'm fine."

The woman in no danger of wasting away pointed to the door. "Coffee pot's already full on the sideboard. Be sure and pour yourself some of that sweet cream into it. You won't be sorry."

In truth, Emilie's stomach rumbled, and the fog in her brain could stand to be washed away by a cup of Cook's strong chicory blend, but Emilie had no mind to drink or dine this morning. She barked an order for her father's breakfast meal to be prepared, then added a hasty apology before escaping to the courtyard.

Water trickled in the fountain, and the shade of the great magnolia tree beckoned. As a child, she could climb so far into the magnolia that even the most agile servant couldn't follow to carry her down. Hidden in the glossy green leaves, Emilie would read about worlds where mothers and fathers loved one another and daughters grew up to marry handsome princes.

Ignoring the strong temptation to attempt the climb just once more, she settled demurely onto the bench and waited. Rather than the breakfast she ordered, Cook emerged with a silver platter. Behind her, three of the kitchen help followed carrying similar items.

"What's this?" Emilie rose. "I specifically asked for a tray."

"Tray's in the dining room," Cook said without sparing her a glance. She stepped into the dining room and went about the business of setting a place for Emilie at the head of the long dining table. "C'mon, honey," she said when she'd finished, "and eat whilst I get your papa's food situated."

"I'll do it." Emilie settled the items on the breakfast tray despite Cook's feeble protest then looked up at the woman who'd stood in her mother's stead since Emilie's birth. "My father and I have some business to discuss, and I would ask that we not be disturbed," she said as she lifted the tray.

Cook nodded and stepped back, her eyes wide. "I told Dell there wasn't a secret in this house that wouldn't someday be made light. The Lord, He promises that in His Word."

Slowly, Emilie guided the tray back to its resting place on the table with only the slightest tremor impeding her progress. Speech was impossible.

"Not much happens in this house that somebody don't know about it." Cook paused. "Honey, sit down. You look like you're 'bout to fall over."

Emilie felt her eyes narrow as the blood rushed to her temples. Without concentration, she might have toppled. Several questions came to mind. She set her focus on the one that plagued her worst of all. "Is there anyone in this house other than me who did not know the truth about my mother?"

The older woman opened her mouth to speak, then must have thought better of it. She pointed to the tray. "Why don't I take this up to him? Likely he's wonderin' where—"

"Cook, please." Emilie hadn't intended to plead, yet her voice failed her. "Please," came out in a near-breathless whisper. "I would have you tell me about my mother."

Her gnarled hand clasped Emilie's sleeve as Cook looked past her to the open window. "I can't speak of such things," she said. "I took a vow not to tell."

"Then you are relieved of that vow." She leaned away from the old woman's grasp. "I know of her death. What I wish to hear is the story of her life."

Cook swayed, one hand on her forehead. "Praise the Lord," she declared as she righted herself and lifted her skirts to dance a jig. "God knew I couldn't carry that secret to my grave, and He's done performed a real life miracle and set me free. Where small hope exists, there does the Lord abide."

How many times had she heard Cook say those words? Too many to count. Enough to hold them in the same esteem as she did those of the ancient Greeks she'd studied at Miss Potter's school.

"If only He chose to perform the same miracle for me," Emilie whispered.

Cook stopped dancing and pointed at Emilie. "Oh, baby girl, He can. You just ask."

Emilie refused to wither under the old woman's stare. "I'm asking you."

"And I'll tell you, but not right now," she said. "There's an old man upstairs who'll have both our hides if he's not fed soon."

Emilie nodded. "Then we shall continue this conversation after breakfast." She reached for the tray once more. "I'll see he finishes quickly."

Unfortunately, Papa was in no mood for finishing his breakfast. Rather, he seemed to want to tarry over his coffee and think. Emilie assumed he was thinking, for he certainly was not speaking as he sat propped against his pillows, staring out the window Emilie insisted remain open.

Finally, she could stand the silence no more. "Papa, I've a topic to discuss if you're a mind." When he did not answer, she pressed on. "My mother. What news have you to tell me? Perhaps something you've withheld that you'd like to confess?"

His jaw slacked, then tightened as he reached for his coffee cup and then turned away. Her hopes of a quick admission of guilt and a passionate request for forgiveness fell away, and in their place, anger began to blossom.

The expansive room became too small. Emilie moved to set his tray on the table, but he held tight to it with his free hand.

"All right, then," she said in a tone she struggled to keep civil, "I'll leave you to eat while I do some tidying up in here."

The room was a mess; this much was true. Papa had refused entry to all but Cook and Mama Dell, neither of whom claimed any domestic skills beyond the kitchen. The chamber pot had seen regular cleaning, but the maids were shooed out should they attempt anything else.

Emilie's motives were not to bring a sparkle to the dust-covered mantel but to wear down her father's resistance. While she dusted, she thought of the seventeenth psalm. She'd read it upon awakening and immediately purposed to commit verse three to memory: "Thou hast proved mine heart; thou hast visited me in the night; thou hast tried me, and shalt find nothing; I am purposed that my mouth shall not transgress."

"My mouth shall not transgress." She would have to work hard to achieve that.

A knock sounded, and one of the kitchen help peered around the door. "I've a letter for the miss," she said.

"Go away," Papa shouted.

Ignoring her father, Emilie accepted the letter and handed the girl the rag. "Please send someone up to clean my father's room," she said. "I want a thorough cleaning. Top to bottom. And have Nate come up and help me move my father to another room while the cleaning is being done."

Wide-eyed, the girl nodded, then scurried out of the room, Jean Gayarre's curses following her. Folding the letter into the pocket of her dress, Emilie closed her eyes and said a quick prayer in hopes that the Lord might provide strength to still her tongue so she might not transgress.

"Father," she finally said, "I would have you stop this nonsense at once. Either you've taken leave of your senses, or you have not. In either case, I demand to know."

"Perhaps I have, Emilie, but I speak the truth." He gave her what almost passed for a pleading look. "If it is any consolation, I loved your mother best. I gave you a life that Sylvie—"

"That I was never entitled to."

His eyes followed her as she walked toward him and took a seat near his bedside. Papa clamped his lips shut and stared. The contents of his breakfast tray shifted as he set his coffee cup down without looking.

"And you let me believe I was the cause

leaving."

Now he stared. "Do you not think th

cult for me as well?"

"For you?" The temper she'd b

free, and she gave voice to h

you, I had no anesthesia for

to the bottle nor knew w

dare you ask me such

bled from the chair

"If I am such

doorway no

would you b

Papa sc

that or

Eve

known in new

forward, obviously warming to the topic. "Twice I took the woman back, and twice Elizabeth bore me a child. In both cases, I never knew whether that child belonged to me or some stranger whose wallet was fatter than mine." With a sweep of his hand, Papa cleared the bed of his breakfast tray. "Be glad not to find yourself in that number, Emilie. You may be the daughter of a slave, but at least I have the satisfaction of knowing you alone of all my children are truly mine."

"Did you know I laid awake and cried for her?"

He looked away. "I was told of it."

of her

s was diffi-

eld at bay broke
er outrage. "Unlike
my loss. I neither took
hat I was missing. How
a question?" Emilie stum-
toward the door.

a bad person, then darken my
nore, Emilie Gayarre. What use
have for a father like me?"

alded the air with another round of curses
ly the slamming of the door could silence.
n as she fell onto the cotton-cloud softness of
er childhood bed a few moments later, Emilie
could still hear the old man's voice ringing in her
ears.

Then, as she had done since childhood, Emilie
rose to open the glass doors and stepped onto the
balcony. Heedless of who might be watching, she
lifted her skirts and climbed over the rail and into
the welcoming arms of the grand magnolia tree
that had sheltered Emilie even when her parents
did not.

By late morning, the weather had turned as sour
as Emilie's temperament, so she retreated to her
bedroom. The biscuit she'd attempted to eat for
breakfast lay heavy as a rock in her stomach, and

her prayers felt as though they bounced off the canopy of her bed and dropped like lead onto the rose-strewn carpet below.

Emilie rolled onto her back and stared up at the blue silk overhead. As a child, she imagined it to be her own piece of the New Orleans sky and wondered what the sky might look like wherever her mother laid her head.

Her mother.

Emilie shook off the thought and left her room to slip into Papa's bedchamber. The room sparkled with the fresh cleaning. Likely, Papa would appreciate the efforts on his behalf once Nate fetched him. Though there was no need to hurry, she hastened nonetheless to retrieve the miniature of Sylvie from the bedside table. Returning to her room, Emilie lay with it beneath her pillow until finally the morning rain gave way to the brilliant fingers of golden afternoon sunlight.

Despite the change in weather, Emilie knew only a return to Fairweather Key would truly lift the melancholy that had settled like a cloud around her. If only she'd ignored the tug of responsibility and had accompanied Reverend Carter on his voyage three days ago.

Darken my doorway no more, Emilie Gayarre.

She rose and crept from her bed for the third time that day. Long gone was the defiant attitude of the morning. In its place was a resolve to leave New

Orleans forever. With her mother dead and her father lost to her, what other purpose did remaining behind serve?

A soft knock was followed by Cook stepping into the darkened room. "Mercy, child, you can't hardly go without eating."

"I couldn't, really," she said as Cook lifted the silver cover to reveal more food than three people could eat.

Cook shook her head. "You barely nibbled at your breakfast, and now you don't want lunch? What happened to that girl I danced a jig with this morning?"

Emilie shrugged and tucked her feet beneath her. "Perhaps you will bring her back by telling me about my mother."

"She was young and fair, and your papa was plumb taken with her," Cook said as she leaned against the door. "And she with him."

Reaching to clutch a pillow to her chest, Emilie regarded the older woman with what she hoped was a calm expression. "Did she love me?"

"Sweet girl, your mother loved the idea of you more than life itself."

"Yet she did not . . ." Tears prevented her from continuing. Cook came to Emilie and wrapped her in an embrace. When Emilie had collected herself, she leaned away. "Yet," she continued, "I never knew her."

"Honey," Cook said as she straightened, "she

was weak from your birth and never recovered. I reckon neither did your papa."

The simple answer made all the other facts fit together. Emilie patted her pocket. "I've taken the miniature of her. I'll not apologize or return it."

"You don't have to explain nothing to me." Cook shrugged. "And likely your papa won't ask where it's gone to."

"And likely he will not ask where I've gone, either."

Cook shook her head but thankfully did not comment.

Emilie glanced at the clock on her mantel. A quarter to two. "I'll need Nate to bring the carriage around."

"Yes'm," she said, "I'll fetch him now."

When Cook had gone, Emilie climbed off the bed and walked past the tray to don her shoes and reach for her handbag. As she leaned over, something slipped from her pocket.

"The letter."

Emilie retrieved it and hurriedly slipped it open. Inside, she read two paragraphs of chatty information from Isabelle, then one more that contained an impassioned plea for her quick return.

"And pray that our father has given his consent to fund the schoolhouse project," Emilie read, *"for I fear Judge Campbell is as stubborn as ever on his deadline of the first day of August."*

A second page followed, this filled with the

scribbled notes of every child who attended Emilie's makeshift classroom school in the parlor of the boardinghouse. Emilie held the letter to her chest as she counted the weeks until the judge's deadline.

"I'm an idiot. I've been so busy worrying myself with the past that I forgot about the future of these children."

The thought carried her all the way to the docks where, under the watchful gaze of Nate, she secured passage on a respectable passenger ship originally headed for Cuba. A few well-placed coins and a stern discussion between Nate and the captain regarding the fact that Emilie was a lady of quality bought her direct passage to Fairweather Key, where she would be deposited before the vessel continued on to Havana.

This accomplished, Emilie walked back toward the carriage with mixed feelings. The portrait now bounced and jostled against her leg from its hiding place in the pocket she'd sewn into her skirt. Two days hence, she would be headed home.

Home. Emilie sighed. When had New Orleans, the place of her birth, stopped being home? The question bore no reason for consideration.

"Home is where You are, Lord," she whispered when she'd settled into the carriage.

"Amen to that," she thought she heard Nate say.

CHAPTER 7

May 22, 1836

Surely they all knew of tomorrow's departure, but no one who lived inside the gates at the Gayarre home seemed willing to mention the fact. Cook greeted Emilie with the same smile at breakfast and said not a word. When the older woman returned with a tray for Papa, Emilie regarded her with surprise.

"I figure you'll be wanting to take this up yourself," Cook said as she turned and made haste out the back door.

"Subtle," Emilie muttered as she rose to fetch the impudent woman. But as she reached the back door, she changed her mind.

Only a coward would slink away without saying good-bye. "And I am not a coward," Emilie shouldered the tray and headed upstairs.

Thankfully, Papa was sleeping, so she left the tray and slipped out of the room without waking him. The same thing happened when his dinner was delivered, making Emilie wonder if the old man was as fearful of holding a conversation as she.

The evening of the twenty-second of May, with her bags packed and waiting by her door for the next day's sail, Emilie decided the ruse was over.

Rather than bring Papa his tray, she instructed Cook to do so, then waited until she heard the sounds of his spoon scraping the plate before she entered the room.

"I've been caught," he said. "Come in and close the door."

She did as he asked but remained near the exit lest he repeat his vile behavior. "Have you been informed of my departure?"

His expression remained unreadable. "According to Delilah, you sail at dawn."

Emilie nodded rather than speak.

"If I wished you safe travel, would you believe I meant it?" Again his face bore no clue of his feelings.

"Yes," she managed, unsure as to where this line of conversation was leading. "I would."

"If I begged you to stay?" His face bore no expression. "What then would you do?"

She sighed and admitted the truth, knowing what it could cost her and the children of Fairweather Key. "Should you require it, I will stay," she finally said.

Papa looked surprised and then pleased. "And if I were to offer a gift, would you accept it?"

Her voice failed for a moment. "That's not necessary," she managed, "although I must confess to taking my mother's miniature." She lowered her gaze a moment before continuing. "As this is all I have of her, might I take it with me?"

Papa inclined his head toward her, then slowly nodded. While she watched, a tear slid down the old man's cheek.

"Oh, Papa," she breathed as she fell toward him. "Thank you."

His arms were thinner, his breathing more labored, but the embrace was as welcome and comforting as the rare hugs from her childhood. More so, she decided, for this might be the last time he offered one.

"I don't have to go," she whispered against his already damp shoulder. "I can stay here until . . ." She couldn't say it.

"You'll go because you're needed there."

She looked up into his eyes. "How did you know?"

"A father knows." He paused. "I'll not allow you to travel unaccompanied. Allow me to send Nate with you."

"Absolutely not, Papa," she said. "You cannot spare him, and I have no need of him. The vessel I've chosen is a respectable ship whose captain produced impeccable references. Nate negotiated the fare and had what appeared to be quite a stern discussion with the captain." She forced a smile. "I'll be traveling directly to Fairweather Key, so the trip will be brief."

Papa seemed to consider her statement. "It will be as you say then," he said as she rested her head against his chest once more.

"Thank you, Papa, for understanding."

"Yes, but, dear Emilie, understand this: I'm an old fool," he said softly as he patted her hair. "You've filled a place in my heart that will remain long after you've gone." He paused again, and Emilie could hear his ragged breath as it seemed to catch in his throat. "Will you forgive me for all I've done?" He paused. "And for all I've failed to do?"

Emilie let out a long breath and tried hard to remember every detail of the moment. To her surprise, her father pushed her away to hold her at arm's length.

"I need to hear it, daughter," he said. "I cannot rest without hearing your words of forgiveness."

His image swam before her until she blinked away the tears. "Yes, Papa. Oh yes, I forgive you." She paused to gather her courage. "There is yet a topic of great importance I wish to speak of, Papa, but I fear you may not want to hear of it."

"Sylvie?"

"No," she said slowly.

Once again, her father held her at arm's length. "Anything, then, ma belle fille."

"Oui, Papa. I wish to speak to you of *Le bon Dieu*. The good Lord." Emilie closed her eyes. *Heavenly Father, give me the words*. When she looked at her father again, Emilie knew what to say and how to say it. The rest she would leave to the Lord.

• • •

May 22
Benning Plantation, Santa Lucida

What the sun did not burn, the relentless mosquitoes stung until, after more than two weeks on the island, Caleb could stand it no more. The letter in his hand, written by lamplight as the waves broke on the beach outside his window, contained an entreaty to Attorney General Butler to forge ahead immediately with any plans he might have for advancing Caleb within the department. He ended with the assurance that with a month's notice, he could be available to travel. It was the second such missive, the first sent just after his arrival on Santa Lucida.

Thus far in looking for someone to undertake management of the plantation, he'd found several qualified candidates among the work crews. Unlike other plantations, those who toiled for the Bennings did so as free men with pay and in conditions that made their employment the envy of all. Like as not, any man chosen would do a fine job restoring the luster to Ian Benning's jewel.

Besides, Fletcher would likely stay behind until he could claim a complete recovery. He could stand in Caleb's stead and help Mother with any decisions. The pair certainly got along famously.

Caleb slapped at another mosquito and tried to

ignore the tug of his conscience as the rebellious thoughts continued. Indeed, a man with his training would, given the time, likely do more harm than good managing such a venture.

That's not it, Spencer. Admit it. You're less fearful of becoming a failure at planting than you are of becoming a success at privateering.

At the thought, Caleb rose and began to pace. True, nothing back in Washington had managed to stir his blood like the sight of the vessel *Hawk's Remedy* limping away defeated after battle. Truer still, only Fletcher's continued improvement and his mother's entreaties kept Caleb tied to dry land poring over the accounting books rather than aboard the *Cormorant* adding his own entries to the ship's log.

It appeared that salt water indeed ran through his veins—a curse of the Bennings, according to his mother. "Well, no one but me shall know," he said as he returned to the desk, "and I shall not speak of it once I am given leave of this place."

The letter lay before him, and he turned his musings toward his mother. How would he explain his hasty departure? The truth stung, yet a lie was impossible. Caleb sighed as he wadded the paper and tossed it into the dying embers of the fire.

Leaning back in his chair, Caleb looked past the billowing curtains to the sea beyond. He'd been back in Santa Lucida less than three weeks. True to his mother's claims, the plantation had suffered under her watch, although the fault did not lay entirely with her.

Where once indigo and cane fields flourished, now fields lay fallow. The fierce storm of September last had dealt a death knell to many other plantations on the island. Those who were able had booked passage and left, practically giving away their lands in the process.

Others, such as the trusted fellow who'd acted as manager since Father died, lost their lives. Though the land suffered, at least Caleb's mother had thrived.

Still, without Ian Benning or John Spencer to guide her, Mary-Margaret Benning Spencer had no one to aid her in making decisions. To her credit, his mother had chosen to purchase several prime properties and now ruled over much of Santa Lucida as its largest landowner.

"All I have to do is make it turn a profit again."

Caleb reached for the ledger he'd hauled up from his grandfather's office on the first floor. Page after page of entries in his grandfather's hand detailed every profit and expense, and the occasional note peppered the pages with bits of the daily goings-on at Benning Plantation. In the margins, his grandfather had jotted ideas for new ways to produce indigo and thoughts on the coming cane season.

Despite his distaste for the subject, Caleb found it fascinating. It seemed as though Ian Benning did have considerable interest in something other than emptying the treasure chests from the vessels of honest seafarers.

"Would that the old pirate had chosen the life of a gentleman planter over this lunacy that still dogs my heels."

He closed the ledger and set it aside, then blew out the lamp. The room plunged into darkness. Slowly, the moon's silver path snaked across the wood floor and silk carpet to puddle on the mosquito netting that covered the massive wooden bed.

Rather than give in to the exhaustion tugging at the corners of his mind, Caleb opened the shutters guarding his door and stepped out onto the balcony that ran the length of the upper floor. The sea breeze tossed the tops of the palms and whipped his shirt away from his body. Casting a glance about to be sure he was alone, Caleb slipped out of the shirt to let the wind cool his sunburned skin.

His hair, already suffering for want of the barber's scissors, tossed about, surely adding to his unkempt appearance. Caleb rubbed his chin, now soft with the growth of the beard his mother detested. In the short while he'd been at Benning Plantation, the man in the mirror had become almost unrecognizable.

Resting his elbows on the rail, Caleb once again allowed his thoughts to wander. Were he of a disposition to allow it, he might content himself learning the intricacies of managing the plantation and forget for a time what he was missing back in Washington. What he'd seen of his grandfather's ledgers told him it was an undertaking not lightly entered into.

But he was a man whose life had been dedicated to the study of the law, a man who had long ago vowed to follow in the footsteps of his father and make a career of righting wrongs.

He should be toiling over a law book or closing the door on his office and returning home to his flat with tomorrow's work tucked under his arm.

"Yet summer is coming, and the capital will not be the most comfortable place for a man to spend his days." Likely the city's households were already in the process of being curtained and cloistered for the long summer days when their halls would be empty of their owners.

Indeed last year—and for much of the decade prior to that—he and a few others had suffered in the heat while those on higher rungs of the ladder summered elsewhere. Had he not prayed for relief more than once?

"Why then am I bothered that the Lord heard and answered?" He smiled. "Caught in a trap of my own devices, as it were."

Perhaps the challenge of learning would fill his days and make the time pass more quickly until he could say good-bye to Benning Plantation and the woman who presided over it. Caleb straightened at the traitorous thought. Though her great beauty had only been slightly faded by the years, her age was apparent in the slowness of her gait.

To think of these weeks and months as exile was to belie the fact God had given Caleb a gift of time he would have otherwise missed. He'd been remiss in using that time to spend with his mother, leaving the entertaining of her to Fletcher, who seemed not to mind.

"I shall not take this for granted, Father," he whispered. "Nor shall I endeavor to do anything but my best for You."

"Talking to yourself, son? I thought you'd given up that habit long ago."

Caleb whirled around to see his mother standing a few yards away. She wore the same clothing she'd donned for dinner, but to the ensemble she'd added a shawl of bright colors threaded with what appeared to be gold. This she wore draped over her shoulders and covering hair that was no longer the color of a raven's wing.

"The wind is fierce," he said as he scrambled to don his shirt once more. "You shouldn't be out here."

She shrugged as she made her way toward him. "You forget this is my home. The wind is nothing."

At her arrival beside him, Caleb wrapped his arm around her. "Can you not sleep, Mother?"

"I'm afraid Mr. Fletcher and I have been embroiled in a battle of epic proportions that has only just concluded."

Caleb laughed. The nightly chess matches between his mother and Fletcher had become legendary for their combination of intensity and humor. Often Caleb remained just to watch.

"Did you let him win again?"

Mother smiled but said nothing. "You mention lack of sleep. I would ask the same of you." Her dark eyes searched his face. "Perhaps you are wishing for the life from which I've stolen you."

"You've stolen nothing," he said, "except for that place in my heart that has always been reserved for you."

Her smile was quick, as was the fading of it. "Yet a man of seven and twenty should have a woman of a much younger age in his heart." She slid a glance in his direction. "Dare I hope there is someone of whom you have yet to speak?"

"Aye, there is." He winked. "And her name is Justice. I've been studying her now for nigh on a decade and I'm certain my love will come to fruition."

Mother gave him a playful nudge. "Your jest falls on deaf ears, son. A mother worries when her son finds nothing to please him save the reading of books and the pursuit of career."

Caleb managed a smile. "Then worry no more, Mother. For I've turned the matter over to the Lord and left Him in charge of my heart."

"As have I," she said, "and perhaps more frequently have I also petitioned Him to move swiftly before my son's intended passes him by while his nose is impossibly wedged into a law book."

Caleb's grin was quick and broad. He reached for his mother's hand and held it to his lips. "Then, perhaps we shall strike a bargain."

Another glance. "And that would be?"

"I shall look up from my law book occasionally to see if she has arrived, and you shall continue to pray that this woman the Lord has fashioned for me will know where to find me." Caleb's chuckle was lost in the sound of the surf. "Oh, and be sure to pray that I will recognize her. I fear the Lord has made me quite blind in that area."

He thought the jest quite clever until his mother stepped away to point her finger in his direction. "You can toy with me, Caleb Spencer, but not with your heavenly Father. This is not a chess game with the ending decided by the cleverest participant."

"I'm sorry, I—"

She held up a hand to stop him, then grasped her shawl as the wind whipped it away. "The prayers have long been whispered to God, my son," she said. "And I know when you meet her, there will be no doubt she is someone special. Indeed, I have asked God to sear her mark onto your soul so that, every time you look into the mirror, you see not yourself but the man she has caused you to become."

Whether it was the wind or the waves or the odd

statement, Caleb found himself completely unable to respond. He pleaded exhaustion and wished his mother a hurried good night.

Back in his room, he threw off his shirt and trousers and slipped behind the nets that did a decent service of keeping the bloodthirsty insects at bay. Long into the night, Caleb lay still, listening not to the sounds outside his door but to the memory of his mother's warning.

Finally, he fell into a restless sleep broken in bits and snatches by the cloaked image of a woman who seared her mark on him with a dueling pistol to his heart. By morning, he'd found humor in the dream.

Any woman who wanted to leave such a mark on him would have to shoot him to do so. She certainly wouldn't find any other way to manage it.

CHAPTER 8

May 26, 1836
Aboard the merchant vessel Sunday Service

Four days at sea, and Emilie felt as green as the dress she wore. "An unfortunate choice of attire," she muttered as she adjusted the strings on her bonnet, then attempted to rise though the floor beneath her seemed to do the same.

Dining thus far had been near to impossible, much more so this morning as most of the night was spent lashed to the bunk with a length of rope. Such was the tossing of the waves that she'd felt certain she would wake to find all her things had been bandied about like toys.

The tiny cabin held fast despite the rolling of the ship, and with the sunrise, Emilie saw that so had her traveling trunk. Carefully lifting the lid, she reached for the tin of food Cook had packed for the journey and nibbled at a few crumbs of cornbread. When that went down successfully, she attempted a few more.

Soon enough, she'd had her fill and replaced the tin atop the other items in the trunk. As she made to shift the items around and close the lid, a small but heavy package landed atop her foot.

"What's this?" She lifted the paper-wrapped bundle and turned it over. "Where did this come from?" Emilie looked into the trunk and saw that her small traveling case had been dislodged during the night and sprung open. Likely someone had placed this inside for her to find upon arrival in Florida.

Emilie held it up, then gave it a good shake. Moving back to her bunk, she sat beneath the gently swaying lantern and pulled at the string that held the package together. When the tie gave, a substantial sum of money and a folded note came tumbling out onto her lap and spilled on the bunk.

Gasping, Emilie reached for the note and folded it open. "'*Pour mon* belle fille, Emilie,'" she read.

" 'This is for the purpose that calls you back to Fairweather Key.' "

She let the note drop and reached to grab a handful of the fortune now decorating her bunk. "For what calls me back to Fairweather Key," she whispered.

The laughter started as a giggle that bubbled up from deep inside. By the time she'd made an accounting of her newfound treasure, the giggle had become a laugh so joyful she doubted her ability to stop.

But stop she must, for the money needed to be safeguarded until she arrived home to present it to the judge. As she had suspected, the amount in her arms was exactly equal to the sum Judge Campbell required to keep the children's education in Fairweather Key.

"How did you know, Papa?" she mused as she collected the money and returned it to the safety of the nondescript package. "Lord, was it You?"

The answer she might never know, but this did not take away one whit from the celebration the town would hold upon her return. Not a penny of this precious money would go to anything but the children's education, but perhaps if the townsfolk were to pool their resources, the festivities would be something to behold.

"Oh, Papa," she said again, overcome with emotions that left her unable to move from the bunk.

A great wave lashed against the vessel, sending

Emilie crashing shoulder first into the cabin wall. A check of the tiny porthole showed the sun still shone bright, so the cause could not be a storm. For this, she quickly gave thanks. The tossing and turning of her stomach, however, seemed greatly magnified when the walls were close enough to see their movement.

And she had great need to celebrate, even if those aboard could never be told the cause.

"Sunshine is exactly the cure for this," she said as she folded the paper and attempted to retie the strings. " 'For these are light and momentary discomforts.' "

The repair of the package complete, she searched about for a place to hide it. Finally, she settled on sliding the package into the secret pocket in her underskirt alongside the miniature of her mother. While it was heavy enough to pull at the waist and tug down on the hem, her green overskirt hid the evidence. That accomplished, she rose and patted her front. Unless someone were to breach the bounds of propriety, the package would remain a secret.

Emilie said a prayer of thanks. Papa might have given the money, but she had no doubt where the idea had come from. She then extinguished the lamp and, with one hand clutching the wall, carefully made her way first to the door of her claustrophobic cabin and then onto the deck. After standing near the rail for a few moments, Emilie found the sunshine did indeed help her queasiness, but the wind buffeted her such that she had to repair to the shadows of the quarterdeck.

Other passengers seemed to have the same idea, for none strayed near the rail. Since they left the river and begun plowing across open water, she had seen very few of her dozen or so fellow travelers. Most, it seemed, kept to themselves and their cabins.

A rather sturdy barrel beckoned, and she managed to settle atop it without toppling it in the process. Before long, she'd become so comfortable there that she closed her eyes and allowed the tangy ocean scent to fill her lungs. Her breathing slowed, and a lovely feeling of peace descended.

The ringing of a bell jarred her, and Emilie scrambled to keep from falling. Where was she? Surely she slept in her bed. No, a bunk, that was it.

A second look revealed she still sat atop the barrel, albeit just beneath the upper deck where the watch bell was situated. The bell rang several more times as Emilie collected herself and attempted to slow her racing heart.

Heat flooded her cheeks as embarrassment set in. Panic quickly followed as she patted her skirt in search of the hidden package.

She finally found it hanging much farther to the side than when she originally had donned the outfit. Obviously during her ill-timed nap, her underskirt had shifted with gravity and taken the package with it. Repairing the damage while above deck was unthinkable, but reaching her cabin without being seen seemed unlikely as well. She stepped off the barrel and did her best to hide the bump now protruding from her right hip by removing her bonnet and holding it atop the problem.

With one hand occupied, the other guided her around the corner and toward the passageway from which she'd come. Emilie had gone only a few steps on the pitching deck when the captain appeared on the quarterdeck above.

"A fine morning it is, Miss Gayarre," the affable captain called down to her. "We'll be making good time today."

"Wonderful," she said as she held the bonnet tight against her side. "If you'll excuse me, Captain."

"Indeed, we shall see port sooner than expected." He lifted his spyglass to peruse the horizon, oblivious to her discomfort. Emilie seized the opportunity to slip away and had almost made it when the captain shouted, "Oh, mercy, no!"

His tone stopped her short. She looked up at the quarterdeck, then over in the direction where the captain seemed to be aiming his spyglass. On the horizon she saw some sort of sailing ship. If she squinted, Emilie could barely make out three large sails.

Nothing about the vessel distinguished it from

the others they'd seen during their voyage thus far. When the bell above began to clang again and men scrambled from all points to gather on the quarter-deck, Emilie knew something about the vessel had caused the alarm.

"You'll have to go below now," the captain called down to her. "And I'll have no sightings of you until someone from my crew comes to tell you 'tis safe to leave your cabin. In the meantime, take all safety precautions."

"Safety precautions?"

"Aye," he said, his tone agitated. "Bolt your door and do not light the lamp no matter how tempting the urge might prove. Answer no one lest they call you by name. In the meantime, we're racing for Havana."

"Havana? But I paid extra to—"

"Miss, those coins won't do either of us any good if they're in the hands of ruffians. Now do as I ask."

Emilie nodded, her fingers fisted around the bonnet.

"And Miss Gayarre?" he called.

"Yes?"

"If someone comes to your door and does not identify themselves as a member of my crew or one of your fellow passengers, do not remove the bolt."

"But that makes no sense, Captain," she said. "Who would come to fetch me except someone from the *Sunday Service*?"

He gestured toward the approaching vessel.

"But that's just a ship." Emilie shielded her eyes and looked over the trim vessel for some sign of ill intention. "Indeed, it appears to be much the same as all the other vessels we've seen on this voyage."

"Indeed it does," he called down, "yet this one seems to be dogging our steps. Now, for a reason known only to her captain, she's begun to chase us down. Could be she's sailing under the Mexican flag and thinks she's found her a slaver to hold until someone comes up with the taxes." His chuckle was dry and humorless. "They call it taxes, but I have another word for it."

"But we're not slaving," Emilie said.

The captain looked indignant. "Indeed not. Yet ours would not be the first to be boarded under the guise of checking." He lifted the spyglass and held it to his eye, then lowered it slowly. "She's too far off course, and she's been toying with us too long. I'd not make her for Mexican navy."

"Are you certain?"

He gave her a stern look, then dismissed her question with a wave of his hands. "Now get below and hide. I'll not concern myself with womenfolk when the care of this vessel and its cargo is my first priority."

Emilie gave the oncoming vessel one last look, then squared her shoulders and quickly found her cabin. The sounds above were muffled in her cell-like room, but nothing sounded amiss.

When the ship lurched, its sails obviously catching in the brisk wind, she let out a long breath. Surely no vessel was a match for this one. They would soon outrun whoever gave chase, and that would be that.

"And indeed all will be well," she said, her voice echoing in the cabin.

The packet now bulging in her skirt, she made to repair the damage. Its weight and bulk, however, made hiding it impossible. Emilie sighed and crossed the cabin to open her trunk. Perhaps there was a way to remedy the situation.

She pulled an underskirt from the trunk and began work on adding a pocket much like the one she wore now. By the time she was done and the money distributed between the two hiding places, a commotion had begun above.

Men shouted. The watch bell clanged. Above it all came the sound of the captain barking orders that made little sense to Emilie's untrained ears.

The shouting stopped and only the bell continued to pierce the silence. Emilie took hope in this. Perhaps the action above was not one of distress but one of welcome. Perhaps the vessel was merely following the same route and had clarified this with some sort of nautical signal.

"Lord," Emilie said as she allowed the idea to sink in and become possible, "would You give that vessel and all aboard safe sailing to their destination?"

Within the hour, a man from the crew came to slip a note beneath Emilie's door, and she lit the lamp for just a moment in order to read it. Dinner would not be served in the dining room for the vessel was still under full sail and in hopes of arriving in Havana at a time to be determined. Until then, all passengers were confined to quarters.

Confined to quarters? Her stomach complained, and she spied the trunk. "Thank you, Cook, for sending supplies."

Emilie found her food quickly, then extinguished the lamp. She nibbled her meal in darkness, an odd situation all around. Somewhere between the rising of the quarter moon and the first light of morning, she fell into a fitful sleep. Awakened by the watch bell, she raced to the tiny window without lighting the lamp.

A deafening roar that could only be cannon fire shook the very floor beneath her feet. Emilie raced for the bunk and tucked her legs up under her. Remembering the captain's warning, she retraced her steps to bolt the door.

Her heart pounding, Emilie felt her way along the wall until she found her bunk and fell into it. Overhead the sounds intensified until it sounded like the roof above her might fall away and a roomful of men shouting and running about would join her.

The ship rocked and shuddered but seemed to

remain steady in the water. Thankfully no further shots were fired, leaving Emilie to return to her theory that it was all a misunderstanding.

She held to that theory until the first man tried to burst through the door. Even then, Emilie never considered she might be leaving the vessel by force.

Until the door splintered.

May 27
Benning Plantation, Santa Lucida

Caleb held the letter carefully, knowing whatever it held would change the careful balance he'd finally found here on the island. His intention in riding to the highest point on the island had been to put space between his thoughts and the home he had come to share with his mother.

Caleb could see the green fields planted under his grandfather's hand. Nearby, the *Cormorant* bobbed at anchor on seas so blue-green that it hurt his eyes to stare at them for long.

None of this, he realized with a start, bore the impression of his father. It seemed as though John Spencer's political and judicial reputation in Washington did not extend to this far-flung corner of the world.

The horse stamped at the damp earth, likely as reluctant as he to remain still when so much of Benning Plantation lay before them. Truly Caleb had found he loved to sit astride a good horse, to give the animal free rein and hang on bareback while the creature flew over the earthy green fields and up into the hills. This mare, Rialto, was his favorite.

"Settle down," he murmured as he patted the horse's flank. "We'll run soon enough."

The letter slid out of his pocket and nearly tumbled to the ground before he caught it. As Caleb broke the attorney general's seal, he held his breath.

Scanning the greeting and first paragraph, his gaze landed on the words he'd hoped for when he left Washington: *Proud to offer this promotion.*

"Promotion. Hurrah!" he shouted as a flock of orangequit took to the skies from their hidden perches in a nearby grove of nance trees.

Once again, he had to settle Rialto before continuing. The next sentence stopped him cold. He read the words again, then slowly said them aloud: "'. . . to the Department of the Navy.'" After he finished reading the last line, he said, "But I'm a lawyer, not a sailor."

"Well, that's a pity," Fletcher said from somewhere behind him. "For I had hoped to entice you to accompany me aboard the *Cormorant* today. I've a mind to test her sails a bit on an errand, and the day's a fine one."

"Well now." Caleb swiveled to see his mentor walking toward him.

No longer did he have the shuffling gait, drawn complexion, and stooped shoulders of a man on the wrong side of health. The only sign of his injuries was the ebony and gold walking stick he barely depended on and the bandages Caleb knew were wrapping his shoulder and chest.

"What say you, lad?" Fletcher removed the ever-present pipe from his pocket and studied it, one hand leaning on the walking stick. "Are we to sail this morning or must I go alone now that you've stated you're not a sailor?"

Caleb laughed even as he determined to steer the subject away from the words he hadn't intended the old man to hear. "A sail, is it? You're looking fit this morning."

"Don't tell your mother." The older man stuck his pipe between his teeth. "I fear she's taking her duties as my nurse quite seriously."

"And I warrant you find nothing to complain of in her caretaking." Caleb laughed. "Indeed, my friend, I wonder if romance is not afoot."

Fletcher's face turned somber. "I'll not have you disrespect the memory of your father, Caleb Spencer. Your mother is a friend, and a friend only."

"Disrespect?" Caleb thrust the letter back into its hiding place and dismounted. "What disrespect do I offer, old friend?"

He lifted his walking stick to point it at Caleb. "Your father was a man of great accomplishment and respect. It's unthinkable to consider Mary-

Margaret might look upon me as his replacement."

Mary-Margaret. Caleb forced his expression to remain neutral. *Indeed, the old man is smitten.*

Caleb snagged the mare's reins and walked toward Fletcher. "My friend," he said as he clasped his hand on the older man's uninjured shoulder, "I have been remiss in thanking you for returning the smile to my mother's face. She's worn her widow's weeds for far too long."

Fletcher gave Caleb the stern look once reserved for correcting youthful misbehavior. "It is your return, not mine, that has your mother smiling. I am but a pet project that fills her time."

"Yes, well," he said as he nodded toward the ocean, "have you my mother's permission to flee her care for an afternoon's sail?"

Fletcher's expression sufficed as an answer.

"Aye then. A sail it is." He gestured to Rialto. "Perhaps you would like to ride?"

Fletcher shook his head. "Thank you all the same, but I'll keep to walking, lad. I fear the jostle is not something that agrees with me just yet."

"Then I shall walk with you."

A short while later, with Rialto handed over to the stable boy, Caleb stood at the rail of the *Cormorant.* As the wind filled the sails and the island of Santa Lucida grew smaller, Caleb turned to Fletcher. "I suspect, my friend, this is not merely an afternoon's whim. Where, dare I ask, is this vessel headed?"

106

"Havana," he said without sparing a glance in Caleb's direction.

"Havana?"

Fletcher nodded as he steadied himself with his cane. "Your mother's idea. She did not specifically say as much, but my guess is she felt you needed some time away from the island."

Caleb looked in the direction from which they'd just come. "And what purpose would this time away serve?"

"Lad," he said, "long ago I stopped trying to understand the logic of women." He smiled. "When your mother asked that I take part in this mission to save you from whatever she believes ails you, what was I to say?"

"Indeed." Caleb leaned against the rail and watched as the vessel skimmed over the froth of waves, then parted a school of shimmering yellowfin tuna. "And how long am I to be banished from Santa Lucida?"

"I have no specific instructions on this," he said, "so I cannot exactly say. She did instruct me to post a packet of letters."

He turned his back to the ocean and braced his feet on the rolling deck. His mentor, a man who relied on a cane and wore bandages to bind him together, seemed to have less trouble remaining upright than Caleb.

Another reminder of Caleb's life of academics rather than adventure.

"Post letters?" He made to smile in order to banish the comparison. "A rather thin excuse given the fact a postal vessel sails past Santa Lucida some ten days hence."

Fletcher retrieved his pipe and studied it. "With Havana a day's sail, my guess is we can see Santa Lucida again in two days, although three would likely please your mother."

"Perhaps."

Three days to decide how to respond to the letter now pressed into his pocket. Perhaps he would look to Fletcher for advice. Indeed, this sort of thing could be best decided when more than one was involved. But before he could speak about it, Caleb knew he had another to consult. "If you'll excuse me, I'll take my leave for a spell."

"A nap this early in the afternoon?" Fletcher chuckled.

"A visit with the Lord," he said. "There's a conversation to be had."

"I see." If his curiosity was piqued, Fletcher's expression gave nothing of it away.

"And when He and I are done, I shall seek you out for some advice if you're of a mind to lend it."

His smile was quick and broad. "Always, lad," he said. "Always."

CHAPTER 9

May 27, 1836
Aboard the Sunday Service

Only the broad back of the stranger was within Emilie's reach, but despite the smoke that burnt her throat and stung her eyes, she fought with all she had. Finally, the man strode back into her cabin and tossed her unceremoniously onto the bunk.

He was a large man, wide of shoulder and clad in rags that looked to have once been elegant clothing. A garish yellow coat barely covered the remains of a fine linen shirt. Atop his mop of filthy blond hair, he wore a gentleman's top hat that had seen better days. Where she expected to see boots, the man was barefoot.

All of this she saw as she plotted the best path to the open door.

Before Emilie could flee, he had her hands. With one knee, he pinned her to the mattress while he lashed a length of rope around her wrists.

"Would that the flames weren't upon us, lassie," he said, his face near and his breath vile. "For a woman of spirit sets my blood a-boilin'."

A crash somewhere near the cabin door caused the man to jolt. Seizing her chance, Emilie pulled away. His lunge sent Emilie skittering to the corner of the bunk. "I'd rather go down with this ship than leave it with you," she said before dissolving into a fit of coughing.

When he came near, she recovered just in time to rake her nails across his cheek. That failed to dissuade him, so she kicked him, landing a blow that sent him backward.

The man rose, and a trickle of blood traced a path down his pock-marked cheek.

"Miss," he said as his chest heaved and the top hat tumbled to the floor, "ye jest got yer wish."

Time skidded to a halt, and Emilie watched the horrible man reach for the pistol hanging from his belt by a red silken cord.

He lifted the pistol.

Checked his aim.

Smiled.

Without warning, a wall of water divided them.

Havana

That evening after a dinner of sumptuous proportions, Caleb finally broached the subject of his letter from the attorney general. Rather than describe it, he simply handed the letter to Fletcher.

"Read it," Caleb said, "and you'll see my need to visit with the Lord this afternoon."

Fletcher quirked an iron-gray brow. "Lad, one never requires a letter from some fellow in Washington to have a need to speak to the Lord."

"Enough of the jest," Caleb said with mock impatience as he lifted the mug of strong coffee. "Read and then I shall entertain your thoughts rather than allowing your thoughts to try and entertain me."

"Clever," he said as he lifted the letter and lowered his gaze.

For a moment, Caleb turned his attention to the brilliantly hued room, its glorious tile and heavy timbers giving the impression they sat in the reception hall of some grand Spanish hacienda. Beneath the light of what seemed to be a thousand lamps twinkling to music provided by a skilled guitarist, all of Havana looked to be in attendance.

Were not men of all kinds dining in the establishment, Caleb might have felt out of place. His overlong, sun-streaked hair and length of beard made him appear as though he'd long ago given up on a barber's skills, yet he looked no worse than some and better than others.

He chuckled at the thought of what his colleagues at the attorney general's office would think of their staid coworker. Glancing down at the golden tan on his arms and calluses on his palms, he knew they'd likely not even recognize him. He rarely recognized his own image in the mirror.

Out of the corner of his eye, Caleb saw Fletcher fold the letter. "Well?"

"A moment," Fletcher said.

Caleb nodded and studied a trio of waiters who

seemed to be racing one another to a table filled with men in uniform. The soldiers appeared to be in the midst of some great debate, and their rapid-fire chatter rose and fell with the sounds of the guitar.

"Aide to the secretary of the navy. Impressive. So." Fletcher leaned back in his chair and gave Caleb a direct look. "What are you going to do?"

"I am going to listen to your sage advice," he said, "and then I shall make my decision."

Fletcher handed the letter back to Caleb. "How well do you know this man?"

"The attorney general?" Caleb shook his head. "Well enough, I suppose, although he was Father's friend, not mine."

"I see." He seemed to be considering something. "And do you think this move is wise?"

"It's a surprising one, most certainly. When I left, I was told the next opening as aide to the AG was mine." He pointed to the letter. "And now this."

Fletcher's eyes narrowed. "What do you make of it?"

"Well, that's the question of the moment, isn't it?"

"No, lad," Fletcher said slowly. "The question of the moment is whether you'll accept the promotion."

"Indeed it is." He toyed with his mug, then lifted his gaze to meet Fletcher's stare. "It appears I must accept it or leave. According to the letter, my job will be filled in my absence."

"Which was the plan all along, correct?"

Caleb inclined his head. "The plan was that my job would be filled when I received the promotion. I certainly never expected the promotion would be into the department of the navy."

"But?"

"I've been trained as a lawyer, Fletcher, and always expected I would follow my father in service to the attorney general. I never considered anything else."

Again he lifted one brow. "Until now."

A statement, not a question.

"Yes, actually," Caleb said slowly. "Until now."

"Then it's settled." Fletcher pushed back from the table and rose, leaning on his cane while he waited for Caleb to join him. "Welcome to the naval department, lad."

As they walked, he tried on his new title. Lieutenant Spencer. Indeed it seemed to fit.

"Did you mention this to your mother?" Fletcher asked.

"No." He paused. "Yet she's sent us on this mission to post mail in Havana."

Fletcher grinned. "Do you think perhaps your mother wanted you out to sea when you spoke to the Lord? It would be a fitting place for a naval officer with promise to spend time with his Creator."

Caleb laughed. "I hesitate to believe a gentlewoman such as my mother might actually contrive to do such a thing. Yet . . ."

"Well, whatever the reason, it was a fine meal we had and a fine sail to get here." He gestured to the bay where the *Cormorant* lay at anchor amongst the countless others under the moon's pale glow. "And tomorrow we'll test her sails and head back to Santa Lucida, eh?"

"But not before I draft a letter accepting the promotion." He stopped short. "Wait, Fletcher. My job is not done in Santa Lucida. How can I leave my mother when she has no one to look after her welfare or the workings of the plantation?"

Fletcher's face was half-hidden in shadows, but what Caleb saw of it held an expression of concern. "I had hoped to have this conversation at a later date," he said. "I'm put in mind of our earlier conversation." He paused. "With your permission, I would like to see to the care of Benning Plantation in your absence."

"And to the care of my mother?"

Fletcher jammed the pipe into his mouth and set off walking. Up ahead, the moon glinted off the mainmast of the *Cormorant* as if leading the way. Caleb picked up his pace to catch up to the older man, who was practically racing toward the vessel.

"Have I hit upon a subject you wish not to discuss? Perhaps you've been giving thought to what I said?" Caleb asked when he fell into stride beside him. "Perhaps I should withdraw the question."

"It would be a healthy idea," Fletcher said, the pipe still clenched between his jaws. "For although you're seed of the Bennings and son of John Spencer, I'll not be answering to you on this particular matter."

"I see."

The older man stopped just short of the dock and whirled around to face Caleb. "And another thing, lad. I'm sure you'll find my devotion to the Bennings as odd and my attention to your mother's welfare as amusing." He paused to pull the pipe from his mouth and jam it into his pocket. "However, you will comment on neither. Do you understand?"

"Clearly."

He tilted his head toward Caleb, his eyes narrowing. "So we're done here?"

"Completely."

"And your mother will know nothing of this conversation."

"Not a word." He gave Fletcher a serious expression. "I've been thinking that perhaps I should have the crew weigh anchor and head back to Santa Lucida tonight rather than wait for daybreak. If we weigh anchor in an hour, we can be home in time for breakfast."

"Do as you wish, lad."

Caleb sidestepped a stack of crates, then returned to the topic at hand. "Might I impose on you to wake the captain and tell him we wish to dine with my mother at dawn?"

"I'll not comment on your reasoning, but I shall inform the captain of your decision."

Stifling a smile, Caleb allowed the indignant man to board the vessel ahead of him. "Thank you."

When Fletcher disappeared below without even sparing a curt good-night, Caleb knew he'd trod on sensitive ground. "No more teasing," he whispered. "It appears my mother may have a suitor."

The thought caused him to smile as he settled into a dark corner of the quarterdeck and made himself comfortable for his evening conversation with God. As he watched, one by one the tiny pinpricks of light pierced the sky.

With each new star, Caleb called to mind a blessing the Lord had bestowed. It was a game he'd learned as a child; who had taught it, he could not remember.

He added a new blessing to the list. "Thank You, Lord, for the man who loves my mother."

Emilie kicked at the water until her tangled skirts bound her legs just as tightly as the rope that still bound her hands. While the gold in her skirts pulled her toward the ocean's floor, salt water stung her eyes and nose and filled her mouth until she could neither see nor breathe.

Save me, Lord.

Somewhere in the distance, a bell sounded, likely from the vessel carrying the thieving criminals. She sank below the surface, and her ears gurgled with the rush of water, ending any hope of hearing from which direction they approached.

Or, she hoped, from which direction they departed.

Please, save me, Lord.

Once again, she bobbed to the surface, this time pitching forward in the hopes of keeping herself afloat by floating, not an easy thing to accomplish given the weight of her father's gold. The thought of what she must look like made her shiver, as very likely she could indeed be dead before anyone other than the ruffians who burned the *Sunday Service* found her.

I cannot do this alone, Lord.

With concerted effort, she threw her head forward and paid for it by striking something hard. Blinking, she tried to see what sort of oddity might be afloat in her vicinity.

Near as she could tell from the feel of it against her cheek, she'd managed to find some remainder of the ship. Still warm to the touch, it likely fell away charred but not completely burned.

Emilie tried in vain to hold onto the floating lumber. Raising her hands over her head, she allowed herself to slip under water then kicked hard and lunged forward again. This time she managed to hold on, albeit suspended half on one side of the log and half on the other.

Hers was a precarious position, one that still allowed the waves to break over her head, but at least she did not have to fear drowning just yet. For a moment, Emilie lay completely still, her arms slightly bent to relieve the ache that had begun to plague her.

Thank You, Lord, for a precious few more minutes.

The bell had stopped, and all the world was silent. Strong was the temptation to call out, to see if she were indeed the lone survivor. To do so, however, might bring the criminals back.

Better to remain silent and be thought dead than to open my mouth and become so. A proverb not found in the Bible yet quite applicable to her current situation. Emilie stifled a giggle and knew she'd completely lost any sense of propriety or sane thinking.

"Forgive me, Lord," she whispered, though the water filled her mouth. "I mean no disrespect."

The bell rang again, this time followed by a blinding arc of light. Some sort of vessel's wake sent her scuttling in one direction while the charred plank went in the other. When the water covered her head, she found her arms were useless.

Exhaustion had set in.

The skirt that had held the promise of a future for Fairweather Key school children now tugged at her and threatened to drag her to the bottom. Where once she fought, now she merely longed for sleep.

As her limbs grew heavier and her lungs screamed for air, Emilie cried out one last time to God: *Save me, Lord.*

When the hand reached out to pluck her from the water, Emilie was certain God had heard her prayer. She rose from the water as if some sort of winged creature had lifted her to safety. The landing, however, was less angelic. She fell hard and skidded to a stop against something that felt as if there might be splinters covering it.

Emilie tried to rub her sore shoulder, then realized her skirts had twisted and scrambled to cover her legs. The wet fabric fought her trembling hands, but with work, she managed the feat. Still Emilie had no idea where she was or with whom she sailed.

Was her arrival in this place truly an angelic visitation? If so, then she must be headed to heaven.

Still, she hadn't expected heaven to smell this, well, vile.

Someone lit a candle, and she saw she'd been snatched by a collection of men who obviously worked for the other side.

A fellow with more pockmarks than teeth inched toward her and placed a hand on her thigh. "What's this?" he asked, his voice thick and his eyes narrowed.

It took Emilie a moment to realize the man had found the bulge in her skirt that gave away the gold's hiding place. Slapping his hand away, she tried to stand but found it impossible on the slippery deck.

Another set of hands reached out and grabbed her, lifting her up to deposit her on shaking knees. Emilie looked up to see she'd drawn quite a crowd.

CHAPTER 10

I demand you release me at once," Emilie said with a bravado she did not feel.

"Do you now?" one of the men taunted. "Well now, if the lady wants to go back into the drink, we ought to let her, don't you think?"

Raucous laughter rose along with comments she didn't dare contemplate. Another man made a grab for her skirt.

"She's got treasure here," he said.

That comment was met with even more ill words and foul humor. Through it all, Emilie bit her lip and tried not to show fear, though her heart pounded and her knees threatened to give way.

"I demand to speak to your captain," she said as she kicked at the offending hand. "And I shall not broach any ill treatment, so mind yourself and step away."

The sheer audacity of her words seemed to stun the crowd. It certainly silenced them, at least temporarily.

"Step aside," someone shouted, and all the men complied.

Slowly, a circle of light moved toward her, the source of which was hidden by the blinding glow. "So you've a treasure?" a deep voice said. "I'll ask you once to give it up. Should you choose not to do so willingly, it will not go so well for you."

A murmur went up in the shadows behind him. Despite her bravado, a tear slipped down Emilie's cheek. *Save me, Lord.*

"I have nothing to give up to you, willingly or otherwise."

The laughter that followed her statement was eclipsed only by the vile things the men said. "Silence!" the holder of the light shouted.

The only sound was the lapping of the waves and the pounding of her heart.

"Hold the lamp," the man said, and someone raced forward to comply.

The man with the deep voice stepped into the golden circle and stared down at Emilie, his yellow coat the color of the light that surrounded him. From just beneath his eye to his jaw was a fresh slash of crimson.

"So we meet again," he said as he reached for his pistol.

"I warrant there be treasure in her skirts, Captain."

He turned toward the source of the voice and made a crude comment that caused Emilie to blush to the roots of her hair. Several others joined the jesting, while the rest merely provided ribald laughter that became for Emilie the symphony of her nightmares.

While the men were thus engaged, she began to work on the fraying end of the rope that bound her hands. If she could only free herself, she might have a chance to escape by falling backward into the sea.

For the first time that day, she gave thanks that she'd chosen a frock of sea green the same color as the ocean on all sides of them. Would that she'd been a proper lady and kept her bonnet handy. It was a slip of propriety that she rarely made.

And will likely never make again.

The knot slipped a bit, and Emilie worked to keep the elation from her face. *Thank You, Lord.*

By the time the man in charge tired of his jokes and turned his attention back to Emilie, she'd nearly made good her escape from the bindings. One last tug and she would be free.

All that remained was an opportunity to flee. For that, she looked skyward.

"That's right," the infidel said as he moved toward her. "Say your prayers, pigeon. For I'm of a mind to send you to the Maker whose ear you now tug upon."

I dare you almost slipped from her slack jaw. Instead, she said nothing.

"Well now," he crowed. "A woman who can hold her tongue. Now there's a rarity."

Still Emilie did not speak.

The man moved close enough to touch a strand of the hair that trailed over her shoulders. "Me, I don't usually like a woman who keeps her silence. It makes me wonder what she's planning."

" 'Silence at the proper season is wisdom, and better than any speech.' " There, let him wonder about that.

"Well now." He released her curl and turned his attention to her face. "Quoting Plutarch, are we?" The man's smile broadened. " 'Freedom is a possession of inestimable value.' " He paused, his fingers inches away from her throat. "Cicero."

"Yes," she said, barely blinking lest he sense her fear. " 'Ignorant men do not know what good they hold in their hands until they've flung it away.' " It was her turn to pause. "Sophocles."

The pirate's hands encircled her wrists and lifted them to allow the loosened ropes to fall free. With a yank, he slammed her against him.

" 'Death may be the greatest of all human blessings,' " he whispered into her ear, his lips so close she could feel the hot breath against her skin. "Socrates."

He looked down from his superior height. "And I feel two suspicious lumps in what is otherwise a lovely dress. My suspicion is that you've hidden something from me besides your virtue. That I will take. The other, this treasure to which my men refer, I would ask that you offer it freely. What say you now, pigeon?"

Emilie swallowed hard and looked past him to the pirates gathered in a circle around them. " 'Verily, verily, I say unto you,' " she began, " 'He that believeth on me hath everlasting life.' " Her gaze collided with his startling blue eyes. "Jesus of Nazareth." She paused. "My Savior."

Abruptly, he released her hands only to lift her into his arms. Seemingly without caring who stood in his way, the pirate hauled her through the crowd and into the bowels of the ship.

"Run dark and silent," he called to someone in the passageway. "See that the men extinguish all lanterns and forsake the watch bells until further notice."

"Aye," the man said, and the passageway plunged into darkness.

"Don't worry, pigeon," the pirate captain said, "I know where I'm going."

He gripped her tighter as he stumbled, then righted himself, liberally cursing as he pressed forward. Her head slammed against walls, as did her feet, but she refused to cry out.

Finally, their journey stopped at a door with a pale orange light pouring from beneath it. With a swift kick, the door flew open, and she found herself dumped unceremoniously onto a bunk that smelled of sweat and unwashed bodies.

Emilie huddled into the corner and reached for the only item within reach, a slim volume she found wedged between the bunk and the wall. The man laughed as he straightened his top hat.

"What? No words of wisdom from some dead philosopher?"

Brandishing the book, Emilie said nothing.

"I've one more word for you before I take my pleasure, then discard you."

She curled away from him.

"Two, actually. I don't intend to kill you, for that would be too kind. Just as I will think of you each time I see the scar on my cheek, so you will think of me and never forget this day."

He let the words hang between them.

"Indeed, never will you look upon yourself without remembering the name of Thomas Hawkins."

"Beggin' yer pardon, sir, but the captain has need of you."

The words cut through Caleb's brain and settled somewhere in the soft cloud of his pillow. When the same voice, a youthful one, spoke the sentence again, Caleb jolted awake.

"The captain, did you say?"

"Aye, sir," the cabin boy said.

"What time is it?" When the youth told him, Caleb sat bolt upright. "What's the cause of this? Is it the *Cormorant*?"

"No, sir," the lad said. "She's fit and fine, but the captain says it's mighty important that you come at once."

"I see." Caleb shook the sleep from his head as he threw on his trousers and stuffed his arms into his shirt. His boots slid on easily, as did his coat, but finding his way across the darkened cabin was not so simple.

"Shall I light the lamp, sir?" the boy asked

Caleb slammed his knee against the desk and bit back a sharp reply. "No time for it," he said, finding the doorframe and then the passageway beyond.

With care, he maneuvered himself through the maze of hallways below and emerged onto the deck where the moonlight gave way to lanterns on the quarterdeck and on the aft bow. Caleb easily found the captain, who stood in a huddle with several sailors.

"What's the emergency?" he called to the captain once he reached the quarterdeck.

"Vessel in trouble, it appears, sir." The captain pointed due north where bits of something that might have been a ship floated in and out of a slender trail of moonlight.

"I'd say the trouble did her in, Captain. From what's floating here, it looks as if she's sunk."

"Aye," he said. "Would you have me leave her be or look for survivors?"

"Send a crew out to search," Caleb said. "Survivors will be brought aboard, of course."

"Of course. I reckon with the tide, we ought to head out more in that direction." He pointed due east.

"Proceed," Caleb said.

As the *Cormorant* plowed closer, the acrid scent of burning timbers rose over the sea spray. While the captain called out orders for the sails to be trimmed, several sailors paced the edges of the vessel, shining lanterns onto the water.

Caleb took up watch on the forward bow. Several pieces of what appeared to be charred wood knocked against the ship, each bouncing away only to collide again. Then he saw what appeared to be a person.

"Fetch a lantern," he called. "I think I see a body in the water."

A sailor raced toward Caleb, the lantern bobbing in his hand. Just before he reached Caleb, a shot rang out and the man fell flat on the deck. The lantern rolled toward Caleb, leaving a trail of fire in its wake. He quickly shed his coat and stamped out the flames, then peered over the rail to see that the supposed body was merely a length of pale cloth wound around a ship's timber.

"Get yourself down," the captain called. "All men to stations."

A roar from behind him caused Caleb to turn. A short distance from the bow, a vessel glided toward them in ghostly silence. Only the flash from a cannon gave proof it was not some spectral vision.

While the captain shouted orders, the *Cormorant* returned fire. Caleb moved the injured man to a safer location, then took up his place beside the other men on the deck. When the attacking ship passed near enough, her name showed plain and clear in the moonlight.

Hawk's Remedy.

Caleb spat on the deck as the blood began to boil in his temples. A lesser man might have cursed the vessel. He preferred to allow the Lord to do that. Instead, Caleb took deadly aim with his grandfather's pistol and dispatched a fellow to the watery depths before he could reload the cannon.

A lad of no more than a dozen years kept Caleb supplied with ammunition while another did the reloading. Caleb switched between pistols until the *Cormorant*'s cannons made a direct hit.

The resulting fire sent the darkened ship gliding away. A second cannon shot made contact with the aft bow, and the vessel soon burned in two places.

A cheer went up aboard the *Cormorant*. "Shall we give assistance, sir?" the captain called down to Caleb.

"This is your vessel, Captain," Caleb responded. "What say you on the matter?"

The captain's fists clenched. "I say we leave the cowards to their own devices. Likely they'll survive well enough, though their vessel appears it will not unless they put out the fires."

"Twice this vessel has plagued us." He stared at the flames now licking both ends of the ship. "Do you know of this vessel?"

The captain shrugged. "Can't say I do, but I'd warrant whoever's at her wheel has a grudge against the Bennings. Seems likely, anyway." He, too, followed Caleb's gaze. "Though I'm thinking the lesson of not firing on a Benning vessel might be well learned now that they're toasting their toes on their own firewood."

"Then proceed to Santa Lucida, sir," he said as he watched Fletcher make his way across the deck. "Did you sleep through the excitement?"

"Hardly." Fletcher looked around him, then at Caleb. "But I did have the good sense to stay out of the line of fire. I saw, however, you did not."

Caleb shrugged. "It's the nature of battle, Fletcher."

The older man smiled. "How like your grandfather you're becoming." He grasped Caleb's shoulder, then squeezed. "Indeed the naval department is getting a fine sailor. Now if there's nothing further to keep my attention, I'll seek solace in my bunk until morning."

"I haven't sent the letter yet," he called to Fletcher's retreating back.

Yet he knew he would. Someday, God willing, he would find a way to combine his love of the law with a love of the ocean he hadn't realized he still had.

Only the Lord, however, could manage such a feat.

"They're turning about," a lad in the riggings called. "All hands, Captain. They're smoking fore and aft, yet they're comin' back fer us full sail."

Caleb strode to the quarterdeck and found the captain with the spyglass to his eye. "What in the world?" the older man muttered.

"I'll have a look." Caleb lifted the glass to his eye. It appeared the vessel was indeed executing a turn that would bring it directly into their path. "Sink them," Caleb said through clenched jaw.

"To the guns," the captain called. "Let's show that tub what the men of the *Cormorant* are made of."

Caleb handed the captain the spyglass and turned to leave. The older man's hand on his shoulder stopped him.

"Might I suggest, sir," the captain began, "that you not make yourself as easily seen this time around?" He held his hands out to silence Caleb's protest. "Meaning no disrespect, but it appears that you may be what the *Hawk's Remedy* is after."

"All the more reason not to back down." Caleb shook his head. "I've fought at their sides on two occasions now. To leave these men to battle alone would be unforgivable."

The captain's gaze shifted away. "I'd greatly appreciate it if you'd let my men do what they do best without having to see to the safety of the Benning heir."

Frustration pounded in every pump of the blood at his temples. Since when had he become some sort of coddled heir to the throne?

"Indeed I see your point," he finally said when he could trust his voice to speak, "but I am as much Benning as Spencer. What would my grandfather have done?"

A smile spread across the captain's wrinkled face. "He would have told me to busy myself with the running of this vessel while he fought alongside his men."

Caleb couldn't help grinning as he snatched up his pistol. "My grandfather's sentiments are mine as well."

CHAPTER 11

Emilie wiped her tears with the corner of her skirt, then settled the torn fabric around her knees. Outside, chaos reigned, but with every fire of the cannons, she gave thanks.

He had not touched her.

Not in the way he'd promised. Not yet, at least.

Indeed, whatever battle raged overhead, it was a welcome interruption in the vile plans Thomas Hawkins had for the evening. Still, when the cannons boomed, the whole ship shuddered.

Emilie moved to the edge of the bunk and slid down until her bare feet touched the floor. Her skirts were much lighter now that the animal had torn away the ones bearing her father's gold. Where he put them, she couldn't say, for she'd closed her eyes and prayed as he laughed.

If only she'd done as Reverend Carter suggested and returned with him. Or, failing that, accepted her father's offer of allowing Nate to accompany her.

But no, her headstrong manner had been her downfall. A lesson learned.

"Still, you've got yourself into quite a fix this time," she whispered, her voice thin and brittle even in the tiny room. "What happened to that woman who was brave enough to teach a slave to read?" She tested her sea legs and found them still worthy, although a bit shaky. "And what of the woman who single-handedly set in motion a plan to wrest a slave from her life of servitude?" The question emboldened her, as did its answer. "I'm still the same woman," she said, her voice stronger. "And I shall escape this."

Emilie squared her shoulders and held her head high. Indeed, she would escape this.

By the light of the small lamp, she adjusted her still-damp clothing, then fashioned her tangled hair into a makeshift braid. The room held little in the way of hiding places, yet she opened every possible chest and looked under everything else to see if her gold might be found.

"Lord," she whispered as she sank into the lone chair in the cabin, "without that money, the children of Fairweather Key won't have their school. Please don't let that happen."

The door flew open, and Emilie shot out of the chair. Her heart racing, she whirled around to see that the man at the door was not Thomas Hawkins.

"I'm to fetch you," the red-haired fellow said. "And you'll need to be bound."

He spoke the words as if he were discussing the weather.

"Have I a choice?"

"Yes," he said. "You can let me do what the captain's told me I must, or I'll do it anyway and likely you'll be the worse for it."

"I see. And then what will happen to me?"

The man ducked as he stepped into the room, a silk ribbon in brilliant scarlet dangling from one hand. "I'm to bring you to the quarterdeck and be hasty about it."

She sighed and met him halfway. "Then let's get this over with."

In truth, nothing could be worse than remaining in the tiny cabin to await the return of the evil captain. At least out in the open she might find the opportunity to fling herself overboard.

That she could not swim mattered less than that she would not remain aboard this vessel.

The man bound her hands, then scooped her up like a sack of potatoes and tossed her over his shoulder. *This is my path to freedom,* she reminded herself as she was jostled on her way up, around, and under the wooden passageways until salt air heavy with the smell of gunpowder and charred wood assaulted her nose.

Immediately, she sneezed.

The activity around her continued as she was carried to her destination like so much baggage.

One more flight of stairs, and she found herself on the highest point of the vessel.

To her right, a knot of sailors worked on a small cannon that looked to have misfired. To the left, another group seemed to be faring well with their weapon. Straight ahead at the wheel stood Thomas Hawkins.

He turned, his greatcoat whirling about, then settling like a cloud under the moonlight. "Welcome, pigeon," he said. "While I regret our evening plans have changed, you're about to become quite useful to me." He nodded to the red-haired man, who quickly retreated. "Walk with me," he said to Emilie. "I've a mind to show you off. See, we have visitors."

She looked where he pointed. A vessel much like the one she'd started this journey aboard came into view. For a moment, she held out hope it might actually be the *Sunday Service* come back to claim her.

"See that ship? She's the *Cormorant*, ship-of-the-line to the pirate Ian Benning," Captain Hawkins said. "She'll either be the life of you or the death of you. I haven't decided which."

"Hold your fire!" Caleb shouted.

"What is it, sir?" the captain called.

"I can't be sure, but I think there's a woman aboard." Caleb snatched the spyglass from the hand of the lad at his side. "Sure enough. There she is."

Hawk's Remedy drew close enough for Caleb to see the woman without the spyglass. Though he couldn't be sure, it appeared she was bound at the wrists.

"What do you make of it?" This from Fletcher, who had come above during a lull in the fray. "I wager she's a ploy."

Caleb considered the statement. "No, there's something in her demeanor that tells me otherwise. Call it instinct, but I think she's a captive."

"Instinct?" Fletcher chuckled. "From a man who has spent his life behind a desk?"

He spared his mentor a sideways glance. "Am I to find insult in that comment?"

"No, lad. You're to find great pride in it." He reached for the spyglass and peered into its depths. "For upon closer inspection, I can see a red cord binding her hands." Fletcher lowered the spyglass. "Likely done to be seen from a great distance."

"I would have your advice," Caleb said.

Fletcher shook his head. "You know what to do, Caleb. Don't ask an old man what you already know."

Caleb nodded and shrugged out of his shirt, then handed Fletcher his pistol and sword. For this, he'd need nothing in the way of extra clothing to impede his ability to swim back to the *Cormorant* if need be.

"You're going unarmed?" Fletcher quirked a gray brow. "Now perhaps I have a comment."

Caleb ignored him to continue his preparation for the mission. Shedding his boots would have been the sensible thing for swimming, but he decided it might be the very thing that alerted the captain of the enemy vessel to his dual motives. Instead, he reached to cut a short length of hemp from the sail ropes and bound his hair, which now fell a good length down his back.

"The better to keep a clear vision," he said as he reached into his boot and pulled out the dagger he'd found among his grandfather's possessions in the cabin. "I've spent my adult life behind a desk, but I do remember a thing or two about the pirate life from my childhood."

The look of pride on Fletcher's face made Caleb smile.

"So you've got a plan."

"I do," Caleb said. "But in order for it to work, you'll have to inform the crew."

Keeping his attention focused on the enemy vessel, Caleb outlined a plan that required good wits, good aim, and good swimming. "What say you?" he asked when he'd finished.

Fletcher gave Caleb a hearty pat on the back. "I'd say you've been reading the ship's log."

"I have," he said with a grin. "Perhaps when we've survived to fight another day, you can tell me all about the last time this ploy was used."

Fletcher laughed and ducked his head a moment. When he lifted it, his smile was gone. "In truth,

136

you would not be here had that plan failed. Thus, I send you with my blessings and prayers."

"Wait." Caleb shook his head. "You mean the woman rescued from the enemy ship was my mother?"

"It was indeed." He shrugged. "She met your father when he required her testimony in court to put away the ruffians who sought to hold her for ransom."

"I never knew."

"There is yet much for you to learn about your family, but now is not the time." Fletcher pointed to the oncoming vessel. "Put your mind to the task at hand, lad. There will be time to tell tales of other adventures."

When *Hawk's Remedy* passed within a few hundred yards of the *Cormorant*, Caleb was ready. He stood at the rail and pointed to the quarterdeck of the other vessel.

"I have a yen for the girl. Give her to me," he called.

A bellowing laugh bounced across the distance between them. "What business does a Benning have with such a fair maiden?"

"My business is just that—mine." Caleb leaned toward Fletcher. "See that the captain gives these men the instruction not to fire until your signal. I'll not have my back filled with grapeshot from my own men."

Fletcher nodded and hurried off to find the captain. In his absence, Caleb stood alone on the quarterdeck, just outside the circle of lamplight. Anyone with a weapon and good aim could have shot him if he moved into the circle.

Less than a ship's length separated them. "What price do you require to release the woman?" Caleb called.

"I require nothing less than the Benning in whose name this vessel sails."

"Payment in gold does not interest you?"

The pirate moved closer to the rail, dragging the woman along with him. While Caleb watched, the fellow scooped her into his arms and held her over the side. "I'll feed her to the fish before I'll take your gold. Bring me the Benning. Nothing else will suffice."

"I suppose I've underestimated you," he said. "A man of commerce such as yourself likely has more treasure than he needs. Of course you'd not be interested in my offer of Benning treasure over Benning flesh." Caleb paused. "Although I must warn you, I've taken a fancy to the woman and would have her at any price."

"Is that so?" He froze, and Caleb knew he must be thinking over the offer. "Name this treasure of gold. Why would I wish to own it over the vast stores I already possess?"

Caleb forced a laugh and hoped it sounded genuine. "Would you possess gold from the Benning vaults or treasure destined for their coffers? I think not, though you've tried more than once to claim it."

"Indeed, Benning treasure is a fit prize. With it I can live to fight the Benning scourge another day." He paused. "But I require two bags of gold. One is but an insult considering the high-born nature of the woman."

"High born?" Caleb shook his head. "Upon what authority do you state this?"

"The woman quotes the Greek philosophers," he said. "And what manner of transfer would you make for the wench?"

Caleb chose his words carefully. "As the chance for receipt of damaged goods is high, I will board your vessel and inspect her before delivering payment of one full bag of gold."

Another laugh. "She's undamaged, much to my disappointment. I'll not have any further discussions until the Benning presents himself and asks me to take his gold." A pause. "Two bags," he added.

"Two?"

"Nothing less. And I want the Benning."

"Then you shall have him." Caleb stepped into the lamplight. "I am the Benning," he said, "and I shall bring your gold and fetch the woman. But first I require your men to stand down from their weapons."

"And should I not?" The pirate took a step backward and dropped the squirming woman onto the deck. For a moment, she disappeared behind the rail.

Caleb held his breath until he saw the woman struggle to her feet. "Then not only will you lose the opportunity for Benning gold, but you shall also lose your life, for three of my best marksmen have weapons trained on your person this very moment. Others are ready upon my signal to open fire." He paused to let his words do their damage. "Thus, you either stand down or lose to a Benning yet again."

Silence fell between them. Slowly, the captain gave his orders. Caleb watched the ragged crew step away from their cannons.

"Now," Caleb said, "drop anchor so I might board your vessel and claim the woman."

"I smell a trick," the villain responded. "You weigh anchor, and we shall each board our boats to meet in between and make the exchange."

Exactly as I planned. Caleb worked hard to keep the satisfaction from his expression. Likely more than one spyglass was trained on him. He began to pace, as much to keep from landing in the sights of some hidden gunman as to convince the pirate of his displeasure over the change.

When he felt he'd accomplished his goal, Caleb stopped short and turned to face the vessel and its captain. "Agreed. I shall send my second and you yours. Mine will carry two bags of gold, and yours the girl."

"No seconds," the pirate shouted. "Only us."

Again Caleb remained straight-faced. "A moment to collect the treasure, and I shall board my boat. You may do the same."

A short while later, Caleb found himself at the oars of the small boat, two bags of the ship's ballast at his feet and a length of hemp connecting him to the *Cormorant* hidden beneath the surface of the water. He'd left his boots aboard the ship, deciding the pirate's pride would never let him notice his adversary had taken precautions in case he was required to swim.

There was no need to light a lantern and find them, for the pirate had one affixed to the front of his vessel, the better to see the feminine prize seated beside him.

" 'Pride goeth before destruction'," Caleb whispered.

"Halt," the pirate called when the boats were several lengths apart. "I'll toss over the rope, and you tie it to your boat. When this is accomplished, give a signal."

Caleb smiled, knowing this meant he could not be seen in the dark that lay outside the lamp's golden circle. Had the pirate been able to make out his image, he would not have asked for the signal.

The rope sailed toward him, and he caught it. When the knot was tight, he called out to the pirate.

"Begin to pull," the pirate said, "and I shall do the same."

Slowly the crafts closed the gap between them until Caleb could almost reach out and touch the other boat. He looked directly into the face of the woman, and for a moment his heart stopped. Her cheek held two things that made his blood boil: a tear that slid over a bruise in the shape of a man's palm.

He quickly finished his assessment, noting she appeared to be of approximately his age and, except for her current situation, seemed to be well fed and well cared for. Her style of dress bespoke serviceable luxury, and her stiff posture told him she'd spent time under the tutelage of someone who valued proper behavior.

Affecting a casual air, he turned his attention to the pirate captain. To his satisfaction, his face was marred by what likely was the woman's handiwork.

"It appears I've been swindled," he said as he pointed toward the man's wounds. "Unless you can swear you received that injury in battle, I'll not be tangling with her no matter how enticing she might be." He gave the woman another look and prayed she could see through his ruse to the man he really was. "I'm not of a mind to require my surgeon to stand by no matter how sweet the prize."

"I warrant you'll tame her soon enough. Until then I'd advise keeping her bound," the pirate said. "Now hand off the treasure before I change my mind and shoot the both of you for my inconvenience."

A gasp escaped the woman, but she did not move nor spare him a glance. *Show her, Lord, that I'm here to save her and not to cause her fear.*

"Upon my signal, we switch," Caleb said. "First the woman, and then the treasure."

The pirate nearly stood up in the craft, such was his obvious displeasure. "Indeed not," he shouted. "You will tie the treasure to our rope. When I pull it in, I will toss the woman to you."

Another gasp, and this time the woman made eye contact with Caleb. *Calm her, Lord, and let her understand I'm doing Your will here.*

"Can you swim?" he called to her.

"She cannot," the pirate said. "Although I have seen her float quite well." He paused to prod her arm. "Better than your shipmates, eh, pigeon?"

It was all Caleb could do not to lunge out of the boat and swim over to throttle the man. Only the need to keep his temper in order to save the woman kept him sitting still.

"Upon my mark," the pirate said. "Have you tied your bags to the rope?"

Caleb leaned into the vessel and pretended to tie the bags, then straightened. "Proceed," he said. "I am prepared."

"And you, pigeon, what say you?"

The woman remained stiff and unresponsive. She did, however, continue to stare at Caleb.

"I shall assume that your silence gives consent." The pirate laughed. "That's from Aristotle," he told Caleb.

"Plato," the woman corrected. "He also said ignorance is the root and stem of all evil." She swiveled to face him. "Which would make you, Mr. Hawkins, an entire orchard and the field beyond."

With that, she pitched backward and disappeared into the water. In the chaos that followed, Caleb dove in and cast about for the woman who would surely drown unless the ribbon encircling her wrists was untied.

"The treasure, Mr. Benning," Caleb heard as he broke the surface. "Else I shall have to shoot."

Caleb swiped the water from his eyes then looked up into the barrel of his opponent's pistol. "The treasure," he repeated.

"I've not yet received what I purchased," Caleb responded as he reached over to grab hold of the pirate's boat, "so I suggest you join me in search of her, else I'll be forced to return to my ship with what I brought."

"You're a fool," he said. "I neither swim nor have the inclination to wait while you do." In one swift motion, the man jumped over him and into Caleb's boat. There he plucked the bags from their resting place and reached for the oars.

Caleb gave a whistle and the lifeline holding the rowboat to the *Cormorant* tightened and caught, sending the vessel speeding toward the big ship. The pirate, unable to leap for fear of drowning, held on tight as he shouted a warning to his crew.

Prepared for this reaction, one of the lads aboard the *Cormorant* began ringing the watch bell. Every time the pirate shouted, the bell rang. Thus, the men aboard *Hawk's Remedy* did not realize their captain was being captured until the men poured over the side of the *Cormorant* and placed him in shackles.

Meanwhile, Caleb reached for the lantern that bobbed from the other boat. He cast a glow across the water until he found the floating figure of the woman. When he reached her, she began to flail about.

"Stop it," he shouted as he gathered her to him, her fists pummeling his back as he fought to remain above the water. Thankfully, her kicking legs seemed to be tangled in her skirts, for he felt nothing but the occasional swipe of a foot. "I am trying to save you, not drown with you."

"Unhand me," she demanded as she continued to struggle. "You're as bad as the other fellow."

A cannonball landed dangerously close, causing the woman to scream and clutch Caleb so tight he began to go under. With a kick, he resurfaced.

"Should you continue this behavior," he said as he turned to find the little boat was drifting farther from reach, "I will leave you to that other fellow. See if he will come rescue you."

The woman stilled.

"Exactly. Likely you'll just be shark food." He shifted positions but did not release her. "It is your choice."

Treading water, he waited, refusing to loosen his grip even if it meant swallowing sea water in the process. Finally her strength left, and she collapsed against him.

"So," he said, "are you done with this foolishness?"

She remained still, saying nothing. Finally he heard a soft yes whispered against his ear.

She remained passive as he pulled her along, his free arm propelling them toward the boat while the other kept her within reach. Once at the side of the boat, he placed her fingers on the side and instructed her to hold tight to the wood while he lifted himself in. To put her in first would be to risk watching her row away without him.

The wild-eyed look she gave him once he righted himself inside the craft told Caleb he'd guessed correctly. "I'm going to pull you in," he shouted over the blast of weaponry from the vessels behind them. "Should you fight me, I will release you to the sharks. Should you think you're going to harm me in any way, be advised I have marksmen watching your every move."

"Fair enough," she said in a voice so shaky he could barely understand.

With a modicum of effort, he hauled her into the

boat and deposited her at his feet. She sat for a moment, seemingly stunned that she was once again on something solid. Then the wild-eyed look returned, and it appeared she might dive back into the ocean.

"Sit there." Caleb pointed to the vacant plank that served as a bench, then forced his breathing to slow. "Should you decide to swim once more, you'll not have my further assistance."

"I'm fine here," she said, her hands clutching either side of the vessel and her back leaning against the plank.

Caleb glanced over at the warring vessels, then back at the woman. Likely her choice to remain lower than he in the water would serve her well should Hawkins have pistols trained on them. He extinguished the lamp and reached for the oar.

"Very well."

He grasped the oars and turned the craft toward the back side of the *Cormorant*. Grapeshot peppered the bow but thankfully hit neither Caleb nor the woman. Through it all, she sat still as a statue, her face pale in the moonlight.

Holding his breath until the *Cormorant* stood between them and *Hawk's Remedy*, Caleb eased the vessel nearer the brig until wood scraped against wood. Immediately, a rope ladder fell to them.

Once aboard, the woman's health quickly returned, and she began shrieking like a banshee. It took four men to catch her and two more to subdue her. The bravest of the bunch, a stout fellow of greater than average girth and height, shouldered her and returned his prize to deposit her at Caleb's feet.

Caleb looked down and knew the moment the woman had the chance, she would once again bolt into the ocean. This time, however, she might not be found alive.

For a moment, he considered speaking privately with her, perhaps even explaining the words he'd blustered to the pirate captain were merely a ruse to lure him away from his vessel. But as the cannons began to fire and the battle renewed, Caleb knew he had no time to try to reason with an irrational female.

"Fletcher, go ahead of these gentlemen and see that my cabin is prepared for our guest." He spared her only a cursory glance before giving his attention to his crew. "Upon Mr. Fletcher's word, I would have you deposit her in my cabin. Perhaps tomorrow she will be willing to listen." He accepted his pistol and sword from Fletcher, then addressed his crew. "Back to your stations," he said. "I've a mind to take breakfast in Santa Lucida come daybreak, but we'll not accomplish that with the pestilence that is the *Hawk's Remedy* chasing us."

"What would you have us do, sir?" the captain called.

Caleb smiled. "Exactly what my grandfather would have ordered."

The captain turned to the crew. "See that the *Hawk's Remedy* will no longer plague any vessel, let alone a Benning ship."

CHAPTER 12

Emilie walked the confines of her gilded cage, unable to stop either her pacing or the recriminations that dogged each step. The phrase *if only* dashed across her mind, followed by thoughts such as: *If only I'd listened to my father and allowed Nate to accompany me. If only I'd chosen a different ship upon which to sail.*

With each *if only* came the realization that her impetuous behavior had finally resulted in consequences even she could not escape. She paused in front of a looking glass that had been bolted to the wall with heavy brackets.

Somewhere outside this tiny room, a battle raged with possession of her and two bags of contraband gold at its center. A cannon fired, and the mirror shook. Men shouted. Was that victory or loss she heard in their tones?

No matter. Whoever won, she would be the loser.

"This time, Emilie Gayarre," she said to the disheveled wreck who stared back at her, "you've really done it. Your foolishness has caused you to be captive to not one pirate, but two."

She tilted her head to see her injured cheek in the amber glow of a lone lamp hung well out of her reach. Though she'd never fancied herself a vain woman, bearing the sign of another man's hand made her blood boil.

Where once her skin had been flawless despite the temptation to expose it to the Florida sun, she now bore a purple splotch where the vile Hawkins fellow had seen fit to strike her. Further examination of the bruise reminded her of other bruises, some from the sinking of the *Sunday Service* and others from fighting for her virtue and her father's gold.

"At least I have one of them." Emilie turned away from the mirror. "And I shall fight to the death before I lose what little honor I have left."

She moved toward a desk that held nothing but ink, a pen, and an aged and mildewed copy of a book on sailor's knots. Stuck within its pages was a slip of paper that looked to be a letter from someone named Spencer to the United States attorney general's office.

"Poor Mr. Spencer must've had his library pilfered and his mail stolen," she said as she slid the book back onto the desk. "The scoundrels."

Another roar went up. This time, the victor's cry was obvious. Emilie walked to the tiny porthole and found the glass to be clean and clear. Unfortunately, her only view was of a night sky and a black sea punctuated with dots of light above and pale, foaming crests that rose and disappeared below.

"I only wished to go home, Lord." She sighed as she traced her finger around the circle of brass holding her window to the world in place. "I am a foolish woman."

"Indeed."

The masculine voice caused Emilie to jump. The door slammed behind a man whose presence not only filled the room but also filled her with dread.

The Benning, as she'd heard Captain Hawkins refer to him, stepped into the light. Whereas before she'd deigned not to give the man the satisfaction of knowing she looked upon him, now she decided a frank and open stare would go far in her campaign to convince him she felt no fear.

As men go, this one was a healthy specimen, broad of shoulder, lean of frame, and thankfully now wearing a linen shirt that was only a bit worse for wear. His skin bore the golden color of one whose days were spent outdoors, and his face—what she could see of it behind a beard that climbed from chin to cheekbone—seemed kind enough despite his earlier behavior.

Oddly his damp and curling hair, which seemed infused with the same golden tone as his skin, had been tethered with a length of the same rope one might hoist a sail with. In all, it appeared neither scissors nor soap had touched him in far too long.

He put her in mind of one of Mr. Defoe's characters in his novel *Robinson Crusoe*. Only his dark leather boots, which met damp and water-stained trousers just below his knee, gave away any sense of the man having ever visited civilization.

The sword at his side and pistol in his sash reminded her this man was dangerous. Someone whose lies would likely sound sweet as honey.

His audacious gaze swept the length of her, but she refused to wither under his stare.

Rather, Emilie squared her shoulders and returned the gesture. "So you've come to claim your prize?" The look of surprise that crossed his features was not what Emilie expected.

"I would have a word with you," he said, his voice firm and even. "And be warned, I'll not tolerate the behavior I witnessed earlier."

Caleb waited for the protest he knew was sure to come. Instead, she went for the desk and seated herself as if she were planning an evening of letter writing. Was she daft?

"Did you hear me?" He pushed away from the door and stepped into the interior of the cabin, breaking his vow not to enter the room and cause further distress to the former captive.

She toyed with his father's book, then reached for the writing pen. This docile creature could not possibly be the woman he had witnessed creating chaos both on his vessel and *Hawk's Remedy*.

Much as she smiled and sat sweetly at the desk, Caleb did not trust her.

Treachery must be afoot. He could feel it.

"Miss? I do not know your name."

The woman glanced up sharply. "Nor I yours." She shook her head, and an inky curl fell from her makeshift braid. "No, forgive me. You are the Benning. A fearsome fellow according to my former shipmates aboard Captain Hawkins's vessel."

Caleb opened his mouth to correct her, then reconsidered. "So you'll not enlighten me with your name?" When the woman shook her head, he felt anger rising. "Tell me, then, about this Captain Hawkins."

"What would you have me say? Are you concerned, perhaps, that he soiled the goods before you had a chance at them?" She rose. "Worry not, for no man has nor will take what is only mine to give."

Dark eyes flashed with an anger that might prove dangerous should he lose his edge. Now, however, with the advantage of superior height, size, and gender he had little to concern himself with save the fact that his captive must not slip past him to perform another dive into the ocean.

"The topic at hand, please." He crossed his arms over his chest and collected his temper before continuing. "Your Captain Hawkins is currently detained below in our brig. He shall be delivered

153

up to the magistrate in Havana as a pirate and likely be hanged, but I would have more information from you as to his crimes."

Her laugh was deep and throaty and might have made him smile had it not held such contempt. "Am I to believe that one pirate would deliver another to the authorities? Why, you speak as if you're on the other side of the law." She stepped away from the desk and crossed her hands behind her back. "Oh, that's quite amusing."

In a few hours I will be sitting at my mother's table. This woman and this voyage will be nothing more than a memory.

Caleb tried again. "Miss, I will require you to accompany the criminal as far as Havana and be prepared to testify against him."

His statement seemed to give her pause. "So you persist in the attempt?"

Just a few hours. "I beg your pardon?"

She faltered before regaining her balance. "I am not a stupid woman, sir. I can see what you're doing."

He gave her a sideways look. "Enlighten me, madam. What am I doing?"

Her sigh was deep and long, and with it she took two steps toward the porthole. "You are attempting to appear the gentleman to catch me off guard."

Hours. Only hours.

"Am I?" Caleb shook his head. "Do tell me what comes next."

She lifted one dark brow.

"Really now," he finally said as he watched her step away from the porthole. "You must understand that the things I said to the pirate were only in the course of rescuing you. Surely you do not believe me capable of such atrocities."

"Are you a man of your word, Mr. Benning?"

"Indeed I am," he said, then realized this spider was weaving a web of entrapment even as she seemed to be inching around the perimeter of the room toward the door. She now stood near enough to reach it in three steps. "Enough of this nonsense."

Brown eyes widened at his change of tone, and for a moment she resembled the woman he'd seen in the boat. Fear. Yes, he saw that, but something else, as well.

One wrong move, one wrong word, and her calm demeanor might once again slip. The last thing he wished to do tonight was lose her to the inky depths.

Not with Santa Lucida so near.

Caleb held his hands out. "What can I do to prove to you that I mean you no harm?"

She looked past him to the door, then back into his eyes. "Let me go."

"I cannot."

Her eyes narrowed. "Then I do not believe you."

Caleb stepped back until he felt the door against his spine. "I am trying to keep you safe," he said.

She laughed. "Oh, of course," she said. "The Benning is going to protect me." Another move forward, and the gap between them closed a bit more. She shifted her weight onto her heels, her arms still curiously behind her back. "From what? Pirates?"

"Yes, actually." He shook his head. "I mean, no, of course not." Finally frustration won over patience, and tact gave way to expediency. "Look, woman, you are alive because I took the time to turn this vessel around and fetch you. I said what I had to say to convince that scoundrel to release you, and may the Lord forgive me for any deception."

"The Lord?" She had the indecency to laugh, though there seemed little humor in it. "I find that hard to believe."

"That I would ask for His forgiveness or that He would grant it?"

A glint of silver caught his attention, and he looked past her to the mirror bolted over his wardrobe. Clearly visible behind the back of the demure brunette was his grandfather's writing pen. She clasped it as if she intended to use it as a dagger.

A second later, the woman lunged at him.

He caught her hand in mid-air, fingers encircling her wrist to easily haul her against him. From that position, he managed to wrest the pen away and toss it a safe distance.

Now came the dilemma. He'd disarmed the woman but still could not be sure releasing her would be safe. Holding her close for any length of time was also not an option.

From his superior height, he could see over her head to the porthole and the stars still twinkling outside. Would this night never end?

Then it occurred to him. Perhaps the woman felt the same.

"Miss," he said carefully, "I wish to release you."

"And I wish that as well," she said against his shoulder. "Rather, I demand it."

"I'm sure you do." Caleb chose his words with care. "For your safety and mine, however, I must insist on a promise of decorum and decent behavior. I cannot risk being stabbed by my grandfather's writing pen. Bad for my health, you know."

Her silence at his poor attempt at a jest spoke volumes, but Caleb pressed on. At least she'd stopped fighting him.

"It is apparent," he continued, "that you do not trust me." The sound she made in response almost made him smile. "Nonetheless, I believe I've a plan to remedy this."

CHAPTER 13

The woman looked up at him. "I fail to see what remedy short of my release will be satisfactory to both of us."

"You wish only to go home."

Again her eyes widened. "How do you know this?"

Caleb tried not to think of how close she stood. For if he thought of it, he lost track of logic—a dangerous state for a man locked in a cabin with a woman already prone to use anything within reach as a weapon. "You stated it yourself," he said when he recalled her first words.

"I didn't think," she said slowly, "that anyone heard."

"Strange as it seems, you and I have the same wish. I know you hold my word worthless, but I warrant you would change your mind if proof were offered. First, tell me what fear you have."

The woman shook her head. "We were just discussing your trustworthiness."

"It is all related," he said, loosening his grip only slightly. "Perhaps I shall answer for you. You are afraid of the men on this vessel, me in particular."

"And Captain Hawkins said you were a dolt."

She gave a good yank and nearly slipped from his grasp. Caleb pulled her close once more, and this time he could smell salt water and sea air in her hair and upon her green frock.

"On the morrow, this vessel will leave me off and continue to Havana. I will give instructions that once you swear out testimony against Captain Hawkins, you are given safe passage for whatever destination you choose."

"You would do that?"

"I give my word."

A knock on the door behind him startled Caleb. "What?" he called.

"Beggin' pardon, sir," came the voice of one of the riggers, "but the captain sent me to see to your safety."

Caleb looked down at the woman still entangled in his grasp. "I remain well and unharmed thus far. Please thank the captain for inquiring."

Another knock. "Beggin' pardon again, Mr. Benning," the youth said, "but the captain also wishes you to know we won't be making port tonight as you hoped."

The woman began to fidget, so Caleb tightened his grip. "And why would that be?"

"There's some work to be done on her, sir," the voice squeaked. "I believe there was a bit of damage to the mainmast."

"A bit?" He leaned against the door as the ship rolled with what seemed to be a large wave.

"Indeed, sir. Captain says it'll take a day, maybe more, to fix her."

A day. Caleb sighed. So much for breakfast at his mother's table.

The woman shook her head. "He's lying. This is a ruse to keep me aboard, and I'll not have it."

"Believe me, woman," Caleb said, his jaw clenched, "were there a way to safely relieve me of your company, I would do so, post haste."

She almost looked as if she believed him, though he did notice her eyeing the spot where the pen had slid beneath the desk. A dangerous one, this female.

"And there's another thing," the youth said.

"Another thing," Caleb echoed as he looked down at the wild-eyed woman whose face showed she bore him nothing but ill will. "Of course there is."

"There's a blow a-comin' from the east. Captain asks permission to shelter her at Langham Island."

"Langham Island? How far is that?"

"We're practically there," he said. "Captain said he could drop anchor in a half hour."

"Permission granted." The woman began to struggle again, and Caleb turned her to place her back to the door. "Is there anything else?"

"No," came the meek reply. "'Cept maybe that the captain said to batten down the hatches until the storm's over."

"Duly noted," Caleb called.

"Storm?"

Caleb looked down to see wide eyes again. This time her face had gone pale. He felt her go slack in his arms and wondered if he might be required to catch her.

"Are you unwell?" When she said nothing, he continued. "You must be exhausted. Perhaps you would consider a few hours' sleep?"

"Alone?" Her laughter was brittle, frantic.

"Surely you don't expect me to stay in here with you." Her stunned expression amused him. "It wouldn't be proper."

The woman quickly recovered. "What assurance have I that you won't attack me in my sleep?"

So, she is one for whom trust does not come easy. Caleb smiled. "Your assurance will be my pistol."

"Your pistol?" Once again she looked up into his eyes. This time her expression softened. "You would give me your pistol?"

"Yes," he said.

"And what if I were to use it on you?" She paused as if thinking the idea through. "I could easily turn on you the second you hand it over."

"Indeed you could," he said. "However, you've seen the loyalty my crew has for me. What do you think would happen to the person who shoots the Benning?"

Caleb could practically see her reasoning out the scenario.

"So," he finally said, "what say we strike a bargain? You shall sleep alone and safe in my bunk, and I shall take up residence outside the door to keep you in and all other trouble out."

161

"I suppose," she said, "this would be a satisfactory compromise."

With care, Caleb loosened his grip. When she could manage it, the woman took a step back and rubbed her wrists against her skirt.

"This pistol belonged to my grandfather," he said as he lifted the sash over his head and held it balanced in his palms. "It will remain in this cabin when you depart in Havana. Do you understand?"

She reached for the weapon, then slowly, as if it might bite her, touched the side plate. Once again, she met his gaze, then lifted the pistol from his palm.

A strange boldness overtook him. Though he handed his weapon to a stranger, one who appeared neither trusting nor trustworthy, he held no fear in doing so. "Do you know how to handle a weapon of this type?"

"I've used one before," she said. "And I'll not be afraid to use one again."

Caleb nodded and reached behind him for the door latch. "Should anyone come through this door tonight with the intention of harming you, shoot him."

She weighed the gun in her hand, then shook her head. "You're serious."

"I am," he said, "but do not think this means you're being given free rein to wander the *Cormorant*. I'll be sleeping with my back to this door. Should you open it, you will have to go past me to escape. I'll not have you jumping overboard and ruining my best pistol."

The woman lifted the cord and slipped it around her neck. "Fair enough," she said.

"Likely the weather will be quite foul," he said. "I recommend lashing yourself to the bunk lest you find yourself sleeping on the floor come daylight."

His captive continued to stare at the weapon. "Yes, thank you," she said in an almost stunned tone.

With nothing left to say, Caleb took his leave. "Then I bid you good night, miss. Perhaps after tomorrow we shall part and likely never see one another again."

"I welcome the thought," she muttered as she backed up three paces and bumped her legs on the chair. "Now, please assume your post outside so I might assume mine."

Back in the passageway, Caleb sunk to the floor and tried to make himself comfortable. Before long, his legs had gone numb. Splinters from the door dug into his back. The floor pitched and rolled as the storm built outside. To make matters worse, the afternoon's battle had his muscles aching and his eyes heavy.

For a moment, he wished for his soft bed back in Washington, but exhaustion rendered him unable to sustain the thought. Finally, he curled onto his side and found brief if fitful rest.

• • •

May 28, 1836

When the first bells of the day called him from his sleep, Caleb rose on stiff legs and hobbled up to the deck feeling twice his age. Finding Fletcher at the quarterdeck, he made his way toward him.

Rather than comment, Fletcher lifted a gray brow.

"Not a word," Caleb said. "Suffice it to say, chivalry can be painful."

"So I see."

Caleb leaned heavily on the rail and took in the beauty that was Langham Island. Once a hideaway for a less than stellar group of runaways from the law, the island had been hit hard by last year's hurricane. In its wake, the storm left nothing of the crude huts and cruder men once populating its hideaways.

Swept clean, the white sand gleamed so bright Caleb had to avert his eyes, while the lush green foliage offered cool shade and a rainbow of birds and fresh fruits. It was, in short, as near to a tropical paradise as Caleb had seen, and it stood completely empty.

He turned to look at the splintered mast being patched together by a veritable army of men, then turned back to Fletcher. "What say you to a trip out to Langham Island while repairs are underway?"

From the map, he knew the island was shaped

like the waning moon, a thin crescent of green outlined in pure white and named for a man whose sole claim to fame was becoming the scourge of the Spanish Armada. The *Cormorant* bobbed at anchor in the dead center of the lagoon, where green water faded to crystal clear as it gently teased the shoreline. The cloudless sky overhead and the slight breeze added to the image of a perfect place.

Or as near to one as could be found this side of heaven.

Fletcher shook his head. "I'm too old for it," he said. "I'd much rather spend the afternoon in the shade with my copy of Mr. Defoe's book."

Caleb laughed. "So you'd rather read about a castaway than pretend to be one for an afternoon?"

"Exactly," Fletcher said. "Though I hardly call my refusal to accompany you good reason for you to stay." He pointed to the island. "Go and enjoy yourself. I warrant we'll not sail until the Benning returns."

Caleb looked at Fletcher, then out across the emerald expanse to the sandy shore. Soon he would be back in Washington, where his only respite from the heat of the day would be a tiny office with one window and a view of the Capitol.

Clasping a hand on Fletcher's shoulder, Caleb grinned. "I wonder if Cook might accommodate me with a bite of breakfast to take along with me."

"Shall I ask?"

Caleb laughed. "Yes, and have him provide something for lunch as well as a Bible if one can be had without disturbing our guest."

When the things Caleb requested had been collected, he deposited them in the same dinghy he'd used last night to pluck the spitfire from the grasp of Thomas Hawkins and pointed the bow toward Langham Island.

Caleb smiled as he thought of the brown-eyed beauty. Perhaps under other circumstances . . .

No.

He pressed on, propelling the craft closer to the beach with every stroke of the oars. Thoughts of the mysterious woman would profit nothing, for unless the Lord generously intervened to rearrange his life, she could never be his.

She knew too much.

CHAPTER 14

Emilie awoke to a knock at the door. She rolled onto her side, feeling the odd pull of something around her middle. Sunlight streamed across her face, blinding her to her surroundings.

Salt air and something akin to frying meat assaulted her senses. Cook must be making breakfast. A pity she wouldn't be going down to partake. Perhaps later she would have someone bring up a tray.

Stretching, she rolled again, this time feeling a

tug not only at her middle but also at her neck. Her fingers felt for the cause and found someone had tied a ribbon around her neck.

Likely her gown had lost some of its ornamentation. Something else for the staff to handle later.

But not now. Not while she was so terribly, terribly sleepy.

Another knock.

She ignored it. Surely the staff had not become so lax in her absence that they'd lost the good manners to leave a sleeping woman be.

"I've your breakfast, miss."

A man's voice. One she did not recognize.

Emilie sat bolt upright, or at least she tried. Something restrained her about the middle, holding her in place. She grappled with the bindings as well as her surroundings. By degrees, she recalled the where and why of her situation.

And then she felt the cord at her neck. It was a ribbon, and at the end of it dangled a pistol.

Lying back, Emilie slid the ribbon over her head and carefully laid the weapon aside. She then went to work on the crudely tied rope that kept her imprisoned on the bunk. At least she knew these bindings were self-imposed due to last night's storm. From the light streaming in, it was apparent they'd all survived the weather to find safe harbor and sunshine.

"I've brought yer breakfast," another male voice called. "You're hungry, ain't you, miss?"

Her stomach complained as if in response, and she swung her legs over to touch her toes on the floor. "Yes," she said, "thank you. I'll just be a minute."

Horrified at the crumpled mess she'd made of her one good frock, Emilie spent a moment in the futile attempt to finger press the wrinkles away. Failing that, she padded to the door and slid it open a notch.

A man she did not recognize held a plate filled with something unidentifiable yet definitely edible, if scent was any indicator. She looked him over and noted he was nearly indistinguishable from the others aboard this vessel. From the hair that begged for a barber to the clothing that likely was purloined from another, the fellow was unique only in the fact that his brilliant blue eyes had a distinct golden ring around their centers.

The scent of food made her throw open the door heedless of her appearance. "Just put it on the desk," she said as she took two steps back to allow the man entrance.

While he positioned the food, Emilie leaned out to peer into the corridor. To the left was a wall while to the right she could see there was some sort of light just around the corner.

Escape teased at her thoughts, but where would she go?

Emilie stepped back inside only to collide with something. A hand snaked around her midsection.

Another hand reached beyond her to slam the door.

A fetid smell overpowered the scent of breakfast and caused her stomach to lurch as a cloth covered her face. She opened her mouth to scream and gagged on a handful of the greasy fabric.

He slammed her against the door, then released her. Woozy from the collision, Emilie nonetheless found the door latch with her hand while maintaining eye contact with the horrible man.

Holding tight to the latch lest her dizziness cause her to fall, Emilie leaned against the door for leverage. In a swift move, she landed a strong kick to the man's ample belly. As he fell, she ran.

Following the pale glow of what appeared to be sunlight, Emilie raced away from the heavy footfalls she could hear as well as feel behind her. Colliding into walls and nearly stumbling more than once, she emerged into the fresh air. Blinded by the light, she ran forward knowing what was ahead could not be worse than that which was behind her.

The ocean beckoned, and she aimed for it. Let the sharks have their way with her. It could be no worse than the vile man who pursued her.

Toward the sounds of shouting she ran. Then, almost as if time had slowed, the ship was behind her, nothing but air beneath her.

Water filled her mouth and stung her eyes while her skirt tangled around her ankles. She kicked toward the blur of green that, she prayed, would indicate land. Soon she found the tide propelling her forward so that she merely had to help it along and keep her head above water.

As she neared the beach, the water became crystal clear, an ocean of glass that gave away the secrets of its depths. Something shone in the sunlight, and she dove down to retrieve a coin of what appeared to be solid gold.

Something for the school, she decided as she clutched it in her fist. Her toes touched something solid. Though some distance remained to reach the shore, she'd reached a place where she no longer had to swim.

Her lungs burned, but her vision had begun to clear. She looked back at the ship, now quite a distance away, and realized no one had followed. At least not yet.

"Thank You, Lord," she whispered as she allowed a wave to lift her up on tiptoe, then send her gently down again. "Even now I feel Your protection. Please make a way for me to leave this place and go home."

It occurred to her as she said the words that she couldn't really state where home was. Certainly not New Orleans, although the women who had raised her remained there. Not exactly Fairweather Key, for she'd only settled there for a brief time, never thinking it would be forever.

She swiped her hair from her face and surged forward, each wave moving her closer to the beach. Finally, the sand beneath her toes began to rise until she walked out of the water and onto dry land.

Once again, Emilie turned back to see if she'd been followed and found nothing but sparkling water between her and the *Cormorant*. Perhaps they'd been too busy with the repairs the Benning fellow told her about to bother noticing their captive had escaped. The best scenario would be for them to reach whatever home port they haunted before realizing her absence. In the interim, perhaps she could coax some friendly fisherman to take her as far as the next port where she could finally find her way back to Fairweather Key.

"I can hope, anyway," she said as she hurried into the cover of the tropical shade to slip the coin in her pocket and shake the sand off her skirt. As she looked around to decide what to do next, she smoothed her tangles into some semblance of a braid.

Her back to the beach, Emilie peered through the thicket. From where she stood, she could see all the way to the other side of the thin sliver of an island and the ocean beyond.

The size of the island dashed her hopes for finding someone who might help her, though she determined the only way to know for sure was to begin hiking until she'd covered every inch of this tropical paradise.

Surely the Lord would provide.

Above her, sunlight filtered through swaying palm fronds and lit a path that seemed to be clear of any sort of creepy crawling creature, much to her relief. One last glance behind her, and Emilie began making her way carefully through the foliage until she reached the other side of the island.

At no point did she see any signs of life other than the brilliantly hued birds that roosted in the topmost canopy of trees. Then she spied something on the beach.

It appeared to be a boat. She moved closer. Indeed, someone had hauled the small wooden craft onto the beach and turned it over on its side as if to fashion a shelter.

Emilie smiled. "Thank You, Lord," even as she wondered how in the world the little vessel would get her all the way to Fairweather Key.

On this side of the island, the beach was deeper and the sand softer. Emilie sank to her ankles in places as she made her way toward the little boat. A few paces away, she heard a strange sound.

Not quite an animal, possibly human. She paused and turned her ear away from the wind. There it was again.

It sounded like snoring.

Emilie crept forward until she saw a pair of boots and an oar leaning against the craft. A few more steps, and she saw feet. Large, male feet.

They moved, and she jumped back. Now what?

Dared she assume that the owner of these feet was friend, or could he be foe?

She paused to think and then decided if none of the men had followed from the *Cormorant*, it was likely this one could be labeled a friend. Thus, Emilie squared her shoulders and marched over to the little boat, then knocked sharply on the wooden hull.

"Excuse me, sir," she said in her most friendly but firm voice, "but I require a favor from you. I assure you I can make this worth your while."

Emilie looked over the edge of the boat in time to see a familiar face staring back at her. "You," she said to the pirate Benning.

"You," the Benning echoed. "Are you real, or have I been in the sun too long?"

She felt the air go out of her. Her only chance, and it turned out to be no chance at all. Emilie flopped unceremoniously on the sand and stared out at the surf.

"Were I not raised a gentleman, I'd take offense to that greeting," he said as he rose and dusted powder-white sand off trousers that had been rolled to the knee.

Emilie ignored him. All was lost, and no amount of levity on his part would relieve the strong need to cry. Only her pride kept the tears at bay. For how long, she did not know.

To her surprise, the pirate plopped down beside her and rested his hands on his knees. For a time he merely stared—as did she—at the emerald waters, the crystal clear surf, and the sky so blue it hurt to look at it for long.

Finally, he leaned toward her. "We have one boat on the *Cormorant*, and it's over there." He gestured toward the upended vessel. "Mind telling me how you came to be on the island?"

She gave him a look that let him know she did not intend to converse. Yet something about his expression softened her resolve. "I swam," she said matter-of-factly.

"You swam?" His brows rose, but for a moment he said nothing. "Looks as if you've ruined your swimming costume," he finally said, his gaze traveling from her face to her dress.

Indeed, the garment was a total ruin, but that was the least of her concerns. She began to calculate the odds of appropriating the boat and rowing away from this island, leaving the Benning to wait for rescue from his pirate companions.

The image that came to mind of her at the oars and him giving chase was comical at best. She actually chuckled, though not from anything she found funny. She was well and truly stuck, a captive.

Heedless of the sand, Emilie fell back and closed her eyes. "What now, Lord? I certainly can't swim home, though You were gracious to get me here."

"You're serious," the Benning said. "You swam here?"

She opened one eye and saw him staring down at her. "I'm not talking to you."

The Benning remained silent, as did the rest of Emilie's prayers. When she'd exhausted her pleas, she turned to the man beside her.

"Go back to that ship and leave me here."

He shook his head. "Cannot do that, madam," he said. "You'd not live out the week." He paused. "You really swam here?"

Emilie ignored him.

"Truly swam?" he continued.

"Yes," she finally said. "It was either that or remain in your cabin and have my virtue compromised by one of your ruffians."

She sat up and turned toward the pirate. An odd thought occurred. Without the beard and length of hair, he might be a handsome man. Emilie tried for a moment to imagine the features that lay beneath the rat's nest of hair and the tangle of beard but could not.

Then the Benning laughed, and her thoughts returned to the situation at hand.

"Do you think I jest, sir?"

"Truly," he said, "your imagination is quite vivid. Did I not leave you with my own pistol for your protection? Surely you cannot still believe my men are bent on your compromise."

Emilie peeled back the still-damp fabric of her sleeve and showed the Benning the fresh bruises on her arm. "Likely the ones covered by this ruined garment are worse."

He reached for her hand and drew her closer,

inspecting her purpled skin with a soft touch then tracing the line of the foul man's hands with his fingers.

"Who did this to you?" he demanded, anger coloring his words and expression.

"I told you." She jerked her arm away. "One of your men."

His fingers fisted, and he looked away. "Tell me more."

She told him of the man who delivered her breakfast, of the rough way he handled her and the things he said. With each statement, the pirate's face clouded more with what could only be anger. When she finished, he climbed to his knees and reached for her.

"Tell me who he is, and I'll see that he swings from the same yardarm as Thomas Hawkins."

Emilie looked past him to the freedom that the ocean offered. "He did not say."

"You could identify him."

She closed her eyes and nodded.

"Then we shall return to the *Cormorant* so this man can be identified and dealt with."

When Emilie opened her eyes, the Benning was standing over her. He reached down to offer his hand. She ignored the gesture to look away.

Finally, he gave up and landed on the sand beside her once more. For a long time, he sat in silence, the only sound between them the crashing waves and salt-tinged breeze.

"I'm not what you think," he said after awhile.

An odd statement, to be sure. "Nor am I," she admitted. What harm did it do to say such a thing aloud? Likely he'd never suspect he carried on a conversation with a woman who was born to a slave.

Again, they fell silent.

Emilie's stomach growled, a reminder of how long she'd gone without food. Of the meal that awaited her back in this man's cabin and the price she nearly paid for it.

Her companion rose to walk over to the boat. He bent down to grab an object, then returned with what appeared to be a scarf stuffed with something.

The reminder of the fabric the vile man had stuffed in her mouth made Emilie turn away to gag.

He set the scarf between them then untied the corners to reveal an appetizing meal. Much as Emilie wished to eat, she declined.

"I assure you it's quite good." The Benning scooped up something that looked like a miniature hard-boiled egg and tossed it into his mouth, making a perfect catch without using his hands. He continued to repeat the process until she finally met his gaze. This time, the pirate lifted a caramel-colored brow and held up two fingers.

Carefully, he chose two and balanced them in his palm. Another quirk of his brow, then the pirate tossed both eggs into the air. Each landed, one after the other, in his mouth.

Emilie suppressed a smile.

"Tough audience," he said. "Should I try for three? To my knowledge, it's never been done."

Her smile finally broke, but not until he tried and failed twice. "That's better," he said, "now eat." He gave her another sideways look. "If for nothing else than to regain the strength you need to escape captivity and row home."

This time her laugh was genuine, yet he quickly sobered. "I'm sorry," he said. "I should not have left my post outside the door. Whatever harm has befallen you is my fault." He met her incredulous stare. "It is my hope that you will find a way to forgive me. Despite what you believe about me, I am an honorable man." He paused. "A man of justice."

The statement rendered Emilie temporarily speechless. What sort of pirate asked forgiveness of his captive?

"There were explicit instructions to leave you alone," he continued.

Emilie felt the odd need to comfort him, to tell the Benning that ultimately she'd not suffered any permanent damage at the hands of the ruffian. After the events of the last two days, she'd expected no less than another man behaving badly.

He reached over to grasp her wrist, his touch gentle. "Might I inspect the damage once more?"

She complied, lifting her hand to allow him to see what the man had inflicted upon her. Then, as if time slowed to a crawl, the Benning lifted the inside of her wrist to his lips.

CHAPTER 15

What had he done? Caleb recoiled in horror lest the poor woman think she was in the presence of yet another man bent on seducing her.

"Forgive me," he said as he reached to gather up the remains of their meal. "I'm afraid I've overstepped the bounds of propriety."

"Mr. Benning," she said in that throaty voice that conveyed humor along with a hint of sarcasm, "I daresay the bounds of propriety were crossed well before now." Her dark eyes widened as a lovely shade of pink crept into her cheeks. "Oh, that did not sound as I planned."

Caleb sighed. "Fear not," he said, "I understand."

"You do." Words spoken so softly he almost missed it.

"Yes," he said. "I do."

This time when their gazes met, Caleb felt the undeniable pull toward her. He hardly knew this woman, and indeed, he could never allow her to truly know him. Yet something about her drew him to her like a moth to the flame.

The vision of what happened to a moth once it found the flame sapped away the need to know more about his captive. To open his heart to anyone was to risk all he'd worked for. All he'd promised his father he would achieve, the position that had never quite been within the elder Spencer's grasp. To be attorney general of the United States was almost beyond a dream, but to rise above the taint of the Benning bloodline, this was attainable.

But only if he kept his lives separate.

Caleb rose and offered his hand to help the woman from her place on the sand. This time she accepted, and soon she fell in beside him on the short walk to the boat.

He righted the craft and made to push it back into the surf when the woman stopped him. "Might we stay a little longer?" she asked.

He must have looked reluctant, for she pressed her case. "I'm not ready to go back and face those who saw me take that jump."

The color still rode high in her cheeks, giving her the look of one who'd stayed in the sun too long. Caleb returned the vessel to its side and positioned it to provide shade for her.

"Thank you," she said as she took a spot at the far edge of the shaded sand.

Deciding there was ample room between them, Caleb took the opposite place, giving himself just enough room to lean back comfortably against the rough wood planks. The sun had traveled past its mid-point and now hung slightly toward the west. In a few hours, darkness would fall and this day would end.

"It's beautiful here. I don't think I knew there

were places like this," she added. "I read of them while at Miss Potter's school, but never have I seen them."

"So that's where you learned to quote the Greeks. Miss Potter's school."

Her smile was beautiful, as was her laugh. "Yes," she said, "though I'm put more in mind of Mr. Defoe's works here." She leaned against the boat and closed her eyes. "*Robinson Crusoe.* Have you read it?"

Caleb nodded, then waited for her to speak again. After awhile he assumed she'd fallen asleep and felt he could do the same. Crossing his hands behind his head, he closed his eyes.

"What's it like to be a pirate?" his companion asked.

Opening his eyes, Caleb studied a lone cloud as it drifted lazily overhead. "I'm not a pirate," he said. "Never have been."

"All right," she said slowly, her tone indicating she neither believed him nor intended to allow this to be his only answer. "Then explain the ship, the crew, the flag, all of that."

Ah, the difficult question. The only thing harder to explain would have been the simple one: Who are you?

"Do you know what a privateer is?" He asked the question carefully, neither admitting nor denying any family participation in the career.

"I've heard of them."

"I see." He paused. "Then perhaps you know this is a trade that is highly regulated and of great service to the government the privateer serves."

The wind blew a curl free from her braid, and it was all Caleb could do not to reach over and touch it. "I seem to recall this is true," she said.

"Then how, might I ask, can you believe my family pirates when there is a longstanding tradition of privateering going back to the first Benning to sail the seas? We have always kept the law, though there are those who might wish to tarnish our reputations."

She turned to face him. "You're serious?"

"Deadly serious."

The woman leaned on her elbow, supporting her head with her palm. "So you're saying there's some code of honor among pir—"

He held up his hand. "Privateers."

"Privateers," she corrected.

"Of which I am not one, and neither was my father."

Her eyes narrowed. "I don't understand. You said—"

"That the Bennings had a tradition of privateering." He nodded. "'Tis true. But I am not a Benning. That's my mother's name. I'm—"

Caleb clamped his mouth shut and tried to keep the panic-stricken feeling from reaching his face. What was it about this woman that made him lose all good sense?

"You're what?" She gave him a curious look. "Or, should I ask, you're who?"

"Oh no," he said, his tone as light as he could make it. "It's your turn. I've revealed enough. Perhaps you could begin by telling me your name."

She turned to stare out at the ocean. "I do not remember agreeing to some game of taking turns," she said.

"It's only a name."

"And yours is?" She paused and swung her gaze to collide with his. "Other than the Benning, that is."

"Fair enough. No more taking turns."

Caleb sat up and dusted the sand from his palms. Soon they would leave this island and likely never meet again. Strange, but the idea saddened him.

"You'll be home soon enough," he said, as much to remind her as himself.

The dark-haired woman seemed not to mind the change of topic. "I'm afraid to believe you," she said.

He leaned closer, impossibly drawn to her. "What can I say to make you understand that I mean you no harm?"

Her eyes closed, and he watched, fascinated, as thick lashes dusted pink cheeks. She looked helpless, this woman whose name he did not know.

Whose name he realized he did not want to know. For if he knew, then he might be tempted to think of her.

And that would not do.

She knew too much already.

Her lids fluttered, drawing him nearer until he leaned impossibly close. Too close to avoid tracing the curve of her jaw and the tilt of her nose.

The woman sat very still, her mouth curling into what might pass for the beginnings of a smile. "Mr. Benning, is this an attempt to have me believe you mean me no harm?"

"No," he said softly, "this is."

He kissed her.

CHAPTER 16

Soon as he realized what he'd done, Caleb scrambled to his feet and began making his apologies. To his surprise, the woman rose as well.

"I assure you I am a gentleman," Caleb continued. "I cannot fathom what came over me, nor will I offer excuses for it."

She straightened her braid, but not before a dark curl escaped to tease her neck. "Sir, if you continue in this vein, I will be forced to believe the experience was so offensive as to be regrettable."

Was she serious? Caleb stuffed his fists into his pockets. "Regrettable?" He shook his head. "Never."

"Repeatable?" She dusted the sand from her skirts.

It was Caleb's turn to smile. Had he not the good sense to know this was an innocent, he would think she was flirting. Something in her tone, however, gave him to believe she truly might not know the answer.

"I am not averse." The woman's smile reappeared, even as she turned and walked away. "So that was not an invitation?" he called.

"It was an inquiry. Nothing more."

He rested his hands on his hips. "And now that I have answered in the positive?"

She ignored him to study the horizon. While she looked to the west, Caleb seized the chance to look at her.

Dark of eye and hair with curls that refused to be tamed, she was not a beauty in the conventional way. Rather, she had a bearing that was striking, with an imperious air that might have been off-putting under other circumstances.

Now, however, as she wandered the ocean's edge, her frock wrinkled and her feet bare, she looked quite the opposite. In fact, she looked quite at home here in this unspoiled paradise.

Unfortunately, the length of the boat's shadow told him their time in paradise was limited. "Excuse me," he called. "Miss Crusoe?"

She turned but said nothing until a wave danced across her feet. Then she giggled, the sound more appropriate to a schoolgirl than a grown woman. Yet it was endearing.

Gathering his wits, Caleb forced his mind back to the topic at hand. "We've a decision to make."

"Oh?" The breeze whipped against her skirts, but their waterlogged hems kept her modesty intact.

"Indeed."

He walked to meet her halfway. She peered up from beneath the curtain of curls that tossed about and obstructed her view. "And what might that be?"

"Simple." Caleb leaned forward but maintained a respectable distance. "We must choose whether Mr. Defoe's man Robinson had the right idea in leaving his island."

Her full lips turned up in the slightest of grins. "What do you mean?"

Caleb noticed she had inched almost imperceptibly toward him. "At the moment, we are two castaways on an island that is ours alone. Our time here, however, is short."

"I see."

"Unless, of course," he said, "we decide to remain here."

She blinked. Twice. "That's preposterous," she said.

"It is, sadly." Caleb reached to offer her his hand. "Then away with you, Miss Crusoe. Your craft awaits."

The woman linked arms with him, and together they strolled at the edge of the surf until they arrived at the little craft he'd used only yesterday to save her from Thomas Hawkins. Now, it seemed, he might be the one in need of rescue.

If only he did not have obligations.

Oblivious to his dilemma, she climbed into the boat while he pushed off into the surf and then joined her. The waves splashed against the vessel, pressing them back toward the beach while Caleb struggled to do the opposite.

How easy it would be to drop the oar and let the vessel find the beach once more.

"There will be questions," she said, "and I would appreciate not having to answer them."

"Are you speaking of the questions I wish to ask or of those that may be asked aboard the *Cormorant*?"

She looked surprised. "Both, I suppose."

Caleb could only nod. "It will be as you ask."

He rowed past the breakers, then turned the craft south. Soon they would be within sight of the *Cormorant*. Across the tiny expanse that separated them, the dark-haired woman seemed preoccupied.

"Miss Crusoe?"

The smile returned.

"I know I agreed you'd not have to answer questions, but I must break that promise." He lifted the oars to stop their forward progress. "For I must ask just one more thing of you, though it will only require a yes or no."

"Go ahead then," she said, her dark eyes sparkling as the sun glinted off the water.

"As one castaway to another, might we share one last kiss before returning to civilization? It would be a memory to cherish," he added, "for where I am going, there is no sandy beach nor anyone as lovely as you."

She smiled. And then she said, "Yes."

The kiss was chaste, and the trip back to the vessel agonizingly quick. Too soon, Caleb lashed the boat to the *Cormorant* and helped the woman aboard.

None dared comment as he walked with her to his cabin, then left her to go inside alone. "The man who frightened you today, I would have a description," he said as she stepped inside.

"There is no need," she said, "for he will be the one with bruises on his belly." She gave Caleb a sideways look. "I may have injured him."

Caleb chuckled. "Then I shall have my men bare their bellies. And pity the fellow who cannot account for any footprints I might find there."

An awkward silence fell between them. She seemed disinclined to ask him to leave, and Caleb did not wish to move away. Yet nothing could be gained by continuing the insanity that had begun on Langham Island.

"I warrant I shall throw whoever is responsible for the reprehensible attack in the brig with Hawkins," he said, "but I cannot assure there are not others who wish to make your acquaintance. You are, Miss Crusoe, a beautiful woman, and that can cause even the most sane man to do foolish things." Caleb paused. "Where is the pistol?"

She looked around then shook her head. "It is not here."

Caleb thought a moment. Surely Fletcher had retrieved the weapon once the woman's antics were made known to him.

"See that you latch the door," he said as he made a note to speak to Fletcher regarding the missing pistol. Even one weapon unaccounted for on a vessel of this size could make for trouble.

Her nod sufficed. Before he could change his mind, Caleb stepped into the passageway. "I wish you safe travel to wherever you're going," he said.

"And you," was her soft answer.

Silence fell between them. Then, as the watch bell rang, Caleb turned and walked away. Should he have remained in her presence another moment, his career in the navy or any other branch of government might have been seriously compromised.

May 29, 1836
Santa Lucida

"Land ho!"

Caleb sat bolt upright. While his casual demeanor with the woman last night had, he hoped, caused her to cease fretting, he had taken the cause up with great vigor. For if one man had tried to have his way with her, likely there were others who might make the attempt.

His concerns were heightened by the fact that

189

neither Fletcher nor any other member of the crew claimed to have removed the weapon from his cabin. Knowing this could spell disaster, he decided a guard was necessary.

With difficulty, Caleb stretched out his legs, then did the same with his arms. Would that there had been someone else he could have trusted with the job. Alas, only Fletcher held his confidence, and he would never ask the old man to sleep in a ship's corridor.

Thus, the job fell to Caleb.

"Land ho!" came the call once again. *Thank You, Lord. You've delivered me home.*

His stomach protested, but he took heart in knowing a feast would await him in Santa Lucida. Caleb leaned back against the door and completed his morning prayers.

"Home," he said under his breath as he thought of what awaited him. "Perhaps it is possible for a man to have two homes: Washington and Santa Lucida."

Washington. The letter to the attorney general must be answered soon, lest the job be offered to another. One last time, he weighed the possibility in his mind, then decided to do what he'd known all along was the right thing.

"What harm can come of trying out a naval position for a spell?" he said as he climbed to his feet and did his best to stretch out the remaining kinks. It might just be the change of pace he needed.

All that remained was to retrieve the letter from his desk and disembark the *Cormorant*. To wait until the ship's return from Havana in order to respond to the naval secretary was impossible. The secretary might give the job to another in his absence, and he'd already lost one job. He'd not lose another.

Caleb pulled the knob and peered inside at the sleeping form of the dark-haired beauty. Rather than risk another awkward good-bye or, worse, be unable to leave her, Caleb decided it was most prudent to allow the beauty to sleep. With care, he pushed the door open just enough to step inside.

Before he reached the desk, something exploded. Caleb felt himself propelled backward. The room upended and went dark.

CHAPTER 17

I shot him.

The words wrapped around Emilie's brain but refused to stick. Yet in her hand was the weapon, its tip white-hot from having discharged.

She'd found it during the night when her fingers felt the cord dangling between the bunk and the wall. At the time, she figured the Lord had provided her with the protection she needed.

Now, she had to wonder if the devil himself had left that pistol where she would find it.

Emilie rolled onto her side, then sat up. Immediately she heaved what little she had in her stomach onto the spot inches from where she'd left her shoes.

Gathering her wits, she stood and tiptoed toward the crumpled heap of a man. The intruder lay face up, his eyes seemingly staring into space and his lids not blinking. His fingers had closed around a piece of paper, its words now made unreadable by the blood pouring down his arm and onto the page.

By degrees, the reality of the situation hit.

The man on the floor was the Benning. The man who'd kissed her not once, but twice.

Oh no. Oh no. Oh no.

Her legs failed her, and Emilie landed on her knees. When she realized she still held the gun, she dropped it. The weapon slid out of sight.

Emilie forced her breathing to slow. *What happened?* She thought it, then said it, then repeated it several more times. Finally, she looked up at the stream of light pouring across the grisly scene.

The sun.

Think, Emilie. Think. What does that mean?

By degrees, she sorted out the facts. The sun shone through the porthole, and the ship no longer moved, thus they had anchored at whatever place the Benning called home.

But why is he here? Why? I thought I could trust him. He promised to . . .

Her gaze fell on his clenched fist. The Benning had obviously come for whatever he held in his hand. Mistaking him for someone who meant to harm her, she'd shot him with his own pistol.

I shot the Benning.

She inched closer to the man whose golden skin had already begun to pale and amended her plea. "No, Lord, please, save this man."

Do something. Help him yourself.

Blood. Stop the blood.

But how? It spread from a wound low on his left shoulder and turned his shirt from pink to red. "So much blood," she whispered as she reached to tear off a strip of her skirt and fashion it into a bandage. "Please, Lord, make it stop."

An old man with a pipe stuck in his teeth burst through the door. "I shot him," she said, looking up from her efforts. "I didn't mean to hurt him," she added, fully realizing how ridiculous the two true statements sounded when strung together.

Things happened quickly. The man with the pipe found and kept the pistol. Other men came and took the body. Still others arrived to bring her something to wear that was not covered in Benning blood.

No one looked her in the eye or spoke a word.

When the door finally shut, Emilie climbed into the bunk and cried until her eyes could no longer stay open and she had not a tear left. Even in her sleep, Emilie saw him. The golden hair, the golden skin, the scarlet blood flowing in a stream that became an ocean upon which she was held captive, then mercifully drowned.

The same man who only yesterday had made her feel beautiful. Had given her hope that someday she, too, might find happiness.

Surely it was a dream. An awful, horrible nightmare of a dream.

Snatches of conversation drifted toward her as she lay motionless, waiting for whatever fate would befall her.

"Havana," one man said from outside the door.

"Soon as possible to keep the men from taking justice into their own hands," another responded.

Other words were said, some of them making sense and others sounding like gibberish. A bell rang, then rang again. Birds screeched, or was it a woman? She couldn't be sure.

Then the man with the pipe came back and offered her something bitter to drink. She took it, not knowing if it was meant to ease her thirst or do her in. She cared little which.

Whether due to the circumstances or the beverage, Emilie soon found herself unable to hold her eyes open. When she awoke, the moon cast a path across the cabin.

The man with the pipe stepped inside without knocking and drew the chair up near the bunk. She didn't have to ask if the Benning was dead. His face told her he must be.

"What will happen now?" she asked, her tongue strangely thick.

"Where do you call home, child?"

"Fairweather Key," she said as she pushed up on her elbows and blinked to bring the room into focus. "I am a teacher to the children there."

Why she added that ridiculous detail, Emilie had no idea.

"Then you shall go home," he said, "and you'll tell no one. You will forget all about what has happened here. Do you understand?"

She didn't really, but Emilie knew the man with the pipe was offering a freedom she did not deserve. "Yes," she whispered.

Though she knew she would never speak of this day, she also knew she would never forget. With every wave that crashed on the beach at Fairweather Key, she would think of the day she was Miss Crusoe and he, well, he was the first man to kiss her.

June 10, 1836
Havana

Emilie straightened her spine and walked through the chaos that was the Havana docks toward the merchant vessel *Felicity*. Though she heard the comments—some in English and French, others in languages she did not recognize—she kept her silence.

When one of the toughs stepped in front of her, Emilie stopped short. "A lady shouldn't be alone in such a place." He leered at her with his good eye. "Or maybe ye ain't a lady after all."

Something inside Emilie snapped. Two weeks of trying to convince herself and seemingly every judge and attorney in Havana that she was a lady and Thomas Hawkins was no gentleman had taken its toll. So had the nightmares of the fallen Benning and his blood-soaked letter.

"Maybe I'm not," she echoed. "I wonder if we've both killed a man recently or if I alone have that distinction. Oh, then there's the fortune in gold I allowed to slip to the bottom of the ocean while fending off pirates." Emilie paused to take a breath, her blood boiling. "Two of them," she added.

It was enough to send the fellow back to his comrades without further comment while Emilie pressed on undisturbed.

Once aboard the richly appointed *Felicity*, Emilie was swept down an elegant passageway to a cabin that the white-suited porter deemed "fit for kings, queens, and royalty of all sorts." When he closed the door, she stood for what seemed an eternity on its threshold, knowing in her heart she did not belong among such splendor.

By degrees, she moved into the center of the room, then turned around completely so as to take it all in. Ironically, the cabin was not unlike her bedchamber back in New Orleans, yet that room, that place, seemed a world away.

As did the woman who resided there. So much had happened since leaving her father's bedside. Would he even recognize her now?

She should write him, but what would she say? *Arrived safely in Havana after shipwreck and abduction by two pirates, one of whom I sent to the gallows and the other I dispatched myself with his own pistol. At least neither discovered I was the daughter of a slave.*

Emilie slipped past an ornate mirror without glancing at the stranger reflected there. Since leaving New Orleans, she'd not seen one familiar face, not even her own.

Lifting her palm to her cheek, she remembered the bruise that had, thankfully, faded and was now all but gone. At least that would be one less thing to explain.

She turned her attention to the task at hand. The voyage to Fairweather Key would be brief, measured in hours rather than days, and she must compose herself before she arrived.

Through events not of her choosing—and one horrible choice—she'd lost the gold that was to have paid for a school as well as compromised her reputation and her ability to provide a good example for the children she desperately wished to continue teaching. She'd also learned she held neither the background nor the qualifications to stand before a roomful of students as a free woman.

Yet she must step off the ship, presenting a good face and giving no hint of any of this trouble. In order to return to her old life, she would have to bury the events of the present one.

Just as someone had buried the Benning.

The reminder stung, as they all had since she pulled back the trigger and changed at least two lives. More, likely.

Forcing her thoughts back on teaching, she contemplated the claim she had filed with the court in Havana. While it was likely the gold in her skirt pockets had gone down with *Hawk's Remedy*, it was also possible the ruffian still possessed it when he met his fate.

There was small hope of this, but Cook always said where small hope existed, there did the Lord abide. If only she could have the faith that Cook possessed.

Rather, if she could only get it back.

Emilie fell onto the bunk and cradled her head in its enveloping softness while she fought the ever-present tears. Sleep beckoned, but she resisted. No need to add to the nightmares plaguing the dark by allowing dreams while there was still daylight.

The sense that she'd left something undone tugged at her until she rose and hung her legs over the side of the bunk. *What now, Lord?*

Outside, the sounds of the docks combined with the screech of gulls and the slap of waves against the ship. Emilie's slow, even breaths seemed loudest of all. Finally, she fell to her knees and looked up, praying the God of all would see and hear her despite her sins.

"How can I live when I've lost the money for the school and taken the life of another? How can You forgive me, God? I know what Your Word says, but dare I even ask?"

She ducked her head and poured out her heart, emptying her soul of the stains she alone had blackened it with. When she was done, Emilie waited.

Surely the clouds would part and God would offer some grand gesture of forgiveness. Instead, slow wave upon wave of peace buffeted her with a love that she could neither completely fathom nor understand. While she might labor the rest of her days to forgive herself, she began to believe her heavenly Father had already done the work of cleansing.

A knock brought her scrambling to her feet. "Come in," she called as she collected herself and swiped at her damp cheeks with her hand-kerchief.

The same jovial porter who had carried her lone carpetbag had returned, this time bearing a single letter on a silver tray.

"But I don't know anyone here," she said. "Are you certain this is for me?"

"You're Miss Gayarre, are you not?" He handed

her a thick letter folded in quarters and fixed at the center with crimson sealing wax. "Perhaps you have an admirer."

"I doubt that," she said as she watched him leave and close the door. "Women like me don't have admirers."

She broke the seal to open the letter. As she did, something fell, and she reached for it.

Her mother's miniature. A catch in her throat became a sob as Emilie saw the nearly ruined but still recognizable face of Sylvie smiling back from the water-damaged frame.

When she could manage it, she set the portrait aside, then turned her attention to the letter. *"All treasures from the criminal Hawkins have been confiscated by the court. This, however, was unmistakably yours."*

Emilie's gaze fell to the bottom of the page. In lieu of a signature was a single letter: *F.*

Fairweather Key

When Emilie stepped off the *Felicity* onto the Fairweather Key docks, it seemed as though the whole town had come out to meet her.

"How did you know?" she asked as she embraced her half-sister Isabelle, then relieved her of the gloriously adorable infant she carried. Bestowing a kiss on the nephew who seemed to have doubled in size since her departure, Emilie looked over his dark head to focus on Isabelle. "I told no one of my travel plans."

The striking woman with the golden hair smiled, and Emilie recognized her father in the grin. For a moment, Emilie wondered what part Isabelle's mother—the woman she had thought was her own mother—played in the elegant features she now saw.

The thought occurred to her that not only did she and Isabelle share the bond of a common father, but they also shared the common loss of their mothers. Emilie felt the pocket of her skirt where the waterlogged miniature lay hidden. *At least I have a picture of mine.*

Isabelle squeezed her arm. "When Reverend Carter received the letter from our father stating your desire to return, we all assumed it would be soon. I've had Josiah inquiring of all the incoming vessels for weeks."

"Then please express my gratitude to him."

Isabelle smiled. "I shall. Now, greet your students properly; then I'll fetch you home for a warm meal and a soft bed. You look exhausted."

Emilie's smile came quickly if not easily. "I am," she said, "but I'll not miss a moment of this homecoming."

The babe tucked into the curve of her arm, Emilie knelt to receive greetings from the boys and girls who studied in her makeshift school. The last in line was William, brother to Isabelle's husband and a strapping lad of nearly twelve.

"Mother and I have been holding class in your absence, Miss Emilie," he said. "Though I'm not the teacher you are."

"Is that so?" She handed her nephew back to Isabelle and rose to embrace the boy who was equal to her in height. "Thank you, William. I'm ever so grateful that you've kept the young ones up on their lessons."

He shrugged out of her embrace, his ears reddening at the tips. "Mother helped with the little ones. They're a bit frustrating."

Isabelle grinned, and Emilie joined in. "Indeed," she said, "they can be difficult. I must thank your mother for the assistance."

"It was a pleasure," Mary Carter, wife of Reverend Carter, said as she joined her son and daughter-in-law in the family circle. "Never have I been so happy as when my husband saw fit to move us near our son." She winked at William. "Our sons, rather, since I cannot imagine our younger one leaving his new home here." She looked over her shoulder to the water. "Where's my Josiah? He should be here to welcome Emilie home."

"He's helping with a repair," Isabelle said. "With the weather closing in, you know the wreckers don't like to have even one boat out of service. Understandable, of course, for what if a vessel were to wreck on the reefs and there weren't enough boats to do the work of saving life and property?"

Emilie glanced over her shoulder and noticed for the first time the dark clouds gathering at the horizon. They mirrored her mood, even as she forced a smile. "Spoken like a true wrecker's wife," she said.

Isabelle sighed. "I never thought I could love this life so much," she said. "We're a long way from New Orleans, aren't we?"

The baby in Isabelle's arms began to squirm. "Might I fetch Joey home for a bath?" Mary Carter asked.

Isabelle offered the smile of an appreciative new mother. "I would be grateful," she said.

"Come, William," Mary called. "Let's leave the sisters to their welcome party."

As the pair strolled away, little Joey smiling from his grandmother's shoulder, Emilie felt a pang akin to jealousy.

"God has blessed Josiah and me so greatly these past two years," Isabelle said as if she'd guessed Emilie's thoughts. "And none of it would have happened without you."

Before Emilie could protest, Isabelle linked arms with her and propelled her down the sidewalk away from the docks. They walked in silence until Emilie could stand it no more.

"What God has done, Isabelle, He would have accomplished without me."

Isabelle slowly smiled. "Indeed," she said, "but He chose this way."

"You haven't asked me about my visit with Father."

Isabelle shook her head. "There will be plenty of time for that." She paused. "Unless something happened that you'd like to discuss."

"What? No," she said quickly. "Nothing exceptional."

"I don't believe you." Isabelle stopped short and pulled Emilie to a halt with her. For an uncomfortable moment, she studied Emilie. By degrees, her face took on a solemn expression. "Surely you did not spend all these weeks with our father and not return changed in some way. I never said so when you determined to go, but my greatest fear was that somehow you would be called to pay for my escape." She paused. "Or worse, that you would return knowing things that were not your business to discover." Another pause. "And you have. I can tell it."

Emilie glanced around and frowned. The normally busy town center seemed overflowing with people, likely due to the ship's arrival. Attempting a private conversation would be impossible. Yet she longed to unload the black mark on her soul, to seek absolution or at least find some measure of relief in sharing her secret.

"There is something, isn't there?" Isabelle's solemn expression turned stricken. "Oh, Em, I never wanted this to happen." She shook her head. "You must understand that it doesn't matter to me at all. Not a bit of it. That's why I burned the letters."

Her head spun with the combined effort of keeping up with the conversation and her racing thoughts. "I must either sit or walk else I fall down," she said.

"Are you unwell? Shall I take you home?"

The thought of spending a moment in the cozy place where she'd lived happy and protected these past two years filled her with panic. "Not yet," she said.

"I'll take you home with me, then."

"No!" Emilie clamped her hand over her mouth. Shouting was not in her character, nor were public displays. She took a deep breath and let it out slowly as she dropped her hand to her side. "I want to walk," she finally said, though she did not make a move to do so.

Her sister waited. She said nothing, though Emilie knew Isabelle well enough to know she desperately wanted to help.

Isabelle was always one to help.

She sighed. Words that had been as yet unspoken begged for release. Finally, she leaned over to whisper in Isabelle's ear. "Yes, I know about our mothers, but there's more. I killed a man, Izzy."

CHAPTER 18

A round them, the activity of Fairweather Key continued as if nothing had changed. Across the way, Judge Campbell carried on what looked like a heated debate with the Ivan brothers, who managed the mercantile, while Mrs. Campbell was deep in conversation with their wives.

When the women looked up and waved, Emilie felt the panic take hold. While Mrs. Campbell was a dear woman and close to a substitute mother for her on occasion, she could not carry on a decent conversation so soon after the admission of her crime. For her part, Isabelle looked too stunned to speak as well.

"I want to walk," Emilie said as she returned the ladies' waves, then pointed in the opposite direction. "That way."

"Fine." Isabelle linked arms with her and followed her lead, neither speaking nor seeming to concern herself with their destination.

With each step, Emilie felt the burden of her crime jostling her conscience. Indeed, she'd gone to God for forgiveness, but translating that into a life that included such an awful sin was not something she could decide how to do. Even during the awful days of testifying against Captain Hawkins and detailing his sins, hers seemed ever present. She had killed a man. How did one redeem that?

She'd never asked Isabelle about her time as a slave, though Emilie knew her sister must have seen awful things. Awful things that were meant for her, not for Isabelle, she reminded herself.

Given the fact she'd been trained as a courtesan in anticipation of her life as a kept woman in the awful tradition of the day, likely Isabelle had done things that tugged at her heart and mind. Yet her countenance was always marked with peace, and it seemed she'd adjusted to her new life of freedom with ease. She'd certainly found happiness with a wonderful, godly husband, a beautiful son, and in-laws who knew of her past and adored her in spite of it.

Perhaps Isabelle can tell me how the forgetting and getting on with life is done.

Indeed, Izzy's journey from slave to wife and mother had the touches of God's hand all over it. From her husband's return to the Lord, to his reunion with his parents and their move to Fairweather Key, all had not only ended well but had made for a beautiful testimony of what God can do.

They stopped on a bluff overlooking a deserted stretch of waterfront. Here the water did not lap against a sandy beach but rather pounded rocks and craggy outcroppings covered with thick vegetation. The only signs of life in this lonely spot were the occasional fishing cabins dotting the distant horizon.

Emilie spied one in particular, a ramshackle place that looked oddly out of place atop the highest rise on the island. It appeared empty and unused, yet the view from its rooms must have been spectacular.

Quite the opposite of how she felt. Though she appeared, she hoped, to still be the same Emilie who had left Fairweather Key many weeks before, she now felt as empty as that cabin looked.

Barren. Lost. Sitting atop a windswept hill with nothing but daylight and darkness for company. Emilie released her grip on Isabelle's arm and wrapped her arms around her chest. Her face lifted to the sky, she closed her eyes and let the sun do its job of warming her face, turning the backs of her eyelids from deep purple to fiery orange.

When she opened her eyes, she found Isabelle staring. Not surprising considering the turn of conversation.

Would Izzy always look at her in that way? As a woman forever marked by the life she had taken?

"I'm terribly sorry for the injustice done to you, Isabelle," she said. "If I could somehow change it, I would."

Isabelle reached to touch her hand. "I'll not speak of this again, nor will you." She met Emilie's gaze. "It is the only way we can move forward without the devil taking a foothold between us."

"Agreed," Emilie said as she unceremoniously flopped onto the grassy ground, caring not what ruin she might be making of the flower-sprigged frock she wore.

What did she care? Even the clothes on her back reminded Emilie of the Benning, for it was the man with the pipe, clearly a member of the Benning clan, who'd brought it to her along with the selection of other dresses that filled her carpetbag. All that was Emilie Gayarre had gone down with the *Sunday Service*, leaving only the shell of a murderous woman and the water-soaked miniature of a mother she never knew. Every stitch of clothing she owned was bought with Benning money.

Or at least the money of the man at whose command Benning's body was removed from that room. The thought of money caused her to think of the gold Papa had given her for the school, gold that was now gone.

"Izzy, I depress myself." She attempted a laugh, but the sound was brittle and humorless.

"Oh, honey."

Emilie watched her sister settle beside her and noticed the unshed tears swimming in her green eyes. Again, she was struck by Isabelle's resemblance to her father. "Forgive me. I should not have burdened you with this."

Her sister reached to take Emilie's hand. "I am honored that you shared your secret." Her gaze met Emilie's then her eyes widened. "It is a secret? Our father does not know?"

"Only you and those aboard the *Cormorant* know."

"The *Cormorant*?"

"The second vessel upon which I was held captive." Another feeble attempt at laughter failed more miserably than the first. "That would be after the sinking of the *Sunday Service* and my capture by the pirate Thomas Hawkins of the *Hawk's Remedy*. He's the one who caused the loss of the money Papa gave me for the school."

"Jean Gayarre gave you money for the school but it was lost to a pirate?" Isabelle shook her head and pushed an errant curl—the lone similarity that marked them as sisters—from her face. "Perhaps you should start at the beginning."

"I don't know if I can," Emilie said. "It's all too much."

"Then start at the end and work backward."

"Backward?" Emilie made to protest, but Isabelle interrupted.

"Just try it," she said.

"I am here with my sister. Half-sister," she corrected.

Isabelle touched Emilie's sleeve. "I take objection. I've never felt fully sister to anyone until you, Emilie. Do not deny me this by qualifying it with technicalities."

Emilie smiled. "Then I shall begin again. I am here with my sister, Isabelle, after arriving from Havana." At Isabelle's nod, she continued. "Where I was present at a trial conducted by the local authorities for the purpose of discerning the guilt of Thomas Hawkins, captain of the *Hawk's Remedy* and a known pirate. I was the lone witness against him, and I testified to his sinking of the *Sunday Service* and his attack on the *Cormorant*."

She paused and looked past the abandoned cottage, to the glittering ocean and the horizon beyond. The threat of foul weather had not touched the horizon on this side of the island. Rather, several fat white clouds hung in the sky, fresh cotton suspended from a canopy of robin's egg blue.

The same color of the canopy she had looked up into every night as a child in New Orleans. Odd that even now as she gazed into the blue, she wished for a mother to ease her aches and kiss away her troubles.

"Emilie?"

Isabelle's voice brought an end to her musings. "Thomas Hawkins had been taken captive in a battle. As had I."

"A battle?" Isabelle sucked in an audible breath. "Oh, Emmy, were you harmed?"

"This backwards story begs continuing," Emilie said, "and then the questions can be answered."

"Of course." The words floated toward her as a whisper on the sea air.

"The battle raged over something, though I am not certain whether it was me or just an incident of pirating. Whatever the case, I was used as barter for two bags of gold—not the same gold Papa gave me, for that had already been forcefully removed from my person—though the transaction was never completed. Before my time on the *Cormorant*, I was aboard Captain Hawkins's vessel *Hawk's Remedy* where it was not gold but my virtue that the pirate demanded."

Emilie let the words hang between them for a moment. "He did not receive it, but I still bear the bruises from his attempt."

"I'm so sorry," Isabelle said. "Was he found guilty of his crimes?"

"He was." A gull soared overhead, then dipped toward the ocean only to climb and soar again. "I elected not to stay and witness his execution, though likely it has happened by now."

"Justice demanded to be served, though it is unfortunate that you had to participate in his trial." She drew her knees to her chest and settled her skirt around her feet. "Emilie, surely you do not believe that you're the reason this Captain Hawkins is dead."

"Hawkins?" How easily she could allow Isabelle her belief and end this conversation. "No," she finally said, "though I certainly did my part to seal his fate."

"But what of this man you . . ."

"Killed?" Emilie buried her head in her hands. "That would be a fellow named Benning. His crew called him the Benning, which I thought odd. He purchased me for the bags of gold, then promptly defaulted on the transaction in order to capture

Hawkins and turn him over to the authorities in Havana." Her voice faltered as the memory pressed in. "Or rather," she said with difficulty as the tears threatened, "a member of his crew saw to the pirate's delivery to the authorities. You see, by then I'd shot the Benning. With his own pistol."

Isabelle inched closer to take Emilie into her arms. "Oh, Emmy, you're a good person. There has to be a reasonable explanation for this."

"No." Emilie pulled away to rise, swiping at the tears scalding her cheeks. "There is no reasonable explanation. He gave me the pistol and told me to use it should any man breach the sanctity of the cabin where I slept."

Her sister stood and swiped at the grass clinging to her skirt. "Then how did you come to shoot him?"

"I awoke to a man standing in the cabin. I found the pistol and pulled the trigger." She shrugged. "A simple explanation, yet that's exactly what happened."

"But why was he in the cabin? Do you think he meant you harm?"

Words caught in her throat and stuck there until she finally managed to say, "I'll never know."

"The reason doesn't matter so much as what you do with the guilt. It will ruin you if you let it." She paused. "So will the anger."

"I believe you." Emilie took a shuddering breath. "I just don't know how."

An eternity passed as Emilie stood staring at the

clouds skittering off beyond the horizon. In their place came the darkening skies that Isabelle had pointed out back on the docks.

The wind turned fresh and whipped around them, its scent ripe with rain.

Isabelle tugged on Emilie's sleeve. "We should go. It'll do neither of us any good to be caught in the downpour that's surely coming."

Emilie followed her sister's lead and turned to retrace her steps to the town. Then came a moment when the burden on her shoulders would not let her take another step toward a place where people expected her to act like the old Emilie.

An outcropping beckoned, and she sat. "Izzy?" she called to Isabelle's retreating back. "Go on without me."

Her sister stopped and turned around, hands on her hips. "I refuse."

The darkening sky mirrored Emilie's mood. "I need to be alone."

Isabelle came and sat beside her. "Then we will be alone together. And when you're ready, I'll walk you home."

Resting her elbows on her knees, Emilie studied the toes of her borrowed shoes. Unburdening seemed her only choice. "I should never have gone to New Orleans. Looks what's come of my greed."

"Greed?" Isabelle met her stare. "You went at the request of our father. How is that greed?"

"I went with the hope that I could coerce him

into offering up some of his wealth to help build a school. I actually hoped to find I'd arrived too late. Are you shocked?"

"Em," Isabelle said slowly, "if only you could know the thoughts I've had in regard to Jean Gayarre."

Thunder rolled in the distance, but Isabelle never removed her attention from Emilie. "Emilie Gayarre," Isabelle finally said, "I will absolutely not have you sitting on a rock one minute longer."

Isabelle rose and reached for Emilie's wrist, yanking her to her feet. For one so tiny, her sister was quite strong.

"And furthermore, where is the sister who led me out of slavery not once, but twice?"

"What do you mean?"

Thunder rolled around them as the wind picked up. "Walk with me, and I will tell you." She waited until Emilie fell in beside her. "You found me and showed me who Jesus was and how He came to save my soul. Then, even when I thought it impossible, you made it possible to leave and have the life I now live."

Emilie paused to smooth her hair from her face. "I fail to see how any of that reflects on what I've done."

"It reflects on who you are." She stepped around a patch of soft grass, then waited for Emilie to do the same. "And who you are right now is the teacher that the children of Fairweather Key have been missing terribly."

"How can I teach them, Izzy? I'm not the example they need. Nor, for that matter, am I qualified by virtue of my birth."

"Expecting perfection, are you? And on top of that, breaking your promise not to speak of our birth already?" Isabelle's green eyes flashed fire. "Well, Emilie Gayarre, for once it is not going to happen. None of us can live up to that standard forever, not even you." She paused. "I'm terribly sorry for what happened to you. I can't imagine how horrible it was, and I know it must have been even more difficult to talk about it. However, if you let this experience immobilize you, then the devil has won, and those who love you have lost. Is that what you want?"

Emilie thought a moment, then squared her shoulders and swiped at her eyes as the first fat raindrop fell. "Really, Isabelle," she said with the slightest grin, "must you keep me out in this weather? If we don't blow away, we'll surely be soaked."

CHAPTER 19

June 12, 1836
Santa Lucida

Caleb's world was filled with dark and murky passageways pierced by the occasional porthole that allowed only pale light to filter through the gloom. Without ceasing, Caleb wandered the unfamiliar halls, looking for the door that would lead him out of the maze.

Each time it seemed as though he might see the end, that a bright light beckoned, he would stumble forward, only to have the door shut. Close inspection would reveal there had, indeed, been no door at all.

Frustration mounted, as did the heat inside the tiny corridors. Caleb tore at his clothes and tried in vain to find relief. Then, when he felt he could stand it no more, the warmth would turn to bitter cold, and he could do nothing but halt his search and shiver, only to have the heat once again return.

This cycle of bright and dark, cold and hot carried on without ceasing until Caleb could go no further. Then the light found him, and he lay in its circle, finally comfortable.

June 13
Fairweather Key

Emilie had been home three days, and already the memories were fading. Not the horror of seeing a man crumpled on the cabin floor, or the abject terror she felt at being held captive not once but twice. Not even the memory of a day spent as Miss Crusoe in paradise.

No, those things would fade over years, not days or even months, if they faded at all.

It was the memories of her father that seemed to slip through her mind like sand through an hourglass. His face, his voice, she struggled to remember these exactly as she left him on their last day together. Even the note he'd written to accompany the gold donated for the school was lost to her, along with the gold.

For to think of Jean Gayarre was to press away thoughts of other things.

Emilie had never managed to ask Isabelle's advice on how to look forward rather than gaze into the past. Knowing that Isabelle loved her despite her confession and the facts of their birth warmed her heart and gave her hope that someday she might love herself as well.

As was her habit, Emilie took her coffee onto the eastward-facing porch of her tiny cottage on the edge of town and waited for God to put on His morning show. With last night's storm safely over and the world washed clean, the day promised to be glorious.

First came the faint smear of purple at the easternmost corner of the sky. It spread like butter melting, the color fading from deepest purple to violet and then to the same blue as Emilie's favorite bonnet.

Like moths drawn to a lantern, boats from the fleet docked east of the city floated toward the horizon. By degrees, the color blue climbed higher in the Florida sky, pushed along by the orange tendrils of a growing flame just below the edge of the ocean.

When the flame rose over the horizon to become a ball of light, Emilie set aside her coffee and picked up her Bible. It was not the Bible of her youth, the one she'd traveled with to New Orleans, then lost with the sinking of the *Sunday Service*. She'd purchased this one in a market in Havana that offered items salvaged from ships. The book had been a rare find and a commodity that held little value for a people whose language was not English.

The bookmark, a fat tangle of multicolored threads made by the schoolchildren as a gift on her last birthday, caused her Bible to open easily to the book of Isaiah. Emilie began reading where she had left off the previous morning at the beginning of chapter 59.

"Behold, the LORD's hand is not shortened, that it cannot save; neither his ear heavy, that it cannot hear: but your iniquities have separated between you and your God, and your sins have hid his face from you, that he will not hear. For your hands are defiled with blood. . . ."

Emily slammed the Bible shut and set it on the porch rail, then looked down at her hands. Defiled. Yes, she felt that way.

Then another verse from Isaiah, one she'd read many times but never appreciated so much as now, came to mind: "Though your sins be as scarlet, they shall be as white as snow; though they be red like crimson, they shall be as wool."

"White as snow." She certainly didn't see that when she looked at her hands. "Perhaps one day."

"Perhaps one day you shall what?" came the booming voice of Hezekiah Carter.

Emilie smiled and rose to greet the pastor, who stood at the edge of the garden path she'd put in just before her departure, the silver knob of his cane glinting in the morning sun. "Just wondering at the Lord's timing," she said. "An everyday occurrence, I assure you."

"As with us all." His expression sobered. "How was my friend when you left?"

Emilie ducked her head then looked up to trace her finger across the corner of the porch post. "His old self, actually," she said. "A bit feisty, a bit weepy."

"I see."

"He listened to me talk about Jesus." Her gaze lifted to meet the pastor's. "And he didn't interrupt me."

"Did he—"

"Profess faith?" She shook her head. "No."

"I see." He shrugged. "So we leave it up to the Lord."

"And His timing." She smiled. "See, yet another thing to wonder about."

Reverend Carter looked away, then returned his gaze to her, seemingly to study her expression.

Emilie felt a bit uncomfortable under his scrutiny but said nothing.

"I got a letter from him, actually," he finally said. "It arrived the day before you did."

"Oh?" She bit her lip. "What did he say?"

"That he gave you a miniature of your mother."

She thought of the tiny painting and made a note to take the pieces apart so they could better dry out. "He did."

A noisy seagull swooped past to land on the roof of the outdoor kitchen. Several others followed, each jostling for position on the tiny structure.

Reverend Carter nodded. "He mentioned something else."

"Oh?" She reached to toy with the edge of the Bible. "Something you wish to share with me, or is this a confidence best left between old chums?"

The pastor tapped her gate with his cane as if he were counting the wooden slats. "His letter states that you left the city on the twenty-second of May."

Her heart sank. While she'd considered what might happen should her misadventures ever come to light, Emilie had never expected it to happen so soon.

When she did not respond, he continued. "Perhaps my old friend has made a mistake. He is, after all, not a well man."

Slowly she returned her attention to her visitor. "Would you like a cup of coffee?"

"Thank you. No." If he had an opinion on why she changed the subject, Reverend Carter wisely kept it to himself. "Actually, I'm here on an errand of a business nature. There's to be a town meeting today."

"I hadn't heard anything about a meeting. Usually the judge makes some announcement. I wonder why he hasn't done that this time."

"Simple, Emilie." Reverend Carter smiled. "Judge Campbell hasn't made the announcement because he doesn't know yet."

"Reverend Carter," she said, her tone light, "dare I ask what you're planning?"

He touched his finger to his lips and winked. "It appears we both have our secrets today. I warrant I shall keep mine, and my guess is you will do the same."

Her nod would have to suffice as an answer. She had no intention of saying anything further on the subject.

The pastor turned to leave, then stopped and tapped his temple. "Oh, one more thing."

"Yes?"

"When I last saw your father, I made him a promise that I would act on his behalf should any suitors come around and express an interest in you."

Emilie felt her breath catch even as embarrassment took hold. "Really," she said as she tried not to show her horror at the turn of the conversation, "that's not necessary."

He shook his head. "I would be honored to stand in your father's stead." The pastor paused. "Unless, of course, you feel I am overstepping my bounds."

"Oh no," she quickly responded. "It's just that, well, there's really no need."

There, she had said it. Some women were made to be wives, and other women were not. From her experience, or the lack of it, she fell into the latter category.

"Actually, there is a need. You see, there's a young man here in Fairweather Key—a close friend of Josiah's—who is entertaining the thought of courting you." He paused and seemed to be trying to gauge her reaction.

She met his gaze. "Surely you're mistaken."

"No," he said, "I'm quite serious."

For a moment Emilie allowed herself to think of what it might be like to have a gentleman caller. Then, harsh reality struck. Eventually, she would have to tell him about who she really was and what she'd done.

"I can tell I've taken you by surprise."

"You have," she said.

"And the thought of being courted is distasteful to you?"

She shook her head. "Surely you understand that a teacher cannot be a married woman. It wouldn't be proper. And there's the issue of my parentage. You cannot believe I am free to marry, so why bother with suitors?"

"This is Fairweather Key, not New Orleans, Emilie. I'm sure it would be fine." Her look must have answered for her. "Then perhaps this is a conversation for another day." He gave her a curt nod, then added a smile. "I shall see you at the courthouse this evening. Five sharp."

The day passed quickly as Emilie busied herself with catching the children up on their lessons. True to his boast, William had done a fine job in teaching the older ones, but the youngest of the students were now more interested in playing than learning.

By the time the last child bade her good-bye for the day, Emilie had need of a nap. If only their boisterous energy could be bottled and saved for moments such as this.

At least she'd been too busy to think. Were she not so occupied, she might have begun to try to guess which of the many single men in Fairweather Key had spoken to Reverend Carter on her behalf.

Emilie pushed away the thought, then gathered up her things and closed the door to the makeshift classroom that had been carved from a front parlor in the boardinghouse. It was a matter of much irritation to the judge that his wife insisted on allowing the school to operate in the establishment she managed.

He was, it seemed, trumped at home by his wife. Emilie suspected this was exactly the reason the old man chose to press the issue of funds for a proper schoolhouse. With the children either gone from his parlor or gone from the island, he could enjoy his meals in quiet.

And despite his size, Judge Campbell did enjoy his meals.

The mantel clock chimed the half-hour as Emilie tiptoed past the kitchen door. "Can you sit a spell?" the judge's wife called. "I've apple dumplings coming out of the oven momentarily, and I know how you love them."

"I do," she said, "but I'm afraid I must hurry home today. Might I beg one for tomorrow's lunch?"

"You might." The older woman turned around and reached for the corner of her apron, then swiped at her forehead. For a moment, she merely stared.

"Something wrong?" Emilie asked.

"Wrong?" She seemed to consider the question a moment longer than necessary. "No, dear, everything's fine. Might I ask the same of you?"

"Fine," she said with a smile. "Now if you'll excuse me, I'll just—"

"Be heading over to the big meeting at the courthouse?" She grinned and let the corner of her apron drop. "Yes, I know all about it. But don't worry. I haven't told the judge a thing. This time around, he's brought whatever's to happen on himself."

"What is going to happen?" she asked. "Do you have any idea what the reverend is up to?"

"Oh, I've a few thoughts on it."

She reached for the dishcloth and opened the oven door. The delicious scent of apples and spices drifted toward Emilie, and her stomach rumbled in protest.

"I heard that," Mrs. Campbell said. "Now sit yourself down and I'll fetch something cold to drink. I promise I'll have you fed and on your way well before the festivities begin."

Emilie left her things at the door and moved toward the big table where Mrs. Campbell did the bulk of her cooking. Taking up a chair nearest the oven, she watched while the older woman's adept moves had the sweet treat sitting on a plate in front of her in short order.

"This is dessert, you know," Emilie said. "I feel awfully decadent having dessert before my dinner."

"Oh, dear Emilie," she said in her singsong voice. "One should eat dessert first upon occasion. I have it on good authority that it's not only beneficial to the body but also to the mind."

She laughed. "And what authority is this?"

"Well me, of course. Now, see what you think. I've tweaked the recipe a bit since you left for that visit with your papa."

The first bite was delicious, even if she did have to blow on it in order to place the delicacy in her mouth. Emilie waited until the second bite before she dared ask her hostess anything further about the evening's meeting.

"You mentioned," Emilie began, "that you might have some ideas of what will happen tonight."

"Did I?" Again, the singsong voice. "Well, I suppose I do." Mrs. Campbell sat across from Emilie and tossed the dishrag over her shoulder. "And I suppose you're being polite by not coming right out and asking what they are."

"I suppose," she said before taking a second bite.

Mrs. Campbell leaned forward. "Well, all right, if you insist. We all know my husband's a good man, but he's just about as stubborn as my daddy's mule. Her name was Sally and . . ." She shook her head. "Well, it doesn't matter what her name was. You get the idea."

Emilie nodded as she chewed.

"I think all of this got started when the judge decided he wanted to find a way to get his parlor back."

"Yes," Emilie said, "and you know how I feel about that."

"I do indeed, but I'll not hear another word of protest. This big drafty house is perfect for a school. There's no need to move it anywhere. Besides, where would you go? Your little house won't fit three grown folks, much less the two dozen youngsters we've got."

"True." She set down the fork and dabbed at her

mouth with the corner of her napkin. "But we must do something."

"I think the reverend's figured out what that something might be." She pressed her palms against the table and rose. "But mark my words. What happens today is going to surprise all of you."

"Don't I get a hint?"

Mrs. Campbell giggled. "If I told you, it would ruin everything."

CHAPTER 20

Judge Campbell stepped out of his office to close up for the night and found the whole town had showed up to walk him home. He shook his finger at the reverend, who merely smiled and joined him on the broad veranda that filled three sides of the combination courthouse, judge's chambers, and jail.

"Welcome to our meeting, Judge," Reverend Carter said. "Since you've been refusing to grant us one, a few of us decided to hold our own." He looked around. "Actually, more than a few of us."

Emilie watched the judge's expression turn from shock to outrage. Even from her spot on the fringe of the crowd, she could see the old man's face go from pale to red.

Out of the corner of her eye, she saw Josiah Carter edging toward her. "Looks like this will be interesting," he said when he arrived at her side.

"Indeed," she responded. "Do you happen to know what your father's planning?"

Josiah shook his head. "Since when does my father tell me things like that?" He chuckled. "I know he's a changed man, but that is one area where he hasn't changed all that much."

Hezekiah Carter sought Emilie out in the crowd and, when he found her, nodded. Emilie returned the gesture, then spied Viola Dumont, her childhood friend. Part of the escape from New Orleans two years ago, Vi had found a talent for nursing and a job practicing her career choice in the town doctor's office. After greeting Viola, Emilie returned her attention to the antics on the veranda.

"And so, Judge Campbell," Reverend Carter said, "the people of Fairweather Key wish to air our grievances on an issue near and dear to all of us. I'm sure you've guessed as the topic has been bandied about, lo, these many months. It's the school our dear Emilie is running."

The judge stepped back as if he'd been slapped. "What of this illegal school that's being run by an amateur teacher with no credentials?"

A gasp went up, and several townsfolk standing near Emilie expressed their disapproval. Someone on the other side of the group yelled a rebuttal while others joined in. Finally, Reverend Carter held up his hands and called for quiet.

"Uh-oh," Josiah said.

"Oh no," Emilie whispered.

"You see, Judge," he continued when the racket died down, "it has come to my attention that this deadline you've set of the month of August is quite arbitrary and may not have any basis in fact or law. Thus, unless you know something I don't about the laws of this country, and you very well might, your decision to put the responsibility for educating our children back on us just won't do."

A cheer went up.

This time it was the judge who called for quiet. "Hezekiah Carter, you might be the preacher in this town, but I'm of a mind to lock you up for inciting a riot."

Reverend Carter had the audacity to laugh, which brought a moan from his son. "I wonder if I should fetch my mother now or wait until the judge sets bail for him."

"Shhh," Emilie said. "I want to hear what he's saying."

"Judge Campbell, I don't see a riot here. What I see is a large and orderly group of people who are upset with how their government is being run." He paused to point out into the crowd with his cane. "Any of you remember the story of the Boston Tea Party?"

A few called out, while others merely laughed.

"Don't worry, Judge. None of us plan to pour anything into the bay, but we do not feel we are being heard. Am I right?"

The townspeople cheered while the judge fumed.

"You're trying to railroad me into something, Carter. Just come out and say what it is."

He grinned. "On behalf of your constituents in Fairweather Key, we demand that a proper school-house be built with municipal funds to house the children of our citizens. I've read up on the law, and nowhere does it say that you or anyone else has the ability to ship our children off to be educated elsewhere."

The judge shook his head. "That's where you're wrong, Carter."

"Prove it, Campbell."

"He's done it now," Josiah whispered.

Hezekiah Carter waved his hands to quiet the crowd. "I propose we allow the judge some time to collect evidence to support what he's saying here." He glanced at Judge Campbell. "What say you to another meeting in this very spot one week from today?"

The old judge crossed his hands over his chest and offered up a smile that seemed to hold no humor. "Now why would I want to do that?"

"Because it's the right thing to do, dear," Mrs. Campbell called from the back of the crowd. She held up a letter, then shook it. "I guess I forgot to mention it, but our dear Jane is coming for a visit next month. Would you really insist on sending our granddaughter to another island for her education when Emilie could teach her just as well if not better right here?"

The judge shook his head. "This is something best left for discussion at home, don't you think?"

"And while I'm on the topic, you do know these poor children are practically sitting one atop the other in that small room." She heaved a dramatic sigh. "It pains my heart to know our Jane will be packed into that tiny room when the funds are surely there for a decent schoolhouse to be built."

This time when the crowd cheered, there was no silencing them. Emilie caught the boardinghouse owner gazing in her direction and smiled. Mrs. Campbell returned the gesture, then winked.

"And one more thing," she called.

"Of course," came the judge's droll response. "There's always one more thing."

"I think our Emilie deserves our applause. Why, before she and her sister arrived on the island we had no school. Those who could read taught their young'uns, and those who didn't passed on their ignorance. Now all the boys and girls have the opportunity that many of us never had. And," she said as she paused to point toward Emilie, "we owe it all to Miss Emilie Gayarre."

"That's right," someone called. "There's no one better than Miss Emilie. Who knows what sort of character will teach them elsewhere? Why, for all we know, we may be sending our children to board with sinners and reprobates. Murderers and thieves, maybe."

"That's a bit harsh," the judge said. "No one like

that is fit to teach a child, and I'm certain that will never happen."

A sick feeling began in the pit of Emilie's stomach that had nothing to do with the excess of apple dessert she'd just consumed. *If only I hadn't lost the gold from Papa. This is when I could have announced his donation.*

She leaned toward Josiah. "I must go," she said.

"You look unwell." He seemed to examine her face. "Should I send Isabelle over to see to you?"

"No, she's busy with the baby. Don't bother her." She paused to gather her wits. "I'm sure I'll be fine tomorrow. Likely the exhaustion from the voyage has finally caught up to me."

Josiah appeared skeptical but said nothing. Emilie was about to make good her escape when she heard her name called. She froze, then turned to see the entire town of Fairweather Key staring in her direction.

"Come on up here, Emilie," Reverend Carter called.

She shook her head and waved away his protests, but he and other vocal citizens insisted. Before she realized what was happening, she'd been pressed onto the porch and stood between Judge Campbell and Reverend Carter.

When the applause died down, the preacher cleared his throat. "Many of you know that I consider this woman like a daughter. Her father and I are old friends. Why, if I told you how long I've known the Gayarre family, you'd never believe I was that old."

A round of laughter peppered the air. Emilie allowed her gaze to bounce from familiar faces to those she did not know so well. It truly seemed as though all of Fairweather Key was in attendance.

"I want you to know that this woman loves your children so much that she undertook a difficult voyage in order to seek the funding of a school for them."

Another wave of nausea hit Emilie, and her knees almost buckled. How would she explain the loss of funds her father had obviously mentioned to Reverend Carter?

"While that trip did not have the result she wished," he continued, "I challenge all of you to see that it was not in vain. Either we need to find a way to build the school our judge requires, or the ruling must be changed to allow the current one to continue."

The old pastor must have noticed her swaying, for he reached to grasp her elbow. "Are you unwell?" he whispered while the crowd cheered.

Emilie managed a nod.

"Then I shall endeavor to make this brief."

"Thank you," she whispered. "I would greatly appreciate that."

"And so would I," the judge said, glaring at Emilie.

Reverend Carter held up his cane to silence the

crowd. "I'm afraid Miss Gayarre is quite overcome with your enthusiasm and not completely recovered from her voyage. On her behalf, I will ask that you allow her to retreat to her home for rest while we continue this meeting."

Emilie thanked the reverend, then stepped with care off the veranda. The crowd parted, every eye on her as she held her head high and put one foot in front of the other to find her way home.

"Until next week, then," Emilie heard the judge say just before she turned the corner. Her cottage beckoned, and despite her shaken condition, she began to run. By the time she threw open the door, she'd nearly exhausted the last of her strength.

She fell fully dressed onto the narrow cot that served as her bed and lay very still until the room stopped spinning. "Lord," she whispered as she reached to extinguish the lamp, "will I ever be who I was before this awful nightmare began?"

As her eyes closed, she saw once again the miniature, the crumpled man, and the bloody letter. She knew the answer.

CHAPTER 21

June 15, 1836
Santa Lucida

Something heavy pressed on Caleb's chest, rendering him unable to move. His chase down the heated and chilled corridors had ended with what felt like a tumble into a light so brilliant he could neither see his way nor find his wits.

So he closed his eyes and listened to the voices: his mother's, Fletcher's, and others he did not recognize. On occasion, another voice quite unlike the others spoke. The words were gentle, soft, familiar: *"I will deliver you for I delight in you."*

Even when the others failed to be heard, this one never left.

June 18
Fairweather Key

Hunger sent Emilie out to Ivan's Mercantile when exhaustion preferred to keep her home. After paying for her items and dodging the attention of other customers, she covered the basket and began the stroll home. As she passed the doctor's office, she heard someone call her name and turned to see her old friend Viola Dumont.

"I've been hoping to see you," Vi said. "Isabelle

told me you'd returned from New Orleans." Her expression seemed calm; her eyes, however, held a worried look. "And you saw your father." A statement, not a question.

"I did," she said.

"Did he mention . . . ?" She looked away, unable or unwilling to continue.

Emilie linked arms with the nurse and patted her hand. "No," she said gently, "he did not mention you or your family, nor did I see them. Perhaps Reverend Carter might have news of them."

For a moment, Vi seemed as if she might respond. Then she shrugged, and they continued their walk until the path heading toward Emilie's cottage loomed ahead. "Would you like to come in for a visit?"

"I would like that very much," Vi said, "but I'm off on an errand to check on the baby who was delivered last night. The doctor's got some concerns, but he's busy setting a fracture that the Gibbons boy sustained."

"Oh my," Emilie said. "Do come and visit when you can."

Vi smiled. "Of course." She squeezed Emilie's hand, then took a step back. "I'm sure we will find plenty to talk about."

Plenty to talk about?

Curiosity and concern mingled as Emilie tried to decipher Vi's statement. Would she ever stop wondering whether people knew her secrets?

• • •

June 20

"You've been awfully quiet all week." Mrs. Campbell rolled out dough for Judge Campbell's favorite coconut pie, yet she managed to keep her attention focused on Emilie.

For a moment, Emilie debated telling the older woman the truth. What good would it serve to tell the town judge's wife that she couldn't seem to shake her nightmares of the man she shot? Even an admission of sleep deprivation would require an explanation, which brought her back to the same point.

"I wonder if your mind's been on this evening's town meeting," Mrs. Campbell said.

Emilie traced the embroidered pattern on the edge of the tablecloth, then rested her palms on the table. "I am a bit curious what will happen."

Mrs. Campbell set her rolling pin aside and reached for the corner of her apron to wipe the flour off her hands. "Curiosity is fine, but don't let yourself be concerned about the outcome. The Lord's got it all in His hands."

Emilie nodded. "He does, doesn't He?"

The kitchen smelled of good food and sunshine, and Emilie felt inclined to stay a bit longer. Unfortunately, from her post by the window, she could see the children coming up the street for their afternoon lessons.

Quickly, Emilie packed away the remains of her lunch and stowed it in her bag. That complete, she looked up to find the judge's wife staring at her in disapproval.

"You don't eat enough to feed a bird," Mrs. Campbell said.

Her laughter followed Emilie into the tiny, makeshift classroom where several dozen children awaited her. True to form, William Carter was already helping a classmate with a particularly vexing arithmetic problem.

It was difficult for Emilie to look around the room and not see what was missing. A proper classroom would have tables and chairs for the students and something resembling a desk for her. The children would have slates or, failing that, at least a book or two of their own.

Lord, might You find a way to provide these? Or, dare I hope, that You might gift us with a real school? This time I promise I won't ruin the work You've done.

She ushered the smaller children away from the others and sat them in a circle for story time. Lacking a storybook, she'd been making up stories. Today's installment of *The Tale of Duckling Dave* was almost over when one of the children pointed to a spot behind Emilie and giggled.

When she turned around to see the cause of the commotion, she found Josiah Carter's friend Micah Tate standing in the doorway doing a fairly decent imitation of a duck. "What sort of nonsense is this?" she said in her most chiding tone before falling into giggles.

"Children, may I borrow your teacher?" the red-haired man said, still using a voice that sounded very much like a duck.

While the children continued to laugh, Emilie rose and dusted off her skirts. "That's enough," she finally said. "Play quietly," she told them, "and do not disturb the older children. I'll just be in the hallway with Duckling Dave, I mean, Mr. Tate."

She stepped into the hall just behind Micah. "I had no idea you possessed a talent as a duck impressionist, Mr. Tate."

He grinned. "I'm a man of many talents."

Mrs. Campbell stuck her head out of the kitchen and waved. "Hello there, Micah," she said. "When you're done talking to Emilie, do come visit me in the kitchen. I've got a fresh batch of sugar cookies and no one to test them out on."

"Yes, ma'am," he said before returning his attention to Emilie. "Actually, I've been working on the *Caroline* again and have ended up with a nice pile of lumber that's still good. I thought maybe, if you're agreeable, I could use it to make tables and benches for the schoolroom."

Emilie glanced skyward. *Lord, that was fast.*

"That would be wonderful, Micah." She paused. "But are you sure you want to do that? It sounds like an awful big job, and I'm sure you could sell the wood elsewhere and make a tidy profit."

"'For what shall it profit a man, if he shall gain the whole world, and lose his own soul?'" Micah shrugged, his cheeks reddening. "Sorry, I've been working on some memorization, and that verse came to mind. Don't know why I blurted it out like that."

His self-conscious demeanor took Emilie by surprise. Where was the serious widower she knew as Josiah Carter's business partner and fellow wrecker?

"So," he continued, "if you'll just let me know what you'd like, I'll build it." He looked around the room. "Not much space here, is there?"

Emilie shook her head.

"You know, it's a shame with all the money Judge Campbell puts into the bank from our wrecking that none of it's going to the children." His eyes narrowed. "I stopped counting how many wrecks we've worked this year, but I can tell you that with each one, the government gets a third of whatever the ship's salvage nets at auction. That's a pretty penny where I come from."

Without a ready response, Emilie remained silent. While she could not see them from her vantage point, she could hear the younger children trying in vain to make the duck noises like their visitor.

"Yes, well, I suppose we'll find out whether

Reverend Carter has made any headway with the judge today." His smile broadened. "I hope he sees the wisdom in doing something about this school situation that doesn't involve closing you down."

"As do I," she said. Behind her, the quacking got louder. "I should get back to my class." Emilie giggled. "Or rather, my ducklings."

He looked beyond her to the children and the potential chaos that was about to break loose. "I can see what you mean. I wonder, though, if I might come back when it's convenient and take some measurements so I know what size to make the tables and benches."

"Yes, of course," she said. "I can make arrangements to arrive early or stay after class." She paused. "Of course, the boardinghouse is always open. I'm sure Mrs. Campbell would be happy to let you into the schoolroom at your convenience."

"Sorry, dear, but I'd rather you handle the affairs of the school," Mrs. Campbell called from the kitchen.

So they'd been spied upon. Emilie grinned. "I suggest you not forget to stop in for your cookies, Micah. Likely she'll chase you down should you make the attempt."

"Come, dear, that would not be appropriate. I would send you instead."

The quacking became louder, forcing Emilie to take action. "Children," she called, "mind your decorum, please. We have a guest."

"Decorum." Micah shook his head. "Do they know what that means?"

"Of course," she said. "See for yourself."

"I see."

When his grin spread, Emilie turned to see the cause. In the corner where she'd left her little ones was a group of little ducklings flapping their wings and whispering barely audible quacks.

"Wonderful," she said with a groan.

Micah affected a serious look. "I'm sorry. I must have misunderstood. I thought you said de-corum." He paused as if studying the quiet chaos. "It looks like what you really said was duck-corum."

At precisely five, Emilie joined the crowd gathering in front of the courthouse. There seemed to be many more in attendance than the previous week, likely owing to the lively discussion around town as to what the judge might have to say. Isabelle and baby Joey had walked over with her, and they now stood near the edge of the crowd.

"It's quite warm today," Isabelle commented. "Josiah said it's hurricane weather."

"I hope he's wrong." Emilie took her gurgling nephew and moved to the shade to shield the infant's tender skin. "It looks as though every business in town has shut down in anticipation of this occasion."

Isabelle leaned toward Emilie. "What do you think the judge will say?"

"Honestly, I've been afraid to speculate." She shifted the baby to her other shoulder and began rubbing his back. "I know what I would like to hear."

"I think we all would," Isabelle said. "I understand Micah Tate paid you a visit today."

Emilie smiled. "He did. He offered to make tables and benches for the schoolroom. It was awfully nice of him."

Before Isabelle could comment, the door to the judge's chambers opened, and Judge Campbell walked out onto the veranda. At his side stood his wife.

"Where's Reverend Carter?" Emilie asked.

"He's here somewhere." Isabelle looked around, then pointed to the far edge of the crowd. "Over there. He's with Mary."

Emilie followed her sister's gaze and found the pastor and his wife in conversation with Micah Tate. All three looked up to find her staring and then waved. Emilie returned the gesture as the judge stepped forward and cleared his throat.

"As you all know, I was challenged on this very spot last week to justify my position on a topic that I've learned is near and dear to many hearts in Fairweather Key. The ruling I made regarding the children's education was done with the best of intentions and with the best interest of your children foremost in my mind."

He paused to look down at his wife. The pair

244

exchanged a smile; then Mrs. Campbell squeezed his hand.

"Let me assure you that my edict regarding the school was both legal and binding, and it was made within the confines of the law as it stands in our part of the Florida Territory."

A smattering of boos peppered the crowd until someone called for quiet.

"I understand your dislike of my decision," he continued. "I have been separated from my children by distance, and it is unpleasant, to say the least. The fact that my granddaughter will finally be paying a visit has given me reason to think in more detail about the education issue."

He paused, and for a moment it appeared the judge might not continue. After another glance down at his wife, he let out a long breath.

"My wife and I have come to a decision. When Jane returns to her parents, we will accompany her. Thus, yesterday I posted a letter to the proper authorities announcing my retirement as your judge effective September 1, or on the first day after the arrival of the new judge."

A cheer went up in the crowd. When the noise died down, Judge Campbell continued. "I will leave the question of the children's education for the new judge to answer."

Emilie exchanged smiles with her sister. "I had hoped he would change his mind, but at least we've got a reprieve."

"Now we pray the new judge is favorable to our cause," Isabelle said.

"Definitely," Emilie replied as she watched the judge and his wife disappear inside the office. "I wonder where they'll find his replacement."

"Well, anyone would be better than Judge Campbell." Isabelle shook her head. "I've never seen such opposition to something that benefits the town. I never understood it."

"Nor did I." Emilie loosened her bonnet strings and turned to face the sea breeze. "Is it unseasonably warm, or am I imagining it?"

"It's not your imagination."

Emilie whirled around to see Josiah walking toward them, Micah Tate at his side. Isabelle met her husband with a smile and a squeeze of his hand. "What is your take on this evening's events, husband?"

"I think Fairweather Key may have trouble finding someone to replace Judge Campbell." He looked to Micah for confirmation. "Unless a man's wanting to get away from politics, he'd do better than to find employment so far south."

Micah nodded. "Not much chance for moving up once you've moved down here."

The men chuckled, while Isabelle and Emilie exchanged glances. The baby began to squirm, and Josiah reached for him. With a few funny faces and a silly sound, he had his son grinning.

"You have a way with babies, Josiah," Emilie said.

"He's a blessing." Josiah gathered his wife to his side. "As is my Isabelle."

Emilie couldn't help but notice that Micah looked away as if watching the happy couple was painful. It was a feeling she knew well. While he was likely thinking of the young wife and baby he had lost before coming to the key, her thoughts were on a sandy beach where she had her first kiss.

And the rowboat where she had her second. And last.

"We should head home," Josiah said. "My old bones tell me a storm's coming in."

"Old bones?" Micah said. "Since when do you have old bones?"

The men continued their jovial bickering until Emilie parted company and headed toward her cottage. She'd almost reached the door when she heard Micah calling her name.

He trotted up the path, then stopped short when he saw her waiting. For a moment, he just stood there.

"Did you need something?" she finally said.

"I was wondering if I might meet you after school tomorrow to do some measuring for the classroom."

"Yes, of course," she said.

Micah nodded but made no move to leave. Rather, he stood awkwardly between the cottage and the street, the afternoon sun shadowing him and turning his hair the same color as its rays.

She looked to the horizon, then back at Micah.

"Josiah says tonight's to be a wet one. I should fetch my laundry off the line."

"I could help," he said.

"I'm afraid that wouldn't be proper." She considered telling him exactly what items of apparel hung there but decided against it. The poor man was skittish enough already without serving up a dose of humiliation, too.

"Well, good evening, then," Emilie finally said.

Her statement seemed to work, as he nodded and turned away. "Good evening, Miss Gayarre," he said when he reached the road.

From the front parlor, Emilie watched the wrecker disappear down the road toward town. She let the curtain fall and headed for the kitchen, where cold chicken and a slice of Mrs. Campbell's coconut pie awaited.

"Well, that was strange," she said. "I wonder what's wrong with Micah Tate."

CHAPTER 22

July 5, 1836
Santa Lucida

The call of the orangequit and the whirl of wings as a flock took flight.

Laughter off in some distant place.

Wisps of lavender on a breeze that likely marked her comings and goings.

The scrape of a razor against his chin.

Caleb took note of each, trying to grasp the thought and hold it captive long enough for it to stick in the blank hall of his memories. Of late, he'd found moderate success in the venture, even recalling the words he'd overhead some indeterminable time ago.

Prayers. That's what he now heard. The prayers of a woman.

His mother.

He tested his fingers and found them willing to move at his command. Slowly, Caleb grasped at whatever he could to discover whether they still held their function.

Then his stomach growled, and Caleb frowned. When had he last dined?

Havana. With Fletcher. He'd had the beef. The conversation had turned to Fletcher. Was his mother mentioned? Possibly. What else? Had he made a decision that day?

Yes, but what was it?

Something about a letter. And a boat.

The prayers had stopped, and the lavender scent announced his mother had drawn near. Perhaps she knew of this letter. He made to ask, but his mouth refused to form the words.

"Caleb? Can you hear me?"

Again he tried and failed to speak.

Someone touched his face. His mother, Caleb decided from the size and softness of the palm. "I know I saw his hands move, Fletcher."

A deep rumble. Perhaps a man's voice.

"I am not imagining things." The palm lifted and was gone. "He's in there trying to come out," she continued. "A mother knows these things. We must continue to pray for his healing."

Healing? Caleb tried to concentrate on what she meant, but as with the others, this idea took wings and flew away.

"I delivered you because I delighted in you."

The voice. The one that stayed when all others left him.

Delivered me from what?

July 6
Fairweather Key

So far July had been wet and warm, but thankfully, Josiah Carter had been wrong about the stormy weather. Other than a few nasty blows and one full week of nothing but drizzling rain, Fairweather Key escaped the foul weather it most feared: hurricanes.

True to his word, Micah had crafted long tables and benches for Emilie's classroom. Two weeks ago, however, the addition of Jane Campbell, granddaughter to the judge, brought the seating to maximum capacity. The next student to enroll would either be seated on the floor or share Emilie's small desk.

When Micah next arrived at the schoolroom, he

did not come bearing plans to build more furniture. Instead, he offered up an alternative location: the old fisherman's shack where he'd been residing since coming to live in Fairweather Key.

"Absolutely not," Emilie said as she reluctantly followed Micah through the center of town, then past the courthouse square. "I refuse to allow you to give up your home. It just wouldn't be right."

Micah stopped short, and Emilie almost slammed into him. "Let's get something straight, Miss Gayarre."

"Emilie." She shrugged. "We've known one another long enough, don't you think?"

"All right." He paused, seemingly to collect his thoughts. "As I said, let me be clear on this. I appreciate your concern for my welfare, but you do not get to decide whether I donate this place as a school or not." Micah leaned toward her, his expression serious. "Do you understand, Emilie?"

Well now. This was a side of Micah Tate she'd not seen before. "I do," she said.

"Then you'll broach no further nonsense. If you don't want to teach the children in the new school once it opens, then maybe someone else will." He turned and continued to walk, leaving her to decide whether to follow.

It occurred to Emilie that she'd seen the place where Micah called home, though she could not recall when. True to his claim, it was a glorified fisherman's shack that looked from the outside to

251

be uninhabited. Somewhere between the original owner and now, few amenities had been added.

The one positive attribute it held other than that it was being offered at no cost was the commanding view the building held. From where she stood, Emilie could see for miles in all directions.

"I kept meaning to fix this place up, but I never got around to it, what with the wrecking business keeping me busy." Micah paused. "But it's clean, and it's kept me dry on many a rainy night."

A memory returned, and she knew why the place looked so familiar. She turned to look to the east and saw the place where she and Isabelle had sat on the day she arrived from Havana. This had been the shack she'd thought looked the same as she felt.

"I was told the fellow who built this was determined to put a lighthouse here." Micah turned his back to the sun and stared off toward the horizon. "The wreckers ran him out of town. Guess they were worried that a lighthouse might put them out of business."

"That's terrible," she said as she joined him on the summit and looked down on the spot where the Fairweather Key lighthouse had eventually been built. "But it is a lovely view."

"Yes," he said slowly, his voice pensive. "With a little work, I think the children will have a decent school," he said, "although they'll have a bit of a walk to get here."

She nodded. A school could be made of the

shack, although it was not her first choice of location. "But, Micah?"

He gave her a sideways look. "Yes?"

"Where will you live?"

"Ah, still worried about me, are you?" He turned to face Emilie with a grin. "I've got a couple of options, actually. Mrs. Campbell's place offers the best of both worlds: a clean bed and more food than I can ever attempt to eat. Then again, I can always bunk aboard the *Caroline*."

"Surely you'll choose the boardinghouse."

He held his hand to his brow to shade his eyes and gazed off toward the horizon. "Actually, I'm leaning toward staying on the *Caroline*."

"You would live aboard your boat?" Emilie shook her head. "I can't imagine sleeping somewhere that's never still."

Her mind slid back to the days spent aboard ship, then dipped dangerously close to the worst of her memories. Memories she'd all but sealed up and hidden away.

Before a return to those awful days could happen, she changed the subject. "So, tell me, Micah, what makes you so interested in the children's education?"

His smile faded. "I just am," he said.

"I see." She didn't, although there was obviously more to his statement, a story still untold. That much she could see. "Then I'm pleased that our school is the recipient of that interest."

"I'm glad you're pleased." His grin broadened. "Let's see if you still feel that way after you've been put to work beautifying this place."

"Put to work?" She offered an expression of mock horror.

"Oh, of course. You're one of those delicate Southern flowers who might wilt if called upon to labor." His poor imitation of a Southern drawl combined with the falsetto pitch of his statement sent her into a fit of laughter.

For a moment, she forgot her upbringing and returned the jest with a quick response in the same tone and accent. As soon as she delivered the line, she covered her mouth with her gloved hands.

"Well now, Emilie," Micah said. "You can be quite funny when you try."

"You sound surprised."

"I've just never seen that side of you. That's all." He shrugged. "I think I'd like to see more of it."

Emilie adjusted her shawl and straightened her backbone, shoulders erect as she'd been taught in finishing school. "I'm afraid my father would not approve," she said, again in the silly accent.

"Perhaps not," Micah said, his voice softening, "but would he approve of me?"

"Of you?" Confusion and Micah's stare marred her ability to develop a witty response.

Silence hung between them until he finally ducked his head. "Yes," he said. "I'm just wondering if he might think me not worthy of spending time with his daughter."

"My father thinks of little but himself," she said, "and even less of the appropriateness of those with whom I spend my time."

"I'm sorry, Emilie. Surely your ma—"

"My mother is dead." Emilie gathered her shawl tighter and gestured toward the shack where she would soon be teaching. "I cannot express how very much I appreciate this kindness. The children and I will be forever in your debt."

Micah reached to touch her sleeve then drew back his hand. "I'm sorry."

"As am I." She shook off the need to add to her reply and gestured toward the future schoolhouse instead. "Could I see the interior?"

He led the way, opening the door to allow her to enter first. Inside, Emilie found a tidy but spare room of roughly twice the dimensions of her current classroom. In one corner, a table and benches matched the ones Micah had delivered to the boardinghouse. The other held a curtained area that was obviously used for sleeping.

She walked toward the kitchen area to peer out the window at a view that was lovelier than the one in the front. Blue skies hung over a slope of gently rolling hillside that spilled out onto a narrow beach and the glassy ocean beyond.

"I never tire of this," Emilie said. As she turned, her attention still on the landscape, she said,

"Fairweather Key is one of the loveliest places—"

A *thud*. Emilie dropped her shawl and knocked her bonnet awry on whatever she'd collided with. She reached down to retrieve her shawl and found it draped over a pair of muddy boots. Only then did she realize she'd run directly into Micah.

Emilie straightened slowly, her crooked bonnet hiding some of the heat that spread in agonizing slowness from her neck up into her cheeks. "We should . . ."

"Go?" Micah supplied as he reached to gently straighten her bonnet.

A nod sufficed in answer. Suddenly, nothing about this setting felt appropriate.

That feeling chased Emilie as she found the door, the path toward home, and finally the gate to her cottage. Only then did she realize Micah had trailed a respectable distance behind her.

"I didn't mean to frighten you, Emilie," he called from the gate.

She paused at the door. What she could not tell him was that the fright did not result from him, but rather from the realization of what this nice man would think of her once he knew the sordid details of her recent past.

And of her birth.

Emilie mumbled a response that she hoped would suffice and slipped inside, her heart pounding from the brisk walk and the encounter with Micah Tate. Her mother's miniature, now in a

256

place of prominence on the mantel, caught her attention, and she walked over to snatch it up.

"I know nothing about men, Sylvie, and less about how to repair the damage I've done. Why aren't you here to advise me?" She shouted the question, then in a fit threw the miniature. It landed on the rug undamaged.

Stepping over the portrait, Emilie walked to the window and caught a glimpse of Micah Tate's red hair disappearing down the path toward town. "You'll make some woman a fine catch," she said as she turned away. "I'm sorry it won't be me."

CHAPTER 23

July 8, 1836
Santa Lucida

Caleb slipped into the stall and made short work of preparing Rialto for their ride. The fact that he felt he must hide his intentions grated at nerves already strung tight by Fletcher's and his mother's constant presence.

He urged the mare into a trot and then, once the terrain leveled out, attempted to bring her to a gallop. Though Rialto was willing, Caleb was not able.

While the world spun, he gripped the reins and tried not to fall into the vortex encircling him. His boots dug into the stirrups, and while he struggled to remain in the saddle, he also gave thanks he hadn't given in to the urge to ride bareback.

Bringing her to a halt was not nearly as difficult as climbing off to try to find solid ground. Rialto spied a patch of grass, and he let her go to take her fill while he rested from the ride.

Another week, maybe two, and his recovery should be complete. Given the fact that the bullet had done its damage some six weeks ago, a recuperation of two months seemed excessive, yet it was far better than the outcome that had been predicted initially. This he knew from Fletcher, who answered any questions posed to him with blunt honesty.

Caleb's mother, however, tended to ignore the difficult queries and only partly answer the others. If Mary-Margaret Benning Spencer had her way, Caleb would believe his injury was nothing more than a flesh wound and his recuperation one lengthy nap.

Likely, this ability to see what she wished was what kept her from giving up. "A talent I've not yet acquired," he said softly as he laced his fingers behind his head.

The sun was warm, but the breeze kept the temperature from being oppressive. Caleb found the shade of a tamarind tree and leaned against its rough bark. Through the feathery fringe of its leaves, dappled sunlight teased his outstretched legs and skittered across his shoulders and chest.

He let out a contented breath. Surely God had taken extra care when He created Santa Lucida.

From his vantage point, Caleb spied the slowly bobbing mainmast of the *Cormorant* and the green sea beyond. While the mainmast made his heart ache for another adventure, the color of the ocean put him in mind of a dark-haired woman in a frock of the same color. He wanted to look into her brown eyes and hear her explanation. To know why she could kiss him and then, mere hours later, shoot him.

Caleb leaned forward and touched the still-tender wound that had nearly taken his life, then tried to muster up the anger that marked his first days of awakening. Now, however, anger had turned to something much more dangerous: the need to find her and exact revenge for what she'd done to him. And to his career. While Caleb had tap-danced at the precipice of eternity, the secretary of the navy had been forced to find another man for the job Caleb had been offered. News of his recovery and subsequent readiness for a new assignment had thus far brought only silence.

Caleb's feeling toward the woman in green was not unlike the emotion that had tempted him to play judge and jury to the vile Thomas Hawkins rather than bundle him off to Havana to allow the authorities there to string him up after a proper trial. He knew how close he had come to ending Hawkins's life with a bullet.

The thought was sobering, yet Caleb could provide more than ample justification for considering the act something other than murder.

"Murder is murder."

Caleb scrambled to his feet in search of the voice.

"I delivered you because I delighted in you."

The bluster went out of him as Caleb nearly fell back into his spot beneath the tamarind tree. Had God really spoken to him? He, a man who plotted murder in his heart and held revenge on his mind?

A man like Paul, perhaps? Or David?

"Father," he whispered, "is that You?"

Silence.

"God?" This time he spoke above a whisper yet not loud enough to attract the attention of anyone who might believe he'd lost his mind.

Silence.

Tiring of the feast, Rialto ambled in his direction, and Caleb rose to grasp the horse's reins. She gave a soft nicker and nuzzled his palm.

"I delivered you because I delighted in you."

Caleb froze. "Delivered me from what?" he shouted, not caring upon whose ears his question fell.

"I delivered you from yourself."

The statement haunted Caleb for days after the encounter. If indeed what happened beneath the tamarind tree could be called an encounter.

Soon he'd begun to believe that he'd been delivered not only from himself but also from the entirety of civilization as it stood outside of Santa Lucida. With no response from the naval department and no one but Fletcher and his mother for company, Caleb was going stark raving mad.

Several times he tried to coerce Fletcher into another visit to Havana, or even a run about the islands to test the seaworthiness of the *Cormorant*'s sails. He accomplished neither, though he did find the empty hours useful for pushing himself and Rialto to faster and longer rides. One week after his first near-disaster with the galloping mare, Caleb was back to full speed.

The sun warmed the stiffness that had settled in his injured shoulder, so he often left off his shirt when he was certain no women were about. His mother teased that he'd soon look like the natives should he continue to brown himself. Something about the fading scar and the fact that he'd survived gave Caleb the ability to laugh at her jokes when he did not feel at all like laughing.

So, day after day, the rides continued. Always he returned to the tamarind tree, though he could never decide whether it was the view or the hope of hearing God's voice again that drew him.

July 16

Caleb pored over his grandfather's ledgers, looking for anything that might catch his interest and relieve his boredom. The margin notes were far more interesting than the accounting of supplies in and crops out that made up the majority of the pages.

Each time he found a gem of wisdom in his grandfather's hand, Caleb would stop and think about it before proceeding. Some were musings on seasons and planting, while others bemoaned the trials and celebrated the victories of a man consigned to live the dual life of pirate and planter.

He rested his chin on his palm. Someone had shaved his beard during the days when he lay between life and death—likely upon the orders of his mother, who detested what she called his savage whiskers. His hair had been cut as well, giving him the appearance of the gentleman he no longer was sure he could call himself.

The only consolation in his altered appearance was that he no longer looked into the mirror and saw the man who'd battled a pirate only to lose to a woman. Where once he had been the Benning, he now appeared to be solidly Spencer.

From Crusoe to . . . What?

Oddly, just as his grandfather expressed in his journals, Caleb felt a bit conflicted by the whole thing. He ran his palm over the spot just above his heart that still plagued him and wondered whether the Lord had allowed his injury as a proverbial thorn in his side much as He'd done with the apostle Paul.

Surely the Lord hadn't used a woman as the

vehicle for such an affliction. Try as he might, Caleb still could not forget the wide brown eyes of the woman whom he thought he was saving. Strange how the best intentions did not prevent the situation from going terribly awry.

"Hard at work?" Fletcher stepped through a broad stripe of dust motes dancing on sunlight to approach the desk, one hand behind his back and his ever-present pipe in the other. "I warrant this will pull you away from Ian's scribblings." He dropped a folded page atop the ledger. Imprinted on the wax was the unmistakable seal of the United States Naval Department.

"Naval department?" Caleb shook his head. "What's this?"

"I'll leave you to read it, lad." He turned to go.

"No," Caleb said. "Stay."

Fletcher lifted one brow as if surprised but made no move to leave as Caleb lifted the seal and unfolded the page. "It appears, my friend, that I've been given a second chance in the naval department."

"Appears?"

"Yes." Caleb folded the letter and put it away. "The good news is I've been offered a full commission as a lieutenant."

Fletcher's brows lifted, but he said nothing.

"The bad news," he said as he took up his pen and turned to reach for the inkwell, "is that I will be assigned an office and not a ship."

"And has this changed how you feel about accepting the position?"

Caleb set his pen down and swiveled to face Fletcher. "No."

"No?" His nod was curt. "And when will you leave us?"

"The letter requests I leave immediately, though I will need a few days to make the arrangements." Caleb gave him a sideways look and a teasing grin. "Us?"

"There's no need for that," Fletcher said, obviously not amused with the jest. "I've come not only to deliver that letter but to speak to you as the head of this household on a matter most delicate. Your impending departure makes a speedy resolution of the greatest importance."

Caleb gestured to the chair nearby. "Sit, then, and speak your mind."

"I prefer to stand."

Was that uncertainty he saw on his mentor's face? "As you wish."

Fletcher seemed to be considering his words carefully. Finally, he nodded and took a deep breath, pressing his palms together. "As you are head of this family, I come to you to state that I would have your mother's hand in marriage, Caleb."

"Would you?" He suppressed a smile in keeping with the seriousness of the occasion. "And what does my mother say to this?"

"Your mother approves but seeks your blessing as well," came the familiar voice of Mary-Margaret Spencer. Soon, obviously, to be . . . ? In all Caleb's life he'd known the man by only one name.

"Come in, Mother," he called.

She complied, easing into the room with an elegance and grace combined with a wink that caused his smile to burst forth. She looked to Fletcher. "I know you wished I wait until you spoke to Caleb privately, but I found it quite impossible not to join you."

Fletcher shook his head. "Perhaps this is a discussion best had later."

"Well, Fletcher," Caleb said as he watched his mother entwine her fingers with the tutor's, "should you marry this woman, I warrant this will be the norm rather than the exception."

"I welcome it," Fletcher said.

"Then there is one final question that must be answered before I give my blessing." Caleb crossed his hands over his chest as if preparing for a serious discussion. "Fletcher, in the two decades I have known you, I've only had one name by which to call you. Now that you and my mother will be wed, what shall she be called?"

The older man smiled. "Mrs. Fletcher, of course."

Caleb could only laugh. "Of course."

CHAPTER 24

July 18, 1836

When not working on their vessels or saving ships stranded on the reef, the wreckers took on the job of bringing the old dwelling up to the standards of a schoolhouse. Their wives, mothers, and daughters had freshened up the interior with colorful curtains and the exterior with a garden and beds of brilliantly blooming flowers. By the middle of July, Micah's shack had become a proper school.

Micah had decided to live aboard the *Caroline*, a curious choice considering the offer of free food Mrs. Campbell had made. As had become her habit, Mrs. Campbell prepared a meal for those who were working at the schoolhouse and sent it with Emilie after school. Usually her arrival was preceded by the sound of hammers or saws or of men's voices discussing the events of the day. So when Emilie arrived at the appointed time, the heavy cast-iron pot in hand, she was stunned to find no work being done and not a single man, woman, or child in sight. She left the food inside and walked around the perimeter of the property until she was certain the site was empty, then went back and retrieved the pot.

Retracing her steps with the intent of returning

the food to Mrs. Campbell at the boardinghouse, she took a shortcut that led her toward the docks and the courthouse beyond. Clustered around the courthouse steps stood most of the men who would normally be fighting over chicken legs and bragging on the quality of Mrs. Campbell's latest pie.

Deciding that whatever was transpiring had the men-only look to it, she kept to the other side of the street and picked up her pace. Surely Isabelle would hear from Josiah what had caused the impromptu meeting and inform her as soon as she could.

Emilie crossed the street just before the boardinghouse and almost got run into by Viola Dumont as she burst out the door of the infirmary. "I'm terribly sorry, Em," Viola said. "I was just with the doctor helping to deliver the Thompson twins when I heard the news."

Emilie shifted the heavy pot to the other hand and shook her head. "What news?"

Isabelle swept past, then stopped short. "Emilie," she said, nearly breathless, "have you heard the news?"

"No," Emilie said. "I have not heard the news, and if someone doesn't tell me the news, I'm going to—"

Isabelle gave her a look then continued walking, Viola at her side. "Aren't we testy today."

"No, we are not testy. We are tired of carrying this heavy pot and tired of guessing what the news is."

"Emilie?"

She turned. Micah Tate approached. He wore his work clothes and swiped at the sawdust on his sleeves as he walked. "I thought I saw you leaving the schoolhouse site. Here, let me carry that." He reached for the pot and easily lifted it from her hands.

Emilie flexed her fingers. "Thank you," she said as she worked the cramps out of her knuckles.

"Where are we going with this?" He turned back toward the docks. "Out to the site?"

"I've just come from there, and no one was around, so I figured I'd take it back to Mrs. Campbell. Say, what's going on down at the court-house?"

"I don't know." Micah gestured to the opposite end of town where the church sat on a rise a few blocks away. "I was helping Reverend Carter with some repair work to the church roof. When I left the schoolhouse, half a dozen men were there."

"They're all down at the courthouse now," Emilie said.

He gestured to the iron pot. "Why don't we drop this off with Mrs. Campbell and see what all the fuss is about?"

Micah loped up the boardinghouse steps, and Mrs. Campbell met him at the door. "Have you heard the news?" she called as she pressed past him.

"No," Emilie and Micah said in unison.

Mrs. Campbell bustled on, gathering her shawl about her shoulders as she turned toward the courthouse. "The mail boat just came. Looks like we've got a new judge." She turned to grin. "And just in time."

Emilie spied Reverend Carter coming her way and waved. "What's this I hear about a new judge?" he asked as he caught up to her.

"Mrs. Campbell said the mail boat came in and brought the news." She reached to dust a smattering of splinters off the old man's shirt front. Obviously, he'd been helping Micah.

"I supposed we'll only get the details if we go down to the courthouse," he said as he pointed his cane in that direction.

The door slammed, and Micah headed down the stairs toward them. "After you."

Reverend Carter led the way on the narrow sidewalk with Emilie a step behind. Micah brought up the rear until they reached a spot where the aging and weathered sidewalk proved particularly treacherous.

"Careful," Micah said as he reached up to place his hand on her elbow and guide her.

The touch of his fingers on her arm caused Emilie to stifle a gasp. "Thank you," she managed to say when she'd gathered her wits.

A few steps later, she reached the courthouse square, where the crowd had gathered around an announcement posted on the judge's door. While

Isabelle waited, the men pressed forward to read the sign.

"Well now," Hezekiah said when he returned with Micah. "It appears our federal government has taken notice of the fine job our wreckers do of filling their coffers."

Emilie watched several wreckers come away from reading the notice, shaking their heads. "Oh?"

Micah nodded. "That letter's direct from President Jackson's office. Judge Campbell's replacement will be some navy fellow from Washington. Said he's been detained but will be here in a month or so."

"Detained? I wonder what that means."

"I'll tell you what that means," Micah said. "It means we're under the iron rule of Judge Campbell for another month, and then we get some tender-foot who'll likely come down here thinking he knows more about us than we do."

August 3
Washington, D.C.

"Admiral Griffin, I assure you the story is quite false."

Caleb stopped his pacing and stood in front of the wide window with the view of the Capitol building and, ironically, his former office when he worked for the attorney general. He flexed his sore

270

shoulder and cursed the damp weather that caused his freshly healed injury to ache even as he gave thanks that the naval department did, after all, wish to have him in their employ.

At least they had wanted him. But now, less than two weeks into the job, it appeared he might be on his way out.

First he'd been shot and nearly killed by one woman, and now he faced a false accusation by another. Staying behind in Santa Lucida to watch the crops grow would have been more pleasurable than this, and he would likely have avoided any further contact with females bent on his destruction. At least he knew his mother didn't want him dead or married. *Scratch that last one. She'd have me married in a heartbeat if she could arrange it.*

Admiral Griffin, Caleb's commanding officer and the highest ranking member of the naval department other than the secretary himself, sat behind his massive desk and stared in astonishment, his jowls shaking. "Are you accusing my Frannie of lying about your intentions?"

"No, but—"

The admiral leaned forward, and the lamplight gleamed off the top of his bald pate. "So you are willing to offer marriage after such a compromise?"

"No, sir," Caleb quickly said as he tried not to consider how very much the woman in question resembled her father. There would likely be no battleship going to sea with her name on it unless her father deigned to put it there.

"I demand you explain yourself."

"There's been some sort of misunderstanding," Caleb began, "and there's absolutely been no compromise of your daughter or any other woman, for that matter. Send for her, and in my presence I am certain she would tell you the same."

"She was quite clear on the events of last evening." His expression gave away nothing. "Crystal clear, Lieutenant Spencer."

"With all due respect, I maintain my innocence, sir."

Last evening. Caleb worked to keep any reaction from his face as he tried to remember where he'd gone and what he'd done. In the two weeks since his return to Washington as an up-and-coming member of the naval department, he'd been feted with suppers, soirees, and the occasional oratorical reading. Last evening had been one in a long line of these events, with the marked exception being his companion.

Yes, he recalled it now. An event at the vice-president's home. An oratorical reading by some literary person-of-the-moment whose voice put Caleb to sleep in the first ten minutes.

But how had he come to share his time with Frannie Griffin?

Ah yes. Upon mentioning he could not stay and assist the admiral in completing paperwork,

Caleb was told he could either stay and miss the event or take along the admiral's daughter, who had been tormenting him mercilessly for an audience with the author.

Funny how doing his superior officer a favor had turned so incredibly wrong.

"Misunderstanding or not, the facts remain," the admiral said through clenched jaw. "I am left with a man of questionable character who keeps company I do not like."

This claim flabbergasted Caleb. It also made him mad enough to fist his fingers, then hide them behind his back lest he use them without properly thinking things through. "Your daughter was at the soiree long after I had taken my leave, thus I fail to understand how any company I keep would—"

"It's quite simple." The admiral toyed with the fat ruby ring jammed on his pinky finger before continuing. "The president has asked the secretary to take on his pet project. That, my boy, is you."

Heat flamed his cheeks, and his blood boiled. "I beg your pardon."

Admiral Griffin held up his hand to silence Caleb. "I don't care how long your father and he were friends, you're no navy man, and you don't belong in my department despite what the secretary has decided." He paused. "And lest you think you can go around me and plead your case to whoever else your father's money and influence has reached from the grave, think on this: I, too, have my supporters. It is likely I will be the next secretary of the navy." Another pause. "With all the power that entails."

Caleb's eyes narrowed even as he bit his tongue. To say anything further would be to risk the career he'd worked so hard to build.

"If it were up to me," the admiral continued, "I'd send you packing back to the attorney general and leave you to his mercy. I understand his wife's nephew has the job he'd slated for you, which is how I ended up with you in the first place. Likely he'd find something for you. Perhaps picking the lint off his robes or seeing that his inkwells are filled."

Caleb took two steps back to keep himself from charging forward and exacting justice in the way no department in Washington would tolerate. *Is this man worth your career?*

He took a deep breath and tried another way of reaching the buffoon. "Sir, I must remind you I had a stellar reputation when I worked under the attorney general." When the admiral's eyebrows shot up, Caleb continued. "I was on track to become a personal aide to the attorney general when I was forced to take a brief leave of absence to see to my widowed mother's interests in Santa Lucida. Then there was the delay caused by an unfortunate accident from which I am thankfully recovered."

"Santa Lucida?" Admiral Griffin leaned forward

and gave Caleb what almost looked like a smile. "Young man, tell me more about this."

So his attempt at placating the admiral had worked. Wary of giving too many of the facts, Caleb decided to be brief. "You may know of the storm that hit the Caribbean last fall. My maternal grandfather's plantation sustained damage, and I was called upon to see to its restoration."

"I see." The admiral steepled his fat fingers and tapped the largest of his chins. "So would you characterize yourself as being a native of that area?"

"A native?" Again, Caleb considered his words before speaking. "It is the land of my mother's birth. I, however, had a more varied upbringing."

"And your father's connection to the president is that he served with him in the Florida Territory, did he not?"

How much more did the man know? "He did," Caleb said carefully. "He was a judge during that period."

Admiral Griffin nodded. "Despite the fact my Frannie will be heartbroken that a potential beau will be leaving the city, I'm sure you will find it convenient and expedient to take whatever assignment is given to you. After all, anyone tied to this sorry excuse of a president we have will soon be glad to turn tail and run."

The only thing worse than enduring the accusations of this man was enduring the attentions of his daughter. But turn tail and run? Never.

His blood boiling, Caleb clenched his jaw and tried to decide whether to hold his silence or apologize later. He decided to do neither.

"Sir, while I can bear the scrutiny of a misunderstood evening with an overly enthusiastic young lady, and I use the term loosely, I will not abide insult to my reputation or to my president."

His fists clenched, Caleb tried to continue but found it utterly and inexplicably impossible. It was as if God had sealed his lips and forbade speech.

"Then it's settled." Admiral Griffin pushed back from his desk and rose to cross the distance between them, his face flushed, yet his smile oddly broad.

Despite the strange grin, Caleb waited for the man to hit him first so he could return the favor. Instead, the admiral reached out to shake Caleb's hand. "Congratulations, Lieutenant Spencer." He tightened his grip as he shook his head. "Judge Spencer," he corrected.

Had he heard the fool correctly? "Judge?"

"It is your good fortune to have crossed me on the same day I am told by the secretary I must provide a candidate for a judgeship that thus far no one will accept. Despite arriving in my offices with your skin tanned the color of an Indian savage, I've read your résumé and know you're a Washington dandy. I'm sure you'll find this assignment perfect. And you're a single man, so there's no concern as to whether the wife will raise a fuss when she hears of it."

Caleb gave no thought to his answer save the fact he'd likely end up in the brig if he worked in this man's employ another day. "When do I take my leave?"

The admiral walked back to his desk, his shoulders shaking from his chuckles. "I'll make the necessary arrangements and write the letters of introduction. Prepare to sail in a week's time."

"But where am I going?"

He grinned. "Let's just say you can leave your overcoat at home when you take this assignment." Admiral Griffin's smile went south. "Now leave my office before I forget you're likely a better shot than I and attempt to send you out horizontally."

CHAPTER 25

August 12, 1836

First came the wind and then the rain, a downpour so hard that the ringing of the bell calling the wreckers to their vessels could barely be heard above it.

Emilie climbed from her bed and padded to the porch, her wrapper whipping in the building gale. The call of "Wreck ashore!" carried across the buildings of the city and bounced up the road to her cottage, rolling onto the porch like the drops falling from her roof.

Over the last two years, she'd grown used to the unpredictable nature of the ocean and its reefs, so a call such as this one rarely drew her from her bed. Tonight, however, she watched the wrecking boats tracing a path from the harbor, their lanterns like fireflies as they bobbed away, and felt as if this time might be different.

The rain slowed until all that remained was the irregular drip from the eaves and the corresponding plopping sound as the water landed in fresh puddles of mud. Emilie was put in mind of New Orleans and the spring downpours that washed the dirt of the city off every surface until it sparkled when the sun finally returned.

Another call of "Wreck ashore!" and then the night was still. Emilie watched for a bit longer as the firefly lanterns clustered around the unfortunate sinking vessel, then one by one carried whatever persons or goods they could back to shore.

She went back to bed with the vessels still shuttling between the wreck and the shore, and her last thought before dozing off was that the wrecked ship must have been quite full with people or goods or both.

A few hours later she had her answer when a knock at the door awakened her from a deep sleep. Throwing on the same wrapper she'd donned earlier in the night, Emilie peered around the half-open door to see Reverend Carter's wife standing just inside the curtain of random raindrops next to a woman with three children huddled in front of her. All of them were soaked to the skin.

"I hope you'll forgive the interruption of your rest," Mrs. Carter said, "but we've a bit of a situation."

"Yes, please," Emilie said as she stepped back to open the door. "Do come in."

Mary Carter ushered the silent travelers in, and Emilie helped get them settled in the parlor. "Emilie Gayarre," Mary said, "this is Ruby O'Shea and her girls." She turned to the bedraggled woman. "I'm sorry. What are their names?"

"Maggie and Carol are the older ones." She lifted her hand to point, then allowed it to drop by her side as if she had no strength to control it. "The little girl's Tess."

While Emilie fetched blankets and dry clothing, Mary bustled about the kitchen, cobbling together a meal from the meager pickings. Though it was warm out, Emilie lit a small fire in the fireplace, an act that brought a smile to all four pale faces.

Depositing the pile of clothing and blankets on the settee, Emilie gestured to the back of the house. "I'll leave you alone now to get warm and dry. Mary and I will be in the kitchen, getting something for you to eat. Just call when you're done."

Emilie turned to go when the woman called her back. She turned to see Ruby holding up one of the dresses the man with the pipe had delivered to Emilie in Havana. The memory made Emilie's stomach do a flip even as the sight of the woman's face made her smile.

"Why are you doing this?" she asked. "If I had something this pretty, I'd never just up and give it to a stranger."

"I'd be honored if you'd take it," Emilie said, "though you've such a tiny waist that it may swallow you." She looked down at the girls. The elder two appeared to be twins, while the younger one held to her mother's damp dress with both fists. All wore blond braids, and none could be a day over nine or ten.

"Oh dear," Emilie said. "I'm afraid you'll have to make do with my nightdresses for tonight. Tomorrow I'll ask some of the girls in my class if they've got anything to spare for you."

Little Tess released her grip on her mother to stare up at Emilie with wide blue eyes. "You look too old to be in school," she said.

Emilie knelt down to look the girl in the eye. "Well, you're right about that. I am too old." She smiled. "But guess what? I'm not a student; I'm the teacher."

"You are?" Her eyes went wider. "You're too pretty to be a teacher."

Emilie laughed. "Oh, thank you, sweetheart," she said, "but I promise I am one. In fact, if you ever decide you'd like to come and see my new school I would love to show it to you and your sisters. With your mama's permission, of course."

"Could I?" She looked up at her mother. "Please?"

The woman looked tired enough to say yes to just about anything, so her nod was not unexpected. "Depends on how long we stay," Ruby said as she swung a tired look toward Emilie.

"What do the children call you?" the girl asked.

"They call me Miss Emilie because Miss Gayarre is a bit difficult for the little ones to say." She upped her smile. "What do they call you?"

"Well, I don't know the children, so I suppose we'll have to wait and see what they call me." She gave Emilie a look that told her exactly what she thought of the question.

"Of course. How silly of me." Emilie looked up at the girls' mother. "I know you'll likely go on as soon as the next ship can take you, but you're most welcome to stay here with me. As long as you don't mind the cramped quarters," she added.

"I'd be much obliged," she said.

"All right, then. I'll leave you ladies to yourselves and go see if I can help Mrs. Carter. You let us know when you're ready." She rose to join Mary in the kitchen.

"I've managed to find a fresh loaf of bread and some mango jam," Mary explained. "It'll have to suffice for tonight."

"I'm sorry," Emilie said. "I had planned to stock up tomorrow."

Mary waved away her concern. "I'm sure after what they've been through, this will be a feast. I'll send Josiah over in the morning with something for breakfast."

"Thank you. That would be wonderful." Emilie reached to pull four plates from the cupboard. "So, what happened to them?"

"The vessel running aground was just the last in a series of things. It seems as though the man in charge of this vessel wasn't exactly who he claimed to be." Mary stopped and seemed to consider her words. "It appears he and his men boarded the ship a day's sail from Havana without anyone's knowledge. This awful fellow claimed the captain's job for his own and sent the real captain overboard."

Emilie covered her open mouth with her hand. She knew too well the possibilities for horror abounded when a villain was in charge.

"Did the wreckers find this man with the ship?"

The pastor's wife shook her head. "No, and the only reason there was anything to salvage is because the pirate took the vessel over for to be his own and loaded all his prizes onto this ship. Best we can tell, he sent the men overboard with the captain and kept the women." She shuddered. "Leastwise they didn't find any men except the ones who were working with that awful Hawkins fellow."

"Did you say Hawkins?"

Mary nodded. "Yes, Emilie. The ladies told the judge the fellow called himself Thomas Hawkins and said he was looking to avenge the sinking of his ship by capturing a bigger and better one." She paused. "Ruby mentioned he was a particularly ruthless fellow. I didn't feel it appropriate to ask her how she came about this knowledge."

"Thomas Hawkins?" Emilie felt her knees buckle, and she sat before she fell.

"Emilie?" Mary called from what sounded like a faraway place. "What's wrong?"

"Thomas Hawkins is dead," she managed through lips that quivered in spite of her.

"Dead?" Mary shook her head. "Honey, what are you talking about? Why would you say such a thing? Josiah told me they were hoping to find him still aboard the ship."

"No," she said, "he can't be aboard that ship. He's dead."

She rested her hands on her hips, her head cocked to one side. "How do you know this?"

"Miss Emilie?" The youngest of the girls stood in the doorway, Emilie's white gown enveloping her and following behind like the train on an elaborate gown.

"Well, don't you look pretty, Tess."

"Like a princess," the pastor's wife added with a nod. "I don't think I've ever seen such a lovely gown as that one, dear."

She curtsied and ran from the room. A few minutes later, all four padded into the kitchen. Ruby O'Shea held a dripping bundle. "Might I trouble you to hang these on a clothesline so's me and the girls can put them back on come morning?"

"Of course," Emilie managed to say in a relatively normal voice. "Do sit down and let Mary serve you a bite while I take care of this."

Emilie took the bundle knowing full well the clothesline was out in the yard where likely the rain still fell in plops and drips from the leaves of the mango trees and shimmied down the feathery leaves of the nearby tamarind. But by taking the clothing outside, she could escape the confines of a kitchen that felt as if the walls were closing in.

Thomas Hawkins is alive.

"He can't be," she whispered as she laid a gown strewn with pink rosebuds over the rope tied between two mango trees. "It's impossible," she continued as she added matching gowns sprigged in yellow and green next to the first. "I heard the judge sentence him to death and saw the gallows being built outside the prison."

Then she held up the last of the bundle, a dress of robin's egg blue.

The same blue as Thomas Hawkins's eyes.

Thomas Hawkins couldn't be alive. For if he were, then she was as good as dead.

Emilie fell to her knees and began to pray. Only God could save her from the fiend should he somehow find her.

CHAPTER 26

August 13, 1836
Fairweather Key

Emilie rose from the rocker where she'd slept and crept into the kitchen to prepare breakfast, stretching out her sore limbs as she walked. True to her promise, Mary Carter had sent someone to deliver a dozen eggs to her back stoop sometime before dawn. Also in the basket was an assortment of goodies that likely had taken the dear woman the remainder of the night to prepare. Beside the basket sat a folded stack of clothing. Emilie knew without looking there would be four dresses, each relatively close if not perfectly matched to the female who would don it.

"Mary, how do you do it?"

She retrieved the food and set it on the table, then fetched in the clothes and went about preparing the eggs. By the time breakfast was ready, all four of her guests were padding around the kitchen, looking much better than when they arrived.

Ruby sat on the chair nearest the window and braided Tess's hair, then started on Carol's. Maggie did her own, then began work on her mother's. By the time Emilie had finished the eggs, all four O'Shea women were perfectly coiffed and ready to eat.

"I wish you hadn't insisted on giving up your bed," Ruby said as she helped set the table. "Though I will tell you it's a fine night's sleep I got, even if these three were sleeping all over the place." She pretended sternness toward little Tess. "And this one thinks it proper to sleep with one foot in my ear and the other stealing my covers."

"It's more comfortable that way," Tess said with a shrug.

"For you, maybe," Ruby said as she shook her head. "But not for me."

"But I'm little and need my sleep." Tess gave Ruby a wide-eyed look. "Isn't that what you tell me?"

The pair continued in this vein, bantering back and forth between bites of breakfast. Emilie shifted her attention to the twins, who seemed unusually quiet.

"Girls, how did you sleep?"

Carol mumbled something under her breath that sounded like *fine,* and Maggie shrugged. Neither seemed particularly interested in the breakfast set before them.

Emilie's stomach growled, and Tess giggled. "Miss Emilie has a tiger in her tummy."

The twins exchanged glances, then rolled their eyes. Evidently Tess's cuteness did not extend to her sisters' perceptions.

"Then I shall feed that tiger, Tess," Emilie said. "What do you think he wants?"

"She," Tess corrected. "You're a girl, so your tiger has to be a girl, too."

"Of course." Emilie looked over the girl's head to her mother. Ruby shrugged.

"Good morning," Isabelle called from outside. "I've got gifts. Are there any little girls here?"

Isabelle stepped onto the back porch as Emilie opened the door. In her hands were two large packages, and in the crook of her arm was a basket matching the one Emilie had found earlier.

"What do you have?" Emilie shut the door, then thought better of it and left the door open.

"What a nice breeze," Ruby said. "We don't have that in . . ." She paused and the twins gave one another a look. "Well, we just don't have that nice breeze where we come from."

"Ruby," Emilie said, "this is my sister, Isabelle." She paused. "Isabelle, meet Ruby O'Shea and her daughters Carol, Maggie, and Tess."

"Very nice to meet you," she said as she placed her bundles on the sideboard. "I've brought clothing for all of you courtesy of Mrs. Carter and the church ladies' committee." Isabelle lifted the cloth on the basket. "And Mrs. Campbell sent lunch."

"I don't know how to thank you," Ruby said.

"Don't thank me," Isabelle said. "I'm only the messenger. You can thank Mrs. Campbell yourself when I come back to fetch you this afternoon and take you over there to stay tonight." Isabelle

287

smiled at Emilie. "I'm sure you'll sleep more comfortably when each of you has your own bed."

Ruby rose and delivered her plate to the dishpan, then began to wash it. "I'll do that," Emilie said. "You're guests here."

Ruby turned, her expression pleading. "Let me do something to thank you."

All eyes were on Emilie. "Yes," she said. "Of course."

"Perhaps we could lay out the clothing," Isabelle said. "The girls could be dressing while you're washing dishes."

Ruby smiled. "I think that's a fine idea."

It took some doing, but the girls all managed to find dresses that not only fit but pleased them. "All right, now take at least one more each," Isabelle said. "It's always good to have an extra frock."

"In case of a party?" Tess asked.

"Exactly," Emilie said.

They watched the girls sort and choose, then fold everything that remained and stack it neatly once more. Ruby walked through the door, the dishtowel still in her hand.

"You've done a good job with them," Isabelle said. "They're very polite and don't fuss at all."

"Oh, they have their moments of friction," Ruby said, "but by and large, they're good girls."

Tess wandered over and grabbed Ruby's hand. "Your turn, Ruby. I mean, Mama."

Ruby allowed the girl to lead her to the stack of

adult-sized clothing. "You can have two," the little girl said. "One for to wear and the other in case of a party."

Ruby looked over at Emilie. She nodded.

It was impossible to miss the fact that while the girls tackled their clothing search with great zeal, Ruby picked the first two off the top and set the others aside. "Don't you want to sort through them and see what you like?" Emilie asked.

"I like these," she said, her eyes downcast. "And I'm grateful for them."

Isabelle touched Emilie's sleeve. "I know you need to get over to the school. I'll be staying here with the ladies until it's time to go over to the boardinghouse."

"Oh no," Ruby said. "The girls and I can find our own way around. I don't need to be bothering you."

"It's no bother," Isabelle said. "And believe me, once my son arrives, you'll see why I'll be glad for four extra sets of hands." She smiled. "Joey is an absolute lamb, but I think he's trying to teeth, and that's not making him very happy."

"The only solution for a fussy baby is to walk 'em." Ruby grinned. "And that's something the girls and I can do, isn't it, girls?"

All three nodded. Tess added a grin.

"Then I suppose I'll be on my way," Emilie said. "The children will take their summer break in a few days, so I will be home should you need anything." She smiled. "Do come and visit once you're settled."

She mouthed a thank-you to Isabelle, then gathered her things for the walk to the schoolhouse. Before Emilie reached the garden gate, she heard a childish voice calling her name.

It was Tess. "Can I come to school with you?" she called.

Emilie smiled. "That's something you and your mama need to discuss. Today's going to be an awfully busy day, what with moving over to the boardinghouse and all. Oh, and it's a lovely boardinghouse. I lived there for quite a while."

Tess looked unconvinced.

"Once you've settled in and been of great help to your mother, then we can talk about school. If you're still here, I'd love to see you girls begin classes in September. We have a little schoolhouse at the top of the summit, and I know the children would welcome new playmates."

Seemingly satisfied, Tess ran back inside. As the door slammed, so did the garden gate. Emilie walked down the ridge toward the school, casting a wary eye out toward the ocean.

If Thomas Hawkins yet lived, he was either out there somewhere or cleverly hiding here in Fairweather Key. Emilie preferred to believe the former, though her worst fear was the latter.

To take her mind off her concerns, she considered the riotous morning and the houseful of females she'd awakened to. It was lovely having the little cottage filled to the brim with visitors, even if it did mean she got a stiff neck in the process.

The way Ruby cared for those girls was a sight to behold. *At least there's one mother who didn't leave her girls.*

Emilie shook off the comparison and picked up her pace. Then she saw the strange man standing outside the schoolhouse. She turned and ran, not stopping until she was racing over the gangplank that connected the *Caroline* to the docks.

"I saw him up by the school," she said when she found Micah sitting on the stern, a fishing line dropped into the water.

"Who did you see?"

Breathless, she leaned forward and gasped until she could talk. "A man. He was at the school."

"Yes," he said patiently, "I understood that part. What I don't understand is what's got you so all-fired upset."

"Come with me, and I'll show you." She straightened and swiped at her forehead with her handkerchief. "I'm afraid it's him."

Micah's eyes narrowed. "Who?"

"Thomas Hawkins."

"The pirate whose ship we salvaged last night?" Micah laughed. "You do have an active imagination, Emilie. That man likely bailed out well before the vessel hit the rocks." He turned to look off into the horizon. "No, I'd predict he's got another ship by now and is back to his dirty tricks."

"But what of the treasure he lost in the wreck?"

Micah smiled. "It was a nice haul indeed."

"Then likely he will want to come back for it." She shook her head. "Don't you think it's possible?"

"I suppose it's possible." He looked down at the fishing line, then back up at Emilie. "Only for you would I do this. Give me a minute to get my boots on."

Emilie looked down and saw bare toes sticking out from his trousers. Then she looked up to see he'd not yet buttoned his shirt nor donned his collar.

"Oh my, I didn't even notice," she said as heat began to flood her cheeks. "I'm sorry for barging onto your boat like this. It was quite inappropriate. I would certainly not walk into your bedroom unannounced. Well, actually, I would never walk into you—" She caught another glimpse of skin. "Oh my. I'm—"

"Emilie," he said in a firm but soft voice. "Stop talking and sit down over there." He pointed to a barrel that had been fashioned into a makeshift chair. "I'll be with you in just a minute."

Slowly, she did as he asked, moving with care across a deck that looked to be freshly scrubbed. He emerged from the cabin fully dressed with boots and collar in place and shirttails tucked in.

Atop it all was a suit jacket that made him look more like a banker than a wrecker.

He must have noticed her stare for he looked down at his garb before returning his gaze to Emilie. "I've business at the courthouse once I get you settled at school." He straightened his collar. "I was appointed the wreck's master last night."

"Congratulations," she said, knowing the first man to the wreck was not only deemed the master, but also given a greater share of the prize. Judging from what she'd heard, it would likely be a large reward.

"Now," he said gently, "show me where you saw this man."

"You're not going to confront him barehanded, are you?"

Micah patted his coat, then lifted it up to show a pistol strapped to his waist belt. "He'll not want for reasons to leave you be," he said. "So just stop your worrying right now."

"Yes, sir," she said as she followed his broad back up the hill.

When they arrived at the schoolhouse, the grounds were deserted. A similar check of the interior proved the same.

"You stay right with me," Micah said. "We're going looking for him."

"We?" she squeaked.

He gave her a patient look. "You could stay here alone, but I figure you'd prefer not to do that."

Emilie nodded and did as he demanded, staying in Micah's shadow until the entire perimeter of the area had been searched and the children had begun to arrive. "It appears he's gone," Micah finally said.

"Yes," she said, "it does."

"Would you like me to come back after my meeting with the judge and see what I can do about flushing the varmint out?" Her hesitation was answer enough for Micah. "I won't be long," he said, his expression serious.

"Thank you." She smiled and led him away from the gathering group of children. "I'm in your debt, Micah," Emilie said.

"Are we keeping accounts now?" He winked. "Then I will have to start paying closer attention. I find you occupy my thoughts far more than you ought. I'm thinking of charging you for the space."

Before she could respond, he turned to leave.

CHAPTER 27

In the two days since Caleb Spencer had arrived anonymously on Fairweather Key, he'd found it hard to keep his identity a secret without resorting to outright lying. The proprietor of the boarding-house, a portly woman of great humor and culinary talents, alternated between feeding him and attempting to identify him.

After working so hard to arrive without fanfare

in order to better learn about the island he would be governing, Caleb's careful plans had nearly been unraveled with one accidental encounter. That he'd been caught surveying the shack that substituted for a schoolhouse nearly undid him. Had the woman not fled, he might have had to offer up an explanation for the early morning visit.

As far as he could tell, she'd only seen him from behind, so his face would not be known to her. The fact that he'd chosen a nondescript outfit rather than full naval uniform also worked to his advantage.

Last night's wreck had nearly caused him to admit his identity, such was his interest in watching the process of salvaging the great ship *Vindication*. The fellow at the mercantile let slip that he'd heard the *Vindication* had a less than illustrious history, first as a slaver and then upon its capture in the waters near Havana as a pirate vessel.

Caleb had been anxious to validate this information, though he'd thus far found no way to ask further questions without arousing suspicion. It was enough to be a stranger in a small village with no visible reason for being there without calling further attention to oneself by inquiring too deeply into anything.

He'd seen the docks where the wreckers and fishermen kept their vessels and the larger quay where oceangoing vessels made port and unloaded their cargo and the mail schooner did its weekly business. In addition to the mercantile, visits had been paid to the barber, the auction house, the tiny but serviceable livery, and the carpentry shop where fine furniture sat next to orders for boat fittings and replacement pieces for gaps in the town's notoriously ill-repaired wooden sidewalks.

The only two places he could not easily investigate were, for obvious reasons, the doctor's office and the funeral parlor. With this visit to the courthouse, his tour of the island would be complete.

Caleb had saved this important venue for last, knowing he would be forced to admit his identity to the outgoing judge in order to gain the information he sought. Considering and discarding the idea of making an appointment, he decided a direct approach and a surprise arrival would be the best means of handling a man whose reputation was known all the way to Washington.

Even those who had heard of Judge Campbell's fiery temperament and penchant for using the jail as his own personal rooming house for unwanted visitors had to admire his ability to earn money from the lucrative wrecking industry.

His was far and away the most profitable island of its size in all of the keys. To be sent to follow him was a daunting task, one Caleb was more than ready to assume.

The idea of doing even better than the old judge filled Caleb with anticipation, while the idea of showing Admiral Griffin he'd not sent Caleb to exile but rather to flourish made him smile.

He made his way past the kitchen where Mrs. Campbell worked with her back to the door. He'd nearly reached the exit when he heard her cheery good-bye. Responding in kind, Caleb rushed out onto the street and turned toward the courthouse square before the persistent woman chased him down.

He found the building easily enough, having been told by the dockhands upon his arrival that the judge, jail, and courthouse were situated in the same spot in the shadows of the great Fairweather Key warehouses.

Inside the nondescript wooden buildings was the bounty salvaged from last night's wreck as well as others awaiting visits from insurance men or auctioneers. Fortunes would be made by ship owners smart enough to purchase insurance for their vessel and cargo, while lesser monies would be doled out to the men who risked their lives to save the trinkets and baubles that would never see their original destination.

Always the first funds were paid to the judge, who then added them to coffers already bulging with the labor of the wreckers. This he knew from the reports turned in by Judge Campbell, the man he now intended to see.

While the massive warehouses held treasure, the squat structure nearby housed something even more important: the office where Caleb would take on his first judgeship.

He took the steps two at a time and swung the door open to find the judge was not alone. "Come on in," Judge Campbell called before Caleb could excuse himself. "Mr. Tate and I were just finishing up our business. He's the master on last evening's wreck."

A lanky redhead rose to offer Caleb a surprisingly strong handshake. "Pleased to meet you, Mr. . . . ?"

"Spencer." Caleb noted the lack of surprise on the judge's face and wondered if the old man had figured out who he was before now. "Congratulations," Caleb said. "Master on a wreck like the *Vindication* is quite an accomplishment."

"Nah, it just means I've got the fastest boat." He gave Caleb a hard look. "Spencer, you say? Is that your first or your last?"

"Last. First name's Caleb. Caleb Spencer."

The wrecker's expression softened, barely. "You passing through or staying awhile?"

"I'm staying," Caleb said, "which is why I'm paying this visit to the judge." He gestured toward Judge Campbell. "I can come back if it's more convenient."

"No," Mr. Tate said. "I need to be going anyway. I promised a lady I'd come back and be sure she was safe."

Judge Campbell frowned. "What's going on, Micah?"

He shrugged. "Emilie saw some fellow nosing around the schoolhouse this morning who she didn't recognize. Came running after me, and we looked but couldn't find him. I told her I'd come check back with her to see that she and the children weren't being bothered."

Now was his chance to speak up. Caleb shrugged. "I fear the man you're looking for is me."

Both men stared at him as if he'd grown an extra ear. The redhead moved an inch closer. "I don't reckon I understand why a man would be nosing around and scaring women when the sun's barely up, but I intend to wait right here until you tell me why."

Had he not the skills to best this man without breaking a sweat, Caleb might have been concerned for his own safety. Rather, he drew out a deep breath and put on his most contrite look.

"Purely accidental, I promise. I followed the road up thinking I would find the island's highest vantage point. The better to get the lay of the land, as it were."

The wrecker didn't budge. "That explains how you got there, but it doesn't tell me what business you had scaring my Emilie."

"Your Emilie?" The judge snickered. "Since when?"

"Hush," he said. "I want to hear what this man's got to say for himself. If he can't explain why he was scaring an innocent schoolteacher, then I plan to swear out a warrant to have him arrested."

"On what grounds?" Judge Campbell asked.

"I'll think of something," came the hotheaded wrecker's response.

"Gentlemen," Caleb said. "There's a simple explanation. I did not intend to frighten anyone. This woman—"

"Emilie," Micah Tate supplied.

"Emilie. Yes, well, she came upon me while I was enjoying the view of the ocean. I did not hear her approach and only heard her leave when she screamed. Thinking there might be something wrong with her, I turned to follow. She ran so fast I decided she was perfectly healthy and merely skittish."

"Skittish?" Tate's face was close to matching his hair. "You'd be skittish too if you expected to be alone but came upon some stranger at your schoolhouse."

It was a stretch, but Caleb supposed he could imagine the scenario. "Then I owe your Emilie an apology."

Obviously, the wrecker had no idea what to do with such a statement. He stared for a moment, then jammed his hat back on his head and looked toward the judge. "He seems like he's all right, Judge Campbell, but I want to reserve the right to have him jailed if I find out he's making any of this up."

"Fair enough," Judge Campbell said.

Micah turned to address Caleb. "The children go home for lunch from eleven to one. I'll have Emilie back up here in Judge Campbell's office by eleven fifteen." He leaned forward with what appeared to be the intention of frightening Caleb.

It failed.

Miserably.

But recognizing this was a man in love, and obviously a man who needed his pride soothed, Caleb made to inch back a notch. "Eleven fifteen," he said and tipped his hat.

The wrecker stormed past without returning the gesture. When he'd gone, Caleb turned his attention to the old judge. "Are all of them like that one?"

"No more than all judges are like me," he said evenly. "That's who you are, isn't it?"

"You've caught me." Caleb gestured to the chair nearest the judge's cluttered desk. "May I?"

He nodded.

"Last I heard, they couldn't find anyone to take my job." He walked around the desk and landed heavily in an ornately carved chair and stared at Caleb. "So," he finally said, "did you lose a bet?"

"I beg your pardon?"

The judge grinned. "Nah, I don't figure you for a betting man." He gave Caleb another long look. "Somebody's daughter?"

The question hit its mark. Still, Caleb made an

301

attempt to deflect the intention. "I'm a legal man who ended up with a navy department position. I couldn't pass up a chance to return to my judicial roots."

The judge cocked his head to one side and peered at Caleb from beneath gray brows in need of a good trim. "It was somebody's daughter, wasn't it?"

"Sir, why can't you believe I would be here only because I want this judgeship?"

The old man leaned forward, elbows on the desk. "Son, nobody wants to come to Fairweather Key, especially not some hotshot lawyer type with career plans."

Caleb decided to take the high road. He also decided this man's poor reputation was well earned. "I wish to see your records and your warehouse, the warehouse first. And," he paused to intentionally speak in the most casual voice possible, "we'll start with last night's wreck."

Judge Campbell paused a moment before nodding. "It's still being catalogued," he said, "and witnesses are being housed at the boardinghouse and in several locations around town."

"I see. And what of the captain of the vessel?" he said, again keeping his interest level as professional as possible. "I would like to interview him first so as to better know what questions to ask the others."

"Well, that's the million-dollar question." Judge

Campbell gathered up a sheath of papers and handed them to Caleb. "When that ship went aground, he and his crew either bailed off her and skedaddled before the wreckers showed, or he wasn't on her to begin with."

"What do you mean?"

"How much do you know about sailing, son?"

Caleb's breath caught but he recovered quickly. "I know some," he said. "Why?"

The judge rose and Caleb followed suit, tucking the papers under his arm. "We had a good rain last night," he said, "but the seas weren't the worst we'd seen by any stretch of the imagination. It was a new moon, so there's a case to be made that they just weren't familiar enough with our waters to keep off the reef."

"Understandable."

"Yes, but here's what's not understandable." He pointed a gnarled finger at Caleb. "That ship was full of treasure. Loaded down with it, which was why it ran aground and stuck. Thing is, it was all up in a subfloor that nobody would have found had it not been wrecked. Why an experienced captain with something to hide would be sailing his vessel so close to me and my jail doesn't make sense." He gestured to the door. "Walk while we talk, Spencer."

Caleb nodded and joined the judge on the porch.

"Warehouse is this way," he said as he headed down the stairs. "Now back to the treasure from the *Vindication*. We see all kinds come through the auction house after they've been wrecked. Pirates, privateers, merchantmen, mail boats." He turned the corner, and Caleb followed. "Never in all my years have I seen a vessel so full that gold bars were used alongside the ballast."

"Gold bars?" Caleb shook his head. "Where would a slaver get treasure like that?"

Judge Campbell stopped short and turned to face Caleb. "How'd you know the *Vindication* used to be a slaver?"

"Just doing my job, sir," he said. "I asked a few questions."

"Well, whoever told you that was right. She's a slaver that someone converted to a treasure carrier." He paused to pull a small ring of keys from his pocket. "Only one kind of ship carries that, and only one kind of captain hides his cargo between floors."

"A pirate," Caleb supplied.

"Indeed." The judge stared a moment, then proceeded toward the first warehouse door. "And one who either hit it big with one strike or kept at it awhile. You hear anything else about that ship?"

"Nothing else about the ship," he answered truthfully as he followed the judge.

He stabbed the key into the lock and easily opened the door. Caleb stepped into a darkened space that smelled of seawater and dampness. Slender streams of sunlight pierced the walls where the chinking and weathering had failed. Otherwise, the vast room was plunged into inky darkness.

"Give me a second," the judge said, "and I'll get the lamps going."

Caleb waited in the dark while he heard the judge fumbling around. In a moment, Judge Campbell's lamp flamed, and a circle of orange light filled one corner of the enormous space. He lit another and handed it to Caleb.

Once his eyes adjusted to the dim light, Caleb faced an amazing sight. Row upon row of items had been neatly stacked in lines that disappeared into the darkness. Upon each item was a tag indicating the name of the vessel and the date it was declared unsalvageable.

"The take from *Vindication*'s over here."

Caleb followed the judge to what seemed to be the midway point in the warehouse. There he saw a stack of what appeared to be ten gold bars with a tag stating its origin on the vessel and a note saying simply *ballast*.

A puddle of something that appeared to be a woman's skirt caught his attention. He reached to touch a tangle of torn white cloth that appeared to have two bundles of coins sewn into it.

"This is odd," Caleb said as he lifted it and felt the coins shift.

Judge Campbell peered over Caleb's shoulder, then nodded. "Not the strangest thing I've seen come off a ship, but yep, that's something different." He moved on and took his circle of light with him. Caleb followed.

"Best we can tell, the *Vindication*'s not insured," the judge said. "You'll have to wait for proof, but once it comes, I suppose you know what that means."

Having studied up on the latest maritime law, Caleb was prepared with the answer. "It all goes to auction without waiting for the insurance claims to pay out. Profits are divided between the wreckers and the municipality, with the wreck's master—that would be Mr. Tate—getting a greater portion than the others."

"Yes, that's right," he said. "But that brings me back to the captain."

Caleb stopped before a waterlogged pistol tied with a red sash. Lifting the weapon, he inspected it, then returned it to its spot.

He kept his expression neutral, his tone deliberately casual. "Any idea who was behind the wheel when it ran aground?"

"I've heard talk, but right now it's all theories and conjecture." The judge turned to head for the door, and Caleb followed. Once outside, the door locked, Judge Campbell paused to scratch his chin. "Whoever he was, he's disappeared faster than the biscuits on my wife's breakfast table."

Caleb chuckled, then quickly sobered. "You have a theory?"

"I do." The judge looked around before returning his attention to Caleb. "Thomas Hawkins. Maybe you've heard of him."

"I have." He shook his head. "But I thought he'd been tried as a pirate and hanged in Havana."

They stepped back into the judge's office, and he headed for his chair. Caleb followed and assumed his earlier seat.

"You heard right, all except the part where he was actually hanged."

Interesting. The mercantile owner's information seemed closer to possible now. "I don't understand."

Judge Campbell chuckled. "Neither do the authorities in Havana. One minute he was locked up tight and ready to hang, and the next he was gone." He leaned forward. "They suspect a woman."

"How so?"

"The fellow standing guard was neither hurt nor bribed, at least as far as anyone could tell. The other prisoners all say the same thing. The guard was visited by a woman and stepped away from his post. That same woman passed by Hawkins's cell on her way out. Every last one of them gives the same description: she was a tiny thing wearing a blue cloak and a shawl that covered her head." He winked. "I doubt that was his mama."

"Likely someone connected with Hawkins. A lady friend, perhaps?"

He shrugged. "Thing is, bad seeds always turn up again somewhere. The Lord rarely lets 'em grow old, fat, and happy."

"So you think we've not heard the last of Thomas Hawkins?"

"Well, someone hasn't heard the last of him." The judge gestured to the desk. "If you've got the time, I'd like to go over what I'll be leaving in your care. Better for you to learn this job while I'm still here rather than to do as I did and figure it out as you go along."

Caleb nodded. "I'd appreciate that."

Judge Campbell walked to a locked cabinet and retrieved several items, depositing them in front of Caleb. "Let's get started, then."

An hour later they'd only begun to scratch the surface of the work the territorial judge was responsible for. "Are you burned out yet, Spencer?"

Caleb looked at the top of a stack of pages he'd covered with scribbled notes. "Not yet, but I'm close. Maybe I need to take this back to my room and study it awhile, then come back later this afternoon."

"Let's make that tomorrow, since I'm on my way out for the day. You're welcome to use my office—rather, your office—to start figuring it out," the judge said. "I know you're one of those Washington types, but I reckon this is a whole other way of doing things."

"I look forward to learning it," he said. "And I'd be grateful for the loan of your office for the day. Until I officially assume the position, it is yours." He paused. "When do you plan to hand the job over to me?"

"Far as I'm concerned, you can start tomorrow." His smile faded as he began to shove the mess on his desk into an orderly stack. "But that would mean you'd have to tell people who you are. You willing to do that?"

"I am."

"Well, that's a relief. My wife's about to bust her buttons trying to figure it out. Just be warned, though. They'll likely have a party to welcome you." He chuckled. "I know they'll have one when I leave. I'm not exactly the most popular person on the island."

"A judge is paid to be right, not popular."

"I didn't expect to like you, Spencer, but it appears we think alike." The judge pushed the papers toward Caleb, then reached for his hat. "Because I like you, I'm going to let you in on a little secret."

"All right."

"It's easy to forget that you don't work for the people of Fairweather Key. Your job is to keep sending money to Washington so they can do whatever it is that they do with it." He paused to don his jacket. "No matter what they want, tell 'em no."

Caleb rose. "What do you mean?"

"There's always some pet project somebody's trying to get the government to pay for. Your job is to see that the government's interests are looked after."

"That makes sense." He gathered the papers and walked around to the other side of the desk.

The judge headed for the door but stopped short. "Oh, and there's one more thing."

Caleb settled into the judge's chair and set the papers in front of him. "What's that?"

"There's a little issue with the schoolhouse that's waiting for you to resolve it." He pointed to the papers. "Details are in there somewhere."

Caleb began to page through the documents. "Any advice on the issue?"

"Yes," he said, "no matter who's asking the question, the answer is no. Take that kind of money out of the funds you've been trusted with, and you're going to have this job forever."

Caleb looked up sharply from his reading. "What do you mean?"

Judge Campbell placed his hand on the doorknob. "You're not fooling me, boy. You might have taken this job because you wanted to call yourself a judge, but I don't believe for a minute you're content to stay in it for any longer than it takes to get yourself a promotion and head back north to Washington."

Caleb said nothing. Did his intentions show that

clearly, or had this man merely developed a strong sense of discernment in what had obviously been many years on the job?

"I'll be back tomorrow morning, so hold your questions until then," he said.

"I will," Caleb responded. "Thank you for the loan of your office."

"No, boy, your office." He gave the knob a yank but did not move to step through the doorway. "So, Spencer," the judge finally said, "who was she?"

He set the papers down and shook his head. "She?"

"Yes, she." The old man grinned, and his eyes narrowed. "The gal who got you shipped out of Washington."

"Ah." Caleb reluctantly returned the smile. "The admiral's daughter. But it's not what you think."

Judge Campbell stepped through the door. "It never is," he called as it closed behind him.

CHAPTER 28

Emilie watched as the last child disappeared down the path toward town. "Thank you for coming back here, Micah," she said. "I feel foolish now."

"Why?" He leaned down to offer her a protective hand as she stepped over the raised threshold and out into the sun.

"Oh, I don't know," she said as she closed the schoolhouse door. "I probably just overreacted."

Micah shook his head. "What I saw wasn't over-reacting," he said. "You were genuinely afraid."

She was but could never tell him the real reason. After all, how would she explain to a good man like Micah Tate that the escaped pirate Thomas Hawkins was likely after her to exact his revenge?

"Emilie?"

"What?" She looked up to see him staring at her with concern. "I'm sorry. It was a late night last night, what with the guests from the wreck, and I'm not myself this morning." She affected a casual tone. "Which is likely the reason for overre-acting."

"Well, I do have some good news for you." He gestured toward town, and she fell in step beside him. "If you don't mind putting your lunch off for a few minutes, I'd like to introduce you to the man who caused all of this unnecessary upset."

"You found him?" An image of Thomas Hawkins safely peering at her from behind the bars of the Fairweather Key jail made her smile. "Thank You, Lord."

"Well, it's not as exciting as all that."

She stopped short. "What do you mean? Capturing a criminal is terribly exciting."

Micah looked at her. "Let's just reserve judg-ment. He seems to be a decent fellow."

A decent fellow? Not the Thomas Hawkins she had encountered.

"Come on," he said as he reached for her elbow.

Emilie allowed him to lead her down the path toward town, then onto the street leading to the courthouse. The day was glorious, the fresh breeze having blown away any remnants of the previous night's showers.

At the courthouse, Micah took the lead, bounding up the steps to stop at the door to Judge Campbell's office. Emilie followed at a slower pace, unsure as to whether she wanted to actually come face to face with the Hawkins fellow again.

As Micah reached for the doorknob, Emilie stopped him. "Wait," she said. "I'm not ready for this."

"It'll be fine," he said. "Besides, that man owes you an apology for scaring you, and I'm here to see you get it." He leaned down and traced the edge of her jaw with his knuckle. "There's no need to be afraid of him, Emilie. I'm here."

Micah Tate was a good man, one of the best, and in his sincere way he obviously had feelings for her. This had not happened before, this feeling of a man's appreciation, and Emilie couldn't say whether she liked it or merely felt uncomfortable. In either case, it seemed wildly inappropriate to continue in this vein on the courthouse steps.

Slowly, she swung her gaze to meet his stare. His eyes were a lovely shade of copper, not quite brown and not so light as to be considered hazel. She stared, transfixed, until the bell on the lookout stand shook her.

"Wreck ashore," the lookout called.

Micah jerked his hand back and opened his mouth to speak, then obviously reconsidered. "I've got to go."

"Yes," she said, "you go."

The bell clanged again, and then the lookout repeated his call. "Go," he repeated. "Now," came out as he turned to leave.

The clanging bell continued until Emilie covered her ears. Likely the thick walls of the judge's office kept the bell from being so obnoxious. Still, with Micah gone, Emilie found no desire to go inside.

What if Thomas Hawkins had convinced Micah and the judge that he was a good fellow? What if he now waited inside for her to open the door, only to pounce and do her in for testifying against him?

"You won't let that happen, will You, Lord?" she whispered.

Emilie inched toward the door just as the awful bell ceased its peals. Her ears ringing, she did her best to peer into the office through the small window in the door.

Her heart skidded to a stop when a face appeared on the other side of the glass. With a jerk, the door flew open.

"You must be Mr. Tate's Emilie," he said before taking a step back. "You," he said as if he'd seen a ghost. "It can't be."

• • •

"I beg your pardon."

She wore his mother's dress. Even if he hadn't recognized the bolt of cloth he'd brought from a trip to Paris, there was no mistaking the dark-haired female who'd haunted his dreams and taunted him in his nightmares.

Miss Crusoe had found him.

"What are you doing here?" he managed, his fingers worrying the door latch until he realized it might show weakness and stopped.

"Micah Tate brought me here." She gave him a puzzled look. "He said the man who frightened me this morning was here to offer an apology." The puzzled look deepened. "Do we know one another?"

Now would be the time to give a truthful answer. He knew none of the details beyond the fact he'd been found by Fletcher clutching the attorney general's letter in his hand.

In hers was the missing pistol, its barrel still smoking.

What now, Lord?

The woman he now knew to be Emilie continued to stare, and Caleb realized she likely did not recognize him. When she'd done her damage, his beard hid his face and his unkempt hair had begged for the barber's shears. His own mother had joked that even she did not know him until she'd had his face shaved clean and his hair trimmed by a local barber during those days when he lay between life and death.

How long he stood staring, Caleb could not say. By degrees, he became aware of a rush of activity on the courthouse square.

"What's happening?" he asked.

"There's a vessel on the reef," she said, still wearing the same puzzled expression. "The wreckers are heading out to save anyone aboard. Then they unload cargo and bring it here." She paused. "Why am I explaining this to you? And where is Judge Campbell?"

Caleb sprang into action. He'd been studying up on the proper procedure for processing a wreck, but the judge's notes were proving hard to decipher.

He went back to the desk to retrieve the ledger from the topmost drawer. In it was a list of the dates, times, and names of masters on every wreck registered in Fairweather Key since the government sent their first judge.

Emilie stood in the doorway, though she'd stopped staring at him in that odd way. Now she seemed to merely observe. Likely she'd soon join the other gawkers he could see through the window who were gathering at the dock.

She certainly seemed to be gawking at him. Yet he saw no recognition in her eyes.

Blind her to who I am, Lord. Don't let my secret be revealed.

"Miss . . ."

"Gayarre," she said, "Emilie Gayarre."

Caleb nodded. "Miss Gayarre, if you will forgive me, I must get out to the dock and see to the supervision of the wrecking process."

Her response was slow in coming. "So are you . . . ?"

"Judge Campbell's replacement? As I said, I am indeed the new judge." He set the ledger aside and walked toward her, offering her his hand in greeting. "Lieutenant Caleb Spencer, United States Navy, at your service."

"Spencer?" fell from her lips in a sound just louder than a whisper. Miss Gayarre shook his hand, then held her grip. "No," she finally said.

"Yes, and I do beg your forgiveness for the fright I gave you this morning. I thought to follow, then decided chasing after you might cause further upset."

"No."

This time she spoke the word with a bit more force. Her grip tightened as well.

Please do not let her see who I really am, Father.

"No?" Caleb gave her what he hoped was a stern look. "I assure you it's all quite true."

Emilie Gayarre continued to stare at him in a manner that put him in mind of the frightened creature he'd hoisted aboard the *Cormorant*.

"Well," he said in what he hoped would be a casual yet firm tone, "I really must go."

317

Still she hung on tight.

Indeed this was a problem. One God seemed to have left up to Caleb to solve.

"Really, Miss Gayarre."

"You're . . ." She seemed unable to say more.

"The new judge," he supplied, hoping his direct manner would deflect any suspicion she might have and cause her to release him. "Caleb Spencer."

"No," she said, slowly, "you're the man I shot. You're the Benning."

Judge Campbell burst through the door, nearly knocking Emilie down in the process. Somehow, the man she knew as the Benning slipped from her grasp. Before she could collect her thoughts and muster them into words, she watched the new judge's broad back disappear down the courthouse steps.

As he turned toward the docks, he cast a quick glance over his shoulder. While the expression on his face was unreadable, the authority in his voice had been unmistakable.

Lieutenant Caleb Spencer, United States Navy, certainly did not seem like a pirate, and he bore neither the unruly mane nor the overgrown beard of the ruffian who'd bartered for her with bags of gold only to steal her heart with a kiss in the shadow of a rowboat.

Yet . . .

It was all so confusing.

"Isabelle," she said as she gathered her wits. "She'll know what to do."

Emilie made her way through the throng heading toward the docks and raced toward the tidy home of Isabelle and Josiah Carter. As was her custom, she knocked twice, then threw open the door.

"Well, Emilie," Josiah's mother exclaimed. "What a nice surprise. You're just in time for lunch. William," she called, "set another place at the table for Miss Emilie."

"No," Emilie said, "I can't stay. I'm looking for Isabelle."

"Why, she's at your cottage with those dear ladies from last night's wreck." She looked perplexed. "Didn't you ask her to keep them company until a room could be found at the boardinghouse?"

"Oh yes, of course." She shrugged. "I'm terribly sorry. I'm just not thinking clearly right now. Do excuse me."

She hurried away toward her cottage, pondering the dilemma of speaking to Isabelle while keeping the actual topic undetectable to the O'Shea ladies. She needn't have bothered, for when Emilie arrived at the gate, laughter was the music of the moment, and it was apparent that conversation would be quite impossible.

Isabelle had moved the party outdoors where she'd spread the feast from her mother-in-law's basket on a board set atop the span between two tree stumps. One of the twins had made a drum from an upturned bucket, and the other sang. Tess, a crown of wildflowers in her tumbledown curls, danced to the symphony of sounds, while Isabelle and Ruby clapped in some semblance of rhythm. Surprisingly, baby Joey slept soundly on his blanket in the shade.

"Oh, Emilie," Isabelle said as she rose. "You've decided to join us."

The music ceased, though Tess continued her dance. Ruby seemed unsure as to whether to remain seated or stand.

"Might I speak to you a moment, Isabelle?" Emilie said lightly, then offered Ruby what she hoped would pass for a genuine smile. "Forgive the interruption. It won't take but a moment."

"Go right ahead," she said.

Isabelle reached Emilie's side and grasped her hand. "What's happened? Is it Josiah?"

"No," Emilie said quickly. "It has nothing to do with him, though the wreckers are out on the reef again."

"Yes, I heard the bell." She paused. "If not Josiah, then what brings you back in the middle of the day?"

"The Benning," she said in a hoarse whisper.

"The Benning?" Isabelle shook her head, then Emilie saw recognition slowly dawn. "The man you shot?"

"Quiet," Emilie said. "No one can know."

She grasped Emilie's sleeve and jerked her closer. "I don't understand. What is that pirate doing in Fairweather Key? He is a pirate, right?"

"Oh, Izzy, I don't know. Right now he's claiming to be Lieutenant Caleb Spencer." She paused to return Tess O'Shea's wave. "He claims to be the next judge."

"Of all the—"

The warning bell in town rang again, and a flock of coal-colored orangequit took flight from the nance tree in the easternmost corner of the clearing.

"That's odd," Emilie said. "Why ring the bell now when the wreck's been announced and the men are already at sea?"

Isabelle's eyes went wide. "Someone's been hurt."

"Don't let your imagination take over. First we pray; then we go see to it." Emilie grasped her sister's hand and beseeched the Lord to protect those at sea and to see to the quick care and healing of whoever had been harmed. She added a silent plea for the safety of Josiah and Micah, then said "Amen."

"Ladies," Isabelle called as she walked back to snatch up her sleeping son, "Emilie and I are going down to the dock. We're a bit concerned about the warning bell. It could be an indication someone was injured."

"Oh no." Ruby rose. "Would you like us to come along?"

"It's not necessary," Emilie said. "Please just enjoy the day and the lunch Mrs. Carter prepared. You've been through enough this week."

Ruby's grateful smile was answer enough.

"Likely we'll return shortly, and all this excitement will have been for naught," Isabelle said.

Isabelle got all the way to the garden gate before she grabbed Emilie's hand. "Tell me everything, but understand until I know my husband's uninjured I may not remember it all," she said as the baby awakened and began to fuss. The baby offered Emilie a wary eye, then stilled.

"I saw the man inside the judge's office. He introduced himself as navy Lieutenant Caleb Spencer. He claims he's Judge Campbell's replacement."

They turned onto the main avenue, where the narrow sidewalk made conversation difficult. Finally, the walkway widened near the courthouse, and Emilie was able to fall into place beside Isabelle. By now, the baby was sound asleep against his mother's shoulder.

"Em," she said, "are you certain it's him?"

Emilie hesitated. "The man I met today had certainly met with the barber's shears since I'd last seen him, but yes, I think it's him."

"You think?"

Joey's eyes opened again, and Emilie reached to

322

touch a lock of his down-soft hair. "I have a strong feeling, Izzy," she said, "and it seemed as though he was, well, I don't know, nervous."

Isabelle gave her a sideways look. "To make such an accusation, you need to have more than just a feeling, strong or otherwise. As for his nerves, perhaps he was struck by your beauty."

Emilie laughed. "Likely not. If so, he would be the first."

"Why do you say such things? Perhaps you just don't see what the rest of us—"

The bell rang again, and they picked up their pace until they reached the edge of the milling throng. Isabelle pointed out Reverend Carter and headed in his direction.

He waved to Isabelle, and when she reached him, he embraced her. "Relax, dear, our Josiah has sent word that he is fine."

"Thank You, Lord," Isabelle said as she leaned heavily on her father-in-law's arm. Emilie relieved Isabelle of Joey so she could compose herself.

Hezekiah looked over Isabelle's head to fix his gaze on Emilie. "I'm sorry," he said. "I know how close you've become to Micah." He reached to take Joey. "Pray," he continued, "because they're looking for him now."

"For Micah?"

He pointed to the water and the horizon beyond where a ship burned to the waterline. Clusters of wrecking vessels fanned out in a half-circle around the flaming hulk, none of which looked to be moving away.

An odd situation entirely, for rarely did a wrecking vessel lay anchor for any amount of time. Such was their lot that fetching and returning was the call of duty, not sitting and waiting.

It could only mean one thing. None would leave until their brother was found.

The world tilted, then righted again. "Tell me," Emilie began with difficulty, "tell me what happened."

"I only know what Josiah has said. They approached the vessel together, he in the *Freedom* and Micah in the *Caroline*. Micah arrived first, making him master of the wreck once again. Though the ship was already burning, he went aboard to secure the vessel and organize the passengers for rescue. The ship was declared evacuated, and Josiah gave the order for the wreckers to lay anchor and board for salvage."

Reverend Carter paused, his attention returning to the drama unfolding in the ocean. Joey snuggled against his grandfather's neck, then stilled. "I was certain that boy would preach alongside me someday," he said softly. "Surely I cannot be mistaken."

CHAPTER 29

School was suspended for the afternoon, much to the delight of the students gathered at the door. For children already anticipating their month-long summer break, this unexpected holiday sent them cheering down the path, their high spirits audible even as the last child disappeared.

When the schoolyard was empty, Emilie returned to her desk until the tears began to spill. "I cannot cry," she said, rising. "There is nothing yet to cry over," she whispered as she stepped into the sunshine and swiped at her cheeks.

Emilie found a soft place near a stand of mango trees and sat, heedless of the mess she might make of her borrowed frock. From her vantage point, she could see the charred and blackened hull of the vessel and the wrecker's boats still gathered nearby.

"Keep Micah safe, Lord, and please hold Your hands of protection around all the wreckers today."

With those words, something inside broke open, and the heart she'd held so closely guarded softened.

How long she sat watching the waves roll past the wreck and its attendants, Emilie had no idea. One by one, the vessels began to weigh anchor and turn toward home.

Emilie picked up her skirts and ran, caring about

neither the looks of the bystanders nor the impropriety of the situation. By the time she reached the dock, the first of the wrecking boats had arrived. She cried out in thanks upon finding it was the *Freedom*.

"We've got him," Josiah called when he spotted her.

"Where is he?" she called as she stepped onto the boat. "What's his condition? And where's the *Caroline*?"

Josiah stilled her by linking arms with her. "Right now I've got to see to Micah." He gestured behind her, and Emilie saw Dr. Hill approaching. "You need to calm down and wait. Can you do that?"

She took a deep breath and let it out slowly, her heart still racing from the run. "I am perfectly calm, Josiah."

He looked at a point behind her. "Judge, would you mind seeing to Miss Gayarre?"

Emilie turned, expecting to see Judge Campbell. Instead, her gaze collided with the Spencer fellow. Or the Benning. Or whoever he was.

"I'm fine," she said even as she knew she was anything but.

Everything about Emilie Gayarre put Caleb on guard. From the way she looked at him to the damage she could do to his career should he persist in identifying him as the Benning.

At the moment, however, she seemed too preoccupied with the fate of her Micah to care that her mere presence grated on his resolve to say nothing of their shared past. Even now, she stared at him as if he were some trussed-up turkey in a shopkeeper's window.

A watch bell clanged, while overhead gulls cried out and swooped in and out of the swells for their afternoon meal. On the horizon, a single white cloud, its southernmost edge blackened with a smear of coal, portended rain.

"Miss Gayarre?"

She barely blinked. "Mr. Spencer."

Even the way she said his name gave him pause. As if she had not yet become convinced he was indeed the man he claimed to be. Caleb sighed.

"Lieutenant Spencer," he corrected, "or Judge Spencer, if you prefer."

She ignored him. Caleb, in turn, tried to ignore the realization that his mother had never looked as lovely as the Gayarre woman did in that dress.

"It appears I am to keep watch over you."

Her snort was neither ladylike nor appreciative. Her defiance he grudgingly appreciated. Emilie Gayarre might be many things, but fearful was not one of them. He'd seen this at sea and now, it appeared, would get a fresh taste of it on land.

Caleb reached for his grandfather's pocket watch, a gift from his mother upon departing for Washington as a freshly appointed lieutenant, and noted the time. "Perhaps you will allow me to see you home as I've other pressing business."

"Thank you, no." She spared him neither a glance nor the courtesy of her attention as she focused on a point somewhere behind him.

No?

He paused to consider the benefits of allowing Emilie Gayarre her wish. Walking away seemed the best choice, yet the wrecker had asked a favor. His word was his bond. "Then perhaps I might offer the use of my office while I am away."

"No." Again her word was a dismissal. She obviously deemed him unworthy of her attention.

Irritation flared anew, and he bit back a sharp retort.

"Despite your promise to my brother-in-law, I bid you leave me, sir."

Irritation flamed to anger, reminding him of the mark she left on his flesh and the threat she had become to his heart and his career. "You appear to need no further coddling, Miss Gayarre." He tipped his hat. "Thus I shall take my leave and make my apologies to your brother-in-law at a later date."

"Coddling?" Her shoulders straightened, and pink stains climbed into her cheeks. "I believe you know quite well from your life as a pirate—excuse me, as a privateer—that I can take care of myself. It is my regret that I shot you, and for that I beg your forgiveness."

Her tone had caught the attention of a few

bystanders, who now stared openly. Caleb forced a smile and reached to grasp Emilie by the elbow. She made to shake him off, then found she could not. For a moment, her eyes widened; then, as if realizing she was caught but standing among friends, they narrowed.

With care, he leaned toward her. "This conversation will not be held in such a public forum. After you, Miss Gayarre," he said.

"Interesting," she said. "Previously you referred to me as Miss Crusoe."

His grip tightened slightly as he led the schoolteacher toward the edge of the crowd. Along the way, he smiled at anyone who stared and made sure, as much as possible, to keep his feelings about Emilie Gayarre's statement off his face.

The far end of the dock looked empty, so he half-led and half-dragged her to that spot. "Madam, I am to be the judge of this district and the highest authority of the law outside of the admiralty court in Key West. Are you certain you would like to make that accusation?"

"Sir," she said as Caleb allowed her to remove herself from his grasp, "you could be President Jackson himself, and I'd make that accusation given the same circumstances."

He felt it prudent not to mention that President Jackson would likely not have the patience Caleb did. At least he'd heard stories to that effect in Washington circles.

"True, you've made a trip to the barber since I saw you last." She pointed to his left shoulder. "But I say that beneath that very proper and official navy uniform is the scar from a bullet wound that obviously did not pierce your heart, though I nearly drove myself to distraction believing it had."

"To distraction?" The question slipped out, surprise being its source. Caleb decided to make light of it. "Why would a woman of such character fret over a pirate?" He paused. "Excuse me, a privateer."

She looked down her nose at him, much as that was possible despite his superior height. "Prove me wrong."

He shook his head and attempted indignation. "Madam, would you honestly have me strip to the waist here in this public place so that you might view my chest? Is that the sort of decorum a schoolteacher should exhibit?" Caleb paused. "I think not."

"You know the reason for it," she said. "And I'll broach no further questions as to my character from one who hides his own."

Ouch. She has a point.

The Gayarre woman turned and fled his company without so much as a backward glance. Caleb touched the spot on his shoulder where the bullet had entered and wondered how many more conversations like today's would happen before he gave his past away.

"Getting to know the locals?"

Caleb turned to see Judge Campbell heading his direction. "Hardly," he said. "What's the status on the wrecker?"

The judge shrugged. "Good news. Just a nasty bump on the head and a broken arm that will likely heal straight and strong in time. It's the strangest thing, though. All that fire, and not a burn on him. His clothes were singed, but not a mark otherwise."

"Interesting. Sort of puts one in mind of Daniel in the Old Testament, doesn't it?"

"It does indeed," Judge Campbell said. "He's going to be fine, but that ship of his is a total loss."

"That's too bad," Caleb said. "Though I understand the fellow was master on two wrecks in two days. Likely he'll manage to find a way to purchase a new boat with some of that."

"Likely," the judge echoed, "but for now our concern is processing what they've brought in." He slapped Caleb on the back and grinned. "We were still working on last night's intake, and now we've got another. Looks like it's going to be a long night for you, Judge Spencer."

"For me?" Caleb shook his head. "You're not leaving all this to me, are you? I've not been trained to—"

Judge Campbell stopped short. "You're not qualified?"

Caught, he could only shrug. "Of course," he

said. "I will do whatever work needs to be done."

"Glad to hear it," he said with a laugh. "The wife planned a big dinner to celebrate my retirement, and I'd like to be home for it." He turned to leave.

"And if I have questions?"

"Ask Mrs. O'Mara," he called over his shoulder. "She's just returned from the mainland at my request. I'm certain you'll find her expertise invaluable."

"Mrs. O'Mara?" Caleb could only watch the old man disappear into the crowd. "Who in the world is Mrs. O'Mara?"

Emilie opened her cottage gate, exhaustion tugging at the corners of her mind. It had been a long day, and from where the sun stood, an even longer time would pass before she could seek the solace of her bed. She walked around to the back and deposited her bonnet on the hook beside the back door. Her shoes came next as she kicked them off along with the sand she'd tracked from the docks.

Finally, she opened the door and stepped inside. The first thing she noticed was the bouquet of flowers on the table. Next to it sat a bowl filled with freshly picked mangoes. Completing the picture was a plate covered with a dish towel.

Her stomach complained as she lifted the dish towel and found two of Mrs. Campbell's biscuits, a serving of smoked ham, and a slice of pie. Then she spied the flashes of color through the window.

Someone, likely Ruby O'Shea, had done the washing. In a neat line were all three of her nightgowns as well as the dress she'd lent Ruby.

What a dear woman.

By now, she and the girls should be comfortably settled in the boardinghouse. "I'll have to thank her when I see her next."

Perhaps she would make a stop there later on her way to visit Micah. At the thought of the wrecker, she sent a prayer of thanks for the miracle that kept her friend from certain death in the fiery inferno of the wreck.

Then her thoughts turned to Lieutenant Spencer.

How could a man move from a pirate vessel to a judgeship, from dead to alive? There had to be a reasonable explanation.

She went over every moment of that last horrible morning aboard the *Cormorant*, from awakening to a man in her room to aiming the pistol at him the moment he turned his back, then shooting.

Realization struck, and had she been standing, she probably would have crumpled. "I shot him when he turned his back. He wasn't coming after me at all."

CHAPTER 30

August 15, 1836

Caleb looked up from the packet of mail to the one who had delivered it. "So you're Mrs. O'Mara."

The older woman, a veritable bundle of energy in what was otherwise a drab and dull office, paused in the middle of singing some obscure hymn whose melody sounded familiar. "I am," she said.

"And what exactly is it that you do?"

"Up until last September when the big storm came through, I was in charge of caring for the prisoners," she said. "If there was no one in the jail, then I took in washing and did a little sewing on the side. That storm sent me heading to the mainland, but I missed this island something awful. Judge Campbell offered me the job of postmistress."

"I see. And to what do I owe the honor today?"

She seemed reluctant to answer, then finally stopped her humming and nodded. "The judge asked me to see to your training, actually."

He shook his head. "Let me get this straight. I'm to be trained by a seamstress?"

She shrugged. "You could do worse. I have worked in this building longer than you," she said. "Though I'm sure you're good at whatever it is you do."

At whatever it is he did? Caleb bit back a stinging retort. What he had done the past two days was to see to the cataloguing of every item taken off the two ships that had wrecked since his arrival. He'd practically begun to count in his sleep, such was the tedious nature of the work.

The postmistress made her excuses and left, the same obscure verse following her until the door shut. Caleb cradled his head in his hands, then jerked upright to swat at one of the ever-present island mosquitoes.

"What have I gotten myself into?" he muttered under his breath as he broke the seal on the mail packet. "No wonder Griffin was so happy to send me off to this judgeship."

Caleb dumped the stack of papers onto his already cluttered desk and began to sort through them. The pile from insurance companies quickly filled one corner of the available space. Each would have to be dealt with, and likely all expected a quick reply. Then came correspondence from the Admiralty Court. That stack was smaller but, to his mind, infinitely more important. A third stack contained three thick letters from his mother and one slender bit of correspondence from Fletcher.

He tossed the packet aside and, to his surprise, a letter fell to the floor. Retrieving it, Caleb checked the front to see where in his rudimentary filing system it might fit. He could find no name for the sender, so he turned it over and broke the seal.

"I know who you are, Benning, and who you are pretending to be."

Dropping the page as if it had burned his fingers, he stared at the handwriting. It gave no clue as to the document's origin, which served to further infuriate him. Kicking at it with his boot only caused the page to slide a few inches, and reading the words made his blood boil. As he studied the flourishes and loops of the fancy handwriting, an idea occurred. This looked more like the work of a woman than a man. A man would be less vague, he decided, and certainly would not resort to this kind of trickery should he have any pride in himself.

No, blackmail was a woman's game. And he knew only one woman who could both write and hold something over his head. Quickly, lest prying eyes return, Caleb picked up the letter.

"So you wish to blackmail me?" He rose, jammed his hat on his head, and reached for his coat, the blood thrumming in his temples. "Well, Miss Gayarre, perhaps you have not yet realized that one cannot blackmail a judge. Perhaps Mrs. O'Mara will find work in her former job as jailer before the day is done."

He got all the way down the sidewalk before he realized he had no idea where to find the woman who likely would never stop plaguing him. To ask for directions would be quite impossible, for he would rather wander about town than have his destination known.

And then he realized that the first place to look for a schoolteacher was at the school.

It was warm, even by August standards, and the dampness that seemed to seep into his pores was nearly visible as he climbed the path to the schoolhouse. Caleb drifted toward the edge of the summit where all of Fairweather Key lay before him, the town to his left and behind him, and the ocean as far as he could see in a complete circle.

He'd discovered on his first week in Fairweather Key that the view from here was nothing short of breathtaking. Pale green water faded to blue as it moved away from the shore. Beyond the patch of blue was a near-perfect line of gray that poured over the horizon and melted into clouds of the same color. Indeed, one had to stare to determine where the water stopped and the clouds began.

God had spent extra time in this place, of that Caleb was certain.

"Judge Spencer, I would advise not remaining in the sun for an extended amount of time." Caleb turned to see Miss Gayarre standing in the shade of the schoolhouse doorway. "It is a known fact that too much sun can wither a brain and cause delusions."

So he'd been correct in his assumption. "Good afternoon, Miss Gayarre. I would have a word with you on a legal matter."

337

She looked at him as if this had already happened, though, to her credit, she did not say so. Rather, she disappeared inside, obviously assuming he would follow her lead.

He did, and when his eyes adjusted to the dimmer light, he found her seated at a desk in the front of what was obviously the classroom. Neat rows of tables were lined by twos, each with benches corresponding to the height of the tables. Toward the front, the tables were lower as if made for small children, while in the back were desks Caleb could have found serviceable if not comfortable.

Someone had tacked up a spelling chart with the alphabet in the center of the wall beside Miss Gayarre's desk. Around this were what looked like folded papers. Upon closer inspection, he noted the papers resembled animals and other objects.

"Origami," she said with what sounded like cool disdain. "It is an ancient Oriental art form."

"I know," he said, "though I am surprised to find you've heard of it."

Her dark brows rose. "Do I look like some sort of cretin, sir?"

"Cretin?" Caleb shook his head, his expression carefully neutral. "Hardly."

Other words came unbidden, but he kept silent. Here in this place with a slanderous and threatening letter in his pocket and a vision in yellow to blame, she was merely another likely suspect.

Even if she was the prettiest suspect he'd ever questioned. And question her he would, as soon as he could gather his wits and remember what to ask.

Emilie sat at the table Micah had built for her and cradled her head in her hands while the new judge paced. It was all too much, this day. Tears threatened, but Emilie refused to allow them to be shed. Not in front of Caleb Spencer or the Benning.

Or whoever he was.

Emilie lifted her head and squared her shoulders. The light seemed to go out of the room in degrees as the sunshine outside faded. The gathering gloom matched her mood.

"You have my attention," she said, "though how long you can maintain it remains to be seen."

He moved a few steps toward her, and then, seemingly distracted by the view, gravitated toward the window. In silhouette, the judge's features sharpened, only serving to highlight his high cheekbones and firm jaw. As if he'd forgotten she was watching, he absentmindedly rubbed a spot on his left shoulder just above his heart, then flexed his shoulder.

He turned to face her. "I would have a handwriting sample from you. Lest you wonder, this is an official request."

She reached for the pen and ink. "What would you have me write?"

His dark brows rose. "So you're willing then?"

What an odd question. But then he was an odd man. "Why would I refuse?"

Judge Spencer seemed a bit confused by the question. "Please write what I tell you." He paused to allow her to prepare. "At the proper time, I will offer a proposition."

"What a strange sentence. Why would you have me write this?"

"You seem genuinely unaware of the words' meaning." He leaned against the window frame and crossed his arms over his chest. "If you are truly innocent, then you will do as I ask and have no concern for the reason."

Emilie rolled her eyes. "I'll need the words again, please."

"At the proper time," he said slowly, "I will offer a proposition."

"At the proper time," she said as she wrote, the lengthening shadows making the writing difficult, "I will propose an offer."

"No," he said quickly. "I will offer a proposition."

She gave him a look meant to let him know exactly how she felt about the prospect of repeating the writing exercise. "This will have to suffice," she said as she pressed the page toward him across the desk. "Now, if that's all, perhaps I can leave."

"Not yet." He walked over to retrieve the paper, then strode to the back of the room to take a seat at

William's desk, where the light from the windows still offered enough illumination to read. "Stay where you are," he said, "while I take a look at this."

"Would you like me to light a lamp?"

"The light is sufficient for my purposes," he said as he seemed to set about ignoring her completely.

Emilie toyed with the edge of her desk, then strained to see the source of the gathering gloom. Judging from the slice of gray she could see from where she sat, one of those Florida late summer storms was imminent. Reverend Carter called them gully washers. Emilie termed them a major inconvenience.

In either case, the storm could be as little as a dusting of raindrops that lowered the heat and chased the mosquitoes away for a few precious hours. It could also send torrents of water over everything and everyone, turning dirt streets into muddy rivers and sending everything in its path downstream to the harbor.

All the more reason to leave this exposed summit before the rains, whether light or strong, blocked her exit. "If you've no further need of me," she said as she rose, leaning against the desk when her knees nearly failed, "I'll be going. I wouldn't advise your lingering, as it appears we're in for bad weather."

The judge stunned her with the intensity of his stare. "Sit."

Sit? Was she now relegated to the status of a house pet?

Emilie made to complain, then thought better of it. When Papa got this way, she'd usually managed to soothe him and get her way not by protest but by placating.

Papa. She stifled a sigh.

"Of course," Emilie said sweetly, though the taste of the words bit at her tongue. "Perhaps this would be the time for me to discuss something with you."

Emilie waited for his response. When there was none, she rested her palms on the desk and said a quick prayer for guidance on what she knew might be a difficult issue to resolve.

That she was in no mood to be pleasant added to the urgent need for prayer.

She decided to begin carefully and with a general statement. "Perhaps Judge Campbell mentioned the issue we've had with schooling our children here on the island."

The judge set her page on the table and pulled something from his jacket pocket. In the process, she watched him wince and rub his left shoulder just above his heart. "Yes, he mentioned it," he said. "I was warned there might be an issue."

His dark head bobbed as he seemed to shift his attention from the page upon which she'd written to whatever he'd pulled from his pocket. Her silence seemed to have gone unnoticed.

Caleb Spencer lifted his gaze to meet her pointed stare. A lock of hair fell across his forehead, and he made no move to sweep it back. "So," he said. "Is that all?"

Outside the wind kicked up and peppered fine, sugary sand through gaps in the boards. It settled between them like the unanswered questions of the day. "I know there are funds for this sort of thing. Wrecking is a profitable industry."

There, let him deny these facts.

Judge Spencer's expression remained unreadable, though a flash of light from outside briefly illuminated the room. "Is that all?"

"Isn't that enough?" Emilie tamped down her rising temper. "Mr. Tate needs his home, and we need a school. There is money for a school." Her fingers curled into fists that she quickly hid in her lap. "Further, it is within your purview to grant this," she said a bit more sweetly.

"I suppose it is." He rose and pushed the bench back under the table. "But I fail to understand why the wrecker cannot just take up lodging at the boardinghouse. If it's suitable for my purposes, I warrant he will find it acceptable for his."

She paused. Caleb Spencer made a valid argument. Yet it just did not seem right that a man who owned a home would be forced to pay to live elsewhere.

A low rumble interrupted her thoughts. "Was that thunder?"

Judge Spencer walked to the window and peered out, and Emilie took a moment to study him. Indeed there was no mistaking the man who had saved her from Thomas Hawkins. His width of shoulder and brevity of speech and the way he seemed to favor his left side marked him as the Benning.

The Benning who'd been shot but lived.

A sigh escaped before Emilie could prevent it. Emilie felt the room sway, likely due to her combined lack of sleep over the past couple of days and difficulty in believing the recent course of events. Only with concentration did she remain upright in the chair. Once the moment passed, she determined to leave this room lest she make a fool of herself by swooning like some insipid schoolgirl.

Perhaps after a good night's rest, she would not see the Benning in this man at all. Indeed, the idea appealed.

Blinking hard, she forced the room to right itself, then waited while the woozy feeling passed. She must find the path to her door before she humiliated herself. She needed the privacy of her cottage and the comforting embrace of the Lord to sort through all He'd allowed since her discovery of the Benning.

Two things stood in the way: her inability to rise, and the man who stood between her and the door.

As if hearing her thoughts, the judge turned to

stare. "Give me one reason I should consider your request," he said, "and please do not attempt to sway me with anything less than logic."

"Meaning?"

He shifted positions, bringing his features into view. "Meaning sentiment will not sway my superiors when I divulge the purpose for what I assume will be quite a large expense."

"I see."

"So, please, the facts, Miss Gayarre." He shook his head. "Tell me one good reason I should even entertain this idea when it is abundantly clear the previous judge did not."

Emilie opened her mouth to speak, but he stopped her with a wave of his hand. "I would have you put that reason in writing and submit it formally."

CHAPTER 31

The handwriting sample she had given proved beyond a shadow of a doubt that Emilie Gayarre had not written the threatening letter. But if she hadn't, who had?

If she gave a response, he did not hear or see it, for the heady scent of damp earth drew him back to his days in Santa Lucida where the rain often came without warning only to leave the island freshly scrubbed and glistening. For the first time since he boarded the *Cormorant* for his trip to

Washington by way of Havana, Caleb felt the tug of his grandfather's ways drawing him back, when in reality, his career aspirations could only draw him forward.

It was a conundrum. The only sure thing in all of his confusion was the fact that he did not belong in Fairweather Key.

There were two ways out; this he knew. He could leave the naval department and go home to Santa Lucida, likely to take over his grandfather's duties, or he could persevere, working to earn his way out of this swamp and back into the drawing rooms of Washington's elite.

A discreet letter to President Jackson might do the trick, although the president was not held in the favor he once had been. An alliance with him now might bring on a worse assignment than Caleb now held.

"Then I shall," he heard the schoolteacher say, though he had to think hard on the words to remember what she referred to.

"I shall await your formal letter."

Caleb glanced out the window as the first fat drops of rain began to fall. Only stubborn stupidity had kept him in the schoolhouse well past the point when he knew he should have made his departure. Now there were two choices: stay here with the Gayarre woman or make his escape and get a good soaking in the process.

While he was not averse to a rainstorm, the lightning did give him pause, especially situated as they were at the highest point on all of Fairweather Key. Caleb glanced through the gloom at Miss Gayarre, who looked even less pleased to be in his company than he was to be in hers.

At least she had not endured a bullet at his hand.

Caleb rolled his shoulders to alleviate the stiffness that accompanied both the fresh onset of rain and the memory of that voyage. Perhaps by staring out at the torrential downpour, he could focus his prayers on changing the weather rather than on the temptation to change his thoughts about what should happen to the woman who shot him.

He knew God's opinion on the subject, but the fact that he'd suffered, that he'd lost the prime posting he'd desired, only to be exiled to this island, was more than ample reason to see that she, too, had suffered consequences.

What sort of consequences, he'd never exactly clarified in his mind. And now, as he thought on it, the whole concept did seem a bit foolish. Instead, he explored the idea of forgetting, just for a time, the crimes against him committed by the schoolteacher with whom he was now well and truly stuck. For from the looks of the weather, things would get much worse before they got better. Another glance at the schoolteacher told him the same just might be true for her.

Caleb decided to lighten the mood. It was better,

he decided, than lighting the lamps. At least in the semi-darkness, he did not have to look upon the beauty that brought such confusion to what had once been a well-ordered life.

Yet look he did.

She sat very still at the makeshift desk, her head cradled in her hands. One dark curl had loosened itself from the confines of the ridiculous bonnet and now snaked about her wrist. Caleb wondered for a moment if the blue-black strands would feel as soft as they looked.

Dangerous thoughts, fool. Watch yourself lest she talk you out of more than just a schoolhouse.

Her shoulders begin to sag. He thought, but could not be sure, he saw a tear glistening and suspended for a second between the fingers of her right hand and the desktop.

When it splashed on the polished wood, Caleb knew for sure. Emilie Gayarre was crying.

He suppressed a groan. Even when faced with the loaded cannons of the larger vessel *Hawk's Remedy*, Caleb had not felt this ill-equipped to handle the situation.

Then, in a moment of clarity, he saw the weeping for what it was: a ploy. Just as Thomas Hawkins had wanted him to believe the pirate vessel was the superior ship, so Emilie Gayarre surely wanted him to believe hers was the superior plan for the education of Fairweather Key schoolchildren. And when he did not immediately fall for her ruse, she set about using her feminine wiles to catch him in her net.

Well, it absolutely would not work. No more than the criminal Hawkins found his ploy successful.

Caleb studied the toes of his boots until he could be sure his temper was securely under control. To think he'd almost fallen into the spider's web with thoughts of glossy curls and wide brown eyes.

When he looked up, she'd begun to sniffle and dab at those eyes with some sort of lacy handkerchief so covered with embroidered flowers that even from here, he wondered whether one would rub off and land on her cheek.

She met his gaze and, rather than hide her affliction, boldly blew her nose.

"Stop that," he snapped.

"Stop lying to me." The schoolteacher looked as stunned to have said the words as he felt to hear them.

"I've not yet told you a lie, and do not intend to do so in the future."

But wasn't allowing someone to believe what was not completely true also a lie? He shoved away the question along with its equally uncomfortable answer.

"You are the Benning." A statement, not a question.

"I am Caleb Spencer, Miss Gayarre, and I defy you to prove otherwise." The moment the words were out, he suppressed a groan.

"Take off your shirt," she said, her voice without inflection. "An unmarked left shoulder will be your defense."

"Surely you jest," was his pathetic response.

"I assure you I am quite serious."

Her expression told him she was. *"And ye shall know the truth, and the truth shall make you free."* Yet the truth felt like a burden rather than an offer of freedom.

Miss Gayarre continued to stare, the handkerchief hanging limp in her hand.

To his utter astonishment, she rose on what appeared to be wobbly legs and walked right past him and out into the storm.

He went out to fetch her and haul her back inside draped over his good shoulder, one arm restraining her kicks and the other swiping the rain from his face.

"Put me down!" the schoolteacher shouted as she beat on his back with fists that carried surprising strength.

Once back inside the schoolhouse, Caleb was faced with a dilemma. As he'd tossed her over his shoulder like a bag of root vegetables—the better to retrieve her without argument or injury to himself—he could now see no gentle way to set her down.

Whether he dropped her or merely placed her feet on the ground, her flailing about would likely cause complications. To hold the woman any tighter would be to further cross the bounds of impropriety.

There was only one thing to do. As commander of this island, he must regain control.

"Cease this immediately," he said with as much authority as he could muster under the circumstances, "or I shall be forced to treat you like the child your behavior emulates."

"Child? How dare you insinuate such a thing? Why . . . ?" She paused, though her struggling continued. "What sort of threat are you making?"

"Well, Miss Gayarre," he said as he shifted the wiggling bundle to ease the twinge in his sore shoulder. "What is it you do when one of your students misbehaves?"

She stilled, but only for a moment. "You wouldn't."

Of course not, but she did not know that. "Are you certain of this?"

Instantly, the fight went out of her. Caleb waited to be sure of it before sliding her to the floor. "I will turn my back to allow you to compose yourself," he said, "but make no mistake: Neither of us is leaving until it is safe to do so."

Even as he let her out of his sight, Caleb was careful to stand between the Gayarre woman and the door. If she tried the foolish move once, she might do it again.

As he waited, Caleb became aware of the silence in the room. Only the rain on the roof and its accompanying thunder broke the stillness.

"May I turn around?"

When she did not answer, he braved a look over his shoulder. She, too, had turned away, and all he could see was a blue bonnet, damp curls, and shoulders sagging forward.

"Miss Gayarre?"

Still no response.

Slowly, Caleb reached out to touch his palm to her shoulder. "Miss Gayarre, please accept my apologies for handling you so roughly. It's just that I feared for your—"

To his surprise, the shoulder beneath his palm stiffened. "It . . . is . . . all . . . too . . . much."

He felt terrible. Her voice, once so strong and defiant, held the tone of the child he'd just accused her of becoming. Worse, she began to tremble.

Caleb jerked back his hand to slide out of his jacket and place it around her. "Miss Gayarre?"

Even with the oversized jacket around her, the schoolteacher continued to shake. Caleb stepped around to stand in front of her. Carefully, he lifted her chin.

Her face was streaked with what had to be tears, not raindrops, and her eyes remained downcast. To see her now made him almost wish for the defiant woman who'd run out into the rain.

"It's all too much," she repeated.

"What's all too much?" he echoed as frustration over his inability to understand rose.

"You were the first man to kiss me, yet . . ."

Tears spattered the toe of his boot as he took a step toward her. Searching for words caused his frustration to soar, and his inability to find them gave him pause to consider his next move.

Her chin tilted up to reveal a face now splotched with red and streaked with tears. Their gazes met. Perhaps he leaned forward, or maybe it was the schoolteacher who made the first move to fall into his embrace. The result was that Emilie Gayarre laid her head against his chest at the very spot where she'd once put a bullet.

CHAPTER 32

How long Emilie cried, her ear against Caleb Spencer's chest and his rapidly beating heart, she had no idea. Reality crept up on her slowly, pushing away the clouds of grief until she saw clearly where she was and what she'd done.

With a start, she backed out of the judge's arms and stood shaking like a fool. What had she been thinking to bare her pain to Caleb Spencer? Worse, to allow him to comfort her?

Clarity brought fresh grief along with the shame of letting her guard down with the last man she ever should have allowed to see her vulnerability. Fresh anger surprised her as the accusation spilled out.

"I believed I was a murderer," Emilie said and felt him sigh. "But I am not."

"No," he said in a voice that was at once soft yet clear enough to be heard over the pounding rain.

She dared not look away, dared not move. "So you admit you are he."

When he did not respond, she felt the tears well up again.

"The island, the kiss," she said. "Will you also deny those?"

He looked away and said nothing, then reached for his pocket watch. "I think there have been enough questions for tonight."

Something fell away from her shoulders, and Emilie realized she'd somehow donned his jacket. The judge reached down to retrieve it, and Emilie seized the opportunity to pick up her skirts and run out into the rain.

At first, her bonnet absorbed the worst of the rain, allowing Emilie to see her way toward the path to town clearly. Then, by degrees, the fabric lost its starch and drooped dangerously into her eyes. In order to swipe it away, she would have to let go of a corner of her skirt, which might then cause her to tumble down the steep hill.

It was, in all, quite the conundrum.

Emile sidestepped a puddle the size of her wash tub only to splash into another that had been hidden in the dark. She tromped on, the hem of her skirt now sodden with enough mud and rainwater to cause her to feel as if she was pulling it rather than wearing it.

Then her shoe caught in soft ground. Only the fact that it slipped off her foot and remained in the bog saved Emilie from a slide toward town on her backside.

"What next, Lord?" she called as lightning zigged dangerously across the sky and thunder cracked in its wake. "That was my best shoe."

The hairs on her arms rose. Likely her shoe would see tomorrow, but if she turned back to fetch it, she might not.

Emilie picked up her pace, slinging her head back to force the sodden bonnet out of her eyes. The resulting rain peppering her face stung her eyes and temporarily blinded her, but to stop until she could see would be to risk allowing the judge to catch up to her.

That could not happen.

It simply could not.

She'd had all she could stand, and even if it meant walking through the worst weather the island had seen since last fall's hurricane, so be it. Anything was better than spending one more minute caged in the small space with that man.

Once she reached the safety of her cottage, all would be well and worth the trouble.

"Miss Gayarre, I really must insist—" she heard just before a particularly loud crash of thunder.

The wind drove raindrops against her ear and through the soaked fabric of the bonnet as if it weren't there. Still she pressed on, taking one step and then another until the ground came close to leveling out.

A group of Geiger trees hid the sharp turn that led to a fork in the road. To the right was the beach, while the left led to town. She took the path to the left by habit rather than sight, as seeing her way was quite impossible except when lightning illuminated her surroundings and cast the world in an eerie silver glow.

Soon the buildings of Fairweather Key's downtown area came into view. Resisting the urge to see if her companion had followed, Emilie ran on until she reached the wooden sidewalk that led past the now-darkened and shuttered businesses. At the parsonage, she paused but a moment, then decided against stopping. There would be time enough to speak to Reverend Carter tomorrow. She pressed on past the trim cottage where her sister's lamps burned bright, past the clinic where no doubt Micah Tate was resting, and past the funeral parlor where it seemed only yesterday that she'd seen to the arrangements for her brother's burial.

Here and there, a curtain would lift and fall, but she saw no one. Likewise, the streets were barren of all signs of life. Faster now, and off across the path to take the road leading to her cottage.

Lightning streaked the sky as if showing her the way. By the time she reached the garden gate, she could barely go any farther. Somehow she climbed the steps, stumbled across the porch, and practically fell inside to slam and latch the door, leaving a trail of mud and rainwater from the parlor to the kitchen.

Emilie threw off her soiled garments and washed without lighting the lamps, then padded into her bedroom to don a fresh gown. It smelled of soap and sunshine, and those were the things she thought of as she fell asleep, heedless of the fact that it was barely past dinnertime.

When the wrecker's warning bell jarred her from her sleep, Emilie rolled over and closed her eyes while the rain pounding on the roof lulled her back to her dreams.

August 16, 1836

The warehouse was full, and so was Caleb's coffee cup. With only a few hours' sleep, he felt as old as the antique silver service that was spread out in pieces on the table nearest the door. He looked around and shook his head. Until a full accounting of all valuables removed from last night's wreck was made, he'd not rest.

"Ready to quit yet?"

Caleb turned to see the injured wrecker Micah Tate in the doorway. "Aren't you supposed to be in the clinic?"

He shrugged, then gestured toward the arm tied up in a black sling. "I'm not one for lying around and waiting to feel better."

"I see."

He took a few steps forward, then stopped. "I'm here to ask for work," he said. "Looks like you're in need of some help, and I know I'm in need of something to occupy my time."

Despite the man's stellar reputation, Caleb was skeptical. "Why here?"

Tate nodded as if considering the question. Slowly, he began to smile. "I reckon I should be honest with you, Judge Spencer."

Caleb leaned against the table and folded his hands over his chest. "That would be best."

"I've got nowhere to go and nothing to do until this arm's back to working right." He paused. "I was master on two wrecks last week, but you and I both know it takes time for that to pay out."

The process was lengthy, this Caleb was just learning. First the insurance companies had to be satisfied and then the owners. Last, the wreckers and the master saw their portions, but not until the auctioneer and the local authorities took their cuts.

"I'm an honest, God-fearing man, Judge Spencer, and I need something to fill my time. I've been talking to the reverend about helping at the church, but that's not going to be anything but part time." Another pause. "Reverend Carter's wanting me to preach."

"So you're a preacher, are you?"

"No, I'm a wrecker, but the reverend, he says the Lord's got plans for me." Micah shrugged. "But I didn't come here to talk about that. Are you going to try and do this all by yourself, or are you going to do the smart thing and hire me?"

Caleb laughed, then met the wrecker halfway to shake his hand. "Welcome aboard, Mr. Tate," he said. "When can you start?"

"Now's as good a time as any," the redhead said. "Where do I begin?"

Ten minutes later Caleb was headed back to his office, secure in the knowledge that Micah Tate would do as good a job as he, possibly better. He sorted through several stacks of papers, but as his eyes began to glaze over, he decided to gather some of them up to take back to the boarding-house.

When he walked in the door, fully expecting to be greeted by the ever-curious Mrs. Campbell, he found a trio of girlish voices harmonizing, while a woman sang the most lovely melody. Caleb crept closer to the kitchen, being careful not to call attention to his arrival.

There he found the woman named Ruby, who now helped Mrs. Campbell, standing at the stove, stirring something that smelled heavenly. At the table, three straw-haired girls bent over what looked like a schoolbook. A second glance showed the item to be a cookbook, though it appeared none of them could read it.

Leaving them to their work, Caleb slipped upstairs to his room and closed the door. Spreading the pages on the cabinet that served as desk and wardrobe, he picked up the most pressing of the group and began to formulate a response.

The attempt at work, however, lasted only as long as it took him to loosen his waistcoat and slip off his boots. He closed his eyes with the purpose of considering a supreme court opinion that seemed applicable to the issue on the page and awoke to the sound of someone calling him to supper.

Caleb sat bolt upright and tried to remember where he was. He'd dreamed of rainstorms and a missing slipper and of the woman who fled from his embrace without retrieving her shoe. She was beautiful, with wide brown eyes and a handkerchief covered with spring flowers and hair that smelled of lavender and salt air.

When she disappeared into a rainstorm, he chased her but could not find her. He spent the rest of the dream searching for the woman with one slipper while grasping its soggy mate in his hand. In the other hand, he held a note that could spell his doom, the ink on the page running in dark rivulets down his hand and leaving a trail in the slick mud.

An altogether odd experience.

"No more naps, and early to bed," he said as he rose to straighten his waistcoat and gather his senses, "lest I begin to believe I've become a part of some strange Brothers Grimm story."

• • •

August 19

Over the next few days, Caleb kept his vow, though it was easier now that he had Micah Tate in his employ. True to the wrecker's word, he had the work done in record time, allowing Caleb to catch up on things the previous judge had let go.

Caleb thanked the Lord for His provision, and thanked Micah Tate by offering him a raise though he'd barely begun his employment.

Among the items Mr. Tate could not handle was the threatening correspondence received on the last mail boat. Caleb locked the soggy remains of the letter in his office and set thoughts of its origin aside. Until further evidence appeared, he could only pass it off as some petty criminal's attempt to rankle a newly appointed judge.

And this judge refused to be rankled, though thoughts of Emilie Gayarre and her schoolhouse came close to accomplishing the feat. On more than one occasion, he'd attempted to research the case of the schoolhouse funding only to find no precedent for or against its construction. Ultimately, he decided, it would come down to whether he could justify the expense.

He concluded he could not. Not if he wanted to return to Washington.

And that, he knew, was what he wanted more than anything.

At least, he believed he did.

Then came the troubling thoughts that plagued him most during the dark nights and while pouring his heart out to the Lord. *"The truth shall set you free."*

But the truth, should it be known, would do just the opposite. The grandson of Ian Benning would never be allowed into the hallowed halls of Washington or, for that matter, be given charge of a seagoing vessel as a member of the United States Navy.

At best, the truth might win him a permanent posting in Fairweather Key. He had only to look at the bitter old judge he'd replaced to know exactly what sort of sentence that was.

Life without hope of parole.

CHAPTER 33

August 22, 1836

The month-long break from school had barely begun, and already Emilie was at her wit's end.

"Good morning, Miss Gayarre," Judge Spencer called. "I wonder if I might have a word with you."

He looked quite fit and rested, a marked contrast from the last time their paths had crossed. The cut of his naval uniform and the swagger in his step served to emphasize this man was not among his peers but rather his constituents. She shook off the memory of their embrace and chose bluster over the embarrassment seizing her.

"With me?" Emilie looked around before shaking her head. "Again?"

Shouldering past a group of dock workers, Caleb Spencer arrived at her side. "Perhaps we should have this conversation elsewhere. In my office?"

"I don't know, Judge Spencer," she said. "Our discussion at the schoolhouse certainly had the gossips' tongues wagging. In the future, perhaps our conversations should be held in a more public place."

"Gossips? Whatever would they find to say about us?" He looked truly perplexed. Then, slowly, understanding dawned. "You mean, they think I, that is we, that . . ."

Heat flamed her cheeks as she recalled the frantic warning Isabelle had given regarding the talk at the mercantile the morning after the storm. It seemed as though someone had been looking out their window at just the right time to see her run past, her skirts raised and at least one foot bare.

Evidently the judge had been close enough behind for the seeds of doubt to be planted. In a town as small as Fairweather Key, it took no time for the word to spread that the new judge had chased the schoolteacher down the hill in a raging storm.

What might they have said if they'd seen Caleb and her moments before she fled the cabin?

In any case, Caleb Spencer seemed to be the only one who hadn't heard the story.

"Don't be ridiculous." He turned to note a gaggle of fishermen's wives staring from their circle near the edge of the docks. "Your reputation, Miss Gayarre," he said as he raised his voice to a level they could not miss, "is beyond reproach, and anyone who might think otherwise is welcome to speak to me personally on the subject."

When he turned to stare at the women, they fled, likely to convene elsewhere and discuss the brazen judge and the horrified schoolteacher. Oblivious to the damage he'd just caused, Judge Spencer wore a satisfied look as he turned his attention to Emilie.

"No, Miss Gayarre, if you would do me the honor of attending a brief meeting in my office, I would be greatly appreciative." Again he looked around, this time catching the attention of several elderly women seemingly out for a morning stroll. "I warrant the subject of your reputation will not be discussed as this is official business."

She stared at him, unable to believe he could make light of something that was extremely vexing to her. As teacher to the children of Fairweather Key, she could not afford the stain of illicit behavior, even if unsubstantiated.

Refusing to allow the situation to escalate, Emilie straightened her spine and walked away. "Perhaps we can discuss whatever bit of business you have while we walk," she called over her shoulder.

Caleb remained rooted in place. He was the judge of Fairweather Key, and this woman, a mere schoolteacher, must understand this. No longer would he play the fool while she issued edicts then walked away.

He watched her disappear into the crowd until all he could see was a sky blue bonnet dipping and bobbing amongst the fishermen, wreckers, and other dock workers. "This concerns the school," he called at a volume he knew she could not miss hearing.

The bonnet stopped but turned neither to the left nor the right. Caleb leaned against the wooden piling, intent on waiting her out rather than being the first to give in.

Several wreckers strolled past and, upon seeing him, stopped to greet him. As he listened to the men's tales of recent wrecks, storms, and other seafaring topics, he kept his attention focused on the bonnet, which still had not moved.

Finally, he drew his focus back to the conversation and soon found himself enjoying talk of a life he'd tasted only briefly. As they spoke of days at sea, Caleb thought of the *Cormorant* and the feel of salt-tinged spray on his face, of the squeal of dolphins playing in the vessel's wake, of waking up tied to his bunk to keep from rolling off when the seas were rough.

"Judge?"

Caleb shook off the reverie and gave the wrecker his attention. "Sorry. For a moment I was back at sea."

He'd said too much, yet among these men the statement seemed nothing more than a truth they shared. None born to the sea strayed long from its waves, it seemed. Besides, he did wear the uniform of a navy lieutenant.

The moment passed, and the joviality continued until a fetching woman with fair hair appeared at the edge of the crowd, calling the name of Henry. The poor chap, one of the men in their circle, reddened about the ears while his fellow wreckers made jokes at his expense.

"Come now, lads," Caleb said. "Let's not give what we cannot ourselves take."

That quieted all but one of them, a lanky fellow barely out of his teens. "I don't know about you poor married folks," he said, "but the judge and I, we don't have wives callin' us home when we don't wish t' be called. Ain't that right, Judge?"

Caleb nodded.

"Yeah, well, the way I heard it, the judge here might not be single much longer," a portly fellow to his right said as he jabbed the fellow next to him with his elbow.

"What have you heard?" Caleb spoke the words evenly and without inflection. "And more important, from whom?"

Silence reigned. Henry slunk away after his wife shouted for him once again. The others looked longingly after their departed friend, but none made the move to depart.

"I would have an answer, sir." Caleb caught sight of the blue bonnet. Had she moved closer? She certainly wasn't walking this way at the moment, and for that he felt only relief.

"The wife," he began, "seems she heard from Miz Ivan's over at the mercantile who heard from Miz Carraway down to the funeral home."

Caleb gave up on trying to follow the logic of the man's statement and focused on controlling the damage. "Did you stop to think that perhaps this was idle gossip and not based in fact?"

As soon as he asked the question, he saw the bonnet begin to move. Toward him. Caleb swallowed hard.

"I didn't mean no harm, Judge," the wrecker said quickly. "If it ain't so, then it ain't so."

"Yes, well," Caleb said as the bonnet disappeared for a moment, "in the future, I suggest you mention to your wife that she cannot believe everything she hears."

The bonnet reappeared and seemed to be picking up speed. If only the docks weren't so crowded this morning.

"If you gents will excuse me, I'll be off." He bolted from the group.

"Nice chatting, Judge Spencer," the younger

wrecker called. "I'm glad t' hear you're not givin' in t' married life like the rest of these blokes."

Caleb waved in response but picked up his pace.

"I'll pass the word on to the wife," the other wrecker shouted. "I told her the idea of you and the schoolteacher carrying on up at the schoolhouse at all hours wasn't to be believed."

He'd almost reached the safety of the crowd. Then Emilie Gayarre appeared. When she saw him heading in her direction, she froze.

CHAPTER 34

A t the sound of male laughter, Emilie paused. When she heard someone mention carrying on at the schoolhouse at all hours, she found herself quite unable to move.

Upon catching sight of her, the men seemed unwilling to continue their banter. Their leader, Caleb Spencer, however, had the nerve to offer a smile.

Each man who stared—and there were many, for it had obviously become quite the sport to watch her spar with the judge—would likely carry the tale home to his wife.

A sick feeling began in her stomach, followed quickly by an anger that burned in her cheeks. Squaring her shoulders, Emilie turned and walked away.

To where, she had no idea. The cottage beckoned, but the idea of the judge following her to that remote location was unthinkable. Should he show up on her doorstep so soon after the incident in the rain, her reputation would never recover.

Pasting a smile on her face, Emilie greeted those she knew while trying not to bowl down those who got in her way. Finally, she reached the courthouse square where the crowd had thinned to just a few vendors and a half-dozen citizens taking in the morning sunshine. She slowed her pace and allowed a deep breath.

Surely given the situation, Judge Spencer would have the good sense to detour into his office and leave her to her own devices. The sooner the nasty rumors of their supposed love affair died down, the better.

Yet the judge caught up to her, heedless of either of their reputations. "I will make this brief," he said as he cut off her escape. "The answer to the question of funding a new school is no."

He turned and walked away.

"Wait." Emilie fell in step beside the judge, then touched his sleeve. "Elaborate, please."

He stopped to stare at her hand until she removed it. "I've given your written request the proper consideration and found I am unable to accommodate your request for a new school in Fairweather Key."

"And any argument I might make to the contrary?"

"Miss Gayarre, has the time not come to set aside our differences?"

When she did not immediately respond, he set off again toward the courthouse. "Wait," she called to his retreating back. He took the steps two at a time and disappeared inside, leaving her to decide whether to follow or retreat to battle another day.

"Emilie?"

She turned to see Micah Tate approaching, one arm in a sling and a child at his side. As he neared, she saw the fair-haired tot was little Tess O'Shea.

"Hello, you two," she said as she strolled toward them. "It's good to see you out, Micah."

"I understand you've met." Micah looked down at the little girl. "Tess, she doesn't look like she swallowed a tiger to me."

"A tiger?" Emilie smiled as she recalled her last conversation with Tess. "Did she explain?"

Micah chuckled. "No."

Emilie gave him a quick explanation, then shared a laugh with him while Tess wandered off to follow a butterfly as it danced from flower to flower. "How are you feeling?" Emilie asked.

"I'm great." Micah's gaze followed the child, and he grinned. "Once this arm's healed, I'll be even better."

She joined him in watching Tess, who had befriended a pair of elderly ladies and seemed to be entertaining them with some sort of tale. "She's a sweet girl," Emilie said. "Not nearly as quiet as her sisters."

"That's the truth," Micah said. "Breakfast at the

boardinghouse won't be the same once Tess leaves." He seemed to reconsider. "All the O'Shea women will be missed."

Emilie smiled. "Why, Micah Tate, if I didn't know you better, I'd think you might have designs on that little girl's mother."

His face turned near the color of his hair. "I wouldn't call it designs," he said, "but Tess's mama's a nice lady who's landed in a set of hard circumstances."

"I can't imagine what it must have been like." Once she'd spoken the words, Emilie realized they weren't true at all. She could imagine seeing a ship go down with little left to show for what was on it.

At least in her case she had a home and family to return to. As far as Emilie could tell, Ruby O'Shea had no one.

"Emilie?"

She looked up at the wrecker, whose face now wore a troubled expression.

"Something wrong?"

Micah nodded. "I've been hearing some things I don't like. I'm a man who believes in going to the source, so I'm coming directly to you." He shuffled his feet, then let out a long breath.

Her heart sank. "This is about the judge, isn't it?"

"I'll let you tell me, Emilie," he said.

"There's nothing to tell." Tess waved, and she returned the gesture. "Nothing," she added for emphasis.

He seemed to consider her statement. "That's not what I've heard, but I'll believe you if you tell me it's the truth."

"Micah," she said, "I have held several discussions with the judge, and I'll be the first to admit that we don't see eye to eye on the issue of funding the schoolhouse. He and I did hold one of those discussions up at the school, but that's the extent of it." She met his gaze. "You have my word."

"I believe you, Emilie."

"Do you?" She crossed her arms over her chest. "I never thought running home in the rain would get me in so much trouble."

Relief crossed his features. "That's what you were doing?" He laughed. "Yes, I can see you'd try to outrun a storm if you'd set your mind to it."

She tried not to smile. "Laugh if you will, Micah Tate, but some people in this town might decide I'm no longer fit to teach their children."

"Impossible." He gestured to Tess. "Say, would you mind doing me a favor? I told her mama I would keep her busy until lunch time and it's about that now."

Emilie glanced back at the courthouse, then shrugged. "I suppose so. There's nothing left to be done here anyway."

She gathered Tess up and walked her back to the boardinghouse, fielding all sorts of questions along the way. By the time she walked into the kitchen and found Ruby setting the table, she was exhausted.

"Looks like my Tess worked her magic again," Ruby said as she sidestepped Emilie to reach for the plates, then sent Tess out to wash up for lunch. "Did Mr. Tate say whether she behaved herself?"

A child's book sat on the table, calling to mind the unwelcome answer she'd received to the question of building a new school.

"I'm sure she was fine," Emilie said, her mind on the issue of the school. "Now if you'll excuse me, I'll be going."

Ruby set the stack of plates on the table, then rested her hand on her hips. "Something's wrong. Did Tess—"

"No, she was fine. Truly." Emilie sighed. "I got some bad news, that's all."

"Sit," Ruby said. "I've got coffee made."

"Coffee won't fix this, Ruby," she said, "but I appreciate the offer." She looked around. "Where's Mrs. Campbell?"

Ruby wiped her hands on the corner of her apron. "Oh, she's gone off to be with her daughter for a week. She left me in charge."

Emilie smiled.

"So tell me about this problem." She shrugged. "I'm not real educated, but I've been told I've got a good head on my shoulders."

"Oh, I don't know," Emilie began. "I was hoping the new judge would approve the building of a real school for our children. He just informed me that wasn't going to happen."

Ruby shook her head. "Why not? Doesn't he know what a treasure children are?"

"That's what I asked him," Emilie said.

"Did he give a reason?" When Emilie shook her head, Ruby continued. "Well, I've always heard if you don't get the answer you want from a man, you go to the next man up for another opinion."

Go to the next man up. Emilie pondered the statement a moment. Who would Caleb Spencer answer to?

"The secretary of the navy." Emilie laughed and reached over to hug the thin woman with the brilliant logic. "Thank you, Ruby," she said. "I think you may have solved the problem."

"I did?"

"Yes," Emilie said, "you did. Starting today, the citizens of Fairweather Key will have their voices heard in Washington, since we obviously haven't had them heard here."

She ran out of the kitchen and out onto the sidewalk with renewed purpose. By the time the mail cutter returned, she and the other concerned citizens of Fairweather Key would see to it the vessel left with a hold full of letters for the secretary of the navy.

And tonight she would hold a meeting at the school to enlist other parents in the effort.

Her first stop was the mercantile. The owners'

wives, mothers of seven of her students, enthusiastically agreed to pass the word of the meeting. Before she went home, Emilie had either seen or left word with most of the parents.

"I pray this is spread as fast as the gossip," she said as she turned for home.

The thought darkened her mood and sent her mind back to Isabelle's warning regarding what was being said about her run through the rain. If only they knew how little truth was in the rumor that she had any sort of relationship with Caleb Spencer.

"For that matter," she whispered as she opened the garden gate, "I suppose their eyebrows would be quite singed should the gossips realize that upon my first meeting with Judge Spencer I shot him."

CHAPTER 35

Y ou've got to do the right thing by her." Micah Tate stood in the doorway of Caleb's office and waited for a response.

"Come in, Micah," Caleb said, refusing to be baited.

"I'll stand here, if you don't mind."

Caleb looked over the wrecker and noted his fisted hands and rigid stance. "Have I done something to offend you?"

He shook his head. "No, but if you don't do something to fix the problem, you might."

"A strong statement," Caleb said. "Unfortunately, I'm at a loss as to its purpose. Why not sit down and tell me what you're talking about." He rose and gestured to the empty chair on the other side of his desk.

"I said I'd stand, sir."

His temper flared, but Caleb held it back. There was nothing to be accomplished by giving free rein to his anger. This was, he reminded himself, a man of good reputation.

"I respect you, Tate," he said slowly, "and I'll listen to whatever you have to say to me. What I won't do is be insulted or dictated to. So either sit down and talk to me, or get out of my office."

"Fair enough." Micah sat, his back ramrod straight. For a time, he seemed to study the floor. Abruptly, he lifted his gaze to meet Caleb's stare. "I've got something on my mind, Judge." Another pause and then a direct look. "There's been talk about you and the schoolteacher."

Was Micah jealous? "Completely unfounded, I assure you."

"Yet that doesn't stop tongues from wagging." Micah pushed back from the desk but made no move to rise. The look on the wrecker's face told Caleb he might be there for a while.

Finally, Caleb let out a long sigh. "Tate," he said slowly, "if you have the prescription for that ailment, please enlighten me."

"Actually, I do." His eyes narrowed. "The gos-

376

sips are talking because it appears you and Emilie are carrying on and don't want anyone to know about it. What's not good hides from the light. That's what the Bible says."

Dread mixed with curiosity caused Caleb to nod. "Go on."

"So it's a simple matter of doing things the right way. Go to the reverend and ask for permission to court her."

"Court her?" Caleb rose, unable to believe his ears. "Are you serious, man? Court Emilie Gayarre?"

The wrecker stood and met his gaze. "Dead serious," he said with the tone of one who would not back down. "And I'd say the alternative's not a pleasant choice."

Caleb could only stare as the blood boiled at his temples and his fingers itched to form fists. "Are you challenging me?"

"No," Tate said. "You'd best me, and I know it. I'm no fool. The others think you're some Washington bureaucrat, but I know that's not all there is to you."

It didn't take a smart man to know this line of conversation could easily veer further into the dangerous. Rather than deflect it, Caleb decided to remain silent.

"I've been watching you, and I think there's more to you than what you're letting on." Caleb worked to keep his expression neutral as Micah returned to his seat. "I see a man with sea legs. Do you know what those are?"

He did. "Isn't that to be expected when a man's a naval officer, Tate?"

The wrecker continued to stare, even as he rested his palms on his knees. "I suppose," he said grudgingly.

The clock behind him struck the noon hour. Time to end this conversation. "Did I misunderstand when you called the schoolteacher your Emilie?"

"I did say that." The wrecker looked away. "But I had plenty of time to think on things while I was laid up over at Doc's place."

Caleb resisted the urge to ask for clarification.

"Long after you've left us, Emilie Gayarre will still be here. I intend to see that she'll be teaching our children as long as she wants."

"And that's why you gave up your home? So Miss Gayarre would stay and teach?" Caleb shook his head. "For a man who believes God has someone else for him, you're certainly sounding besotted."

Micah Tate rose with a look in his eye that told Caleb he'd gone too far. "I don't have to explain my motives to you, Judge Spencer. Emilie Gayarre is a good woman, but people are saying bad things about her, and it all comes back to you. I know more than I've said, and I'm not allowing this situation to continue without doing something about it."

"Is that so?"

The wrecker dipped his head. "It is."

"And what would that be?"

"I'm starting with trying to talk some sense into you."

Caleb crossed his arms over his chest. "Save your breath. I'm not building a school, and no amount of coercion is going to change my mind."

Micah shook his head. "I'm an honest man. The Lord doesn't honor anything but the truth, and He surely doesn't honor coercion."

"Agreed."

Micah leaned forward. "Right now, the truth is that my friend is in a fix, and you're the only man who can repair the damage. What say you?"

"I say it's my own business if and how I do anything, Tate." Caleb swallowed the rest of his irritation, then let out a long breath. "I will give what you've suggested some consideration. Beyond that, I cannot say what I will do."

Micah stared, then gave a curt nod. "Fair enough."

Caleb glanced at the clock and back at the stack of papers waiting to be attended to. "Was there anything else?"

"Just one more thing." He paused. "Does the name Benning mean anything to you?"

Caleb felt as if he'd been punched in the gut. He walked to the door, then stormed back to stand over the wrecker. "What kind of question is that?"

"I asked that myself," the redhead said slowly. "Seems like a popular name."

Caleb sank into the chair and waited for Micah to elaborate.

"First there's Hawkins."

"Go on," Caleb said evenly.

"I think that Hawkins fellow wants his treasure back." He shrugged. "And maybe he's looking to find the man he thinks robbed him of it."

"Me," Caleb said.

"Well," Micah said, slowly, "actually, the way Miss O'Shea tells it, he's looking for some woman who testified against him at his trial and a fellow he calls Benning." He leaned forward. "Funny thing is he's got it in his mind you're him."

"Any idea why?"

Micah shook his head. "Then there's these two fellows who showed up down at the docks a couple of days ago. Said they were looking for work, so I hired them for the afternoon to help me salvage what I could of the *Caroline*." He paused to look over at Caleb. "They mentioned a man named Benning, too."

"In what way?"

He shrugged. "Just in passing. It seemed odd, though, that they would be interested in whether I knew of that particular fellow since Miss O'Shea told me Hawkins had a hankering to find him as well."

Caleb leaned forward in his chair and rested his

palms on his knees. "I would have you point out these men to me. Would you do that?"

He lifted a brow. "Intending to investigate, are you?"

The question felt much less casual than Micah made it seem. "That's my job, isn't it?"

"Depends."

Anything he might have said would've been either foolish or wrong, so Caleb said nothing. When he gathered his wits, he rose again. "Thank you, Micah," he said. "You've given me plenty to think about."

The wrecker stood and reached to shake Caleb's hand. "I want you to know I'll stand with you should this Hawkins fellow prove a problem. The other wreckers, they will, too."

"I appreciate that," Caleb said.

"But this situation with Emilie," Micah continued, "I won't be standing by you if you let her take the blame for something that's not her fault."

Fresh anger spiked. "So you're telling me to start courting Emilie Gayarre or lose the support of the wreckers should the pirate Hawkins come after me?"

"No," he said calmly. "I'm telling you to do what's right, and we'll do the same."

With those cryptic words, Micah Tate took his leave. As Caleb watched him through the window, he wondered whether he'd won that round or lost it.

The noose that was the Benning legacy seemed to come close to tightening around his neck, yet he'd slid free without deceit or deception. The next time, would he be so lucky?

"We cannot allow the loss of our freedom," Emilie said at that evening's hastily arranged meeting at the schoolhouse. Half the town of Fairweather Key had turned out for the event.

"So you're saying all we need to do is write letters to the secretary of the navy and we'll get us a school?" someone called from the back of the crowd. Several others voiced skepticism, while some argued the other side.

Emilie raised her hand for silence. "None of us knows whether this will work, but we all know that what we've done so far has not. Is there anyone here who does not feel beholden to Micah Tate for offering up this place to educate our children?"

A smattering of claps grew into full-fledged applause when Micah joined Emilie at the front of the crowd. "Listen to your teacher," he said, then smiled as the audience laughed. "I say, what can it hurt to try this?"

"Anyone got the address?" a woman up front asked.

"I do," Emilie said. Before the night was done, she'd given that address out to every person in the schoolyard. When the mail cutter returned on the twenty-ninth of the month, it left the harbor the next day with more letters than had ever been posted from Fairweather Key.

And a large number of them were addressed to the secretary of the navy in Washington, D.C.

CHAPTER 36

October 3, 1836

Caleb had been quietly looking for familiar faces since his conversation with Micah Tate regarding the Benning name. Twice now Micah had reported items missing from the warehouse, things that went in but did not make the log book.

Any other man might have brought suspicion on himself with the claim, but Tate seemed to care not for the guilt he might appear to have. Rather, Caleb knew him to be honest above all other things. Thus, the claim was duly noted and a plan decided upon.

No longer would the warehouse go unguarded. Now a man would be stationed at either end of the building night and day, except during times when they were called to duty at sea. Then the fishermen would take over. All men answered to Micah Tate.

And Micah answered only to Caleb.

It was a plan that, while elaborate, seemed to work. There had been no further loss of cargo since its implementation.

The only other strange activity in town seemed to center around the mail cutter. When it departed the first week in September, the craft had been laden with a high volume of letters. The same thing happened each Monday of the month.

As judge, he wondered what sort of foolishness was going on. Why, did it seem that everyone in town had decided to write letters?

Even Mrs. O'Mara had remained silent on the subject and refused to allow him to inspect the cargo. When he'd arrived on the dock the last two times the vessel had dropped anchor, she not only refused him entry to the hold, but she had also ordered him off the vessel.

"You can have a peek at these items if we don't make it past the reef," she called. "If we do, then it's none of your business."

When they parted, she'd been humming some obscure verse from one of his mother's favorite hymns. Caleb could only smile, even as he wondered what sort of trickery might be going on.

Today, however, he intended to get to the bottom of this, even if it meant throwing the former jailer in the brig. He adjusted his hat and stepped out of his office into the warmth of the October Monday morning.

Back in Washington, things were likely covered in ice. Perhaps even a dusting of snow. But here the sun shone and the skies were blue. Were he not so far from the place where the real work of justice went on, he might actually enjoy living in such a place.

With a nod to the pastor's wife and her daughter-in-law, Caleb turned toward the docks where the mail cutter looked ready to depart. "Mrs. O'Mara," he called as he spied the postmistress.

"Judge Spencer." She waved. "Come on aboard," she said, "unless you're of a mind to raid the hold again."

Caleb stopped short and weighed his options. He decided to try flattery. "Do I look like the kind of man who would interfere with the business of the mail system, especially with one so competent in charge?"

Resting her hands on her hips, Mrs. O'Mara shook her head. "Yes, actually, you do."

So much for flattery. "Madam, I am the judge in Fairweather Key, and as such I demand you tell me exactly what is going on with all of this mail. If there's a crime being committed and I am not informed, I feel I should warn you that you will also be considered a party to it."

He paused to let the threat sink in. Whatever bite he'd put into the words seemed not to have caught her attention at all.

With nothing more than a grin and a wave, she bade him good-bye and stepped off the vessel. "You'll need to go with her, Judge," the captain called from the quarterdeck, "unless you're interested in coming along."

Caleb looked back at Mrs. O'Mara, then up at the captain. "Oh, I don't know. Where are you going? Maybe I'll ride along with all those letters you're carrying."

"Don't you tell him, Captain," the postmistress said. "He's not authorized for that information."

Shaking his head, Caleb headed down the gang-plank and returned to dry land without his answers. As he neared Mrs. O'Mara, he paused. "Should I ever decide to leave my position as judge, I shall recommend you be named as my successor."

"And I'll accept. I've been running this island for years. The judge just didn't know it." The older woman laughed. "Isn't that right, Miss Emilie?"

Miss Emilie?

He turned to see Emilie Gayarre gliding toward him in a frock of pale violet with a bonnet to match. "Mrs. O'Mara, how lovely to see you," she said. "Judge," she added as an afterthought.

"A pleasure to see you again, Miss Gayarre," he said, though he'd only just had the distinct discomfort of sitting in the pew in front of her at Sunday services yesterday. All through Mrs. Carter's solo and Reverend Carter's sermon, he could feel her staring.

Afterward, he'd taken pains to speak at length with Mr. Benson at the auction house until she finally exited the church. How much longer he could continue to deal with the dual need to see her and stay away was beyond his understanding.

Something, it seemed, would have to change, and soon.

Still, he'd managed to deflect her questions until she stopped asking them. Perhaps after several more months passed, she would be amenable to a fresh start without the accusation that he was the Benning.

The complication in that plan was the fact that, indeed, she was correct.

"Well now," Mrs. O'Mara said. "What's gotten into you two?" She linked one arm with Emilie and the other with Caleb. "When I heard the talk that you two were slipping around having some sort of secret romance, I knew it couldn't be true. Now I wonder."

Stunned, Caleb attempted to step back, but her iron grip remained on his arm. Emilie's face went beet red.

"Hear me out. Two people who don't care a fig for one another are easy to spot. They don't show an opinion as to whether the other's around or not." She paused to look first at Emilie and then at Caleb. "But you two, well, you're like two long-tailed cats in a room full of rocking chairs."

She released her grip, and Caleb half-expected Emilie to bolt and run. On principle alone, he remained rooted in place.

"What you two need to do is stop dancing around each other and let the Lord do what He wants to do with you. Why, it's as plain as day you're meant for one another." The older woman shook her head. "All I've got to say is youth is wasted on the young," she said as she turned and walked away without looking back.

"Ridiculous," Emilie said. "I've never heard such nonsense."

Caleb said nothing. Indeed, the more he tried to work up irritation at the woman, the more he was reminded of Langham Island and the barefoot beauty who swam up to meet him during his nap.

Even yesterday in church, as he felt her eyes on him, Caleb wondered whether his jacket might have a spot of lint on it or if he'd missed a place on his jaw while shaving.

Emilie was right about one thing: It was ridiculous.

"Emilie?" Mrs. O'Mara was back, this time with a letter in hand. "Something for you from the mailbag."

The former Miss Crusoe retrieved the letter, scanned the front, then quickly folded it in half and held it behind her back. "Thank you, Mrs. O'Mara," she said. "Always lovely to see you." She bustled away without so much as a parting word to Caleb.

"See," Mrs. O'Mara said, "she's got it bad for you."

Caleb laughed as he watched the haughty female hurry out of sight. "For someone who claims to know people, you've missed the mark on that one."

Postmistress O'Mara reached to grasp Caleb by the arm. "Ah, but she didn't miss the mark, did she, Judge Spencer?"

Caleb thought back to that morning aboard the *Cormorant*, then smiled down at the older woman. "Thankfully, Mrs. O'Mara, she did."

He returned to his office and a desk full of newly delivered mail. There were also two men with familiar faces sorting through the documents.

Caleb reached for the pistol at his waist and aimed it at the bigger of the pair. "I can only shoot one of you at a time, but I can certainly take you both."

Two sets of hands shot up, and they stepped away from the desk like errant schoolchildren. "There's no need for that," said the shorter man, a fellow with close-cropped hair and a distinctly French accent. "We are all on the same side here."

Caleb stilled his trigger finger but never removed his attention from the men. "Who are you?"

"Actually," the man said as he gave his partner in crime a sideways look, "Mr. Fletcher sent us to find Monsieur Benning."

Caleb's finger tightened against the trigger as the blood pulsed in his temples.

The bigger of the pair, a buffoon with a scar that traveled from the corner of his mouth to his hairline, said nothing. It occurred to Caleb that he could dispatch both men and solve the problem.

The door opened behind him. "A word with you, Judge Spencer," Emilie Gayarre said.

Caleb dared not look at her. "Not now, miss," he said.

The men exchanged glances. Caleb lifted the weapon to aim, being careful to keep it out of Emilie's sight.

"Yes, now," she said. "This won't wait."

Caleb resisted the urge to turn and look at her. Rather, he slid one hand behind his back and pointed to the door. "Go," he said, his jaw clenched. "Now." As an afterthought, he added, "Please."

Of course she ignored him. With each footstep in his direction, Caleb's temper rose.

Emilie came into view, a puzzled look on her face. "What's wrong with you?"

"Madam, I will ask you again to leave the office."

A smirk rose on the smaller man's face. "Well then," the Frenchman said, "we will be going." He inched away from the desk, his companion following a step behind.

"Parlez-vous Francais?" Emilie asked.

"Oui," the man responded, and the pair began conversing. The door closed, and just as Emilie came around to stand beside him, Caleb lowered the weapon to his side. His expression, however, told the men he would use the pistol if provoked.

• • •

To Emilie's mind, Judge Spencer appeared even more grumpy than usual. In contrast, his guests were both hospitable and refined. The gentleman from Lyon was especially nice, even asking questions about the island in general and Emilie's home in particular. It seemed he had been giving thought to settling in Fairweather Key and finding employment along with two former partners in a shipping venture.

She was about to tell the judge this when the men bade a quick good-bye and slipped past. The French fellow offered a curt nod to the judge, then a broad smile to Emilie. His friend merely grinned over his shoulder as he exited a few steps behind.

When they were gone, the judge walked over to the desk to make order of what was an awful mess. Snatching up an envelope with an important-looking seal that looked eerily similar to the one she'd opened a short while ago, he looked up at Emilie. "Would you excuse me one minute?"

"Of course." As she planned to stay until her business was conducted, Emilie found the nearest chair and settled there, arranging her skirts around her ankles and pulling off her gloves.

The letter seemed to remove all thought of company from Judge Spencer's mind, so Emilie was free to study him undetected. A vast physical improvement had happened since their day on Langham Island, most markedly in the cut of his hair and the clean-shaven condition of his chin. The smiles that came so easily that day, however, had not been appreciated.

Would that she could recall them, for his expression stood in stark contrast. "Something amiss, Judge?" she called, though it appeared her question had not pierced the thick veil of his thoughts.

No matter, for she had her own concerns. Once the contents of her letter were known, likely the former pirate would have no need of his grin for a long time.

Abruptly, the subject of her thoughts looked up. He appeared to be forming a statement or, perhaps, a question. Failing that, he set the paper atop the collection on his desk and merely stared.

Too young and handsome to be judge and jury of anything—that was her thought as she watched him rest against the edge of the desk and study the toe of his boot. She took the opportunity to notice the breadth of his shoulders and to wonder where the bullet had entered. Surely a lesser man would have died. So much blood. Eyes staring up from a place where no recognition could be had. Voices outside, shouting. Bells ringing. A man with a pipe.

The recall made her shiver, even as it rendered her unable to look away. When the lieutenant's gaze lifted, he caught her staring.

"Indeed you look troubled," she said to cover her discomfort. "Might you need some cheering?

Perhaps a day in the sun on some tropical island would soothe your temperament."

"Should you continue to make reference to some sort of past experience you believe we had, I shall be forced to rethink my decision to allow a school to be built once the proper location can be secured."

"Interesting, Judge Spencer," she said as she rose, her confidence soaring. "For I did not mention this island might figure into some sort of shared past experience. Only the Benning would know of our day on Langham Island. Only the Benning would . . ."

Realization dawned even as she watched the color drain from the judge's face. "Did you say you were going to allow the school to be built?"

CHAPTER 37

Even as he condemned himself for the unforgivable blunder, Caleb was rendered speechless at the sight of Emilie Gayarre rushing toward him. When she threw herself into his arms, he didn't know whether to participate in the embrace or flee.

The foolish man in him elected to do the former, while his good sense chose the latter.

Miss Gayarre spoke, for he heard the words, but the feel of her in his arms brought back the scent of salt water, the scratch of sand, and time spent in the shade of an upended rowboat. For a brief moment he was Crusoe, and she his companion.

She stepped back, and the last of the sand crashed through the hourglass of their past. "Miss Gayarre, you're staring. Again," he added.

Biting her lip, she held her silence; an uncharacteristic gesture for one usually so forthright. Slowly she seemed to animate, first with a sparkle in her eyes and then, with deliberate slowness, the upturn of her soft lips.

That he remembered their fullness, their softness, plagued Caleb even now.

Why is she still in my life, Lord? Send her to someone who can appreciate her. No, he amended, *to someone who is free to love her.*

"I did not misunderstand. Your intention is to build our school."

"It is," he said, forcing sternness into a voice that only wanted to be tender. "Given, of course, that a proper site is found and the materials and—"

"Come with me." Strong fingers encircled his wrist and dragged him upright.

"Miss Gayarre, I assure you—"

She had the audacity to reach up and close his lips with her forefinger. "I propose we form an alliance, Caleb. May I call you Caleb?"

He nodded, her finger still firmly resting against his mouth.

"Wonderful, and I am, of course, Emilie." She paused. "An alliance will suit us both, I believe, for I have the answers to the questions you seek."

Caleb stared. He dared not move. *The Lord alone has the answers, for you cannot fathom the questions.*

Yet the Lord had remained strangely silent on the subject of Emilie Gayarre.

She lifted her finger but held it mere inches from his lips. "Unless you've pressing business to attend to, I would like very much to show you what I believe is the perfect spot for construction of the Fairweather Key school."

He nodded, unsure of his voice. As she stepped out of his reach, he swallowed hard.

Someday she would know that she owed her school not to any benevolence on his part but to the letter now on his desk from the secretary of the navy. The mystery of the full mail boat was quickly explained in the words of the secretary's letter:

Popular demand compels me to come and inspect the Fairweather Key school personally. As luck would have it, I will be traveling south in November and would relish an appointment with you to discuss said schoolhouse personally. In addition, I've had an interesting conversation with the attorney general regarding your services, though I am loath to recommend your transfer back to him with such an issue hanging in the balance.

"Lead on, Emilie," he said as he retrieved his hat.

Lead him she did, all the way to the lane that ran beside her cottage. He knew of the location, even as he knew never to venture near it—or her—lest he fall into a trap such as the one he'd just tumbled into back in his office.

He cursed himself as a fool, even as he fell into step beside Emilie on the broad lane that wound behind the downtown district and turned toward a low bluff jutting over the bay. As her cottage appeared on the horizon, Caleb felt her tug on his wrist.

"Hurry," she said, though he hadn't realized he'd slowed his pace.

Loosening her grip, Emilie fairly ran ahead of him, the ribbons of her bonnet forming blue streamers that followed in her wake. He, too, followed, a foolish man who could never forget her nor ever pursue her.

She rushed past her home and the tidy fence that surrounded it to stop in an expanse of flat land bordered on two sides by nance and mango groves. The remaining edges were hemmed in by the ocean to the west and Emilie's cottage to the east.

Caleb stepped carefully off the path and past the woman who'd stopped to allow him to admire her choice on his own. He did so silently, taking his time to state what he knew from the moment he saw the property.

"It is a fine location," he said without turning to

face her. "All that remains is to find the owner and secure a purchase." Now he turned, finding to his relief that she'd stayed put. "I warn you, Emilie, though I am giving in to your town's demand for a proper school, I will not raid our coffers for an extravagant purchase."

She pursed her lips then formed a slow smile. "And what," she said slowly, "would you consider a fair price for such a lovely location?"

Caleb shrugged, then named an amount he knew to be vastly under what was surely the cost of this place where he now stood. He watched her nod, purse her lips once more, then nod again.

"And what of the budget for the building? Have you a figure in mind?"

He did not, though he'd prefer she not realize how early in the plan to placate the secretary it was. Again, he named an amount he felt was not up to her expectations. Again, she considered it then nodded.

"Anything else you would like to know, Emilie?" he asked, though as soon as the words had fallen from his mouth, he wished to snatch them back.

"Of course," she said, eyes sparking, "but with your permission, I would ask that I reserve that right for a later date."

"Permission granted," he said, not knowing whether he'd just found his reprieve or signed his death warrant.

"Then shall we talk business?" She gestured to her cottage. "Might I offer a cup of coffee or a glass of something cool to drink while we converse?"

Caleb followed her to her porch, then settled onto a bench while she went inside. The view was spectacular from here, almost as breathtaking as that of the current schoolhouse. While most of Fairweather Key's downtown area lay in a low point between two hills, Emilie's cottage sat above the city within sight of the harbor and the ocean beyond.

He leaned back and listened to the orangequit's song until a memory of Santa Lucida beckoned. *"I delivered you because I delighted in you."*

Caleb stretched out his legs and crossed them at the ankles, remembering the strong presence of God that day. Had the time only been measured in months? It felt like years, decades, since he had heard the Lord's voice so clearly.

Sounds inside the cottage mixed with the sound of birds and the rush of tree limbs on the salt-tinged breeze to form a symphony he knew he would never tire of hearing. A symphony he would never hear once he returned to Washington.

What had once been the lofty goal of keeping a promise to his earthly father suddenly began to feel like betraying one to his heavenly Father. He thought back to a moment long sealed in the farthest reaches of his memory. Of his father lying near death in Santa Lucida, and the words he whispered. "Take up the cause of justice, Caleb. Promise me you will achieve it."

It.

That was, he had decided, the position of ultimate justice. The attorney general's post. More than once, he'd heard his father and the men who kept company with him talk of John Spencer's nomination to the post. Had an accident not felled him, likely the position would have been his.

Though he had been a lad of barely ten, Caleb had both taken up the cause of justice as he'd promised and ignored the call of the sea that he'd so loved.

With Fletcher to guide him and his skills as a jurist to recommend him, every goal had been reached save one: He was not yet the attorney general his father had desired him to be.

Time, however, was his friend, as he had many years of service to his country ahead. And with the construction of this school and the restored good graces of the secretary of the navy, the position would one day be his.

The secretary had hinted as much in his letter. With all his dreams coming true, why did he feel as if the life had been drained from him? As if he'd somehow left the real Caleb Spencer back on Langham Island, never to be found again?

I miss You, Lord. This admission led him to another. *Somehow I've left Your path. Help me find it again.*

A cloud drifted lazily on the horizon, propelled across a sapphire sky by the trade winds. Beneath it, a three-masted schooner, its sails as white as the cotton above it, made for what looked like the edge of the earth. Then as he watched, it slipped from view, leaving sparkling diamonds of cresting waves in its wake.

All was still. Quiet. Serene. Caleb closed his eyes against the sunshine shining on his face as he weaved his fingers together behind his head.

"I delivered you because I delighted in you."

Caleb sat bolt upright, nearly toppling the bench in the process. Much as he wanted to call out to the Lord, he hesitated to bring Emilie running.

Instead, he opened his heart and waited in hopes that God would remember him as one of His own. *Help me, Lord. I feel like I've fallen off the face of the earth. What do I do to find You again?*

A rustling of tree branches and the tang of ocean air, then silence. *"The truth shall make you free."*

The truth. Anything but that, please.

Silence.

All right, Lord. Where do I start?

"Did you think I'd fallen off the face of the earth?" Emilie called from somewhere inside the cottage. Her footsteps neared, barely audible over the pounding of his heart. "We can start with this," she said when she emerged, balancing a tray in her hands.

She set before him some sort of food and drink,

though he barely took notice. Not since his ride with Rialto on Santa Lucida had he felt this way. To waste the moment sipping sweet drinks and making small talk seemed unthinkable.

Yet he did until Emilie finally turned the course of conversation from the mundane to the specific. "You've stated a budget for the property and construction. Correct?" When he nodded, she continued. "That's a fair number. Might I have it in writing?"

He lifted a brow in amusement. "Of course. Would you like me to do this now?"

"If you would." She rose to step inside, returning a moment later with pen and ink as well as a sheaf of papers. "Just a simple note as to what we've discussed here will suffice."

"Don't you trust me?" he asked, even as he accepted the items from her.

It was her turn to raise a dark brow.

"Fair enough," he said. Caleb did as she asked, generously adding a small percentage to the number she'd stated.

She read over the words, then set the document aside to take up her glass. "Shall we toast to your generosity?"

As he raised his glass to touch hers in a smart clink, he could not meet her gaze. For what she termed generous was just one more thing he must do to climb the ladder his father had set before him.

His earthly father.

"A few items of business, then," Emilie said. "I propose a committee to be formed of men from the community who will see to the building of the school."

"Micah Tate might be a good man to head it up," Caleb said as he struggled to regain his composure. "Much as I hate to spare him, I fear he's ready to work somewhere besides the warehouses."

"I shall bow to you on the selection, though I admit Micah is an excellent choice." Emilie paused to touch her lip with a flower-strewn napkin. "Might I have some input as to the arrangement of the interior? We've a serviceable collection of tables and benches courtesy of Mr. Tate, though I would hope the new location will be bigger and thus in need of more of these items."

"I had hoped you would offer to assist us. Assist me, actually," Caleb corrected.

Her smile was slow in coming but sweet nonetheless. "Now, about the budget."

His guard went up. "I knew this was all too easy." Caleb set down his glass and waited for her to begin.

Emilie held up her hands as if to fend him off. "I'll not contest any of it," she said. "Rather, I'd hoped to confirm the amount."

"The paper confirms it," Caleb said.

Her satisfied smile worried him more than the potential of protest. "Excellent," she said as she reached once more for her glass. "That will build a nice school for the children."

"It will," he agreed.

"Especially since all the funds can be spent on the building." She met his gaze, a twinkle in her brown eyes. "The property belongs to me, Caleb. I am donating it to the cause."

"You tricked me," he said with equal parts surprise and admiration.

"Did I?" Her expression remained neutral, though the merriment in her eyes was unmistakable.

"Indeed you did." He paused. "I thought you a woman of quality, dear schoolteacher. With this discovery, you've wounded me."

Wounded me. Emilie froze. As she lowered her glass to set it on the tray, her hand shook. She seemed to attempt a smile, but it did not quite appear.

Silence fell. Even the breeze ceased, it seemed, and the birds no longer chirped. The cloud had slid from view, leaving the sky a blue that hurt Caleb's eyes.

Yet that's all he could do, for he certainly could not look at Emilie Gayarre.

"Forgive me?" she asked, and he wondered whether they were now talking about the school or something else.

Had Micah Tate not opened the garden gate, Caleb might have discovered the answer. As it was, he discovered only his need for it.

And soon, perhaps, the Lord would show him how to proceed.

"Judge," Micah said after greeting Emilie, "there's a problem down at the warehouse and you're needed right away."

Caleb said his good-byes, then fell into step beside Micah.

"I hated to come and get you," the wrecker said, "but the men are a might riled up."

They arrived at the warehouse to find a crowd had gathered. Josiah Carter shook his hand. "I speak for the wreckers in asking you to see if we can't get to the bottom of this situation." He gestured to the warehouse. "My master's log for the wreck two nights ago and Micah's warehouse log for that same wreck don't match. If he weren't my best friend, I'd be demanding you throw him in jail."

The other men joined in, each stating their opinion. Caleb lifted his hands to silence them.

"Are you saying one of you is pocketing items before they get to the warehouse?"

Josiah shook his head. "I'm not blaming anyone, least of all these men here. In the two years since I arrived on this island, I've never seen a dishonest man in the group."

"Until now," Micah said.

Again, the men began to murmur.

"If not one of them, then who?" Caleb asked.

"The fishermen wouldn't have access." Josiah

glanced at Micah. "We think it might be someone spending time at the wharf. Possibly even someone with a vessel docked here." He looked at Caleb. "My guess is it's someone who is familiar with the process and has access to the items."

Caleb stepped back feeling as if he'd been punched in the gut. "Are you suggesting I might have something to do with this?"

"No," Josiah quickly said.

Micah agreed, and so did many of the men.

"We just want the criminals caught," Josiah continued. "And until they are, I'd like permission to organize our men into shifts to up the watches."

"Of course," Caleb said.

"One more thing," Micah added. "Someone's going to have to stand guard on the docks. Someone trustworthy."

"I'll leave that to you men," Caleb said, "though I must tell you I'd thought to hire Micah away from the warehouse."

Tate looked surprised.

"You see, I've just informed our schoolteacher that Fairweather Key will have a new schoolhouse paid for by government funds." He reached to grasp the wrecker's shoulder. "I'd like to offer Micah the job as foreman of the project."

A cheer went up as Caleb lost the men to a jubilant celebration that included much cheering and backslapping. "Thank you, Judge," Micah said

405

when he broke away from the group. "I'll do right by the job."

"I know you will," Caleb said, "but there's another matter I'd like to discuss."

"Certainly."

"The place we've chosen is within sight of Emilie's home. I'd be much obliged if, while you're out there, you'd keep an eye on her for me."

He nodded.

"Thank you," Caleb said. "What with this recent crime spree and a few odd characters coming around, I'd not want to think harm could befall her."

But as he walked away, Caleb had to wonder if Emilie needed more to guard her safety than a wrecker's presence at a building site next door.

CHAPTER 38

October 17, 1836

By the time the mail boat arrived, construction had already begun in earnest on the schoolhouse. With Micah gone from the warehouse, Caleb found his attention divided between the work of his office and the tedious cataloguing that had to be done in his warehouse.

To hire another man to replace Micah was out of the question. Thus far, he'd found none he could trust. Thankfully, Fairweather Key was a quiet town with little to concern Caleb in the way of crime. The handful of men who'd graced his jail thus far were transients brought in with the tide and leaving in the same manner.

Perhaps the two characters who'd called him out as a Benning had done the same. When they did not return, he assumed they'd either met their match elsewhere or deemed him not the man they thought him to be. Either was fine as long as they kept away from his island.

He lifted the seal on a letter from his mother. She was happy, blissfully so, and had much to say in the way of recommending marital bliss. Caleb smiled, though he ignored her advice to find someone and settle down soon lest he miss the opportunity.

He read on as the handwriting changed from hers to Fletcher's. In Caleb's absence, the work of the plantation had gone on. With help from Fletcher, the men who worked the land had organized themselves into a cooperative that not only surpassed previous years' crops but also found new ways to reduce cost. It was, Fletcher noted, a profitable agreement for all.

Caleb closed the letter without reading the rest. Likely more notes on domestic happiness. He could read those at length another time. Today, however, he had an appointment with Emilie Gayarre.

With the building taking shape, the schoolteacher had decided now was the time to begin discussing details of the interior. As Caleb rose and donned his hat, he felt his heart jump at the thought of spending time with Emilie.

For two weeks he'd only seen her across the crowded pews of the Fairweather Key church. Such was his life that any thought of time spent in any activity other than paperwork or cataloguing of items was unimaginable.

Now as he hurried up the lane to her home, he was stunned to find she did not wait for his arrival alone. He recognized two familiar faces among those on her porch and one he'd never seen.

She looked up to wave. "Welcome, Judge Spencer," she called. "Perhaps you remember these gentlemen?"

"Bonjour," the little man said. Though he wore much more elegant clothing, as did his companions, none of them seemed quite accustomed to their finery.

Caleb stepped through the gate and glared at the Frenchman, then took note of the other two. The larger man refused to meet Caleb's gaze, while the other, a fellow not much removed from his youth, stared slack-jawed.

"If you will excuse us, gentlemen, Miss Gayarre and I have business to discuss." He walked past the trio to nod at Emilie then reach for her hand. Before she could comment, he raised her to her feet. "I'm sure you understand," he added to the suspicious characters, "but we've a schedule to maintain."

When no one moved or commented, Caleb chose the Frenchman to address. "Did you forget who is in charge in Fairweather Key?"

The little man rose slowly, deliberately, his teacup still in his hand. *"Non,"* he said. "It would be impossible to forget who you are, sir." He set the cup on the tray and reached to take Emilie's hand, but Caleb blocked the move. "Yes, well, I do thank you for your courtesy, Miss Gayarre," he said, pointedly ignoring Caleb. "Perhaps on our next visit, you will allow me to bring—"

"There will be no next visit," Caleb said.

"Really, Caleb, I must—"

He stopped her protest with a glare, then turned his attention to the men still loitering on her porch. "My office at four," he said, this time allowing his gaze to rest on the other two before landing on the Frenchman. "Consider this a demand, and not a request."

The man offered a smirk. "And what is the difference?"

"Ignoring a demand from the judge could land a man in jail," he said.

A giggle erupted from the youngest of the trio. "So what's a request get someone?"

Caleb cut him down with his glare, then casually allowed his free hand to graze his coat sufficiently to show his weapon strapped to his belt. "I wouldn't know. I don't make them."

• • •

Emilie slipped from the judge's grasp but held her silence. Once the trio was on its way, she turned on the puffed-up buffoon. "How dare you come to my home and behave that way?"

She intended to say more but, under his withering glare, elected not to.

A muscle in his jaw tensed. "Do you know those men?"

"Well, of course I do. I only made Ben's acquaintance today. He's the young man, but the other two I met in your office. They are quite well-mannered." She paused for effect. "Unlike you."

The comment seemed to miss its mark, as the judge was staring past her and paid it no heed. She swiveled to follow his gaze, then watched as the men disappeared around the bend on the path toward town.

"Come with me." A demand, not a request. She followed as he took her to the site of the school building, the location of their planned meeting that had now gone so strangely wrong.

Caleb seemed oblivious to her presence as he walked to the edge of the bluff and stared out at the ocean. She moved to stand at his side, though he continued to ignore her.

A thought occurred, as did a possible explanation for his rude behavior. "Caleb, perhaps I owe you an apology."

He gave her a sideways look, one brow raised. "Perhaps?"

Emilie nodded, though she needn't have bothered, for he'd already returned his attention to the horizon. "Yes, well," she began slowly, "I had only the best of intentions when I called the parent meeting that began the letter-writing campaign."

She cast a glance up at him. A muscle worked in his jaw, but otherwise he stood stock still.

"So what I envisioned as a nice, quiet, yet firm way of circumventing what I and others felt was an authoritative position on the subject of the new school became a—"

"Emilie, please." He moved to catch her wrist. "Do you think this is about a group of disgruntled citizens writing letters to Washington?"

"Yes, well, I . . ." Her breath caught when his grip tightened. "I suppose I did, and for my part in any trouble this may have caused you, I do apologize."

He stared.

"I would ask that you unhand me, sir." Emilie squared her shoulders and returned the glare. "And I would remind you that I have now asked your forgiveness for . . ." Again she paused. "For all of it."

Caleb shook his head. "Were I to persist in holding the offense against you, I fear I would only harm myself." Emilie lost him to the sea once more. "This I am still learning but endeavor to put into practice."

"Thank you," she said. "I, too, have difficulty in that area."

He turned abruptly. "With me? Have I—"

"No," she said. "It's of a more personal nature." She shrugged. What damage could the truth do with one who had no idea of the parties involved? "I struggle with an offense I have only recently become aware of."

His silence this time begged her to continue.

"My father," she added, "whom I share with Isabelle, favored me over her." Another pause. "Favored my mother over hers. Isabelle has managed to live with the fact, though it caused her great personal sacrifice and pain. She has forgiven. I, knowing I did not deserve the favor, have not." She lifted her gaze. "Why am I telling you this?"

He reached for her hand once more, this time entwining his fingers with hers. "There is some measure of safety in a shared past, Emilie."

A shared past.

His fingers tightened around hers.

" 'The truth will set you free.' " He spoke the words so softly they were almost lost on the wind.

"I wish I believed that," she said, "for I feel as though upon knowing the truth, I have become imprisoned by it."

Caleb lifted her fingers to his lips and held them there. Emilie dared not move, even to slowing her breathing, lest he move away.

"A prison is something we construct around ourselves, Emilie," he said, this time staring openly as if watching for her reaction.

"A strange statement coming from the man who holds the keys to the jail."

He shook his head, even as he released her. "Say that again."

She stared down at her fingers, still warm from his touch. "I said you hold the key to the jail, Caleb."

"I do, don't I?" A smile broke, one Emilie hadn't seen since Langham Island. In a swift move, Caleb placed his hands around her waist and lifted her off the ground, circling as he let out a yelp more suited to a boy of ten than a man near thirty.

"Put. Me. Down."

He did, and the earth continued to spin until her feet were once again airborne. This time Caleb lifted her into an embrace and, in a stunning turn of events, kissed her soundly.

When he placed her on her feet again, Emilie fully expected an apology for his ungentlemanly behavior. What she got was another smile that nearly had her asking for another kiss.

Rather, she elected to act the prim schoolteacher. An act she hoped she could maintain. "What on earth has gotten into you, Judge Spencer?" she managed as she repaired her hair with a shaking hand.

"The truth, Emilie," he said, "is setting me free."

She tried to think of a response, but none came. Perhaps it was because her head still spun.

"I am the Benning."

"I know," she whispered.

His curt nod put her in mind of the stern judge and not the man who'd just danced a jig in her field. "When my father died, I tried to become him." Another pause. "It was my duty."

This time she reached for his hand, and after a moment he curled his fingers around hers. "Duty is a difficult taskmaster."

"Indeed."

"How did he die?" she asked softly.

"Yellow fever," Caleb said. "He came home to Santa Lucida to die. And to draft the son he rarely saw for the cause."

She held his hand and waited, thinking of what it must have been like to sit at the bedside of a dying father at the age of ten. It had been hard enough at twenty-one.

Again the ocean had his attention. She thought of their first meeting, the tangling of frightened captive and blustering rescuer in the dark waters between two warring ships. Theirs had been a spectacular introduction, complete with cannon fire, grapeshot, and two bags of gold.

Emilie felt him move beside her and turned her attention to him. He did not smile, nor did he frown. Rather, he appeared to be either confused or surprised.

"I could love you quite easily, Emilie Gayarre."

CHAPTER 39

There, he'd said it. The truth, all of it, was out. Caleb stood on the edge of the cliff feeling as if the woman beside him held the power to hurl him off it. Emilie seemed as stunned as he at the admission.

"Perhaps I should have kept silent on this," he finally said. "I can see I've caught you off guard."

"Off guard?" She shook her head even as she pulled away. "That's not it."

Panic the likes of which he'd not felt even in battle rose. "Emilie, say something."

It took far too long, but finally she met his stare. Still, she seemed disinclined to speak.

"I cannot require a response," he paused to force a smile, "but I can request it."

Slowly, she seemed to come back to herself. "I cannot," she murmured.

Blood began to pound at his temples. Surely she would not rebuff him. Not his Miss Crusoe. "You cannot what?"

"I cannot continue this conversation," she said as she whirled around to practically run across the field.

Caleb caught her easily but resisted the urge to haul her back. As with the times he'd heard God speak, there was no forcing a moment beyond its natural end. And it appeared the conversation that set him dancing for joy like King David had reached its end.

At the gate she neither paused nor offered a good-bye. When the door closed behind her, something also shut tight in his heart.

He'd almost reached his office when he realized he hadn't warned Emilie about the three characters who insisted on pretending a friendship with her. Unless he missed his guess, they were scouts sent by Thomas Hawkins.

The day passed in a numbing routine of conversations, work, and silence until Caleb though he would lose his sanity. At precisely four, he spied the trio walking toward the office.

"Afternoon, Judge Spencer," the Frenchman called.

He waited until all three had assembled inside to raise his pistol.

"What is this? Are you jealous of that pretty girl?" the younger one asked.

"Emilie is her name, yes?" the Frenchman said.

Caleb pulled back on the hammer.

"You're not going to shoot us," the big man said. "There's three of us, and you've only got one pistol."

The blood pounded at his temples. The truth had imprisoned him once again. A fitting fate for these wharf rats as well.

He pointed to the door that connected the jail with his office, a passageway Judge Campbell had been wise to commission. "If you're with Hawkins, you know I'm a fair shot. If you're not, then you're about to find out."

None spoke, though the words did have the effect of taming their bluster.

"So you've got a choice," he said, fueling his words with the dual anger of their threat to Emilie and their connection to Hawkins. "All three of you find safety in my jail or at least one of you, likely all, will be carried out by the undertaker."

He was almost disappointed when they chose the jail.

November 7, 1836

As word spread that the jail had three new occupants, so did the rumor that Caleb had caught the men who'd stolen goods from the wrecks. He could make no such accusation without proof, however, and he had none.

According to the letter Mrs. O'Mara had delivered along with the men's afternoon meal, he also had little time to find the proof he needed. The navy secretary's arrival in Fairweather Key was imminent, likely the second week of November. He would be hard pressed to explain three men detained without charges, even if he and the rest of Fairweather Key did believe they were guilty.

Thus when Reverend Carter arrived at the boardinghouse to interrupt his dinner, Caleb was not

417

exactly receptive to his invitation for an evening stroll. With a promise from Ruby to keep his dinner warm, Caleb agreed.

"Forgive the intrusion," the pastor said as he made for the door, "but I warrant you'll want to hear what I have to say." He paused to allow Caleb to step out ahead of him into the deepening twilight. "Or," he said slowly, "perhaps not."

"Go on," Caleb said as they set off walking down the middle of the empty street, the lights of homes on either side of them and the moon above guiding their way.

Reverend Carter's cane clacked a rhythm on the hard pavement even as his sprightly gait offered up no evidence of its need. "I've spoken to Emilie."

At the mention of her name, Caleb's heart sank. So the schoolteacher had spoken of him? Likely only to say how she heard his admission of love, then turned her back on it. A laugh was surely had at his expense.

"And?" Caleb offered.

"And being a man who only had sons, she and Isabelle are like daughters to me. That said, understand that our conversation did not encompass anything personal in relation to the two of you, much to my regret." The pastor paused to lean on his cane. "I have strong feelings on that particular subject."

"Oh?" He glanced at the old man. "Anything you'd care to share with me?"

"Oh, I'd care to share it," he said, "but I haven't pastored a church this long without learning when to speak and when to keep my mouth closed."

"Fair enough." They resumed walking. "So might I ask what words of wisdom Emilie has for me?"

"Emilie feels you've incarcerated those men without cause."

Irritation struck. "Then let her tell me."

The pastor held up his hand to silence Caleb's protest. "Or, possibly, for a cause that's not quite good enough to get a man jailed."

Caleb bit back the sharp response he wished to release. "And what cause would that be?"

Reverend Carter seemed reluctant to speak. "Could you be paying these men back for keeping a little company with Emilie?"

"Did she say that?" he exclaimed, his tone much harsher and his voice much louder than he intended.

The preacher seemed unfazed. "She mentioned a situation where you walked up on them having refreshments on her porch."

His blood boiled, and if he hadn't made a point of steering clear of the schoolteacher, Caleb might have stormed up to her cottage on the hill and told her exactly what he thought of her conclusions and the fact that she'd decided to share them with others.

"Reverend Carter," he said as gently as he could manage, "I'm afraid Emilie is mistaken."

He gave Caleb a hard look then slowly nodded. "I've known you to be a fair man," he said, "and I believe you've known me to be an honest one."

"I have," Caleb said.

"Then I must be honest with you. I'll not require proof of these men's guilt, nor will I offer any that they're innocent. What I ask is whether you have either."

Caleb said nothing.

"It's likely they were involved in those thefts. My son tells me nothing's gone missing since they were thrown in jail."

"That's true."

"But we're still living in Florida Territory, and a man cannot be locked up indefinitely without a proper trial." He paused. "And I figure maybe Emilie's right in saying you'd formed an opinion before you decided they were to be locked up."

He had to consider the statement a minute before grudgingly agreeing to its truth. "Should I release them, I fear for Emilie's safety."

Reverend Carter's eyes narrowed. "You'll need to be more specific about this, son."

"I'm sorry, sir," Caleb said, "but I cannot."

"Then I'll ask again that these men be released. I don't want to take this to the people, but I will if need be."

Caleb shook his head. "Why would you do that? I'm trying to keep those people safe."

"Here's the thing, son," the old pastor said. "Sometimes safety isn't worth the price."

"What do you mean?"

Reverend Carter rested his hand on Caleb's shoulder. "I admire you," he said. "You're a good man, and if she weren't so stubborn, you'd be a good husband to my Emilie. But much as you've got good intentions here, Fairweather Key's already been under the rule of one tyrant, and we will not tolerate another."

They passed the lights of town and walked under a canopy of stars. In the distance, the rise and fall of waves against the shore echoed. "Is that what you've called me away from my dinner to tell me?"

"It is," the pastor said.

"Then you've said it." Caleb stopped, and Reverend Carter followed suit. "If there's nothing further, I'll be returning to Ruby's stew."

"So we're clear," he said, "you understand what you're facing should you continue to hold these men without charges."

Caleb pondered the statement—carefully worded not to be a question—and worked his anger down to a mild upset. "Reverend, I will take what you've said under advisement. So we're clear," he added, "I am still the judge of this part of Florida Territory, and I will do my duty with concern for one thing: the law."

Hezekiah Carter gave a curt nod. "That is all I can hope for, son," he said.

"Then we're clear."

"We are." The reverend placed his hand on Caleb's sleeve. "There's just one more thing."

Caleb expelled a long breath. "What would that be?"

"Emilie."

The name hung between them. Caleb resisted the urge to speak as they left the starry night behind and turned onto the street leading through town. Up ahead, the single spire of the church beckoned, as did the lights in the window of the rectory.

"I want her to smile again," Reverend Carter finally said.

Dipping his head, Caleb felt his heart lurch. "Tell her that," he said.

They walked in silence, then paused in front of the church. Reverend Carter seemed ready to say something further on the subject, but Caleb held up his hands to stop him.

"I'm going to ask something of you, Reverend," he said. "I have reason to believe those men wish harm to Emilie. I'll not reveal anything further than that. You will have to ask her for details."

"Fair enough."

A door opened in the rectory, and Mary Carter called to them. "Good evening, ma'am," Caleb responded. After turning down a meal and dessert, he made his excuses and turned to leave.

"Judge," the reverend called.

Caleb stopped but did not respond.

"I'll see she comes to stay with us or Isabelle and Josiah for a few days. How's that?"

"Thank you," he said, only later realizing the statement meant he'd already decided to release the criminals.

November 8

The last of the wharf rats scurried from the jail like vermin set loose. Rather than lecture the men on proper behavior while visiting the city, Caleb decided to allow the men from whom they'd stolen to escort them aboard their vessel and see to their departure.

Caleb watched from the docks as the trio's vessel slipped over the horizon, a parade of wrecking vessels in its wake. As they turned to head back to port, Caleb went back inside.

He'd done the right thing in releasing the men, of this he was certain. Legally, he'd performed his duty. Whether justice had been served was another matter altogether. For now, men who presented an obvious threat were walking free, and Emilie Gayarre was closeted behind the lace curtains at Josiah and Isabelle Carter's home.

Where was the justice?

Micah stepped inside, a grin on his face and his red hair suffering from the windy ride back into port. "Likely they'll not be bothering us again," he said.

"Thank you," was all Caleb could muster.

The wrecker came to stand across the desk from Caleb. "You're looking a bit worse for wear, Judge," he said. "I was about to try out my sea legs on my new boat. Want to come along?"

It didn't take much in the way of talking to convince Caleb to step aboard the as-yet-unnamed wrecking vessel. Getting his own sea legs back was another matter entirely.

While he wasn't pitched into the drink, he did tumble twice. "You'll do better next time," Micah offered.

"Next time?" Caleb shook his head as he stepped off the vessel. "You'd have me back? For a navy man, I'm a poor example of a seaman."

"But you weren't always, were you?"

The wrecker's question took him by surprise. "No," he finally said, "I wasn't."

Micah nodded but said nothing further on the subject. "You think they'll be back?" he finally asked.

"Those three?" Caleb looked around to see who might be listening, then gave Micah his attention. "I do."

He seemed to think on the admission a moment. "I do, too."

"I would have you continue to keep an eye on Emilie. I don't trust these men, and I think their purpose here was not petty thievery."

"No," he said, "they were hunting down the

Benning and the woman who caused their captain nearly to be hanged."

Caleb put out a hand to stop the wrecker. "How did you know of this?"

"I pay attention to things," Micah said.

"Such as?"

"The warehouse stands right next to the jail. Have you noticed that?"

"Not until now." He paused to allow a pair of ladies to pass. "What else do you know?"

"Thomas Hawkins is alive and royally aggrieved that he nearly swung from the rope in Havana."

He nodded. "This much I knew."

"You see, I've been keeping tabs on those fellows because I thought maybe they were here after Ruby. She was on that vessel with those girls." When Caleb nodded, he continued. "Now I'm certain they have no idea she and the girls survived. I was in that warehouse a number of hours every day, and they never spoke of Ruby." Another pause. "They did, however, talk at length about you and Emilie."

Caleb knew he was well and truly caught. "So you know."

"That you're the Benning?" He nodded. "What I don't know or care about is what in the world that means."

Relief washed across his worries. "I appreciate your reluctance to pry. What I can tell you is this:

The threat to Emilie is real and, unless I miss my guess, imminent."

"He'll touch a hair on her head only over my dead body," Micah said.

"No," Caleb responded. "Over mine."

"Be careful what you say, Judge," Micah said. "Else I'll think you're serious."

"But I am." Caleb looked out over the horizon then turned to Micah. "She won't let me near enough to keep her safe. So I'll have to go to the source of the trouble."

"Hawkins?"

Caleb nodded.

"How will you find him?"

"I won't." He shrugged. "He's going to find me."

CHAPTER 40

November 19, 1836

Caleb's letter went out on the fourteenth of November. Owing to the stiff trade winds and the hefty sack of gold in the captain's private safe, the mail cutter arrived at the dock in Santa Lucida the next morning. This Caleb had learned Friday night when Fletcher walked into the boardinghouse.

Theirs was a long overdue reunion, and Saturday morning, even in the light of what was to come, Caleb found reason to smile. Of course, waking up aboard the *Cormorant* helped.

Fletcher joined him on the deck, the ever-present pipe missing. "What happened?" Caleb inquired as he sipped the bracing coffee that he'd become accustomed to at his mother's table.

"A casualty of marriage," he said of the missing pipe, "though what I have gained far exceeds any loss I might feel."

Caleb grinned. "I half-expected she might join you."

"Oh, she might have if given the opportunity." He glanced at Caleb. "Believe it or not, she actually listens to me."

He hoped his chuckle conveyed the proper amusement. Fletcher, however, was obviously not fooled.

"Your request that I come at once was not based on nostalgia, was it, Caleb?"

"No," he said. "Hawkins is back."

Fletcher looked away. "You have a plan, I presume?"

"I do, but I must warn you," he said, leaning against the gunwale, "the *Cormorant* and her crew will be in danger."

"My boy," Fletcher said, "do you not think those aboard wouldn't follow where you lead?"

He thought of only one: Emilie Gayarre.

"None who haven't already done so," he said as he watched the tide ebb and flow against the shallows below the docks.

"So there's a woman."

He jerked his attention to Fletcher. "Am I that obvious?"

"Was I?"

Caleb nodded. "Point taken."

To his credit, Fletcher stepped away to allow Caleb to brood in silence. He might have stood at the gunwale all morning had he not seen a vessel flying the flag of the United States of America appear on the horizon.

"Emilie, how long are you going to sit by the window pretending to read that novel?" Isabelle stepped into the room, her son in her arms. "I know you cannot possibly enjoy something so much that you read it through twice."

It was three times, but what did it matter? She could never tell Isabelle that reading *Robinson Crusoe* was as much about enjoying the novel as it was basking in the memory of a stolen kiss.

Two, to be exact.

Because remembering those two kisses always brought her to the third kiss, the one they'd shared just before she walked out of his life.

Tears came afresh, and she did not bother to stop them. The book swam before her, and she reluctantly closed it.

Isabelle left the room only to return without Joey. She knelt before Emilie and wrapped her in an embrace. No words were necessary. Each had shed tears over the same dilemma.

Finally, Isabelle pulled away to stand. "You must tell him," she said. "If he loves you, it won't matter who your parents were."

"Who my mother was," she corrected. "And it will always matter. What you're suggesting is against the law."

"Those are man's laws," Isabelle said as she pulled her handkerchief out and handed it to Emilie. "Let God tell you what to do."

Emilie nodded and blew her nose, then tucked the handkerchief into her apron pocket. "Izzy, I'm afraid. What if he doesn't want me after he learns who I really am?"

Her sister knelt before her once again. "Then he was not the man for you. God makes no mistakes, even if we do."

"Then I must tell him."

"Yes," Isabelle said, "you must."

They rose together, and Emilie cast about for her bonnet.

"Em, you can't just go find him and blurt this out," Isabelle said. "You must pray over this and make a plan." She opened the desk drawer and reached for writing paper. "Write him a note and have him meet you somewhere private. There you can have your talk. If he's the one the Lord has for you, nothing will keep you apart." She smiled. "Josiah and I are living proof."

Indeed they were. Still, Emilie held her doubts close as she wrote a brief note asking Caleb to

429

meet her at the old schoolhouse to discuss their future. To be sure he understood, she folded the paper and tucked it into the pages of the novel.

Emilie would let *Robinson Crusoe* say what she as yet could not.

When she'd accomplished her task, Emilie donned her bonnet and hurried to the boardinghouse. Thankfully, the judge was not at the table with the other boarders. She caught Ruby and took her aside.

"Might you do a favor for me later this morning? I've a book I need delivered to Judge Spencer." She handed Ruby the book. "Be careful to point out to Caleb that there's a note inside."

The younger woman grinned. "I'm always happy to advance the course of true love."

"Oh, I don't know about all that," Emilie said. *Though I can hope,* she thought.

"Don't make me do this." Claire O'Connor leaned against the side of Tucker's Feed and Supply and closed her eyes, the book still clutched to her chest.

"I saw the woman go into the boardinghouse," Jean Luc said. "And I know she gave you the book, for she was carrying it when she went in but not when she departed."

Thomas Hawkins's second-in-command snatched the book from her and thumbed through the pages until he found the note. A smile dawned, and he stepped away from Claire.

Claire's gaze darted to the only exit from the alley she'd blindly allowed Jean Luc to trick her into entering. When it came to men, she'd never been known to have good sense.

Ben and Jamie Hawkins, Thomas's younger brothers, had been stationed at the end of the alley, either keeping watch or watching Jean Luc. As yet, it seemed to be the latter.

She returned her attention to the Frenchman who'd courted her right under Thomas's nose. Perhaps the spark of interest had not yet completely died.

"Jean Luc," she said as she leaned forward to grasp his shoulders and draw him near. "I owe this woman a favor. Let me do that favor for her; then maybe we can find time to be alone and talk about what I might do for you."

"Sweet Claire," he whispered as he touched his lips to her neck. "You grow more beautiful every day." Abruptly, he grasped her hands and held them against his chest. "But Thomas, he grows more tired of waiting."

"Please give me back the book, Jean Luc."

The Frenchman pointed to the paper, and Jamie Hawkins delivered it to him. He broke the seal and read the document, then handed it back to Jamie. "We're going to take this to the judge ourselves. Make amends with him, as it were."

"You are?" Her smile was genuine. "How can I thank you, Jean Luc?"

He nuzzled close, his breath smelling of whatever he'd had for dinner. "In the usual way, Claire," he murmured. "And if you don't show tonight, I'll have to go to Thomas. Thus far, the three of us have kept our mouths shut."

Ben and Jamie nodded.

Claire yanked the book away and slipped past the three men to emerge onto the sidewalk. By the time she reached the boardinghouse, she'd become Ruby O'Shea again.

Emilie waited at her cottage until the mantel clock struck nine. Caleb was late.

Or perhaps he wasn't coming at all.

She moved from the parlor to the porch rocker and took her Bible with her. It was dark, too dark to read, but the feel of the book in her hand gave her comfort.

When the garden gate opened, she rose. "Caleb. You came."

But it wasn't Caleb.

"Hello, pigeon." Emilie opened her mouth to scream but found her voice strangely silenced. When the gag went in, she cast about for its source and found the formerly polite Frenchman standing behind her.

Time began to move faster. She jerked at the gag. Her hands were caught. Tied together. Blindfolded. The smell of something akin to medicine. Something like what her father took when the pain was too bad to stand.

"Good work, Jean Luc," Hawkins said. "Now show me the way out of here. I'll not risk having myself found out. Might be bad for business."

The world upended and the sounds stopped.

CHAPTER 41

November 20, 1836

Good morning, Mr. Secretary," Caleb said as he arrived in his office to find the secretary of the navy sitting at his desk. "I trust you slept well."

"What sort of ship are you running here, Spencer?" he said as he opened each desk drawer, then slammed it shut.

"A tight ship," Caleb said. "You've seen the log book. The men here are doing an impressive amount of business for the government. Even with the expenditure for the schoolhouse, there's a substantial sum in the coffers."

He looked up. "Tell me more about this school."

Caleb told him what he knew, then concluded with an offer to visit the location. "Let's," the secretary said. "I'm impressed you would think of such a thing."

"It was not my idea, sir, as you might have gathered from the letters the townspeople sent."

The older man nodded. "Indeed, though I must tell you most were complimentary of you, even as they complained about their school."

433

"Oh?"

"Perhaps we should see this school," he said. "I've told the press in Washington of the largesse of the United States Navy. I should view the building I've laid claim to thinking of!"

"You've laid claim to the idea?" Caleb chuckled.

"Yes, sir," he said. "And a brilliant idea it is."

They walked toward the school, and the secretary fell silent. As the town slipped behind them, he cleared his throat. "You know, Spencer, I was skeptical about taking you into the department. Your father, well, he had a good reputation over at the attorney general's office, and we who knew him always thought you'd follow in his footsteps."

"Indeed, sir, that has been my aim."

He smiled. "I'm glad to hear it," he said. "I've been talking to the AG."

"The attorney general?"

"Seems his aide's a bit of a disappointment. He suggested I might want to swap one of my navy boys for this fellow. Send him out in the field and bring my man to Washington." He slapped Caleb on the back. "Problem is you've earned a bit of a reputation thanks to the admiral's daughter."

"Sir, I never touched her. Never said an untoward—"

He held his hand up to silence Caleb. "I believe you," he said, "which is why I feel safe in sending the man who has helped me catch the eye of the president over to the AG."

Caleb stopped abruptly. "Wait. You're sending me back to Washington to work as aide to the attorney general?"

The secretary nodded. "Let me see if I can explain this. See, we're taking a beating in the press on this Indian war issue. Nasty business fighting with the Seminoles." He shrugged. "So naturally building schools in the same territory where the nastiness is happening sort of evens things out."

Realization dawned. "So you didn't request I go forward with the school because of those letters?"

"Oh, they helped. Without them, I'd never have heard of this mosquito-ridden backwater." He pointed to the clearing ahead. "Is that the school?"

"No," Caleb said. "That's the schoolteacher's home."

"Excellent. Take me to meet her." He reached for the garden gate and a moment later was banging on her door.

"I think she's staying in town with her sister," Caleb finally said. "Perhaps we'll find her there."

But when they reached Isabelle Carter's doorstep, she said, "No, I haven't seen Emilie since she set off to meet you yesterday."

"Meet me?" Caleb shook his head. "I was never informed of a meeting."

"Oh, dear," Isabelle said. "I assumed . . ." Her eyes widened. "Oh dear."

"Isabelle," he said slowly though his heart beat

in his throat and his blood raced. "When and where was the meeting to take place?"

She shook her head. "Let me think. The time, I'm not clear, but the location was her home. This I know."

"But we just returned from there," the secretary said, "and that place was empty."

"Oh dear," Isabelle repeated. "If only Josiah hadn't taken his father and the missionaries down to Key West aboard the *Freedom*. He would know what to do."

"What about Micah?" Caleb asked. "Might he know where Emilie is?"

Again she shook her head. "He's with them."

Gradually, light encroached on the darkness. Emilie lay back against the bunk and tried not to cry. With her hands tied, it made wiping her tears or swiping at her nose quite impossible.

Thus far, the horrible pirate had left her alone. She'd been taken aboard a ship, this she remembered, then somehow transported to dry land. Now, with the rocking beneath her, she knew she was back aboard a seagoing vessel.

Shouting erupted above her, and a great lurch followed. The rocking increased until it felt more like a pitch and roll than a forward motion. Then it all stopped.

Abruptly.

The noise was deafening.

Then, silence.

• • •

"Wreck ashore," the lookout called as Caleb and the secretary were coming out of the Carter home. "Wreck ashore," he said again.

"Someone's on the reef," Caleb said to the secretary. "Now the men will go out and fetch first the passengers, then the crew. When they are safely in, the men will board the vessel for anything of value."

"Splendid," the secretary said. "Let's go."

Caleb shook his head. "You want to go aboard a wrecking vessel?"

"I do," he said.

He shrugged. "Then we should hurry. Likely they'll be loading up and leaving soon."

They reached the dock as the last boat was loosening the lines. The man at the helm pointed to Micah's vacant vessel. "We need all the help we can get," he said. "Judge, can you operate a wrecking ship?"

"I'll vouch for the fact he can."

Caleb turned to see Fletcher and several of the crew from the *Cormorant* standing dockside. One of them held the Benning flag across his arm. Lifting a brow, he sent a silent question to Fletcher, who shrugged. Quick introductions were made as Micah's vessel set out to follow the others.

"The men said the Benning should only fly under his own flag," Fletcher said when he'd sidled up beside Caleb. "Anything less would be a lie."

Interesting. He said nothing, instead continuing the task of heading the craft toward the ship now sinking on the horizon.

The first boats to the scene dropped anchor, and a master was chosen. While Caleb watched, grapeshot began to pepper the would-be rescuers. One by one, the vessels lifted anchor and pulled away.

"Raise the flag," Caleb shouted.

"What flag?" the secretary called.

Caleb smiled. "The Benning flag," he said.

Once the banner was hoisted, the cannons adjusted their aim. Then came the man with whom Caleb had sparred mere months ago. Thomas Hawkins stood on the deck, the familiar red ribbon tying a pistol to his neck.

Blood rushed to Caleb's temples. "Mr. Secretary," he said, "I suggest you go below until this scrap is over."

When he complied, Caleb shouted the orders that would bring an end to Thomas Hawkins. With care, Fletcher eased Micah's vessel close to Hawkins's ship. A cannon fired, and grapeshot peppered the deck, serving only to inflame Caleb's temper.

When the vessels were close, Caleb made the jump and landed on the tilting deck of the pirate's vessel. Hawkins charged but lost his battle at the hands of Caleb's pistol. He fell backward into the water, and Caleb made to go after him. An explosion beneath him caused Caleb to abandon his mission.

"Get these men back to my jail," he called to Fletcher. "I'm going to look for Emilie."

He found her in the hold, knee deep in water that swam with galley rats. When he gathered her to him, she fought him off. Only when they reached the sunshine did she realize who held her.

And hold her he did, all the way back to Fairweather Key.

At the docks, he stepped onto dry land with Emilie still in his arms. "I'm taking you to be checked by the doctor," he said as he turned toward town.

"No." She leaned her head on his shoulder. "Please."

Caleb nodded. "I'll not leave you out at your cottage, but I will take you to the *Cormorant*. What say you to this, Emilie?"

Emilie closed her eyes and nodded. By the time he settled her onto his bunk, she'd fallen asleep.

"Laudanum is my guess," Fletcher said. "We found enough of the stuff in his safe to kill someone."

The thought sent ice through Caleb's veins.

"She's safe now," Fletcher said.

Caleb smiled. "Yes," he said slowly, "she is."

When Emilie awoke, the first face she saw was Caleb's. "You found me," she said.

"I did." Caleb gathered her into his arms. "Did he harm you?"

She shook her head, then settled against his chest.

"I love you, Emilie," he said. "And that will not change even if you choose to walk away again."

She looked up into his eyes. "You cannot love me, Caleb. You don't know who I am."

"Then tell me," he said, "though I warn you it will not matter."

"My mother," she said as she averted her gaze, "was my father's concubine." She paused to risk a glance in his direction. "A slave."

Emilie waited for what she knew would be his rejection. "Marry me, Emilie," he said instead.

"Did you hear me, Caleb? My mother was a slave."

"And mine was a pirate."

"What?" She shook her head. "Your mother?"

"She was the daughter, granddaughter, and great-granddaughter of pirates." Caleb laughed. "We're quite the pair, aren't we?"

She nodded, never lifting her head from his chest.

"Arrest that man for piracy." Emilie looked up to see a strange man in a navy uniform standing at the door.

Before she could protest, she was unceremoniously dumped on the bunk and Caleb Spencer was off to be locked up in his own jail.

• • •

This time when Emilie called a meeting of the Fairweather Key school parents it was not about writing letters to the Secretary of the Navy. Rather, it was about protesting an innocent man's arrest.

Several men had already begun a loud discussion of just what they thought should happen to the secretary for making such accusations against the judge. To his credit, Micah was doing a decent job of calming them.

"I don't understand," Ruby O'Shea said as she walked up and shifted a sleepy Tess to her other hip. "How can they think the judge would be one of those *pirates?*"

Something in the way she said the word made Emilie wonder what Ruby knew of such men. She shook off the odd thought and addressed the woman who practically ran the boardinghouse single-handedly. "He's not, and that's all there is to it."

Ruby seemed to think a moment before nodding. "True enough," she said. "And I'd be willing to say so with my hand on a Bible if need be." Again, Emilie wondered at the woman's meaning, but she had no time to contemplate it, for the secretary of the navy himself stepped onto the porch. "What is the meaning of this?" he called.

"The meaning, sir," Emilie said as she pressed past those in attendance, "is that you have imprisoned an innocent man."

Voices old and young, familiar and unfamiliar echoed Emilie's statement.

"Would that you were correct," he said, "but my eyes saw what they saw, and this man flew under a pirate's flag. How am I to believe the man I thought worthy of a judgeship has not turned pirate like his father and grandfather before him?"

"Now see here, mister," Ruby shouted. "I haven't known these people long, but I have had the misfortune of knowing a pirate or two in my time. I don't know why the judge was flying the Benning flag, but I do know any man who does would strike fear in the hearts of the sort of fellow you *should* be putting in that brig of yours. You let the judge out, and I'll prove I'm right."

Emilie stared at Ruby, shock rendering her unable to speak.

"That won't be necessary," a man called from the edge of the crowd.

"Who are you?" the secretary asked.

"My name is Fitzgerald." He pulled a packet from his coat and lifted it into the air. "Mr. Secretary, I bring letters of introduction that will prove what these people have said about your prisoner."

"Come forward, please."

Mr. Fitzgerald pressed past Emilie and climbed the steps to stand beside the secretary. "Please understand, Mr. Secretary, that I am charged by the highest authority with seeing to the safety of the man you've thrown into that jail." Again Mr.

Fitzgerald lifted the packet, then slowly lowered it. "A part of that charge is protecting him from false accusations."

It was all Emilie could do not to run up those steps and snatch the letters away to read them herself.

The secretary cleared his throat. "Upon whose authority?"

"The President of these United States."

The cell was dark, the air dank and nearly void of oxygen. Caleb took deep gulps and tried to sleep, but rest would not come. He lay on the wooden bunk and stared into the darkness with only God as his companion.

"Whatever you want of me," Caleb said, even as he prayed the Lord would set him free.

The door swung open, and Mrs. O'Mara stepped inside, humming her usual obscure verse from some hymn he'd not heard in years. His stomach complained, yet she had not brought his meal.

"I'm here to take you for sentencing," she said.

He offered up his hands for restraints, and she shoved them away. "Just get on with yourself, Judge. A whole lot of people are waiting to see you."

He followed her down the short distance to the office that had once been his. When Mrs. O'Mara opened the door, he saw the office was crowded with people. So full, in fact, that the crowd spilled out onto the porch, down the stairs, and onto the lawn.

As he walked, they parted until he could see his desk and the secretary of the navy seated there. Beside him stood Emilie.

"Caleb Spencer," he said. "It appears the truth has set you free."

"What do you mean?" He looked around at smiling faces, most of whom he knew.

"I've heard more testimony as to your character than I ever wanted to hear." He cast a glance around the room. "You've got friends here, my boy, but I want to make you an offer."

"Oh?" he said, though he couldn't take his eyes off Emilie. She seemed to have a similar problem.

"Indeed, a fine man like you deserves to be where you can do the most good. I'm going to speak to the AG on your behalf. Congratulations, Caleb, it looks like you're going back to Washington."

Washington. His goal. Caleb shook his head. No, that was his father's goal.

"Mr. Secretary, I respectfully decline your invitation and ask for something else instead."

"Is that so?" He rose. "What would that be?"

Caleb reached Emilie to entwine her fingers with his. "I request, sir, that as an admiral, you stand in lieu of the reverend who is away and officiate at a marriage."

"A marriage? To whom?" he blustered.

Caleb dropped to one knee, his fingers still wrapped around Emilie's. "Will you have me as your husband, Emilie?"

"Yes," she said as the first tear fell.

"Hold on here," a voice called, and Caleb turned to see Hezekiah Carter making his way through the crowd. "If there's to be a marriage, I'll be the one doing the officiating."

"And I'd ask a blessing of you as well," Caleb said to the old pastor.

"That you have," he said. "Now let's all get these two down to the church and have a wedding before they change their minds."

EPILOGUE

Santa Lucida

"A daughter at last," Caleb's mother said as she gathered Emilie into her arms. "Thank You, Lord, You've answered my prayers."

"And mine," Emilie managed as she felt her husband's arm wrap around her waist.

"And mine," Caleb added, "though if you and Fletcher will excuse us, Mrs. Spencer and I have a honeymoon to get to."

"Caleb!" Emilie ducked her head just as Caleb lifted her into his arms and carried her from the room. "Where are we going?" she demanded.

He grinned. "Keep quiet, Mrs. Crusoe," he said. "Tonight you're my captive."

She buried her face in his neck and held on tight. "Tonight and always."

ABOUT THE AUTHOR

KATHLEEN Y'BARBO

Kathleen first discovered her love of books when, at the age of four, she stumbled upon her grandmother's encyclopedias. Letters became words, and words became stories of faraway places and interesting people. By the time she entered kindergarten, Kathleen had learned to read and found that her love of stories could carry her off to places far beyond her small East Texas town. Eventually she hit the road for real—earning a degree in Marketing from Texas A&M before setting off on a path that would take her to such far-flung locales as Jakarta, Tokyo, Bali, Sydney, Hong Kong, and Singapore. Finally, though, the road led back to Texas and to writing and publicizing books.

Kathleen is a bestselling author of more than thirty novels, novellas, and young adult books. In all, more than half a million copies of her books are currently in print in the U.S. and abroad. She has been named as a finalist in the American Christian Fiction Writers Book of the Year contest every year since its inception in 2003, often for more than one book.

In addition to her skills as an author, Kathleen is also a publicist at Books & Such Literary

Agency. She is a member of American Christian Fiction Writers, Romance Writers of America, the Public Relations Society of America, Words for the Journey Christian Writers Guild, and the Authors Guild. She is also a former treasurer of the American Christian Fiction Writers. Kathleen has three grown sons and a teenage daughter.

You can read more about Kathleen at www.kathleenybarbo.com.

Center Point Publishing

600 Brooks Road • PO Box 1
Thorndike ME 04986-0001 USA

(207) 568-3717

US & Canada:
1 800 929-9108
www.centerpointlargeprint.com